NOR TOLERATE

AMONG US

ALSO BY CHARLES WILLIAMS

In Close Proximity
-an action/thriller-

Higher Than The Angels
-a novel of life and of fighter pilots in Spain-

I. Xombi
-a comedic play

13, 13, 13
-another comedic play

NOR TOLERATE AMONG US

CHARLES WILLIAMS

This novel is a work of fiction. Any references to historical events,
to real people, living or dead, or to real locales are intended only
to give the fiction a setting in historical reality.
Other names, characters, places, and incidents
are the product of the author's imagination or are used fictitiously,
and their resemblance, if any, to actual persons, living or dead,
is entirely coincidental.

Cover and interior design by Charles Williams

ISBN-13: 9781095304334

ACKNOWLEDGEMENTS AND DEDICATIONS

I truly appreciate those friends who have read, critiqued, and offered correction to my work. Thank you especially Ky Webb, Hamp Heard, Rob Spence, Sabrina Afflixio, Jeff Jacobs, and Lynda Kalantzakis.

Special thanks to Meredith Kelly for your professional editing suggestions as well as enlightening notes and comments that helped me turn a verbose epic into a marketable novel.

I consider myself extremely fortunate that my parents, Kenneth and Charlene, were always so supportive of me. My loving mother read everything I wrote, every novel I drafted or published or planned to publish. My father was and is my favorite veteran. I have never known a more loving, caring, dedicated man. A better role model no son ever had. Thank you, mom and dad. I miss you both.

My loving brothers:

Paul Wayne, a fellow United States Air Force Academy Graduate now American Airlines Captain, who read, critiqued, and edited the first 800 page draft of my first novel many years ago. I miss you, bro.

Jeff Alan, who reads my work even when he does not have time to between working for NASA and playing with his martins or his plants. Your strength and intelligence have always inspired me.

Forrest Taylor Kirk Williams, who created my first website for me. Thank you. You are a fine son and a talented man.

And finally, always, my beautiful wife – and guara grower – my angel of unconditional love, my most trusted advisor, my closest friend. Karen, you are the love of my life.

FORWARD

As a contemporary graduate of USAFA with the author, I have a distinct appreciation of the story Charles Williams has woven in his latest novel. I enjoyed the accurate remembrances of cadet life, both uplifting and depressing, from regulation and ritual, through the demands on time, mind, and body, to the valuable, identity-forming human interaction and relationships with other cadets.

While cadets are normal (mostly!) college-age youth with the same immaturity and social needs as their civilian college peers, they live in a pressure cooker of hardened rules and expectations. This life is on full display in Williams' novel.

But this is not a documentary on AFA cadet life. The Academy serves as a stage on which Williams has placed his characters, and the story is much more about their actions and reactions to the environment and, more importantly, to their friends and nemeses.

The title of the novel reminds us of the corollary tenet of the AFA Honor Code which holds that cadets must hold their fellow cadets to the same high standard of honor required of themselves. In my day, teamwork, esprit de corps and looking out for your brother cadet was stressed in training. A soldier will say that the prime motivation for bravery, heroism, and reliable performance in combat is that unquenchable desire to protect and support your brother soldiers. Not tolerating, hence snitching or ratting out a fellow cadet thus poses a moral dilemma for a young man. Williams weaves this conflict into his story.

I admire Williams' skill in overlaying a poignant human story on a deeper moral framework that will speak to every reader, regardless of your connection to service academies or the military.

Stephen Kentucky (Ky) Webb
USAFA Class of 1976

WHAT READERS SAY ABOUT
NOR TOLERATE AMONG US

What a gift an author has to make his characters come alive as we feel those characters' joy and sorrow, excitement and introspection. Keep up the Good Work, Charles! I anxiously await your next book!

Lynda DeWitt Kalantzakis

Great book! Actually teared up at the end. I loved reading it entirely! Thank You!

Hamp Heard, Class of '77

Five Squadrons, 5 Groups in 5 years (including Basic). Charles Williams knows the "Blue Zoo" better than most.
He offers insights and experiences
all generations will enjoy.

John Hope, Class of 1976

This book was a lifetime in the making, with many years of writes, rewrites, and editing, and the end result is not at all what I anticipated.
Were you to ask me if I would want to read a book about the Air Force Academy, my honest answer would be no. While I hold those who attended USAFA in high esteem, I prefer, likely due to my degree in English Literature, to read character-based novels that draw me into the story and leave me wanting more.
To my surprise and great delight, this book offers just that—engaging characters we care about and with whom we can identify. I enjoyed the literary quality of the writing and quickly became immersed in the narrative. I was anxious to see how the characters coped with life's challenges in their strange and unique world and, not surprisingly, discovered that I had that sad, lost feeling that sometimes lingers on at the end of a good story involving characters we will miss.

Karen Kirk-Williams, Wife and Best Friend

For Paul, Hamp, and Kentucky,
and all other cadets that have or will
spend four years of their lives
attending a service academy

and for Karen

PROLOGUE

When Vincent Nebraska Book was a toddler, his Gram nicknamed him "Skye." The tag stuck because it suited him. He was tall with pale blue eyes, wavy blond hair that arrayed his head like golden clouds, and blessed with an intellect that soared above his peers. He was likeable and fun and the bravest person I have ever known. Nothing that was true could scare him.

But truth is a glass palace built on an island of shifting sand.

If I am to tell his truth, and that is the sole purpose of this narrative, I must avoid the most treacherous sinkhole of all, the lie of omission. Everything must be revealed, however painful. I owe that much to him.

It begins near the end.

I rode through the dark hours alone, desiring neither the comforting solace of another human hand nor the refreshing renewal to be gained from sleep. Rather, I wished to remain as I was, gritty and raw, inside and out. I craved every candid emotion that might prey upon whatever self-righteous pretense I claimed to possess. Only then could I hope to be cleansed, perhaps even reborn.

Exiting I-25, I passed through the South Gate as soon as the airman guarding the entrance would allow. Ignoring his stern but silent admonition, I continued on slowly as if in a processional. Meandering northward past the airstrip and the stadium, I reflected in stoic silence as the Colorado sunrise brought all that was before me into focus. At Academy Drive I turned left, putting the rising sun at my back. Turning into the second overlook, I shut the big twin down and sat unmoving for a moment or two before lowering the kickstand to the pavement.

I dismounted and walked to the edge where the ground descended steeply below and away from me. Removing my helmet, I stood erect, my legs spread wide in an outward show of bravado that belied my inner angst. I took a deep breath of the crisp morning air.

Lush green athletic fields stretched languidly in the valley beneath me like fertile pastureland preserved exclusively for the most exceptional lambs. To the south, beyond the fields, the aging aluminum structure of the Cadet Area rose to my level in stark contrast to the natural grace of the pale pink and gray foothills peppered with firs and pines. To the west, the Rocky Mountains ascended heavenward in timeless indifference to the Academy, and me. The rising sun bathed the mountains in morning glory as I sought for and found the bald face of Eagle Peak. The air was calm and quiet where I stood, but I could distinctly hear the call harkening me back.

It is often those places where our reflection grows darkest that we are most compelled to return, as the sinner to the scene.

I returned my focus to the Cadet Area. Despite the years, the view seemed little changed from the first time I had taken it all in. At that initial viewing, poised high above it all, I felt certain I was ready for whatever could befall me. Standing now at the edge of what my beloved younger brother had once called the "lookout," I felt the mirror of my past drawing me into the abyss.

My knees buckled as I fought to catch my breath, my mind engulfed in a flood of youthful memories. Forced thus into penitence, I prayed for the will to fight my way out, to be finally free of the torturous shackles of regret.

This was my last chance.

PART ONE

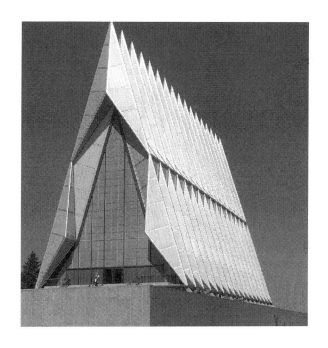

"Man is the measure of all things."

Protagoras

CHAPTER ONE

I n late May of the year that changed my life, seventeen and far from worldly, I graduated from high school in an obscure southeastern Texas town whose only enduring claim to fame—other than its proximity to what certain authorities have declared the "most irreversibly polluted city in the United States"—was that it harbored an undying belief, still held by many, that Jesus once appeared on the screen door of a small house near the river. Some say the door still exists, carefully preserved in storage somewhere, perhaps awaiting a second coming.

More is known of this than of William Q. Rigby—the great grandson of the town's founding father—who rose to become a powerful if not prestigious United States Congressman. Congressman Rigby was a diminutive, combatively pious man with large, radar-like ears that gathered all sides of every argument then distilled the facts to fit his preferred perception of the world.

Despite, or perhaps because of his second billing, the Honorable Congressman stated on numerous occasions that he wished only to remember his roots and be remembered for his service. This shrewd persona—a simple man putting his constituency first while denying even a glimmer of personal ambition—would for 37 years keep him and his family in the relatively sophisticated climate of Washington, DC—far, far away from the sweltering depression of our polluted little town.

I found it a dubious honor to be nominated to attend the Academy— albeit as his second alternate—by this man who served as the Vice Chairman of the Committee on Veteran Affairs despite never having the privilege of serving in the armed forces himself.

Rigby's primary candidate was the son of his close friend, Judge Durwood B. Krull, a nod in the judge's direction of little consequence as the boy had no desire to attend the institution. To make his intentions crystal clear, DB Jr. married his pregnant high school sweetheart during a quick stop at the Justice of the Peace before continuing on to our senior prom.

The Congressman's first alternate, Nicholai Delgado, was an All-State quarterback from the nearby county seat, the majority of whose residents it is safe to say knew far less of the Academy than they did of their hometown hero. Recruited by several state universities, the venerated football and track star with his flowing auburn hair and chiseled physique also missed the cut, destined rather to loll away the stifling East Texas summer retaking Algebra II by day and cruising the Gateway Strip by night in a beefed-up El Camino he painted maroon and white to match the school colors of Texas A&M.

Thus, the honor fell to me, uncelebrated and of little consequence as I was.

While Nicki weathered the Dog Days of summer speeding down the saltmarsh backroads in an inebriated fog, thrilling young maidens and evading the authorities, I soberly endured the better part of July and August with 1400 other fledgling males double-timing in combat boots and olive drab fatigues against the backdrop of the Rocky Mountains.

Summer was just beginning when my father drove my mother, my brother, and me from the east coast of Texas to the southern range of the Colorado Rockies. We left earlier than was necessary, freeing up time to explore the Academy and surrounding area before I was to report.

My first glimpse of the Academy from Interstate 25 remains eternally etched upon my mind. The Cadet Chapel—acute and angular—seemed to suddenly erupt against the rugged mountainous backdrop in calculated contrast to the level dry plains to the east and the flat-roofed dormitories and academic buildings that formed the perimeter of the Cadet Area like subservient adjuncts beneath the Chapel's watchful eye. Together they fashioned a shimmering monument to what my friend Whit Whittaker would come to call "Man's desire to out-God God."

As we drove west along the rolling stretch of road beyond the Academy's North Gate, the accordion design of the Chapel vanished then reappeared like a pulsating beacon saying, "This is the way. Stay on the narrow path, that you might stand tall with me."

I felt then I was gazing upon the place from which I would arise in well-honed glory, my body physically strong like the mountains, my mind rugged enough to keep the honor code as my own, my spirit as grandiose and singularly unique as the Cadet Chapel.

Ah, the Chapel. That iconic symbol that seemed to have wedged its way through the pale granite foundation beneath the academy grounds, welling up like a sacred relic longing to free itself from the secular bonds of earth. A massive hunk of angular architecture with its seventeen spires, the Chapel was at once a beloved monument to young cadet hearts and an aluminum prod in our highly disciplined asses that served to remind us of our devotion to God and country. The seventeen spires, as cadet lore explained, were so numbered in honor of the twelve disciples and the five chiefs of staff, the priority, I suppose, being determined from which direction you began counting. I often wondered which of those spires belonged to Judas.

Perhaps to impress upon me the significance of my appointment, my father stopped at the second overlook north of the cadet athletic fields. As he killed the blue Chevrolet Impala's engine, I considered the contrast between this magnificent spot and the soggy salt marsh and sprawling petroleum refineries of that corner of Texas we called home. The dismal image of a town dominated by processing towers spewing unknown chemicals into the Texas night air gave way to this sculpted testimonial to man and God that radiated an aluminum glory making all things possible.

I jumped from the confining backseat of the Chevy, followed immediately by my younger brother, who tiptoed to avoid crushing the yellow currants in bloom at the edge of the asphalt. The green fields of athletic endeavor—of which I held to be my greatest asset—lay before Tyson and me, beckoning us like the sirens to Odysseus. On impulse and exhilaration, I ran down the hill, dodging the small islands of scrub brush and yellow flowers desperately rooted in the rocky gravel of the slippery slope.

Tyson followed as closely as he could—as he would throughout his life—falling and skinning his unprotected knees but rising immediately without complaint or even taking the time to remove the small sharp stones imbedded in his soft skin. I was his hero, but I don't think he ever understood how much I revered him. While I was quick to grumble and slow to praise, Tyson did not live for glory, and no regrets shadowed his character. He was antithesis and synthesis rolled into one neat eleven-year-old ball of willful humanity.

Sprawling expanses of freshly mowed grass greeted us as we emerged from the rocky surroundings of all else that was unnurtured or otherwise quarantined from this isolated Eden. The grass was lush like back home, but the air was drier, fresher, and the smell of dust and pine replaced the smell of burning butane that until that moment had been my most ingrained olfactory memory.

I slowed when I reached the wooden fence of the baseball outfield to allow Tyson to catch up. My desire in racing down the barren hill to this green spot was to gain a more level perspective, but an out-of-place discovery outshines all else I remember of this day. Sitting on a horizontal beam of the fence like a relic upon a shelf was the perfectly preserved skeleton of a starfish roughly ten inches in diameter. While I could not know how it came to be there, it did not seem out of place. In fact, I looked at it as just another indicator of my special life. Why should I not be greeted by such an unusual, suggestive find in a place where I intended to star?

I gingerly removed the starfish and turned it over in my hands. It was very much intact, dried blond by the sun but otherwise un-weathered, plain yet detailed, hardened yet vulnerable, imperfect and yet unique.

"How did that get here?" Tyson asked. "There's no beach."

"Doesn't have to be," I said. "Not anymore, anyway. Maybe it's a fossil."

"Nope," Tyson said, taking it from me. "It's real, not rock." He examined the hollow ridges of the underside. "What are we going to do with it?"

I took it from him. "It's not ours."

Tyson looked around. Except for our parents waving at us from the overlook a quarter mile away, we were the only breathing things here. "I don't think it's anybody's. Let's take it with us. Show dad."

"No." I placed it on the fence exactly as I had found it and looked up into the mountains. Many of the promotional photographs I had seen depicted the Cadet Area nestled beneath the watchful magnificence of Pikes Peak, rising to the west above the foothills just as I imagined

Kilimanjaro would off the Serengeti. Such majestic composition was, to me, the compelling allure of the Academy.

The iconic peak was not visible from where we stood.

"There's an honor code here," I said.

"There is?"

I nodded. "They kick you out if you break it." I looked south to the Cadet Area. I could just see the spires of the Chapel above Vandenberg Hall, what the cadets called the Old Dorm. "We will not lie, steal, or cheat, nor tolerate among us anyone who does."

"How do you tolerate?"

"You don't here."

"But how would you?"

"You let someone else get away with lying or stealing. Or cheating."

"Not tell on them."

"Right."

"So, you don't tolerate. You snitch."

"It's not the same," I said, shaking my head. "It's more like not baring false witness. I wouldn't tolerate anyone who tried to tell a lie about you."

"I wouldn't let anyone lie about you either," Tyson said emphatically. "I'd make 'em pay!"

"Really. How?"

Tyson held up his young fists and made his best boxing move toward me. I grabbed his bony wrists and held them behind his skinny back.

"I'm watching out for you!" he protested, squirming to break free.

"And I'm watching out for you, squirt, so you don't do something to bring your young life to a premature end." I released his wrists and started running back up the hill with my brother in hot pursuit. He slowed to a walk only when I did. I told him I wasn't winded—which, at 7000 feet above sea level, I was—but that I was waiting for him.

I took in a lasting image of my parents standing together at the "lookout." My father's muscular bulk and shortly cropped buzz cut stood in sharp contrast to my mother's long flowing red hair and petite, almost frail feminine frame.

When we were nearly to the top, Tyson turned to me and said, "I'm going to miss you."

Before I could answer, he exploded into a quick uphill sprint, reaching the crest before me. I smiled inwardly. I would miss him, too.

On the edge of the overlook these many years later, I labored to regain my composure as I rose to my feet, gazing from past to present with weathered and mournfully wiser eyes. I thought it a good thing to remember the deceptive nature of such innocent exhilarations.

Pulling back the sleeve of my jacket, I glanced at my watch. The Reunion Committee had organized a tour to emphasize the cultural changes reflected in the life of the 21st Century cadet. Among other things, women were now a decidedly integral part of the cadet wing. Prior to my senior year, there had been none.

Striding back to the Indian Chief, I noted for the first time that the yellow flowers I had seen there so long ago were now gone. I fired up the big twin as my mind composed a picture of the pink gaura that adorned my yard back home, still in bloom and dancing with the bees seeking their drops of sweetness.

Turning off the perimeter road, I parked near Harmon Hall and doffed my waterproof jacket—replacing it with my black cloth one—and locked the waterproof and my helmet in the saddlebag out of habit. I checked the mirror. I was clean enough, although it appeared I could do with a shave.

Pausing to study the elongated administration building, I searched for shadows beyond the tinted windows before turning away to follow a group of tourists strolling up Cadet Drive. With the Chapel directly in front of me, I paused, gazing upward as if in meditation.

Where I stood was hallowed ground.

I peered intently at the spires, trying to remember where the bullet holes were. Every physical trace had been skillfully buffed away decades ago, but I knew the scars, like those on my soul, remained deeply embedded beneath a polished, superficial façade.

High above the road to the west, between the Chapel and the mountains, a hawk floated on a breath of wind I could not feel. As I watched the raptor circle to gain altitude, an apparition emerged from the depths of my mind, a face gripped with pain just as I had last seen it.

Lowering my head, I turned and walked north, passing the wall where Melody Book once waited for me many years ago, an image so permanently etched in my heart that I was sure I could identify the precise spot where she sat as she flashed her enigmatic smile below the barely visible tear-shaped scar that seemed to trickle from her eye.

My pace quickened as I descended the Chapel ramp. I shifted my gaze to the large quad on my right, an angular expanse of grass surrounded on all sides by the terrazzo tiles and intersecting marble strips of the predominant walkway cadets refer to simply as the Terrazzo. In stoic attestation of the superiority of the US Air Force, a decommissioned fighter rested in perpetuity in each ordinal corner of the quad, facing outward as if guarding the manicured greenery from foreign intrusion.

Striding toward Vandenberg Hall, I marched a few steps along one of the long marble strips, momentarily infused with a memory of my first year at the Academy when this was the only pathway allowed to Fourth Classmen.

I joined a small group of reunion attendees assigned to Cadet Second Class Wesley who, after introducing himself as our tour guide, led us down one of the Old Dorm's many hallways to an alcove with one door opened to a neat, almost sterile cadet room.

The cultural changes were immediately evident. Carpeting now covered the tiled floor my classmates and I labored late into many a Friday night waxing and buffing, a softer veneer to a harder time. I was surprised to see boxes of breakfast cereal on shelves where I had been allowed books, pictures, and stereo speakers but never anything reminiscent of my mother's pantry.

Two twin beds, covered with red blankets tightly folded in the distinctive presentation reserved for Saturday Morning Inspections, lined the side walls. The metal chairs and desks seemed smoother now, and footlockers replaced the dressers I had prepared for inspection more times than I could recall. Drawn curtains hid the large window that ran the width of the far wall, giving the room a claustrophobic air.

"Those are supposed to be open," Cadet Wesley said, pointing to the curtains. He strode the length of the room and pulled them apart, revealing the Chapel and, above and beyond, the bald face of Eagle Peak rising like an unmoving sentinel focused on some distant, unknowable future.

A guttural gasp of recognition escaped my throat, inciting a former classmate's wife to ask if I was all right.

I nodded in the affirmative. I don't know why, exactly, but the turn on the old joke ran swiftly through my head: 'If the Air Force wanted you to have a wife, they would have issued you one.' Like my friend and classmate, Henry Francis Cruce, I had never married.

My heart racing, I stepped through the all too familiar doorway as if being sucked into the vacuum of my past.

"Please sir, you will need to stay in the alcove," Cadet Wesley instructed as he turned from the window. "Everyone will be allowed to look in from there."

Ah yes, I thought. Unlike the cadets to whom this room temporarily belonged, we were neither obligated to uphold the honor code nor protected by it.

Nodding as Cadet Wesley gestured toward the hallway, I concocted the necessary lie. "This was my room," I said, not moving. "I'd just like to look around for a moment. See what's changed."

Cadet Wesley glanced quickly at the others in my group. The classmate's wife nodded with a winning smile.

"Please don't disturb anything," Cadet Wesley said.

I nodded again. "I won't." Shifting sand.

I crossed the threshold, flooded with memories that bade me enter a world I had labored decades to forget.

CHAPTER TWO

O n the dawn of the day that heralded the beginning of my cadet career, I woke early from a fitful dream. Many weeks would pass before the luxury of sleeping-in was again an option for me.

I rose from the hotel bed I shared with Tyson and stood in the shadows, reveling in the notion that I would soon be awash in the light of a red-letter day. I threw open the heavy window curtains, allowing indirect sunlight to flood the room. Somewhere beyond my view, the Academy awaited my arrival.

An awkward silence suffused our car as my father, wearing the inscrutable smile of the Sphinx, negotiated the Interstate traffic. As we closed in on the Academy, my mother looked around almost frenetically. She was moments from handing over her firstborn to a cadre of military college students she had never met who would discipline him in ways she could not begin to imagine. My father held a better understanding of what lay ahead for me, having enlisted in the Navy in the middle of the Second World War. I had no idea then how completely those years had pummeled the innocence of his youth.

The stream of cars approaching the drop-off area advanced at a slow but steady pace as airport buses from Denver and Colorado Springs unloaded anxious teenagers arriving on one-way tickets from every corner of America and beyond. Fourteen hundred forty-five of us in all. Through various means of attrition, little more than half that number would graduate. A fair number of those who fell short were in many ways like me—wide-eyed and green, intrepid but naïve, enamored more with the idea of being a cadet than with anticipation of the rigorous training meant to harden our bodies and transform our minds.

In the shadow of the "Bring Me Men" ramp, bedecked in the armor of my high school letter jacket, I emerged from the Impala's backseat holding the USAFA recruitment booklet under my arm. Full of myself, I turned to face my family. My father grasped my outstretched hand and shook it gruffly. He tried to give me my suitcase, but my mother flew between us, embracing me in a near desperate hug that seemed overly tight and a bit too lengthy.

Tyson reached to shake my hand, but youthful emotion won out, and he grabbed my waist in a tight hug. "I don't want you to go!" he said.

I staged a laugh. "That's how come I'm going, squirt."

He nodded. "Be sure to not... tolerate." Through blurry blue eyes he gazed inquisitively at my face before releasing me to tuck himself away in the backseat.

A cadet clad in summer blues, white gloves, and a wheel cap indicated it was time for me to go. My father placed my suitcase in my left hand as I eyed the cadet in admiration, imagining that would soon be me. I recalled my high school counselor's favorite George Washington quote: "Associate with men of high esteem if you value your own reputation." More than anything, I wished to be esteemed. There seemed no finer place to begin that quest than where I stood at that moment.

I wheeled away from my family and followed the cadet, certain there was nothing the Academy could throw at me that I could not overcome.

I was assigned to Jaguar Squadron along with 145 other basic cadets. The cadre took our civilian clothes and quarantined them in a locked squadron storage room. I managed to keep my letter jacket and proudly hung it in the closet amid my newly acquired military uniforms—olive drab fatigues, pale blue shirts, black combat boots, and a gray robe.

In the first two days, we were instructed in the art of shining our boots, aligning our belt buckles with our tightly tucked uniform shirts, making our beds, organizing our clothes, standing at attention, and tucking our chins as tightly against our necks as was humanly possible.

I was ahead of the game in the "tidy room" department. My mother always insisted we keep our rooms clean and our beds neatly made, complete with hospital corners. Some people worry about being in a car accident while wearing ragged underwear. My mother feared the embarrassment wrought by grieving relatives arriving at our home to discover a distasteful discordance of disheveled rooms and dismantled beds.

We marched or double-timed from one activity to the next, each with its own focused purpose in facilitating the transition from our former lives to one of conformity that would soon become Hell-lite. We were advised to use any "spare" time to learn everything we could about the Air Force from our little book of knowledge called "Contrails."

After lunch on the third day, we took our first trip to the cadet post office to check our mailboxes. My roommate, Adam Carroll, and I were among the lucky few who met this first mail check with success.

I had two letters, both postmarked the day of my departure from the salt marsh of my youth. One was from my mother, obviously written while I was yet at home packing. The other was a sweet smelling pink one from Noelle Stanquist, the girl I had taken to my senior prom, towed on skis behind my father's boat, and with whom I had never come close to rounding the bases.

Adam had three letters from his mother, and one from his sister.

The cadre granted us a short respite from their supervision that we might read these sacred words of love and longing in the relative privacy of our room.

My mother's caring missive conveyed encouragement, optimism, and support, all of which Adam's letters were completely devoid. As he read, he groaned in a way clearly meant to elicit a response from me.

"Bad news?" I asked as I reread the letter from Noelle. Our "free time" was limited, and I was anxious to discern whether she was pining for me or in active pursuit of someone new to fill the void.

"My sister and my mother... they are not happy," Adam whined. "And both of them have written about Tiffany."

"Your girlfriend?"

His head slumped. "My Maltese. Mom says when they got home from shipping me off to this hellhole, Tiffany ran all over the house trying to find me. When she could not, she just lay down and stared at them."

I thought this a bit melodramatic, but I could tell he needed encouragement. "Yeah, my family misses me, too," I offered.

He pulled a Polaroid from the envelope which he stared at soulfully before showing it to me. "She looks so heartbroken," he moaned. "And she is such a good dog!"

"Never pees on the rug," I said, sounding more cynical than I intended.

Adam glanced at me. Genuine pain contorted his face. I expected tears at any moment.

"My girl misses me, I think," I said to Adam, "but she doesn't seem heartbroken. I told her I'd be home for Christmas." I almost added 'Unless she pees on the rug,' but I held my tongue.

"But you cannot tell a dog that!" Adam answered in exaggerated anguish. "Dogs do not understand. All they know is you are there or you are not."

"She'll probably be excited to see you in your uniform," I said, but I was envisioning Noelle's reaction more than that of Adam's Maltese.

He stared forlornly at the photograph, a faint mist forming in his eyes. "If she still remembers me."

I thought he might be needing that offer of sympathy we were all craving. "Dogs remember," I offered. "Sometimes better than people."

"Maybe. But in the meantime, she suffers."

"Maltese," I said. "Small and fluffy, right?"

Adam did not answer, returning his attention to his sister's four-page letter. I glanced at him out of the corner of my eye. Disappointment and shame seemed to hover over his head like a dismal cloud. He released an emotive sigh, the first of many to come.

"I am going to the latrine," he said finally. He tucked the letters in a pants pocket of his fatigues and placed his baseball cap on his head. "Oh, I meant to tell you. Our element sergeant, Cadet... something or other, said you need to put your letter jacket in storage."

I had received the precious jacket only a month earlier, having lettered in track, mostly because I was a senior. But it meant something to me, a symbol as much as anything else. At least I had tried. "If he wants me to get rid of it," I said, "he can tell me himself."

Adam rose and walked to the open door, coming face to face with Cadet Technical Sergeant Janson who knocked rudely on the doorframe.

I turned to him as he entered.

14

Janson eyed me evenly. "Call the room to attention when an upperclassman enters," he said. This was a recent instruction, one of dozens we would learn to obey in the next six weeks.

"Okay," I said. "Room, attention."

"And call me and all upperclassmen 'sir.'"

"Sir, yes sir," I said.

"One sir per statement."

"Sir, yes..."

"Just say 'Yes sir' Townsend."

"Yes sir."

"Element meeting before the evening meal formation," Janson said. "Fatigues and baseball caps. Move it gentlemen!" His manner was suddenly harsh in ominous contrast to the preceding days.

He walked to my closet and slid the door open. Eying me, he pointed to my letter jacket. "Get rid of that. We're all lettermen here."

That rang true enough, even if it was a slight exaggeration. All new cadets brought something equally special with them.

Adam tossed me a glance that reeked of condescension. In his eyes, we were not all equal. On our first day together, he informed me he ate Continental style, as he said most sophisticated people did. "I hope that is not a problem with the cadre."

"Continental style?" I had queried.

With a patronizing sigh, he explained, "I keep my fork in my left hand. When I cut the meat, I do not change hands. It is part of my breeding."

After Janson departed, we scrambled to stow our letters in our desks, checked each other's tuck and gig-line, then lined up at attention in the hallway with the rest of our element.

We would not discuss Tiffany again.

CHAPTER THREE

T he evening air of that third day was warm, dry, and still. Jaguars formed up on the Terrazzo to march to the evening meal with the other nine basic cadet squadrons. We faced east with our backs to the mountains and the Chapel, perhaps to minimize the visual distractions that might impair our attention to the little gray Contrails book of cadet knowledge.

When all were present, our Squadron commander, Cadet Lieutenant Colonel Nash, called us to attention. I tucked my Contrails book into my fatigue pants pocket and stood erect and silent.

"If you're taller than the man in front of you, move up!" Nash commanded.

We shuffled timidly, comparing height and moving forward or backward as stature dictated. Momentary stalemates arose here and there, the final resolution being determined by an upperclassman. Adams was the tallest in our element and so moved to the head of the line. Three other members of my element were also blessed with taller genes and moved forward, placing me just a little ahead of the middle. I thought of this sometimes, the fact that the guys in front were there due to aesthetics rather than merit. But this asymmetry made us look better when we moved as a unit.

Once we were organized, the Summer Group Commander called the squadrons to attention, at which point Nash bellowed, "Jaguars! Left ... face!"

We pivoted to face Vandenberg Hall, and I felt the warmth of the sun on my cheek. A central command of our indoctrination mandated we keep our eyes "caged" forward when in formation or when addressing a superior. But bathed in this western glow, I squinted and turned my head involuntarily to glimpse the majesty of the Colorado Rockies and the sun hovering above them on its downward journey.

Philip Quince stood at attention to my left. In the preceding days, I had taken little interest in him, except to note that he had reported to the Academy on day one with his hair already cropped short. Against the glare of the evening sun, I took in the contours of his face which even from this angle appeared exaggerated. His nose was comically small compared to his protruding lips and forehead. His skin glowed as from a perpetual sunburn, making his angular head appear like a bulbous over-ripe tomato balanced awkwardly on the thin stem of his neck.

Quince furtively shifted his eyes, though not his head, in my direction. In that brief instant, I detected both admonition and annoyance, a look from those dark orbs I would come to know all too well. I turned my head back to the north.

Across the Terrazzo, a group of thirty unknown upperclass cadets stood at attention in three rows, silently staring at us with collective intensity from beneath the brims of their wheel caps.

The awkward silence that accompanied this face-off was jarringly shattered by a startling "Boom!" that reverberated off the mountains and echoed back into the strident aluminum structures of the Cadet Area as if corralled in the confines of what was now the extent of our world.

Were you to focus on this place in history and withdraw from the scene such that the players, then the Terrazzo, and finally the entire Cadet Area were nothing more than a speck on a pale blue dot at the edge of the galaxy, you would certainly ascertain no significance to this ritual.

From my very earthly perspective, I observed the upperclass cadets erupting like a disturbed hill of ants upon 1445 wide-eyed boys who would never be able to erase this moment from their memory.

They charged, penetrating our ranks as cavalry engaging an enemy.

Suddenly, an angry face was inches from my stunned one, yelling wildly, accusing me of horrid transgressions that until this point in my life were freedoms I took for granted. He had seen me turn to look at the mountains which infuriated him beyond the bounds of sanity. The now vacuous space between us was infused with the frenetic froth of his hot breath as the bill of his cap pushed against mine. Reacting to this violation of my personal space, I involuntarily pulled back my head which enraged him even further. In a flaming diatribe fraught with expletives and saliva, he branded me the lowest form of life on the planet. Whale shit decomposing on the bottom of the ocean was higher up the food chain than me. I was a smack, a maggot, a—

"Squat! I want to see chins!" he yelled. "Double time in place!"

I tucked my chin against my throat and began to run in place.

"Get those knees up, smack!" He placed his hand, palm down, at waist level in front of me, a target for my knees. "Get 'em up!"

All around me shouts of "Yes sir!" and "No sir!" and "No excuse sir!" were intermixed with a ravenous roar of demands and commands spewed forth by our new group of antagonists. After an interminable amount of time, a second cannon shot resounded above the chaos, and the upperclassmen abruptly ceased their immutable barrage of fault-finding tirades and took their places in the ranks at the back of the formation for the evening meal march.

Upon our arrival at Mitchell Hall, we endured constant verbal molestation from the upperclass cadre as we maneuvered amid the ensuing chaos in search of our assigned tables. Once there, we weathered a stream of nonstop criticisms, condemnations, and mind-numbing questions from the two cadre members presiding over the table as we poured water and tea for our tablemates.

I felt myself nearing the brink of my mental endurance when a voice boomed over the loudspeaker, "Group! Attennnnnnnnnn-hut!!"

All conversation ceased. The Summer Group Commander came to the microphone, but I could not see him. I stood stiffly erect, chin tucked in as close to my chest as I could force it, my forehead straight, my eyes cast down to the table.

"Gentlemen, welcome to Basic Cadet Training," he said simply. "Be seated!"

Adam Carroll quickly discovered the cadre did in fact have a problem with his Continental-style fork management. We ate one small bite at a time, "grounding" our forks between each until the process of chewing was accomplished and the bite swallowed before retrieving the fork to repeat the process. Visions of the comforts of home danced in my head as I chewed each morsel amid the incessant disparaging denigrations dispatched by our new supervisors.

The change of command signaled not only the radical shift from the cadre's comparatively parental attitude of the previous days, it also changed who and what held dominion over our lives. Reduced to the lowest form of living matter with everything to prove, nothing accepted as collateral, our dubious character our largest liability, we were a collective of 1445 individual souls unified by a common quest for survival, fighting our own solitary battles while exhibiting a solidarity unrivaled by the vast majority of the world's institutions for higher learning.

After eating perhaps a third of what was on our plates, we were informed the meal was over. The delectable desserts that adorned each table—this night it was chocolate cake with chocolate icing—went untouched.

We stood at attention behind our seats until the table commandant posted us to regroup in squadron formation outside of Mitchell Hall for the march west to the cadet student center named after the commanding general of the Army Air Forces during World War II, Henry H. "Hap" Arnold.

Rising like a vertical extension of the tiled Terrazzo, Arnold Hall was starkly pale. And like every other major structure in the Cadet Area— with the exception of the Chapel—the building was a grandiose squared-off frame with a flat roof. The west wall, made almost entirely of glass, faced the planetarium—emerging like an enormous half-buried golf ball—and beyond that, the mountains. The other three sides facing the Terrazzo and dormitories were rock-solid and gray. In the coming years, I would attend concerts, plays, movies, wing meetings, pep rallies, Saturday Morning training, and class assemblies here. I would dance in the ballroom and drink 3.2 beer in the Richter Lounge.

When we reached Arnold Hall, we were dismissed and corralled into the auditorium.   I sat next to Adam as the rest of the basic cadets entered amid a soft buzz that never rose above the mass equivalent of a raspy whisper. Adam appeared deeply embroiled in an inner battle, his eyes flickering from one side of the stage to the other where three officers and one scholarly-looking civilian sat, legs and arms crossed as they surveyed our subdued migration.

It seemed civilians were always studying us. Perhaps that is why the dormitories were constructed as they were—flat with large windows like glass slides on a microscope.

"Stand up, please gentleman," the civilian said, and 1445 anxious young boys snapped stringently to attention. "Take it easy," he said. "I'm not your commander." He laughed to ease our newfound rigidity. "This will be a fun little experiment. Relax."

I shook my arms a bit like an athlete loosening up before a game.

"What you are going to do is, you are all going to hold your arms outstretched to your sides, forming a cross," he suggested. "And no, this is not a religious test." He chuckled again.

In unison, 2890 arms flew into position. Some of us even chuckled with him.

"Now, what you are going to do next is very simple," he said. "You're going to hold your arms outstretched like that for as long as you can. When your arms go down, you sit down."

A muffled murmur arose from our ranks. A challenge had been issued. Some fun was involved. The thought occurred to me, as I am certain it did to many, that the longer we held out our arms, the more time would pass before we were returned to the rigorous keep of our new taskmasters.

Several quick minutes elapsed with no quitters. After some time, boys began to cull themselves from the herd. The enlightened ones were among the first to lower their arms. Perhaps they questioned the futility of the exercise, sensing that no reward would come from pain borne out of a meaningless struggle. From the comfort of their seats, they watched with casual amusement as the rest of us pursued the dubious eminence of being the best at this pointless game.

Murmurs turned to groans as fatigued arms dropped like flags lowered in surrender. Philip Quince sat down suddenly as if to say, 'Enough of this!' Arriving that first day at the Academy with a buzz haircut had been painless enough. This took a bit more effort.

More arms drooped, and many acquiesced only when fellow classmates joked that the angle of their arms formed more of an arrow than a cross. Others refused to quit without pain. Henry Francis Cruce— who preferred to be called Hank—was one of these. To occupy my mind against the task at hand, I focused on Cruce.

He was shorter than most of our classmates, slightly built, lean but wiry. His shortly cropped hair receded from the sides of his forehead in an exaggerated widow's peak that reminded me of Eddie Munster. His ears were oddly asymmetrical. The small right one pressed tightly against his elongated head and seemed too far removed from his temple while his left ear was perfectly centered. Looking at his profile from left and right, you would swear you were looking at two different people.

When Hank was finally forced to resign, his eyes rolled toward the back of his head as he verbalized angry frustration in himself.

My arms began to ache. My shoulders were on fire. I looked around at my competition. There were maybe a dozen remaining who had to be hurting as I was. The lone Black member of my element, Lewis Carpenter, lowered his arms as he exchanged glances with a statuesque blond kid across the aisle.

At some point, I reached a compromise with myself, rationalizing that I would not have the energy to make it through the rigors of tomorrow if I did not quit now. Survive to fight another day and all that. Uttering a low groan, I put down my arms and sat beside Adam to await the winner.

The tall blond fellow remained standing. I watched in silent awe as he stared at the ceiling as if hypnotized by the lights, his square jaw enhanced in profile. He stood erect like a legionnaire offered up in willing sacrifice, his face awash in the glow that comes from focused suffering.

Mesmerized by his concentration, I noticed the boy sitting next to him was tapping him gently. The blond fellow blinked and glanced around as if awakened from a transcendental state. Realizing he alone remained standing, he kept his form a few seconds more as if lowering his arms would require more effort than keeping them aloft. Another moment and he dropped them slowly to his side, poised briefly above the rest of us like a monument before bowing into his seat.

"What fortitude!" the civilian said. "Commendable, young man!" He returned to his place behind the lectern and addressed us. "Lieutenant General Thomas S. Moorman is quoted as saying, 'If it is possible to sum up the programs of the academy in a single word, that word is *challenge*.' You might find it interesting that studies such as we simulated here tonight show that a person's endurance in this little experiment is in direct proportion to his determination to stay at the Academy."

Adam turned to me to whisper, "That is just so much **BS**."

I would later decide he was right, at least about this. Unless they documented every single cadet as he lowered his arms and then compared those names and numbers to the actual attrition lists, there was no way they could make any meaningful correlation. It was a story meant to plant something else in our heads.

Still, I went to bed reveling in my own personal glory. I contemplated the boost of esteem this was certain to bring me in the eyes of my peers. But merit ebbs and flows. The "what" you were yesterday means little if it is not replenished by the "who" you are tomorrow.

No one in my element ever mentioned that I almost won.

After two more nights of exaggerated sighs, Adam was gone. On his last day he ate at a table with other out-processing cadets. Despite their transitional status, they were forced to endure the Academy's protocols to the end, sitting and eating at attention. Above the din of the meal, I could hear Adam's high-pitched voice at regular intervals yelling "Yes **sir!**" in a nasal tone that spewed sarcasm melded with contempt.

I managed to slip Adam my P O Box number before he left, but he never wrote. He simply washed his hands of that one brief week at the edge of the Rockies. In my mind, his time there was insufficient to understand what he was leaving. But perhaps it was enough for him. The rest of us had little more than an inkling of what we were yet to face.

There were those among us who had seen the real world in a way many of us never would. Having overcome so much worse in their previous lives, to them this academy party was one ant short of a picnic. Some might struggle with making grades or meeting the minimum physical requirements, but what they lacked in intelligence or aptitude they would make up for with sheer willpower and hard work. Others, like Lewis Carpenter, were motivated to excel beyond what any initial assessment might have indicated.

Upon Adam Carroll's departure, we all moved up one slot in formation. But whoever had been next in line in the hierarchy of the congressman that appointed Carroll to attend the Academy would not be offered the chance to take Adam's place, regardless of how likely he might have been to keep his arms up. That ship had sailed.

There was other shuffling as well, and Hank Cruce became my new roommate. This pleased him because, as our element started with thirteen, he had been sharing a crowded room with Philip Quince and Lewis Carpenter. They too were pleased.

In the nights that followed Adam Carroll's departure, I thought about Tiffany. In nature, dogs don't care about rugs. They pee wherever they want. But doing what is good does not necessarily mean doing what is natural. Sometimes, it's quite the opposite. And if we cannot define good for ourselves, someone will always be there ready to do so for us.

I did hope Tiffany would reward Adam with a jubilant display of affection upon his return.

CHAPTER FOUR

We were regulated by a system of rewards and punishments. If we performed poorly, we were subjected to physical trials designed to gauge our ability to endure. If we performed well, we were rewarded with encouraging words as we endured those same physical trials.

I looked forward to the end, knowing it could not last forever. Night would come, and we would be allowed to sleep. Morning would come, and we would be allowed to eat. Everything had a beginning and an end. I endured the melancholy that sometimes accompanied my days at the Academy with the anticipation of promised rewards. Parent's Weekend, squadron parties, weekends downtown, Christmas Leave, stereos, recognition as upperclassmen, cars, and, finally, graduation. There was always a carrot.

We often sang when we moved in formation, songs I had never heard nor, due to my strict religious breeding, would have imagined existed. Songs about sex. Songs about killing. Songs with words I had never used. Sometimes, in deference to my nurtured innocence, I sang different words to obscure the vulgarity. Still, all in all it was quite liberating. The world was far more risqué than I had imagined.

I don't think any of my fellow basic cadets ever noticed my word changes because they were usually trying to drown out Hank Cruce, who approached singing as he approached everything else. He either did not know or did not care that his warbling style was abhorrent. My mother would have said he had "no ear" for music. But the concept of natural talent meant nothing to him.

The third Sunday of Basic Cadet Training marked the completion of what cadets called First Beast. And we rested. This was the day of the Basic Cadet Dining Out, the few hours outside the Cadet Area we had lived for since hearing of it two weeks earlier. Our first big carrot.

On this Sunday morning, we did not sing. For the first time, we dressed in our recently acquired Service Foxtrot—Air Force blue pants, pale blue shirt, black dress shoes and blue flight cap. In deference to our attire, we marched wordlessly to Mitchell Hall as the Air Force Academy Band played selections by John Philip Sousa.

We ate our breakfast in a quiet, leisurely atmosphere. There was no yelling. No derogation. The morning was an island of civility amid a turbulent sea of discipline.

After breakfast, we proceeded to the Chapel for mandatory church services. At times, the Chapel could feel cavernous and hollow, even lonely. But it was also a safe haven. There was no sitting at attention, no spouting-off knowledge, and the soul was the only thing under inspection.

The Chaplains were celebrities, and they knew it. The services they conducted were as much performances as they were a means of communal worship, a spectacle for tourists and cadets and their families designed to demonstrate that those who stood ready to kill in defense of their country could still pray for peace. You knew it was a show because while the congregation bowed their heads in supple submissive prayer, the players—the leaders—were always getting ready for the next act—turning pages, consulting notes, adjusting robes and stoles, walking to the next part of the stage, confident that God Almighty understood the necessity of their deferred reverence.

We sang songs on which I was raised—rather than the ones about Stella who took me down to her cellar, or the Chicago Department Store where the wares always had something to do with sex. Like the caged bird, I sang boldly, reveling in my own voice through the litany of hymns I knew by heart. I craved the comfort this music offered my soul.

When we sang "Lord Guard and Guide the Men Who Fly," I lowered my head and the tears came. I doubt I was the only one. There

were many bowed heads that morning, including Hank Cruce, who
expressed a subtle piety that belied his usual irreverence for anything
spiritual.

I cannot recall the name of the captain who took Hank, Josh
Steinway, Lewis Carpenter, Philip Quince, and me to his modest duplex
in Douglas Valley. He seemed excited to have his small house full of well-
mannered, clean-cut young cadets. While his wife worked in the cramped
kitchen preparing a tasty home-cooked meal, the captain sat in the living
room with us as we guzzled Dr. Pepper, apparently the house favorite.

"Thanks for the pop, sir," Lewis said suppressing mild burps of
pleasure. "It's been three weeks."

Hank Cruce gazed curiously at Lewis. "Pop?"

"What do *you* call it?" Quince asked.

"Coke," Hank answered.

"But it's Dr. Pepper," Steinway put in.

"In the south," Hank answered, "when someone asks if you want to
go out for a coke, they don't just mean Coca Cola." He looked to me for
confirmation.

"In Jersey, it's soda," Steinway said.

"Pop, soda, coke... I don't really care what ya'll call it," I said, turning
to the captain. "Can I have another?"

"Help yourself," the captain said.

When the five of us returned from the kitchen with a second round,
the captain continued to answer our questions about the Air Force. He
seemed a nice enough man who could envision no life's purpose other
than to serve as a career officer. No doubt, he, like the other sponsors,
had been briefed to portray the military in a very positive light.

When I asked what would happen if, after our five year commitment,
an officer decided to get out of the Air Force, he seemed taken aback.

"Oh," he said as if considering it for the first time, "if you want out
you need to put the skids on, let the Air Force know, so you aren't
considered for promotion."

His wife stuck her head into the living room for a moment, listening
to this exchange before returning to the kitchen without speaking.

I tried to backtrack, as if I never even remotely considered leaving,
but I think what I said made him suspicious. My companions remained
silent on the subject. They no doubt grasped the wisdom of an important

tenet that had been drilled into our heads from the beginning of our training: Never volunteer information.

We sat to eat around a large oak table made longer by the addition of two leaves. Shortly after the captain offered up the prayer, Hank asked if attending chapel was mandatory in the Air Force like it was at the Academy.

"Well, no," the captain answered. "But it's good for you guys. Being a good Christian is essential for being a good officer."

Cruce nodded solemnly, but he looked away with a mocking smile.

Philip Quince moved his large head in an exaggerated nod. "Yes, sir. Faith is the most important thing."

The captain turned to him. "Well, I wouldn't say most."

Quince retreated. "Yessir. But... very..." He lowered his head.

Steinway shuffled in his seat. I followed his gaze to the small wooden cross nailed above the entrance to the kitchen. He was noticeably subdued for the remainder of this afternoon. Perhaps if I had been more versed in the ways of the world, I would have been more attuned to his discomfort.

With the meal over, we took turns calling home from the privacy of our sponsors' bedroom. When my turn came, Mom picked up on the first ring and accepted the charges. Moments later, Dad was on the extension. I had asked in a letter if Noelle could be there as well, but she was not. Perhaps my parents thought to suppress anything that might cause me to consider giving it all up. The soft cooing voice of a young girl pining away back home would certainly have qualified.

I imagine the conversation with my parents mirrored so many others that day, especially their questions: 'Are they working you hard?' 'Are you getting enough to eat?' 'Are you making friends?' Among the questions noticeably absent was, 'Are you happy?'

After our calls, we were treated to a fantastic dessert of chocolate cake and ice cream before crowding into the captain's station wagon for the ride into Colorado Springs to see a movie. I still recall the excitement I felt, being off the Academy grounds with no upperclassmen in sight. While we waited in line for tickets, the captain snuggled up to his pretty wife, nuzzling her neck from behind. It seemed like a show for our benefit.

Hank poked me in the ribs. "Captain's gonna get some nasty tonight," he whispered.

I said nothing, which only made Hank laugh and add, "Doggie style!" I nodded.

He poked me again. "And I'll be chokin' the chicken."

At this point in my life, the only completely naked woman I had ever seen was in a Playboy magazine that my best friend snuck into my hospital room where I was recovering from a broken arm. A curtain separated my bed from the older man who shared the room, but he later told me he could tell we were looking at a "girly magazine" by the way we were giggling.

Watching the movie, I felt my face flush just as it had after my hospital roommate exposed my boyish transgression. There were naked women on the screen, some being raped, others in the throes of passionate love making, and all being strangled to death by neckties.

I wanted to believe our captain had no previous knowledge of the storyline. Surely, he could not have thought a movie about sex, rape, and murder was just the ticket for young boys who had not seen a girl in three weeks.

After the movie, the captain's wife dropped him off at their house in Douglas Valley before taking us back to Vandenberg Hall. It was a quiet ride. We were all too aware that, while we luxuriated in this six-hour respite, the first BCT cadre was packing up to leave as their replacements settled in.

We dutifully thanked the captain's wife and walked away in single file, delivered as we were into the hands of the Beast.

At 1915 hours, our new masters burst forth into the squadron hallways, bellowing orders through our open doors. "Shower formation! Skivvies and shower clogs! Now, squats!"

"I don't wanna see anything but assholes and elbows!" our new squadron commander, Cadet Lieutenant Colonel Hart, yelled above the din. "Move it wads!"

Within moments, the hallways were lined with basic cadets wearing only whitey-tighties and flip flops. We carried our towels on our arms, but quickly dropped them to the floor, removed our flip flops, and began to run in place.

"Knees up, maggots!" the cadre members yelled.

Hart stopped in front of me and held his hand at waist level. "Hit my hand, wad!" he barked.

I pumped my legs higher until my knees touched his hand.

He continued down the line, his face in a deep scowl, his hand tacitly demanding compliance.

.

CHAPTER FIVE

I met Skye Book, as I did most people who would have a dramatic effect on my life, by accident rather than design. At that initial introduction, veiled as it was amid the dust and sweat that was Jack's Valley, I could not know I had met the one person who would alter my perspective as none have before or since.

Three days after the Dining Out, dressed in fatigues and combat boots, with M-1 rifles on our shoulders and metal helmets balanced on our heads, fourteen hundred of us marched down the winding dusty road to the Valley.

Spawned from the generation that survived the Second World War, we were children of the Sixties. Our knowledge of the world beyond our home was largely informed by a little country torn by civil war in Southeast Asia. How we felt about it was largely determined by the opinions of our parents. Few of us could recall a time when there was no Vietnam conflict or active military draft. We were volunteers yet to be soldiers, draft eligible yet untouched by the specter of conscription so long as we remained at the Academy.

During a brief rest stop midway between the Cadet Area and the Valley, I recognized the fair-haired winner of the arm-raising challenge sitting cross-legged among a circle of our squadron mates. Some were picking the little yellow flowers that grew beside the gravel road and putting them in their rifle barrels like the war protesters we had seen on TV. Others were reveling in this light-hearted jab at the training in death and destruction to which we would all soon be exposed.

The Valley was to be the instrument that forged our class spirit and cohesion—a shared experience to establish and enhance solidarity and to discover what we were capable of accomplishing as a unit, despite our differences in breeding.

Still, even as the Valley sought to bring us together, it separated us like a jeweler sorts his diamonds by their attributes.

Several aspects of our training in the Valley were predicated on playing soldier. In some ways, it was much like I had done as a kid. The difference was we donned real steel helmets and dressed in real fatigues and shouldered real M-1s that shot blanks. We were given maps and compasses and instructed to find our way to different checkpoints amid a hostile environment created by upperclass cadre who sought to ambush us as we worked our way through the wooded areas of the Valley.

At mid-morning, the moss on the trees seemed almost damp. Concealed behind the trunk of a fallen pine on the crest of a ridge, Philip Quince and I watched our element-mates descend through the trees with questionable stealth to cross the road below us one-by-one.

When Hank disappeared into the undergrowth beyond the dirt road, I grabbed my rifle and stood carefully. "See you on the other side," I whispered to Quince. "Cover me."

"Cover you?" Quince hissed.

I took a step over the fallen tree then stopped, afraid to move. From the left below us, two olive drab military vans appeared. They pulled up suddenly at the point where the other members of our element had crossed. The drivers, upperclassmen wearing the cadre's distinctive ascots and berets, put on the emergency brakes and scrambled out followed by three or four others from the back of each van.

Less than twenty yards away, none of them looked up the hill in our direction. I stood transfixed as the upperclassman disappeared into the woods in gleeful pursuit of Cruce and the rest of our element. I pulled back my leg and crouched next to Quince behind the rotting, moss-covered tree.

"Now what?" I whispered.

"Don't make a sound," a new voice growled from behind us. "And don't move."

"Yes sir!" I said hoarsely.

"Quiet!" the voice said. A tall fellow with cropped blond hair knelt to my left as he surveyed the road and the vans.

"I've been waiting for those guys to come back," he said, barely moving his head to indicate the vans. The smeared dirt on his face camouflaged his high cheek bones and handsome nose. I glanced at his name tag. I could read 'Bo...' The rest was covered by dirt and grime. Then it hit me. Kneeling beside me was the winner of the cross endurance contest from that night in Arnold Hall. The little yellow flowers no longer adorned his gun barrel.

"Where's your element?" I whispered, regaining my composure.

"The bad guys ambushed 'em. Probably came back here looking for me." He pointed up the hill. "I've been hiding over there."

"They went after our element," I said, eying his profile.

He nodded. "It's a set-up." He paused, turned his attention to the dirt road below, then rose to a half-stance. "Okay... let's go!"

Quince stared at him. "Go? Go where?"

He looked at us and smiled broadly. "We're gonna take those vans."

"We can't do that!" Quince protested. "We'll get in all kinds of trouble." He settled lower with his back to the fallen tree.

The blond guy rose slowly. "We'll be heroes."

I groaned. "They'll skin our asses so bad that when we stand up, our pants will fall off."

"It's a challenge."

"Don't do this!" Quince whispered to me as he eyed the blond kid. "The best way to keep out of trouble is to just stay put."

The blond guy studied him evenly, but his lips formed a crooked smile of disdain. He turned to look at my nametag. "No guts, no glory,

Townsend." His lively blue eyes widened with electric determination accompanied by a tinge of mania. "Bayonets forward. Let's go!"

Before I could object, he hurtled the fallen tree and began sliding in the decaying pine needles down the side of the hill, any thought of stealth now a thing of the past.

I started down after him, stopping momentarily to check for Quince. He was still behind the tree trunk. "Come on!" I said. "Bayonets forward!"

Quince frowned, his protruding lip turned down in defiance. "It's his funeral." He lowered himself until only his eyes and forehead remained exposed above the fallen tree.

I turned and skidded down the slope in reckless abandon behind the crazed blond kid now crouched at the edge of the dusty road.

The vans were still running. My companion took a quick look inside the trailing van, then signaled me with his rifle, indicating I was to take the driver's seat. "Hop in!" he said rather loudly, the grin of his white teeth accentuated by the dirt on his face.

He trotted to the lead van and disappeared inside.

I jumped in the driver's seat of my van but hesitated for a moment before putting it into gear, imagining how I would explain to my father that I had been kicked out of the Academy for stealing a government vehicle. The van in front of me jerked forward. My heart was beating wildly, my guts threatening at any moment to empty themselves in all their glory. I released the brake.

The lead van stopped suddenly, and I crushed the brake pedal, nearly rear-ending it as the blond kid reemerged and raced back to me. "Better idea!" he said, dangling the keys like he was ringing a bell.

"Yeah!" I answered. "We grab Quince and get outta here!"

He squinted, looking in the direction the cadre had gone. "Who's Quince?"

I pointed in the other direction up the hill.

"Oh. The chickenshit." He eyed me as if judging the worth of saving Quince by the look on my face. When I said nothing, he grabbed the keys from the ignition and threw both sets under my van. "Over there," he said, indicating a group of boulders rising like icebergs from beneath the crusty soil.

34

Feeling like a schoolboy charmed by a newfound idol, I followed him. Ducking behind our granite fortress, I glanced up the hill. Through the cover of trees, beyond the camouflage of his ripe-red face, the whites of Philip Quince's eyes exposed both his physical location and his mental distress. "Quince..." I began.

He raised an eyebrow and smiled at me briefly. "It's his funeral."

I took a deep breath. "Now what?"

"We wait." He ducked lower. "Here they come!"

The members of my element emerged from the trees carrying their weapons in one hand, the other placed on their helmeted heads. The upperclass cadre strolled behind them covering them with their own rifles. As the cadre ushered my guys inside the vans, I noticed Lewis Carpenter was not among them.

"Now!" The blond kid was up and running before I could understand what was happening. He pointed briefly at the rear van as he rushed to the other one, brazenly brandishing his rifle through the open door at the driver.

"Bang bang, sir!! You're captured!" he yelled.

I followed suit, pointing my M-1 with a bit less confidence at the other driver. "Sir, this van is... confiscated..." I said, my voice lacking the certainty of my companion's declaration.

Cadet Captain Percival stared down the rifle barrel before raising his eyes to meet mine. Glaring menacingly, he fumed, "There better not be a chambered round in that weapon, squat!"

"No sir!" I said. I had no idea if my companion had adhered to this safety rule.

I retreated a few steps as Percival jumped from the van to face me.

"Where are the keys?!" he bellowed.

I stood my ground in fearful silence.

His scowl emphasized his impatience. "Lower your weapon and give me the keys!"

"Sir, you are my prisoner..." I said, trying to sound defiant.

The driver of the other van stepped onto the road, ignoring my companion's aggressive stance. He walked toward me. "The keys, smack!" he said. "Where are they?"

"Sir, I do not have them," I said honestly.

The other cadre members emptied from the vehicles and into the fray. The blond kid and I were surrounded and critically outmanned.

Percival turned to the blond kid. "Book, squat! You have 'em?"

"He doesn't!" I said before the blond kid could answer.

Percival glared at me. "Did you see who took 'em?"

"Yes sir!" I said.

Book jerked his head, a questioning look on his face.

"Have you seen him before?" Percival asked. "Who is he?"

"Probably Jacobs!" another cadre member said before I could answer. "From Executioners. He's been trying to get us back for the thing we did to his sleeping bag." He turned to me. "Tall blond guy? Kinda goofy looking? Big feet?"

I cracked a shallow grin and nodded slowly as if trying to remember.

"Jacobs!" the other one said.

Percival glared at me. "Did you see where he went?"

"Sir, yes sir!"

"One sir per statement, squat."

"Yes sir!"

"Where did he go?"

I pointed directly at the group of boulders. "Sir, there were two of them. They started off that way."

From the corner of my eye I caught the amused look of my companion.

"Sir," Book said, "you are our prisoners."

Percival swiveled to face Book, his hands on his hips. "You think you've captured us, smack?!" he smirked.

"Sir, yes sir!" I said for him.

Percival glared menacingly at me.

"Yes sir," I corrected.

Suddenly, Quince descended noisily from his hiding place. "Sir, I have you caught... cap... captured," he declared awkwardly. The upperclassmen pivoted in his direction.

Book nodded to me as if to say, 'So, the chickenshit wants to play the hero now.'

"And I saw where they put the keys," Quince volunteered, adding, "Sir."

36

I stared at Quince in disbelief, unable to understand why he would expose our felony and accuse us of a lie. Quince glanced at me then said, "One of them threw the keys under that van!"

A couple of the upperclassmen bent down to look under the vehicle. Amid the dusty median of the road, the keys glimmered like a lost treasure.

Percival glared at me as he banged on the side of the nearest van. "Squats!" He yelled. "Get the hell out of there!"

Percival eyed Quince and growled, "If I see any of you again before the evening meal..." He grabbed one set of keys, jumped into the driver's seat, and gunned the engine. Staring intensely at Book, then at me as if committing our faces to memory, he slammed the driver's door shut, leaving his open-ended threat hanging in the dry morning air.

As the last of my element jumped from the vans, the cadre members climbed in and the two vehicles disappeared down the road in a storm of angry dust.

Turning to Quince, Book said, "I can't believe you nearly busted us." There was something in his expressive eyes that made even the thought of betrayal unforgiveable.

Quince recoiled defensively. "I didn't..."

"Might as well have."

"But he didn't," I interjected in Quince's defense.

Holding his rifle at port-arms across his chest, Quince squared off to Book. "I heard the lie."

Book gestured toward me. "Everything Townsend said was true."

"It was a lie of omission," Quince said. "I'm not about to get kicked out of here for tolerating that!"

Cruce appeared next to me. "We ain't under the code yet, Quince. No harm, no foul."

Book nodded in agreement. "It was a very slick truth." He looked at me in sudden admiration. "There's more honor in covering for your buddy than there is in being some chickenshit Johnny-come-lately."

Lewis Carpenter appeared from the far side of the woods. "We gotta go guys! There's more cadre around that curve!"

"Where were you?" I asked.

Carpenter grinned. "Halfway up the hill. I slipped when the bad guys showed up, so I stayed down. One of them almost stepped on me."

"How'd you stay hidden?" Quince asked.

Carpenter gave him a snarky close-lipped smile. "I kept my eyes shut." He shook his head and looked at me.

"You saw everything?" I asked.

"Yeah."

"You heard what happened," Quince said.

"I couldn't hear much." Carpenter turned and passed a knowing nod to Book. "I was too far away."

"Let's go!" Cruce said. "We gotta make our marker in..." He glanced at his watch. "...seven minutes."

I nodded and looked at my blond compatriot. "You going with us?"

Skye Book shook his head. "I'll find my group. Turn myself in."

"For..." I hesitated.

"The exercise," he said, looking amused. "I'm sure I've got some squat-thrusts coming my way." He smirked, shouldered his rifle, performed a crisp about-face and marched down the dusty road toward the camp. I was sure I heard him whistling.

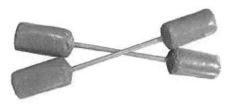

CHAPTER SIX

T he image that pervades every cadet's memory—one I think most of us wish we could forget—is that of the Assault Course where, like the Spartans, we trained in hand-to-hand combat. If my memory is disproportionally laden with the image of running through that simulated battlefield with a bayonet attached to my rifle, perhaps it is because the wounds I sustained while dodging and weaving my way through my years at the Academy might have left fewer scars had the armor of my character possessed fewer chinks.

I fared well enough on the Confidence Course, swinging boldly over murky water, balancing on narrow wooden beams, climbing the high wooden structures with near reckless abandon. These small acts of courage were tethered to my father's athletic affinities. More importantly, the confidence I held in myself then was nurtured by a mother who had always insisted I was exceptional.

I was less effective on the Leadership Course, where I learned that good ideas unaccompanied by charisma make people ignore them and you.

Skye Book, on the other hand, ascended to quasi-legendary status as word of his skills spread through the Valley. The thirteen members of his element solved more of the challenges on the Leadership Course than any other group. And the rumor was that Skye masterminded most, if not all, of their solutions. His element members may have seen it differently. But legends are what people remember.

It was rumored Skye had a chance of breaking the Assault Course record for the fastest time. That chance arrived when Jaguar Squadron's final run at the Assault Course was scheduled on our second Sunday in the Valley.

On any day, the Assault Course was an irreverent spectacle of mindless vulgarity and profane brutality, a mind-hardening, soul-stabbing, emotion-quelling, mercy-denying, horror-inflicting indoctrination to war. But with ten squadrons of basic cadets in need of training, there could be no day of rest.

Within my own element's olive drab twelve-man tent dwelt a microcosm of the diversity that composed the cadet wing, embodying varied perspectives from across America and beyond. Whatever great or little faith we possessed came frothing to the surface on this morning amid the sacrilege of spending an otherwise spiritual day running a course designed to demean the holiness of life through the instruction of killing with a bayonet.

"What a monkey shit way to spend a Sunday!" Hank Cruce complained as our element dressed for the morning. I don't think the fact that it was Sunday mattered to him. Like the bulk of us, he simply hated the idea of the Assault Course, regardless of the day.

From the far end of the tent, Philip Quince said, "Just remember, *I can do all things through Christ who strengthens me.*"

Cruce stiffened, sitting upright on his cot with his back to Quince. His large nose protruded rudely from his narrow face as he tilted his head upward. It seemed oddly balanced with the mountainous Adam's apple that erupted volcanically from his long skinny throat as he swallowed. "The word of God," he said as he pulled on his boots. His green eyes flashed with amusement. I could see he was fighting the temptation to laugh.

"It is," Quince said.

"Are you a student of the Bible?" Cruce asked without looking at him.

"I am. Well, I have studied it," Quince answered warily. "The important parts."

Cruce tied his boots. "You'd be better off reading the Sunday comics." He shook his head and returned to his rant. "It's immoral! Sunday's supposed to be a day of rest!"

"I don't think that counts in the Valley," Lewis Carpenter said. He winked at Cruce.

"We went to the obstacle course on the Sabbath," Josh Steinway said.

"That was Saturday," Cruce answered.

Steinway nodded slowly.

"The most sacred thing about Saturday is college football!" Quince said with a quick laugh.

Steinway opened his mouth to speak but refrained.

"Monkey shit!" Cruce said loudly. "If liquor stores are closed on Sunday, the assault course should be, too."

"When did you suddenly get all religious?" I asked.

"Last night," Cruce said, grabbing his rifle off his cot.

"Yeah," Lewis said wryly. "I thought I smelled something."

After an abbreviated mandatory nondenominational religious service, followed by an inspection of our tents and ourselves, the twelve dozen reluctant teenagers of Jaguar Squadron began a final run along the flat dusty road to the Assault Course. We were delivered into the hands of the training cadre who immediately began barking demands and insults reminiscent of the change of command ceremony. Holding our M-1 rifles at port arms, our ill-fitting helmets bouncing on our shorn heads, we ran in place while the cadre moved freely among us spewing insightful disparagements of our character. Redemption from their lowly opinion of our worth would be possible only if we convinced them otherwise by "putting out" on the course.

Never again in our Air Force careers would we perform the primal actions of the soldier, the practice of assault, the fixing of a bayonet, the hardening of the mind to the idea of stripping another man of his life with our eyes fixed keenly on his.

But this was not really training in the use of the bayonet. Only repeated practice over the years could maintain the mastery required to survive this form of combat. Rather, it was meant to flip a switch from being a peace-loving civilian to a fighting warrior who in later years could brief a wing commander on how he would deliver a nuclear weapon against a heavily defended target while accepting the collateral damage of reducing the skin of babes to dust in the charred arms of their mothers.

The years have not blurred the lines of that day. I remember being sweaty and dirty and profoundly fatigued. Bayonets fitted and forward, we ran the course for time as loudspeakers secured to tall poles reproduced the sound of machine guns and musketry, and blank shells discharged from US Army Reserve tanks echoed along the perimeter of the course. Some members of the cadre carried bullhorns to amplify their wrathful diatribes above the ear-splitting agony of what McArthur called the "mournful mutter of the battlefield."

We got gritty and suffered and ached as we struggled to advance our young war-weary bodies under barbed wire, beneath camouflaged netting, and through corrugated tubes. We labored to put out enough to keep the cadre off our backs, knowing all the while that none of us had a chance in hell of crawling under the radar of their insatiable ire.

As each of us completed the course, we immediately returned to the edge of the battlefield to encourage those of our squadron yet engaged with the "enemy." We yelled and clapped and even ran in place without being so ordered as a testament to our class unity.

I took up station at the obstacle I hated most, the "rabbit-hole," consisting of three long camouflaged tunnels placed side by side. This arrangement allowed three aggressors to crawl through the tunnels at once, thereby facilitating efficiency in both the time and agony required to complete the obstacle.

As I shouted encouragement to my classmates, my mind returned to the memory of our first visit to the Assault Course. An upperclassman named Remington had demonstrated the proper means of negotiating the rabbit-hole, diving energetically into an opening at the far end. In awestruck silence, we watched as the beefy Second Classman scrambled through the tunnel at an unbelievable pace. Although we could not see him once he entered the hole, we could hear him rumbling his way along, kicking up dust, slapping the sides with his hammer-like fists until he appeared on the far side, sweaty, dirty, but barely winded. The man was a beast, it seemed.

My thoughts returned to the present when I noticed the six-foot-three frame of Skye Book lumbering toward me. His head and his rifle held high, he raced past two of our panting classmates as if they were standing still. He ran like a true warrior—his chin level, his legs strong, his stride fluid and smooth.

His cheeks and forehead were gritty from dust and sweat, but his eyes glowed with a fire born of sheer guts and indomitable spirit. I admired him as he approached, even as I realized he encompassed all of something I would never be.

The cadre should have been proud of his effort, cheering him on to a magnificent finish, perhaps even a record run.

But something happened.

When Book emerged at the far end of the rabbit-hole, Remington was immediately there in his face. The rumble of the cannon amid the chaotic clamor of the battlefield made his angry words unintelligible, but Remington's meaning was clear. Without hesitation, Book turned and double-timed back to the entrance, diving to the ground to repeat the obstacle. When he reappeared on the far side, Remington confronted him again. It seemed nothing would satisfy him short of Skye Book flying through the hole.

Again, Skye returned to the entrance. I realized then why he was being forced to suffer this repetitive torment.

He was smiling.

This brazen insolence had infuriated Remington. After three trips through the hole, he allowed Skye to continue on, but there was no chance of him breaking the record now. Still, I doubt that dampened his spirit. It seemed Skye Book's only real competition was himself, or more precisely, his perception of himself. If he felt that he was honestly doing his best, no outside measure could alter that perspective.

When the last of us had crossed the finish line, we were told to reform into our elements around sets of pugil sticks and assorted protective equipment.

A single-elimination contest to determine who was "The Meanest Mother in the Valley" was ostensibly designed as a form of bayonet training, but it was really a chance to beat the hell out of your buddy. As we stood in the circle, Jaguars' squadron commander, Hart, suddenly appeared and grabbed my fatigue shirt and Philip Quince's sleeve.

"Quince! Townsend! Get in there!" he yelled, pushing us inside the ring.

Quince and I avoided each other's eyes as we double-timed to the center of the circle and dutifully donned the fighting gear of caged helmet and padded gloves. A white pugil stick was thrust into my hands as I watched Quince grab his from the dusty ground.

Hart grabbed my collar. "Are you going to put out for me...?" He glanced at my nametag. "Townsend? You want to be the Meanest Mutha in the Valley, right?!"

There being no other acceptable answer, I shouted, "Yes sir!"

Hart released me. "You will *not* swing your pugil stick like a baseball bat," he warned. "You *will* keep one hand at each end of your weapon at all times. You *will* try to hurt your opponent. And you *will* disengage when your opponent goes down."

Years later, I would think back on this, remembering how Skye had been down and how Quince and his conspirators continued to pummel him.

I adjusted my helmet to better protect my chin and glanced at Quince. In his eyes I saw fear and reticence but also a grim determination to avoid embarrassment. We stood facing each other wondering who would be the first to take a swing.

Finally, I lunged, catching him across the side of his helmet. The look in his eyes went from shock to confusion to anger. I expected a retaliatory strike to my head, but he crouched and thrust one end of the pugil stick like a bayonet into my stomach. I recoiled in surprise, fighting to catch my breath. Quince's eyes narrowed as he sought to gauge how deeply he had stirred my wrath.

I made a wild thrust but missed as he dipped to his left. The momentum took me down on one knee near the edge of the circle of my classmates. As helping hands reached for me, I quickly jumped to my feet and turned to face my adversary. Quince took a half-hearted swipe that just missed my chin. I ducked and stabbed at him, catching him with a light but solid blow to his knees. He jabbed at my left shoulder, and I pivoted to parry the blow.

"Goddammit! Let's go you babies!" Hart yelled. He grabbed my helmet like a high school football coach would and thrust his face against the grill. I felt the raw anger of his breath flow around the padding. "Never back down! Fight!"

He threw me against Quince, who allowed me one step in retreat before hitting me hard on my shoulder. The sting that followed was born of humiliation from the cheap shot, but I had no time to moralize as Quince jumped into me, pummeling left and right like he was rowing a sinking kayak away from a waterfall. I took a step back.

"No retreat, Townsend!" Hart yelled from behind me.

There was fire in my blood now, and I could barely resist the urge to take a wild swing at Hart.

I thrust the blunt end of the padded stick into Quince's gut at the same time he landed another solid blow against my chin. We both fell to our knees. My nose was bleeding. Quince was gasping for breath.

"You smacks are goddam worthless!" Hart fumed.

Quince glanced away, and I laid a salvo of solid blows against his head that sent him reeling over on his side. I struck at his neck, then rose to my feet and stood over him, my pugil stick inches from his chin.

"That's enough!" Hart yelled, grabbing the padded end of my stick behind my shoulders. "Doff your gear and get back in formation!"

I removed my battle regalia and returned to the edge of the circle where I stood breathing heavily at parade rest, avoiding Quince's eyes.

Once the Meanest Mutha was determined—Hank Cruce was briefly in the running, but I cannot remember who came out on top—we assembled in formation, dirty and sweaty, our polished boots, clean rifles, and pressed fatigues now soiled casualties of the afternoon's training.

I could think of nothing but the hot shower, warm dinner, and cool canvas cots that awaited us at the end of this day. I glanced cautiously at my sweaty classmates with helmets balanced awkwardly on young heads, wide eyes glowing white on faces caked in dry mud.

"Jaguars!" Hart howled suddenly from the front of our formation. "I'm goddammed disappointed in you! Your performance was pathetic!"

Hart paced back and forth as his rant intensified. "You have to learn to work together as a class, not a bunch of goddam individuals!" He paused. "So, we're gonna run a little more!"

Silent depression enveloped us like a fog.

Our rifles at port arms, we shuffled silently through the dry dust that would take us to our rest, barely lifting our feet off the road. I spotted Skye Book at the far front end of the squadron, his head bobbing in unison with the rest of us but to a cadence he alone could hear. I wondered if Hart was punishing us out of disappointment in Skye's failure to break the Assault Course record. That would have reflected well on him, I suppose.

I tried to draw renewed determination from Skye's strength, but my mind faltered, and I looked away.

The sweat started anew, and the blood and grime on my face formed a red stream of mud. I lowered my head, catching a glimpse of my boots. It would take some time to shake the dust from them. The rifle was so heavy. I felt as if my arms might drop from my shoulders, and my shoulders might sag into my chest. As I spotted the turn in the road that would take us to our tents, I felt a certain degree of rejuvenation. I was contemplating starting a chant when I realized we were not turning. We continued down the road.

The sun was dipping toward the mountains. I thought of the sunsets on the lake back home, one of which had illuminated my first kiss with Noelle. For the first time, I thought about quitting, about going home. I thought of Adam Carroll and Nicki Delgado and wondered how they were spending what remained of this glorious summer.

I must have leaned against Lewis Carpenter because he pushed me away with his shoulder. We finally turned and ran back up the road to the living area. Hart stopped but made us run in place for what seemed an eternity.

"Jaguars!" Hart bellowed. "Don't ever let me down again ever. Don't ever let your classmates down again! Ever! Understand?"

"Yes sir!" we answered in unison.

"Nothing matters more! You stick together! Always! Right?!"

"Yes sir!" we yelled as loudly as our exhausted lungs would allow.

I pondered how Quince and me beating the devil out of each other could somehow motivate us to stick together.

"Get showered up and eat!" Hart ordered. "Lights out at twenty-one hundred hours!"

We'd be polishing our boots in the dark again.

"Dismissed!"

Shortly before lights out, I removed my boots and wiped the pale red dust from the black leather. I placed my polish and brush where I could get to them in the dark, undressed to my skivvies and crawled into my sleeping bag.

Lewis Carpenter lay on his back in the cot next to mine. He sighed heavily. "I'm done in." He voiced no incrimination for my earlier weakness.

"Me, too," I said. "The rabbit hole kicked my butt."

Lewis looked at me. "I saw what Remington made Book do."

I nodded. "Remington..." I decided against further comment.

Lewis returned his gaze upward. "You know how he does it, don't you?"

"Who? Does what?"

"Remington," Lewis said softly so only I could hear. "I should say Remingtons." He laughed briefly. "They're brothers. Identical twins. One of them jumps into the hole and starts crawling wildly. The other one's hidden halfway down the tunnel. He picks up the movements and emerges like a hero at the far end." Lewis looked at me for my reaction.

I shook my head, unclear how Lewis could know this. "Well, that's a neat trick," I said finally.

Lewis sighed and glanced around the tent at our element mates readying themselves for bed. The air in our tent smelled hotter than it really was, but there was enough of a breeze to keep the heat of the day and our collective aromas at bay.

"How'd you do today?" I asked.

Lewis looked at me before returning his gaze to the top of the tent. "I had the fastest time."

My head jerked as I turned to look at him. No one had mentioned this. Not Hart. Not anybody. "They should acknowledge that," I said.

"What difference would that make?" Lewis asked. He closed his eyes and turned away.

CHAPTER SEVEN

My old pastor once told me, "Whatever gets your attention, gets you." So, while I had labored to learn the knowledge imbedded in our little Contrails book, I sought to cull the things I thought important from the things I considered trivial. But the upperclassmen considered every trivial thing in that little book important.

On the evening my class was to be sworn in under the Cadet Honor Code we were back at Mitchell Hall, enjoying another sumptuous evening meal one bite at a time. Basic Cadet Training was all but over, yet the dining hall still growled with the usual back and forth between upperclass knowledge questions and subsequent admonishments with the requisite "Yes sir!" "No sir!" "No excuse sir!" responses from my classmates.

"Quince!" Percival, our table commandant, bellowed through a mouthful of bread.

Sitting to my right at the opposite end of the table, Quince immediately grounded his fork and stopped chewing. "Yes sir!" he yelped, fighting to swallow a bit of chicken breast.

We all stopped eating. It was like someone yelling at a room full of puppies. One of us was being singled out, but we all cringed in dread of the anger in that voice. I chewed quickly, swallowing as soon as possible.

"Don't talk with your mouth full, squat!" Percival bellowed.

Quince swallowed. "Yes sir!"

"And always finish chewing!"

"Yes sir!"

My head was up but my eyes were down, focused on my plate. I could only assume the two cadre members were gazing at Quince with malicious discontent.

"On what day did the United States Congress authorize the construction of USAFA?" Percival asked.

I knew this! It was a fact hidden amid the longer articles in the little Book of Knowledge. April First. An easy date to remember. The Academy being signed into existence on April Fool's Day struck an ironic chord for many of us.

I knew Quince was eye to eye with Percival as his mind searched for the answer.

"Quince! Squat!"

"Yes sir!"

"I'm waiting!"

I reached my right hand surreptitiously under the table and started to spell out "April" on his leg. He jerked subtly, and I knew he was trying desperately to deal with two things at once, not yet realizing they were immediately related.

Percival was obviously enjoying his mind game. "Quince, wad! You think because basic training is nearly over you can kiss-off learning your knowledge?!"

"No sir!" Quince whimpered.

Suddenly, Lewis Carpenter looked up at the one person we were allowed to address without permission. "Mr. Garcia!" Lewis called to the waiter. "Could we have some more of this chicken that must have been cooked last April?!"

A helpful hint for Quince. It was brilliant.

"Sir, it was April..." Quince began.

"When in April?" Percival queried.

Quince hesitated.

I was repeatedly tracing a "one" on his thigh.

"Just one more," Lewis said to Mr. Garcia. "One, thank you."

The light bulb came on. "April First!" Quince said.

I grinned slightly.

Percival suddenly turned his ire on me. "Townsend wad!"

"Yes sir!" I answered, looking up.

"Townsend! Why didn't you help your classmate like Mr. Carpenter?"

I was surprised. "Sir, I was..."

Percival glared at me. "Townsend, I watched you. You did nothing!"

Quince had to know I was trying to help him. He could have asked to make a statement and then told them what I had done. But he sat at attention, motionless, volunteering nothing.

"Townsend! Stand up, smack!" Percival commanded.

I was immediately on my feet, my head erect, my eyes on Percival.

"About face!"

Confused, I lowered my eyes and performed a crisp one-eighty.

"Bring your eyes up, squat!"

My mind reeled. I looked up. Other members of the cadre were staring at me.

"Townsend!" Percival growled. "Look at your classmates! Your honest classmates! You do not deserve to be in their company!"

I did another about-face and looked at Percival. It was inconceivable to me that one of such power, a cadet—the concept of which I still highly esteemed—would question my honesty without discussion. I thought of Skye Book and the vans and how that might relate to my present torment.

"Sir, may I make a statement?!" I asked.

"No! Sit down."

"Sir, I..."

"Sit! Townsend! I don't want to hear another word from your lying lips! You may not be under the honor code yet, but that doesn't make you any less a liar!"

I took my seat, unsure what else to do. I had no recourse. I sat at attention, as stiff as I could, and stared at my plate. It started in my stomach and swelled into my chest. I feared I would start crying, but I held on.

My tablemates had stopped eating.

"Gentlemen, you are dismissed!" Percival snorted.

As if choreographed, my seven classmates immediately placed their napkins beside their plates, grabbed their hats from under their seats, and rose. They wavered, unsure what to do next. Carpenter turned, squared the corner, and walked rapidly toward the far wall. The others followed in quick succession.

I stayed, hoping for the chance to redeem myself.

Percival glared at me. "Get out of here!"

I turned to leave, remembered my wheel hat, retrieved it, and followed my classmates. Percival may have assumed it was over for me, that I would resign. But I was innocent. No false witness could force me out.

The welcoming sun above the mountains greeted me as I exited the dining hall. I longed to close my eyes and turn my face to its warmth and solace. Tears being the only outlet, they flowed as I marched alone in silence to rejoin my classmates in Arnold Hall. I was outraged. I quaked with anger and pain. Quince alone held the power to tell Percival the truth. He had not then. Nor would he later.

That evening, 1380 of us swore an oath to the Honor Code.

"We will not lie, steal, or cheat, nor tolerate among us anyone who does."

They told us that whether we recited it or not, we were obligated. They said the code was purposefully strict. They said the toleration clause made us all stewards and guardians of the code, that without it, the oath was without meaning, that it alone was our one true path to gaining personal integrity.

CHAPTER EIGHT

My mother once asked me what I would do if I "had to room with a negro" at the Academy. I answered that I hoped I would. As strange as it seems now, my answer was quite liberal in light of the conservative environment from which I emerged.

The percentage of minorities in our class did not represent the American demographic. There were more cadets from Texas alone than there were Blacks in the entire Wing. And while there was but a modest chance I would have a Black roommate at some point, every Black cadet would room with a white guy almost exclusively.

Lewis Carpenter and I were assigned to 23rd Squadron for our first academic year, along with Cruce, Quince, Steinway, and twenty-nine other Jaguars. I did not believe in fate and therefore saw it only as coincidence that Lewis and I would share a room for the first three months of the fall semester.

Lewis and I got along quite well. Despite his minority, he seemed comfortable in a way I don't think I would have been if the tables were turned. He possessed a wry sense of humor, and I treasured our friendship. He was essentially the opposite of what many of my hometown friends told me I should expect from a northern Black man. And by northern, I mean about as far north as you can get in the continental United States. Minot, North Dakota.

His father, Matthew Carpenter, a retired Air Force master sergeant, encouraged Lewis to apply for an appointment to the Academy because he wanted a life for his son different from the world he had known. Only later would I learn how dark that world had been. Carpenter's parents must have been fairly devout Catholics. He was the only uncircumcised guy I had ever known, or at least seen.

Lewis and I used what leisure time we had to help each other memorize the quotations in our Contrails book and learn the names of our chain-of-command along with their hometowns. Chief among them was our Flight Commander from South Carolina, Cadet Captain John Jackson Newell, Jr.

Rumors were spreading that US involvement in the war in Vietnam was winding down, and that the draft would wind down with it. Through no provocation from me, Lewis began talking one day about the Confederacy and how it had instated a draft because too few southern men were signing up to fight for "the glorious cause." A year later, the North followed suit. Southern men could avoid the draft by paying someone to join for them. So then as now, as Lewis said, "Rich men pay poor men to fight their wars for them."

I realized then that freedom is a slave to economics.

On the Friday before our first home football game, the cadet wing was busy preparing for a Saturday Morning Inspection, an In Ranks Inspection, and a parade. Cadets called this a "triple threat" because, among other things, there were three opportunities to screw up, all crammed into one Saturday morning.

Triple Threats were thankfully rare, but when we had them, it completely killed Friday night. Enterprising upperclassmen exploited the Doolies, allowing us to listen to their stereos in return for making their SAMI beds and buffing their floors. The upperclassmen would then go to Arnold Hall to drink 3.2 beer while the Doolies labored soberly in dubious gratitude.

While Cruce and I prepared Newell's room for inspection, two doors down Lewis buffed the floor for our Black Sergeant Major, Cadet Master Sergeant Brian T. Robinette.

Cruce and I made Newell's SAMI bed and dusted his room while we listened to *Déjà Vu* on his stereo. Being a Crosby, Stills, Nash, and Young fan, it was the first and only album I had bought at the Academy.

"I hope Newell doesn't find out what we're listening to," Cruce said laughing as I flipped the album to side two. "I can almost smell the weed."

Newell came from a long line of soldiers. On the desk in his room was a framed faded photo of his grandfather sporting the uniform and mustard gas marks that adorned so many infantrymen who fought the war to end all wars. Twenty-five years later, this scarred man's son took a bullet at Kasserine Pass that nearly killed him, which of course would have meant no John junior.

But it was the Civil War, which Newell only half-jokingly called the "War of Northern Aggression," that obsessed him. He boasted his great grandfather fought under Robert E. Lee at Gettysburg and Spotsylvania. To him, the Civil War was a question of state's rights at least as much as it was about slavery, and I don't think he considered either subject settled.

Newell carried a personal memory of a war he never experienced as if he fought the Yankees himself. Raised on tales of heroes fighting for independence, he tended a wound he never received, nursed a blood-grudge for a war he never knew, and viewed the world through the eyes of self-righteous bigotry. He captained our squadron intramural football team where he encouraged us to let loose with the "rebel yell" on every kickoff. Cruce suggested he might not celebrate Independence Day, though I doubted that was true.

He was a product of his environment—of breeding and experience—but in my mind, Newell in no way represented the south as I wished it to be known. While *Gone With the Wind* was a favorite of mine, I harbored no desire to return to those days of slavery, inequality, and white supremacy. Newell pined for them, I think, as one might hopelessly yearn for some former golden age to rise like a Phoenix from the ashes.

Once Newell's room was dusted and buffed, I went to help Lewis with our room. We scrambled through the hours, dusting, organizing, and making our SAMI beds. Our turn with the buffer did not come until after midnight.

The Wing marched to breakfast the next morning abuzz with speculation. Somewhere in the night, the F-104, nick-named the "Missile with a Man in it," had been moved from its corner on the grassy quad of the Terrazzo and was now blocking the western entrance to Mitchell Hall.

One hour later, Lewis and I stood at parade rest at our respective beds. Through the open door, we listened to Newell's progression down the hallway as other cadets in our flight called their room to attention when he arrived and to parade rest when he exited.

I called the room to attention when he appeared at our threshold. Newell was in Service Alpha, wheel cap on his head, his sheathed saber at his side clipped to the white strap that crossed his chest, white gloves on his small hands. His Flight Sergeant, Cadet Second Class Odem, followed behind him, pad in hand, ready to write down our discrepancies.

Newell walked directly to me, stopping to perform a brisk right face that brought us eye to eye. He stared at me, waiting. His eyes were intensely blue and mean. His nose was upturned, almost pig-like. He had wide ears I found difficult not to stare at, his hair was short and curly. The smile that sometimes spread his incredibly thin lips into a garish crescent seemed to have been sucked into his boyish face. He was a little shorter than me, and as he leaned to place his nose two inches from mine, I came to rigid attention.

Newell stared for a moment, challenging me to return his gaze. I concentrated on the silver-lined bill of his wheel cap. After a moment, he turned his attention to my hairline. My hair was still short, and yet he lingered, leaning first to my left, then to my right, coming within inches of each side of my head as he performed his inspection. I could hear him breathing through his nose like a dentist in close examination of a problematic tooth.

Satisfied with my grooming, Newell took one step back, performed a crisp about face, and went quickly to Lewis. He ignored Lewis's hair and went right to his uniform. "There's some kind of crap on your jacket," he said. "Did you inspect it?"

"Yes sir!" Lewis had the boldest 'Yes sir!' of us all.

"Did you have your classmate police you?"

"Yes sir!"

"So it's Townsend's fault."

"No sir!"

"Townsend policed you but missed this, is that right?"

"No sir!"

"If I ask Townsend, he'll say he policed you?"

Lewis hesitated for a moment, then said, "Yes sir!"

I expected Newell to come back to me now. Instead, he shook his head slowly and turned to examine Lewis's desk. He ran the white forefinger of his gloved hand along the edge and looked at it. "Dust," he said.

Odem wrote furiously.

Holding the finger up to Lewis he said, "It looks dark, like dirt." He turned to the window, his back to both of us. "Townsend!"

"Yes sir!"

"Give me Patton's quote from *War as I Knew It.*"

"Sir! '*Never tell people how to do things. Tell them what to do and they will surprise you with their ingenuity*' sir!"

He nodded. "Carpenter!" He turned and eyed Lewis. "Give me Robert E. Lee's quote concerning duty."

Without hesitation, Lewis spouted the quote. "Sir! General Robert E. Lee's quote concerning duty: '*Duty, then, is the sublimest word in the English language. You can never do more. You should never wish to do less*' sir!"

Newell nodded and crossed the room to my dresser. The three drawers were open in the stair-step manner mandated for inspection. He lifted the tray from the top drawer, revealing a pair of socks I had forgotten to fold. He clasped the socks between the tips of his fingers and removed them like he was removing a pile of tissue from a backed-up toilet. He placed them on top of the dresser, shaking his head.

He wheeled and left the room with Odem in tow.

I nodded at Lewis, and together we went to parade rest. I looked at his uniform. If there was something there, it was too small for me to see. I glanced out the door and then to the socks. I thought to grab them quickly, fold them and put them back in the drawer. As I turned toward the dresser, Lewis called the room to attention. I immediately struck the pose and waited as our squadron commander entered the room with Robinette. The commander went right to the socks. He brushed them with his gloved hand and turned quickly to leave the room.

Robinette glared at each of us. "You squats!" he said angrily in his drawn out manner, "Had better get your shit together!" Without another word, he turned and left the room.

Moments after that, we heard Robinette's voice from down the hallway, "Twenty-third squadron, attennnn-hut!"

We snapped to attention, an interesting thing since there was no one watching to ensure we did so.

"Twenty-third Squadron! Dismissed!"

I exhaled loudly. "Man, I'm tired of Robinette telling us to consolidate our feces in a single pile." I glanced at Lewis, hoping he would laugh and not think I was disparaging Robinette's ethnicity.

Lewis remained silent. I knew he was angry at me for the socks, but there was something else in his eyes. I would understand it later when he received a Form 10 with four demerits for his uniform discrepancy and the dust on his desk. I expected a Form 10 for the socks, but it never came.

CHAPTER NINE

Cadet attendance at home games was free. It was also mandatory. Air Force Academy football players were not highly recruited semi-professionals on special scholarships. When you watched an Academy team play, you were watching a group of fast, determined, smart young men who, after the game, would go back to being cadets with the same academic demands, the same rigid discipline, and the same graduation requirements and military commitments as the cadets rooting for them in the stands.

We left the stadium in mid-afternoon as proud winners and returned to the Cadet Area to discover that the F-104 had been returned to its corner of the grass quad. A small chain was snaked around its landing gear, ostensibly as a deterrent to its being moved again. Time would prove the ineffectiveness of such modest tethering.

I went to my squadron and signed out for my first off-duty privilege, my first trip into Colorado Springs alone. Fourth Classmen were not allowed to wear civilian clothes off campus until after Christmas, so Doolies walking the streets wearing Service Bravo suits stuck out like police at a peace rally.

This was a time in our country's history, so foreign from today, when going to war had painted the military in perhaps the worst possible light. In the eyes of many, we were blood-thirsty, warmongering, napalm-dropping scourges of a world that teetered dangerously on the edge, a mere finger-press away from nuclear annihilation. We were not applauded when we came onto airplanes. Few thanked us for our service. Sports figures did not wear uniforms with camouflage motifs. Americans were tired of war, and many of them were tired of us.

But being a civilian college-age kid in this era carried its own risks. Those of the Woodstock generation, embroiled in the most public anti-war movement in US history, put themselves in danger, simply by speaking their minds. They were beaten by the dubious representatives of the "Silent Majority," and shot by guardsmen tasked with fighting the war on American soil.

I felt inclined to treat the downtown streets as hostile territory. I did not fear the physical possibilities near so much as the verbal ones—the oral abuse, the ridicule, the derision. Hoping to diminish my profile, I packed a shoebox with an Air Force issue blue denim shirt along with a pair of civilian slacks I had purchased at the Cadet Store.

Not that I wasn't proud of being a cadet. I just wanted to feel some separation, some normalcy, some chance to once again commune with the society I had discarded three months earlier.

Like a genie in a bottle, I hoped my shoebox would transform me into an everyday guy walking the streets of C-Springs who just happened to have short hair and preferred wearing polished black dress shoes with his denim and double-knit.

With one last look in the mirror, I tucked my shoebox snuggly under my arm and departed Vandenburg Hall, entering the zone where I was not required to walk at attention.

Fall was in the air. Soon the wind would turn brisk, the aspens would glow red and gold, and the real college freshmen would revel in their first autumn of higher learning.

I wished so much to be a part of that world without sacrificing the benefits of the Academy. I had checks in my pocket that almost any business in Colorado Springs would readily cash. I had a place to sleep at night safe from the uncertainties of the world. If I stuck it out, in my senior year, I would have the privilege as well as the means to buy a new sports car, and, upon graduation, a guaranteed job.

For now, I wanted to meet college girls, many of whom were jealously guarded by college boys unable to compete with the secular assets of cadets.

Sitting outside on the bench below Vandenberg Hall where cadets needing a ride downtown often waited, I spotted Lewis walking down the hill toward me. When he was within speaking distance, I said, "You decided to head into town, too."

"Yeah." He had no shoe box.

"Where?" I asked. I had given only passing consideration as to where I would go or how I could store my Service Bravo uniform if I did manage to get a ride into town.

"To rent a car."

"A car," I said. "You can afford that?"

"You can get a cadet rate for five dollars a day."

"Wow."

"I signed out for a weekend," Lewis said.

"Ah." He would not have to return by 0130 like I would. He could stay away all night.

I turned to see a car coming toward us, a white Pontiac Trans Am with a big black and blue firebird decal on the hood and a metal Confederate flag bolted to the front license plate holder. As it approached, I recognized Newell behind the wheel. He brought the car to a stop and rolled down the passenger side window.

"Ya'll need a ride?"

I glanced at Lewis. "Sir, I do not know."

"Get in," Newell said to me. He looked at Lewis. "I only have room for one." There was a stack of clothes on the undersized backseat. He probably could have moved them.

I glanced at Lewis.

"Go on," he said. His words seemed like a challenge.

I hesitated.

"Get in if you want a ride," Newell repeated, looking directly at me.

"Yes sir." I tucked my shoebox under my arm, opened the passenger side door, and ducked inside Newell's Pontiac.

Closing the door, I glanced back at Lewis, unsure what to say next.

"Thank you, sir," I said.

Newell eyed me. "When we get past that parking lot, you don't need to call me sir."

I nodded.

"Lock your seat belt."

"Yes sir." I could not help myself. I knew if I addressed him as "Jim" I would regret it until sometime the following May. Maybe longer. "I mean ... what should I call you?"

"Call me Cadet Newell."

Ah, I thought, no first names just yet. "Yes si... okay."

"What's in the box?"

I'm sure he could guess. "A shirt and pants," I said. "I've heard there are people in C-Springs who don't like cadets."

We rode in silence a while, so I took the conversational lull to mean I should not try to get too familiar. I looked around the interior of the Trans Am as one might gaze upon a trophy to be won in some future contest. It had deep red leather seats and an instrument panel that reminded me of metallic fish scales. I think Newell bought the Trans Am because he couldn't imagine anyone else from his hometown being able to afford one.

My eyes settled on Newell's right hand and the star sapphire senior ring that adorned his finger as he gripped the thick black steering wheel.

"Carpenter's your roommate," Newell said, breaking the silence.

"Yes."

"You're okay with that?"

"It's okay," I said.

"Uh huh," Newell said, going silent again.

Without saying so outright, Lewis made me aware Black cadets had to maintain a certain balance. If a few Black cadets were hanging around together, as often happened in Mitchell Hall at the end of the evening meal, a cadet with but a modicum of Newell's xenophobia might irrationally fear something was up. It is the fear of difference that makes us intolerant.

"Where can I drop you?" Newell asked when we were through the South Gate.

I knew of only one place. "I've heard a lot of cadets go to Giuseppe's for pizza," I said. "So, I guess there."

"Not exactly on my way," he said. "I can drop you close."

After an extended silence, he asked, "Where was Carpenter going? To the movies to see *Superfly*?"

I considered Newell might be feeling his conscience, thinking he should have made room for Lewis. "He said he was going to rent a car."

Newell nodded. "Probably going to Denver." He paused. "They go to parties up there."

"Who does, sir?"

He glanced at me.

"Sorry," I said.

He gripped the wheel tightly for a moment. "All week, the blacks wear their skull caps to keep their greased hair down. Then on weekends, they go to Denver, comb their hair out into afros that are against regs, and they party."

"Oh," I said.

Newell pulled over, braked to a halt, and looked at me.

I glanced around. I had no idea where I was, but I opened the door. Newell pointed and said, "Giuseppe's is a couple blocks that way. Take a left at the light." He then added, "Why don't you just leave that box with me." It was not a question. "I'll get it back to you."

Reluctantly, I placed the box containing my civilian armor on the console and turned to get out. "Be careful," he said, tossing my box backward on top of his clothes. "Try not to get too drunk."

"Yes sir," I said, then remembered. "Okay."

"Okay, Cadet Newell."

"Okay, Cadet Newell. Thanks for the ride, Cadet Newell."

"One 'Cadet Newell' per statement," he said, smiling his peculiar 'I totally own your ass' smile.

I wondered if I would see the box again. I knew he couldn't lie to me, and he couldn't steal my civilian clothes, even though I wasn't supposed to have them. I thought briefly of those lucky cadets from Colorado Springs. They could see their family every weekend if they wanted. Their girlfriends, too. And they knew the places they could wear civilian clothes with little chance of getting caught.

A Patton quote we were required to memorize came to mind: *If you can't get them to salute when they should salute or wear the clothes you tell them to wear, how are you going to get them to die for their country.*

Walking alone along the route Newell said I should take, an image of soldiers in the rice paddies of Vietnam formed in my head. Trudging slowly, ever wary of an ambush, their rifles held at chest level, their eyes darting back and forth, searching for the insidious dangers that lurked among the nearby tall grass or in the trees beyond.

When I found Giuseppe's, there were two other Fourth Classmen in uniform standing near the door smoking cigarettes. I walked to the entrance.

"You here for the pizza...?" one asked, looking at my name tag. "Townsend? Or beer."

I did not answer immediately. I wondered how we looked to the unaffected observer. Three greenhorns in blue cadet uniforms with our nametags, fourth class shoulder boards and our only authorized decoration, the National Defense Service ribbon, the one referred to as "alive in 65," pinned above our left breast pocket.

"Beer then," his companion said exhaling smoke. "For starters." His nametag declared him to be Zusman. "I'm Waldo F. Dumbsquat," he said in an accent I associated with New York. He pointed to his smoking buddy. "Nino Balducci," he joked, referencing the fictitious cadet who legend said wondered around the Academy year after year having never graduated.

I nodded. I looked at the nametag of Zusman's buddy. Vlastok. "Yeah..." I had no idea how to pronounce his name. "I'm Gene."

"Bernie," Vlastok said. He flipped his thumb toward Zusman. "Joe."

Joe Zusman dropped his cigarette on the sidewalk and crushed it with the sole of his polished black shoe. As he tilted his head to look at his watch, I caught a glimpse of the pale scar that ran the length of his right cheek. "Beer-thirty," he said.

Vlastok flicked his cigarette in an arc toward the street and reached for the door.

Zusman lowered his head, studying me from beneath his broad forehead and protruding eyebrows. "There'll be chicks in here. So, it's all for one and one for all and every man for himself."

Vlastok pointed to his own chest. "What woman wouldn't want this?"

We laughed, but not much as we went into the restaurant and surveyed our options.

Zusman and I followed Vlastok in single file to a booth in the corner where we sat hunched over the table. The two of them sat together facing the front entrance. I slid onto the bench across from them with an unimpeded view of the hallway leading to bathrooms in the back.

"You know any girls?" Zusman asked as his eyes moved around the front room.

"The only girl I know is a thousand miles from here," I said. "How 'bout ya'll?"

Zusman smirked. "Ya'll?"

"I met a girl at the first cattle call," Vlastok said, referring to the mixer dance the Academy had put on for Doolies in September.

"So, where is she?" Zusman asked while eying me.

Vlastok shrugged. "Probably still running."

Zusman lowered his head as he held my gaze. "A thousand miles," he said. "That's..."

"Texas," I said. "How 'bout ya... uh... you?"

"Da Bronx."

"Texas!" Vlastok gasped with playful incredulity. "I thought so." He shook his head. "We can forget about getting laid tonight." He looked at me. "So, do your cheerleaders say 'Ya'll yea-ell?'"

I nodded to mask my embarrassment. "If we're not yellin' enough."

Zusman pulled a pack of cigarettes from his coat. I pointed to the "No Smoking" sign on the wall behind his head. He turned to read it, sighed, and put away his smokes.

We ordered a pitcher of 3.2 beer.

Vlastok reeled back as if sitting at attention and nudged Zusman who nodded in tacit acknowledgement. Following Vlastok's impetuous stare, I swiveled in my seat to see a group of four college-age girls giggling their way to a booth on the far wall.

"Aha!" Vlastok murmured in subdued interest.

"Yeah, aha," Zusman echoed with decidedly less vigor.

The girls took their seats, flashing no interested looks in our direction.

"They want us," Vlastok said.

Turning my gaze from the females, I caught the glare of four guys watching us from a table in the center of the room. There were whispers accented by frowns that suggested we were trespassing in hostile territory.

The waitress, a nice looking but somewhat weathered lady I pegged to be in her mid-twenties, placed a pitcher and three mugs before us. Under Zusman's watchful eye, I inexpertly poured myself half a glass.

"Your Texas damsel," Zusman said tilting the pitcher to top off my beer, "is she literary?"

I looked at Zusman. "Literal? You mean real?"

"Does she write? This babe back In Texas?"

"About once a week," I said feeling my face flush.

"Lucky bastard," Vlastok said, shaking his head. "Scented letters?"
I nodded in the affirmative. "Sometimes."

Vlastok pursed his lips before saying, "The only reason I check my mailbox is to feed my spider."

"So, you haven't met any ladies here," Zusman said to me. He lowered his head, his eyes weighing my response beneath his well-defined brow.

"I didn't say that. I'm just not ready to latch on to the first one that comes along."

Again Zusman topped off my glass. "You'd better get to latching. You won't make much of a fighter pilot if you go blind."

I spied a familiar silhouette walking down the hallway leading to the restrooms. Lewis Carpenter reemerged shortly wearing civilian clothes. When our eyes met, he nodded in wordless acknowledgment and continued past our table to one near the windows. After a few minutes, I turned as stealthily as possible to see him engaged in conversation with a pretty girl wearing a sundress and matching hairband. They were the only Blacks in the restaurant. Suddenly the uniform that set me off from the other patrons did not seem so stark in comparison, nor were my surroundings nearly as hostile.

When our pizza came, Zusman ordered another pitcher of beer as Vlastok separated the sliced pieces to allow them to cool. I glanced toward the table of girls. They seemed oblivious to the various suitors eying them at regular intervals. The guys at the center table seemed to be as interested in us as they were the girls, and I sensed trouble. I stopped looking in their direction altogether.

When the pizza was gone, the conversation turned again to possible strategies for approaching the girls. I had imbibed in perhaps a third of the first pitcher. Vlastok, with some help from Zusman, had polished off two more, courting the courage necessary to make a move beyond failed attempts at eye contact. We blamed the lack of interest on the uniform. Eventually, the girls left, leaving us to stew in the squalor of our inaction.

As we rose to leave, I saw Lewis walking with his girl toward the exit. Just outside, I tapped him on the shoulder.

"Sorry about Newell," I said.

He nodded. "It worked out."

"You're being kind of bold, aren't you?" I said. I was a tinge jealous that he had somehow managed to sneak civilian clothes downtown in a way I had not.

Lewis looked over my shoulder without answering, his eyebrows furrowed as if considering a great mystery. When he did not speak, I turned to see the guys from the center table bearing down on us.

"Hey, baby-killers," one of them said.

"What are you zoom-bags doing here?" his bigger buddy asked contemptuously. "You escape from the Blue Zoo?"

Zusman and Vlastok stepped closer to me as Lewis pulled his girl toward his back. I felt a rush of adrenaline as the civilians stopped a few feet away, seemingly ready to pounce. I tried to picture what my first move would be once the fists began to fly.

A fifth guy in civilian clothes and sporting a newsboy cap made of light blue plastic appeared stealthily behind them. My apprehension eased a bit when the familiar tall blond figure cleared his throat. Two of our adversaries glanced up over their shoulders to see Skye Book returning their questioning gaze with a grin.

A voice behind me said, "Everything okay here, Townsend?"

Keeping one eye on our aggressors, I turned to see Newell and three other First Classmen all looking welcomingly large.

"Yes, si... Cadet Newell," I said.

We now outnumbered our antagonists. The four guys glared in brief silence before walking cautiously away down the sidewalk. Crossing the street a block away, one of them yelled over his shoulder, "Fuckin' zoomies!"

I turned to address Skye, but he was no longer there.

"You do anything to bring that on?" Newell asked me.

I looked at him. "No," I said. "We were just fixin' to leave."

Newell turned his gaze on Lewis in his unauthorized civilian attire. "You got a car?"

"Yes sir," Lewis said involuntarily. I know he felt embarrassed in front of his girl.

"Why don't you give these guys a ride back," Newell said.

Lewis nodded.

"Uh..." Newell began.

"Yes sir," Lewis said.

Newell and his friends sidestepped us and went through the door into Giuseppe's.

"There's a cadet bus pickup near here," Zusman said.

"Yeah," I said, turning to Lewis. "We'll find a ride."

Lewis shook his head and looked briefly at the girl, whose eyes were wide with concern. "I'll take you back," he said. "I don't think that was a suggestion."

I looked again to see if I could spot Skye among those entering or leaving the restaurant, but he had vanished as if he had never been there. I almost convinced myself he had not. The strange plastic cap he was wearing made his appearance seem more of a fantasy. Lewis made no mention of having seen him, and, with the exception of Vlastok's snoring, the ride back to Vandenburg was very quiet.

CHAPTER TEN

Despite the demands of those first months at the Academy, I found time to be lonely. I longed for the comforts of home and family and anything else that would nurture my soul. Weeks passed, and dusk came earlier and the dawns later.

By December, the evenings were shrouded in a mixture of darkness and artificial light from the academy buildings. A week before the Winter Solstice we received what many in the cadet wing saw as a long-awaited Christmas gift.

It was a bitterly cold day. We marched to the evening meal wearing our athletic jackets layered beneath our black parkas.

The parkas had pointed hoods which made us look like 40 clusters of some monastic order trudging to the great hall. They were designed so the hood could be unzipped to form a flap in the back that allowed us to wear wheel hats. This day was too cold for that, although it was not too cold for marching. It seldom was.

Within the warmth of Mitchell Hall, I stood stiffly at the foot of the dining table, pouring tea into glasses that Hank Cruce filled with ice and handed to me. Lewis Carpenter then passed the filled glasses to the upperclassmen.

"Cruce!" Newell barked down the table from the far end.

Midway into scooping ice from the bucket, Hank managed to deftly lower both the scoop and the glass to the table as he hit an incredibly rigid stance and turned his head to face Newell. "Yes sir!"

"No ice in mine! My nipples are still frozen."

"Yes sir!" Hank went back to his task. He poured the ice from the glass back into the bucket.

"Cruce, squat!" Newell barked.

This time, ice did go flying as Hank again lowered the glass and scoop. "Yes sir!"

Newell shook his head in disgust. "Pass up my glass!"

I filled the glass while Hank held it. He passed it forward, bypassing Lewis.

Hank picked up the next glass.

"Cruce!" Robinette barked.

Hank again placed the glass on the table, snapping to an even more rigid form of attention as he made multiple chins. "Yes sir!" he bellowed.

I knew it was coming.

"Get... your shit... together!" Robinette said.

After calling the hall to attention, the Wing Adjutant made the simple announcement. The United States Supreme Court had ruled mandatory chapel to be unconstitutional. When we returned after Christmas Leave, chapel attendance would be at the discretion of the individual cadet. A roar of approval arose above the applause.

Cadet Robinette was ecstatic. "Fuckin' A!" he said, slapping the table. "Fuckin' A right!"

When the smoking light was lit and the Seniors were excused, Robinette allowed us to sit at rest. He was in good humor. Hank and I talked guardedly, not wishing to take excessive advantage of a good thing.

"No more chapel!" Hank whispered gleefully.

"No more mandatory chapel," I corrected.

"Fuckin' A!"

As we finished our dessert, Cruce pulled out a pen and filled in the Air Force Form 0-96, which one Doolie at each table was required to do before we were dismissed. If everything had gone fair enough with the service and the meal itself, the Doolie was obliged to check the boxes that reported as much. The first indicated how quickly the meal had arrived. The box to mark was: Fast. Then the server's appearance, which was: Neat. The meal portion: Average. The server's demeanor: Friendly. The food itself: Good. The overall rating: also Good. Fast neat average friendly good good. A fair description of the majority of cadets.

"You smacks going to the honor board tonight?" Robinette asked.

"Yes sir!" I said in unison with Cruce.

Lewis remained silent.

"Good," Robinette said. "You guys get out of here!"

We wiped our mouths rapidly and stood to don our blue athletic jackets followed by our black parkas.

"No post tonight," Robinette interjected as we pulled our hoods over our wool-cap covered heads.

We wheeled away from the table and headed to the big glass doors where Lewis parted ways with us. I had thought he would go along, but he was still smarting from the tours he had marched after Newell wrote him up yet again for some minor uniform-related infraction.

We walked the marble strips to the boardroom where the honor hearing was to take place. Doolies were encouraged to attend a Wing Honor Board sometime in that first year. The very fact that the Academy knew there would be honor boards available for us to witness seemed a bit calloused.

Once inside, we spotted Josh Steinway already seated among the growing audience and moved in next to him. The air in the room was somber and bleak, and most of the light was directed at the far end of the room where the honor board members sat ready to face the accused. The cadet honor prosecutors sat at a smaller table with their backs to us. Another cadet honor rep sat at an adjacent table with the cadet on trial.

The eyes of the accused darted around the room like a cornered animal looking for some means of escape. His deep sighs accentuated the anguish in his face. I think he would have preferred to merely resign and thus avoid all this formal embarrassment.

"Has a cadet ever won one of these things?" I whispered to Hank.

"Not likely," Hank said. "He's all but gone."

I shrugged noncommittally.

"So what are you doing for Chrissmyth?" Cruce asked me. "I mean, now that you no longer have to go to church?"

I glanced at Steinway before saying, "Was that on purpose?"

Hank smiled devilishly. "Yeth." He looked at Josh. "How about it, Steinway?"

Josh looked annoyed. "I'll probably sleep in and go to a movie."

Cruce laughed softly. "Yeah! No more mandatory chapel!"

Steinway's eyes met mine. "It doesn't affect me," he said. "I never went to synagogue because the Academy said I had to."

"Synagogue." Cruce grinned slyly. "You're still Jewish?" He could be a shit sometimes. "Well, you're free now."

"It means nothing," Steinway said looking forward again.

Feeling a nudge, I turned to see Skye Book taking the seat next to mine. I nodded.

"Criminal Townsend," he whispered. He looked past me to Cruce and Steinway. "Is the chickenshit here?"

"I don't know," I said honestly. I looked around but did not see Quince. He and I were now roommates for the winter "go-around," but we had not discussed attending together.

Skye noted my reconnaissance. "Do you know what this is about?"

"What?" I looked at the accused. "The honor board?"

Skye nodded.

"No," I said.

"He's a Firstie from my squadron." Skye glanced at me. "Evil Eight." "Oh."

"He lied about attending mandatory chapel," Skye said. "Went to his girlfriend's apartment instead. Seems God has a sense of humor." He looked at me for my reaction.

I nodded solemnly. I felt intimidated by Skye's presence. I thought to ask about the brief encounter at Giuseppe's and what he would have done had Newell and his gang not arrived, but I did not want to say anything that might make me sound ignorant.

Skye said nothing more, so neither did I.

That evening, I learned emphatically that honor knows no season. If the respondent was found guilty—which he was—there would be no forgiveness of the sin of breaking the honor code, no second chance for redemption, no savior. The fact that he was six months from graduation made no difference. As far as the Academy was concerned, his Christmas vacation could last the rest of his life.

And he would not care if attending chapel was mandatory or not.

Striding toward the mountains in my retreat from the carnage of the honor board, the magic of the Chapel's colors made me slow my pace en route to the Old Dorm.

As my years at the Academy progressed, I would develop a tepid hostility for the Chapel, as it, above all else, symbolized my voluntary incarceration in the half square mile that was the Cadet Area.

But in these earlier times, anything that reminded me of the goodness of Christmas—family, warmth, home, spiritual yearnings—fed my loneliness and my anticipation. It was comforting to know that time could not be suspended, and that, no matter what, Christmas would come, and I could go home.

Alone on the Terrazzo, I gazed soulfully upon the Chapel without fear of reprisal. The stained glass of the majestic Protestant sanctuary glowed like a beacon through the crisp wintry air. The first three vertical rows were primarily yellow and blue, followed by many rows of blue and red. Despite the stark angular shape, the refracted light served to soften the seventeen tetrahedronal spires that pierced the evening sky like rapiers.

I had decided the yellow glass represented the Trinity. I would later learn this scheme was meant to signify a soul coming from darkness into the light.

There were also stained-glass windows downstairs where the Catholics and Jews worshipped, but within the confines of my cultural knowledge, I was unaware of any story hidden behind those.

I stopped briefly, closing my eyes a moment before turning right to continue on across the Terrazzo to Vandenberg. Over my shoulder, I could almost hear the organ music. I tried to play Handel's Hallelujah Chorus in my mind, but what I heard was the somber yet powerful organ fugue of the Protestant choral director, James Roger Boyd, and his melancholy progression of chords.

The organ, which dominated the sanctuary loft over the entrance to the chapel, was a magnificent piece of human endeavor that Saint Cecilia would certainly have admired. A Möller designed by Walter Holtkamp, the tiered pipes, stacked and layered on six windchests, rose behind the choir and above the organ in an unquenchable blaze of awe-inspiring grandeur.

If I squinted, I could imagine two eyes separated by a noble nose and cleft chin, the lower pipes forming a veil, and the horns at the apex a crown of thorns. The lower platforms were spread wide, appearing to me as welcoming—or perhaps questioning—arms. You almost expected the service doors to fly open and the Messiah to step forth to begin His thousand-year reign.

I can still see Mr. Boyd, his visage framed in a thick snowy beard and full head of white hair, his shoulders working as he caressed the keys. Perched at the console high in the balcony, seated with his back to the congregation and opposite the huge aluminum cross with horizontal cross-members shaped like a pair of wings, he looked every bit like an aging phantom of the opera. The sound would swell, filling the Protestant sanctuary as the chords progressed until the music saturated the air, music that made me feel at once inspired and melancholy.

Hour after hour, night after night, often days at a time, the organ was silent. Inanimate. Like a resting beast patiently waiting to breathe its dominance over the believers.

Then Mr. Boyd would unlock the keyboard and move a switch one inch to start the flow of ions that fed the machinery that pumped the air that brought the magnificent beast to life. When he pulled out the stops and the wind rushed through the pipes, the ethereal emanations could make the most stoic among us shiver with emotion.

In the first six months of my cadet career, I spent an hour every Sunday in the Protestant Chapel, huddled in a pew, insulated by the music that fueled my quest for spiritual strength. Beguiled by the instrument's whispering gales of joy and wrath suffused with mournful lamentations, I would often contemplate the majestic aluminum cross hanging above the altar opposite the organ and Mr. Boyd.

If only there had been wings on the Savior's cross, to do what the angels had apparently been unable to do. Fly Him out of there.

CHAPTER ELEVEN

As the Texas International DC-3 descended toward Southeast Texas Regional Airport, the lights of decorated homes below and the glow of the refinery along the riverbank to the north served to fuel my nostalgic inclinations. The soft blue and green airport taxiway lights were like luminaries to me, the headlights of cars pulling into driveways like so many stars guiding me home.

When I strolled into the terminal, Tyson and my parents greeted me like a returning hero. On the short trip home, we all talked at once as if trying to catch up on months of separation in one fifteen-minute car ride.

I could not remember when our house was filled with so much joy. I would have been hard-pressed to ask any more of my family, so pleased were we all to be together again. Tyson was especially clingy, at least as much as an eleven-year old boy will allow himself to be. He seemed to glow whenever I call him "squirt."

My mother and father appeared to be as pleased with each other as they were with me, which was very comforting. In recent years, a wall had begun to form between them as they struggled to balance their dreams with the reality of living. I felt especially glorified that my new role of Air Force Academy cadet far away from home was breathing new life into their lack-luster marriage.

When things were going well enough for my family, every few months or so my father would break out the slide projector and later, after little Tyson was born, the home movie projector.

I treasured seeing the images of our past projected on the end wall of the dark living room. This Christmas was especially intriguing as there were new things I had not seen, a passage of family time minus me.

Dad was proud of his compositions, and he made a big production of it: the unpacking—everything was neatly stored in boxes—the setup, the sorting, and finally, the "show." Through the magic of focused light, we could view the exposed parts of our lives any time we wanted, even in reverse.

I can still smell the heat of the lightbulb mixed and diffused by the cooling fan, still hear the hum of whirring machinery that brought the past to life. And in my mind's eye, I reach out to gently swirl the particles of dust hovering beyond the lens in the widening expanse of light that projected a portrait of my life onto the wall.

The tiny specks appeared from nowhere as if irrepressibly drawn to the past like moths to a flame. Sometimes, they would take on the more brilliant colors of the image, as if the only way to really see was through these tiny bits of sluffed-off skin suspended in space and time.

Despite my mother's diligent dusting, I am sure some of these memory moths still swirl in the air like stars and galaxies or linger in the cracks and secluded corners of the house that for twenty years we called home.

When I phoned Noelle, her homecoming greeting to me was warm enough, but there was something in her voice that put me on edge.

Dressing for our first date in six months, I took my favorite shirt out of my closet. As I buttoned it, the front rippled in a series of waves like bacon curling on a hot skillet. Seeing what months of military training had done to render my wardrobe obsolete, my mother disappeared into her sewing room and returned with an early Christmas present. Designed to fit snugly, the new shirt did every bit of that, bulging in slight exaggeration of my academy-enhanced muscles.

I had packed my high school letter jacket for the trip home, thinking I might wear it in glory and honor. It seemed superfluous now. I hung it in my closet. I would not wear it again.

Noelle's house was near the high school, so I took a scenic detour past my alma mater. The purple and white mosaic of an Indian chief in feathered headdress that adorned the entrance to the school was illuminated by a single white flood light.

It had been dark for some time, but the buildings and the football field were well lit, I suppose to discourage the spurious vandalistic tendencies that could sometimes arise in our local guys with too little to do and too much time to do it.

Driving slowly along the wide street that fronted the school, I imagined hearing the beating of the war drums, ritualistically announcing another athletic contest with a rival school.

My town had a reputation for being in a good school district. The population was growing, and the money from taxes and sporting event attendance was growing as well. The citizens of Rigby's Bluff adored their Cherokees, and many boasted that they "bled purple and white." During a time when many of the larger nearby cities were beginning to integrate their schools, there were no Black residents in Rigby's Bluff—and very few Hispanics. So, if you worked at one of the refineries, wanted your child to get a good education, loved sports, and were white, my little town was the place for you.

Noelle answered the door when I knocked, which surprised me. Usually her mother met me, which allowed her to give me the once over before letting me in.

"Merry Christmas," Noelle said. I detected a subtle intake of air as she lowered her eyes from my short haircut to my torso and the tight shirt that covered it.

"Happy New Year," I answered. My eyes went to her hand as she reached to touch the little silver cross that dangled around her neck. Her summer color had faded, but the cut of her blouse was low enough that I could just detect the tan lines from her bikini. She wore tight white pants that made her thighs look good. I looked into her crinkly eyes which were smiling more than her lips. I knew I had noticed her the way she wanted me to. "Are you ready?" I asked.

"In a minute," she said. "Come say hi to the parents."

This was the part I hated. I had the impression Mr. Stanquist approved of me only as a placeholder until Noelle found the real keeper. I envisioned him threatening my existence for merely thinking about touching any part of his daughter that was not already exposed. Every encounter between us seemed a contest of intention versus dissuasion. I was an easy mark. My upbringing rendered even the notion of going beyond second base absolutely taboo. Not that I didn't think about it.

I followed Noelle inside. Through the opening that connected the kitchen to the den, I could see Mrs. Stanquist in her apron busying herself with the after-dinner cleanup.

The far wall of the den was arrayed with the family's ever-growing collection of crosses. All types and sizes were displayed in a manner that seemed to me rather haphazard. I'm sure Noelle's father had an excellent explanation for why they were arranged as they were, but I had never asked.

Mr. Stanquist was in his easy chair reading the newspaper and smoking a pipe. A framed picture of the Pope hung on the wall behind his head. Definitely home court advantage.

But I was bringing new things to the table since our last encounter. I was an older college kid now, more worldly, and likely sporting fresh ideas that spawned fresh concerns. I doubt he would have believed that my exposure to the opposite sex in the last six months had been so limited as to actually result in a regression of my social skills.

"Gene," Mr. Stanquist greeted me, looking up from his paper over his readers. "Or should I call you Cadet Townsend?" He smiled.

"Hi, Mr. Stanquist." I laughed a little. "Merry Christmas." I reached to shake his hand while he remained seated.

"Same to you," he said, leaning just enough to clasp my outstretched hand when it was within reach. His small pale fingers seemed to almost disappear in mine. "How's school? I'll bet you're glad to be home." He released my hand quickly and folded the paper in his lap, indicating I now had his full attention.

"The Academy's a little tough," I said. "But I'm doing okay. I think I'll make the Dean's List."

"Congratulations." Mr. Stanquist pulled his pipe from his teeth and tapped the ashes into a butterfly-shaped ashtray on the end table. "Have you seen much of Colorado?"

Over time I had learned what it meant to have a conversation with Mr. Stanquist. His innocuous statements were shrouded in subtle inuendo. 'Congratulations' meant 'I expect no less from the guy dating my daughter'. 'How's school' meant 'Are you going to stick it out?' 'Have you seen much of Colorado?' meant 'I don't care what you've learned out west, don't try any of that on my little girl.'

"Doolies don't get out much," I said.

"Doolies?"

"Fourth Classmen. Freshmen. We can only leave the Academy twice a month. I get two weekends a semester where I can stay out overnight."

"I see." Which meant 'I'm not sure if that's good or bad.'

I was still a virgin. As was Noelle, so far as I knew. I was also sure Mr. Stanquist took both of those facts for granted. He tacitly demanded no change in the status quo.

"Where are you guys going tonight?"

"To a movie." I was sure he already knew our plans.

"Who's in it?"

"John Wayne," I said. I was sure he knew that, too.

He looked at me.

"PG," I said to his unspoken question.

Noelle came into the room. She had changed into a button down black dress with a short hemline and a V-neck that plunged a bit lower than the blouse she had been wearing five minutes earlier. Her touchable areas had expanded favorably. She stood strategically behind her father's chair and kissed him on top of his head.

Noelle's mother glided into the room, still in her apron and drying her hands on a kitchen towel. "It's good to see you, Eugene," she said.

I hated that she felt compelled to address me by my given name. I had not been called Eugene since elementary school. Not even by my mother. Except when she was mad at me. Then it was "Eugene Oliver," followed by a detailed delineation of whatever sin I had just committed.

"You, too, Mrs. Stanquist," I said honestly.

"Are you enjoying your Christmas break?" she asked sweetly.

"Every moment of it."

"How long do you have off?"

"Two weeks."

"Well, we hope to see a lot of you."

Mr. Stanquist twisted in his chair, noting Noelle's wardrobe change for the first time. He opened his mouth to say something but closed it again when his wife caught his eye.

I glanced at my watch.

"Well, you kids have fun," Mrs. Stanquist said. She slipped Noelle a house key on a ribbon and kissed her on the forehead. "Don't stay out too late."

We departed into the night, walking briskly to the Chevy Impala. I opened the passenger side door for Noelle. By the time I got around to the driver's side, she had worked her way across the bench seat, allowing me just enough room to slide in behind the wheel. After I closed the door and the light was off, she kissed me with open eyes. "I've missed you," she said, taking my hand in her lap.

"I've missed you, too," I said.

I decided to drive out of Noelle's neighborhood via the back road, which took us past the small fenced-in white building that had been the town's first post office. When I was young, I asked my father about this building, sitting alone in an otherwise vacant lot, looking forlorn and lonely. Without flinching, he told me it was the jailhouse.

I think my father took that opportunity to induce a bit of disciplinary fear into my impressionable mind. He saw nothing wrong with a little white lie meant to keep at bay the waywardness that simmers in most young boys.

With Noelle still holding my hand, I followed the road along the river and turned onto Atlantic.

She nestled in tightly against me. Resting her head on my shoulder, she kissed my neck.

Karen Carpenter was singing *Superstar* on the radio. As she faded out, The Temptations sang to us how "Papa Was a Rollin' Stone." Despite the anti-war, drug cultured, free-love atmosphere of the seventies, we, like our music, were much softer then than we are now. Musicians did not glorify making money as drug dealers. No singer grabbed his crotch while bragging about sexual exploits. There were no video games where soldiers blew other soldiers to bits. We played "Pong."

With one hand on the wheel, I steered the blue sedan along Atlantic, our way illuminated by the bright yellow glow of the refinery. With the escaping fog-like vapors from the lighted distillation towers rising tall into the night sky, the refinery took on the look of some futuristic space city. We slowed briefly in the evening "rush hour" traffic brought on by shift change at the plant before turning downtown on Gateway, what we called "The Drag."

Noelle tried to talk me into ditching John Wayne in favor of Woody Allen's *Everything You Always Wanted to Know About Sex*. I knew I'd never be able to lie to my parents about a movie my father had probably already seen, so I told her we would do John Wayne now and that Woody could wait until later.

We arrived at the Twin Cinema just when the movie was to begin. I turned off the engine but left the radio on.

The Moody Blues were singing about the strangeness of life as I placed my arm around Noelle's shoulder and kissed her soft lips.

She closed her eyes and her lips parted.

Her breathing became quicker and shallower as I stroked her thigh.

Suddenly she pulled away from me. "Oh," she said, looking at her watch. "We're going to miss the start of the movie."

I sighed heavily as she checked her hair in the rearview mirror.

"I really have missed you," she said.

"Have you been a good girl while I was gone?" I asked.

"Yes," she said as she pushed a curl back in place. "Have you?"

"Been a good girl? Not exactly."

She pulled slightly away. "Really?"

"I've been a good cadet," I said. "There hasn't been much opportunity to be anything else."

"You haven't met some irresistible Colorado ski bunny?"

I shook my head. "I haven't even met a resistible one."

For the next three nights, Noelle was unable to go out with me for one reason or another. Finally, on Christmas Eve, she invited me to Midnight Mass. My Methodist parents were none too thrilled with the idea, but they gave in reluctantly when I promised to attend our church's Christmas Eve candlelight service earlier that evening. Dad even half-jokingly said, "Okay, you can go. Just be home by midnight."

The carols sung by the choir in prelude to the mass were beautiful, and the lights were like magic. Noelle was also more beautiful than I had ever seen her, and there was magic in our goodnight kiss. I got home at 1:30 Christmas morning. Six hours later, Tyson had us all up, and Dad never asked what time I got in. It was one of my best Christmases ever. I was immersed in the spiritual side of Christmas on Christmas Eve and the secular side of it on Christmas Day. At the time, I really did not think about the possibility of a third side.

.

CHAPTER TWELVE

B y mid-January, the "dark ages," as cadets called the time between Christmas and Spring Break, had settled in somber and deep. The mountains were covered in snow, and at times there was little clear distinction between them and the slate-tinted sky. Sometimes, the mountains disappeared altogether.

These dismal days were not unlike those of medieval history. We had a lot of time on our hands to concoct baseless notions and wild imaginings. When the air cleared enough that the tops of the mountains reappeared, I could see the angling white outline of Cheyenne Mountain to the south which led me to contemplate the ongoing rumor that a nuclear missile silo, controlled remotely from the complex, lay hidden beneath the shallow grassy mound near the southeast corner of the Terrazzo.

The snowfall seemed unending, as if making up for lost time in December. The white blanket that settled on the Cadet Area would have undoubtedly remained until the spring thaw had the powers-that-were not commissioned bulldozers to work constantly at keeping the Terrazzo clear. Perhaps they feared we would forget how to march.

In early February, protocol was sidelined along with the snowplows in resignation to the fact that Nature had, for the time, won out. As the powder rose to near belt-level, the Doolies could no longer be confined to the marble strips because we could not see them.

With the cold of the Colorado winter came the howl of the Rocky Mountain wind. Some nights, it filled the glass stairwells of the Old Dorm with a ghostly wail. When it was especially strong, the pressure sucked the stairwell doors shut so forcefully that a mournful bellowing of wind followed by the crushing sound of metal on metal reverberated down the corridors.

Against the chill of winter, cadets wore heavy wool uniforms that, when damp, exuded a pungency unrivaled by anything short of three-day-old socks. Add to that the fact that wintertime meant more indoor time, and you have the perfect storm of stink.

It was during these dank and desolate dark ages that cadets became most annoyed with each other. Perhaps this is why we Doolies were made to change roommates every three months. As I think back on it, rooming with Philip Quince during this time was by far the most aromatic three months of my cadet career.

Once, when we took time out from our evening studies to talk about the world situation, he jokingly told me he considered the most imminent threat to his existence to be the smell of my feet.

"Still," Quince said, "it's nothing like my two weeks with Carpenter during BCT."

I ignored this along with most of what Quince said. In the three months I shared a room with Lewis, I found him to be the cleanest guy I had ever known. By contrast, Quince made our room smell like a gym locker. Bathing was not a daily concern for him as getting prepared for and walking at attention to and from the showers took up too much of the time he preferred to spend cleaning his uniform and shining his shoes, which he did quite a bit more than I.

Quince and I got along well enough, despite our past discords. This was due in part to a mutual belief that, as classmates, we had to support each other. Quince had a more personal reason for our peaceful coexistence. He wanted to make the Commandants List, an accolade reserved for the top one third of the class's Military Order of Merit.

Quince reminded me of his ambition on numerous occasions, as he did with all our squadron classmates. Forgoing any reference to our history, he sacrificed a touch of dignity to secure my vote.

His lobbying paid off. When my classmates and I ranked one another for the first time, in what was essentially a popularity contest, he was granted the Commandant's silver wreath. He tried to act humble about it, but that did not suit him. He nurtured an air of arrogance kept aloft by what he assumed was the esteem of his peers.

I thought differently of him and was surprised when he made the list and I did not. In fact, I was ranked in the third quartile. One of my anonymous classmates even ranked me last, citing as his explanation that he believed I had been dishonest with an upperclassman during BCT. I was fairly sure I knew who that was.

The sorting had begun.

I did make the Dean's List. I was proud to wear the star, especially as I considered it an achievement garnered by my own work versus an arbitrary assessment of my peers. Still, I would have readily worn the wreath as well, to join the elite members on the Superintendent's List.

In late February, I signed up for a weekend retreat sponsored by the Academy chaplains. Two days and two nights that offered a chance to be normal, even among upperclassmen.

I was not sure if Quince knew about it. I never mentioned it to him, and he never brought it up.

I decided to approach Lewis Carpenter about going. I knew he liked to get away from the Academy when it suited him. He was doing well both academically and militarily, having made the "Supe's" List along with his winter roommate, Joshua Steinway.

"Nah, thanks," Lewis said when I went to his room, disturbing his studies with my invitation. "Catholics aren't much into retreats."

I guess he did not care to take the chance of falling off the Supe's List just to attend a weekend-long boondoggle.

I nodded and turned to Steinway.

Reading my mind, Josh shook his head and smiled knowingly. "Doesn't sound kosher."

"Oh. Yeah," I said in embarrassment at my unspoken thought. "Guess not."

Still, having a wry-witted Jew at a Christian retreat might have proven interesting.

When I mentioned the retreat to Hank, he signed up without hesitation.

"Having doubts?" I asked.

Hank shook his head and grinned. "Far from it."

I nodded. "Still the atheist."

"It would be immoral of me to be anything else."

"Yet you're willing to submit yourself to a weekend of propaganda."

"If it means two nights away from this hole," he said, "let the fuckers do their worst."

The daily snowstorms failed to diminish as the weekend approached, causing me concern that my soul's desperate need for revival would be cancelled due to inclement weather.

But Friday arrived with the retreat still a go, and my depression was replaced with the exciting prospect of a brief reprieve from the demands of Doolie-hood.

We boarded the blue Air Force bus wearing civilian clothes with no overt indicators of rank. My hair was getting longer and, except for the conditioned fourth class response to social situations triggered by months of subservience, I blended well enough with the upperclassmen.

The retreat would be an open and relaxing foray into faith, spiritual uplifting, and, above all, a glorious, if not brief, retreat from the crushing repressions of cadet life. Rank would be abandoned, for the most part, and we could all be brothers on a first name basis.

As we drove into the mountains and away from the Academy, I felt the fetters of the Fourth Class system falling from my mind as I gazed out on the white winter wonderland from my window seat. I began to feel invigorated and free and just the opposite of a cadet.

The facility for the retreat was part of the Farish Recreation Area, named after a soldier who died during World War II and donated to the Academy by his parents. The bus followed the mountain roads northwest through a surreal snow-covered valley and finally north from Woodland Park. As the crow flies, we were barely six miles west of the Cadet Area. But we had drifted into a different world, a reality altered by time and snow and pretense.

The sky was gray and overcast with low clouds dipping into the valley, enveloping the houses and trees and roads in a delicate fog. The bus barely crept along at times as the driver negotiated the frozen Fountain

Creek Valley Road. It could have been a treacherous journey, but the worst of it was brief.

Growing up in Texas, I had seen snow only once. I had gone to bed after a day of playing with my plastic soldiers in the dead grass that sparingly covered the front yard of our small beige home. I awoke to a world miraculously transformed by a layer of soft white velvet, a magical landscape of fleeting splendor that closed my elementary school for the day.

The neighborhood kids and I were fashioning imperfect snowballs and hurling them with amateurish glee, giving little thought to defense when Mrs. Daily, the friendly young blonde who lived in the pale green house next to ours, sought to redirect our energies.

She had no children of her own. We rarely saw her husband, who usually slept during the day to work the night shift making tires at the plant.

Mrs. Daily instructed us to work together piling the fresh snow into a rounded base. I could not make a good snowball, so she scooped up some snow in her gloved hand and made one for me. Snowflakes gathered on her lashes as she vigorously compacted the snow between her palms. I got a faint whiff of her perfume when she tossed the snowball to me, instructing me to make it into a head. I rolled my little snowball and was delighted to see it growing larger to the point where I had to push it with both hands.

Mrs. Daily monitored my work as she helped the other kids pile on to our snowman's body, encouraging them to make him fat but unique. She cooed inspiration amid broad laughter that made it all the more fun. She was probably beautiful, but at my age, I cared less about looks and more about character. I do remember her long blonde curls flowing over the collar made by the red scarf that, smelling faintly of mothballs and Chanel, was wrapped twice around her slender neck. We had little need for scarves in this part of Texas, and the thought occurred to me that she must have obtained it in earlier days somewhere up north.

My little snowman's head grew, adding on snow like memories along Life's path, and it became harder and harder for me to roll. I tried to stay on level ground, avoiding the ditch that, although easy to descend into, would require much more uphill effort to escape. I looked up from time to time to assess our snowman's progress. I remember seeing my father's face on the far side of the large living room window of our house, tipping his cup as he followed Mrs. Daily's movements. I expected him to join us, but he just sipped his coffee and watched.

When my head was large enough, Mrs. Daily put it in place and instructed us to dig into the snow under a tallow tree to gather leaves. She broke off two long branches, sticking one on each side of our snowman, widely spread as if our creation was delivering an oration on some irrefutable truth. We put the leaves on top of the head like a laurel wreath, and Mrs. Daily finished it off by wrapping her scarf around the snowman's fat neck.

Finally, we rested, standing back to admire our creation.

The day warmed rapidly, and by mid-afternoon, our handiwork was reduced to a faded lump of slush, leaves, sticks and wool.

It was dark when the Air Force bus arrived at the Farish complex. We walked outside among the buildings, the snow muffling our steps and our voices in a way that insulated us from a harsh world that awaited our return to the Academy. I wore a yellow ski jacket I had purchased at the Cadet Store specifically for this weekend, and it wrapped me in a protective layer of polyester and down that made me feel like a hardened mountain man.

I decided on that day that if I ever regained control of my life, I would come back to live forever in this valley with the mountains all around, far from the Gulf Coast refineries of Texas and the far-reaching flatness surrounding them.

The first thing the retreat organizers did was feed us. There were cadets of all classes gathering at whatever tables they desired. No one stood at attention with downcast eyes. No one called anyone "sir."

Hank and I migrated toward a table where three other cadets, obviously Fourth Classmen, stood behind their chairs, subliminally segregating ourselves.

Hank looked around the table. "God, I hate fried chicken," he said.

"What would you prefer?" I whispered.

"I like beef stroke-me-off."

An upper classman I recognized from the Protestant Chapel Chorale took a microphone offered by another cadet and said, "Gentlemen, please bow your heads."

We obeyed.

"Dear Father," he began, "we just want to thank you for this opportunity to come together. And Lord, we just want to praise Your name for all the blessings You have bestowed on us, and Lord, we just want to basically show our love for You and just give you our hearts and our minds in Your service and just celebrate Your Son, Jesus Christ, and Lord we just..."

I could smell the fried chicken getting cold.

Cruce leaned close to me. "This isn't a retreat," he rasped softly. "It's an ambush."

I watched the prayer leader as he continued to listen to his own voice praise God and tell Him all we would do this weekend to worship Him and show our love for Him and... I cannot remember all he said, but his mantra is forever etched in my mind.

"He must think God has a short memory," Cruce whispered to me.

After the Amen, I said, "Short memory?"

Cruce smiled. "He kept reminding God that he was talking to Him."

When I did not answer, he said, "It staggers the imagination."

"Yes, you do," I said.

Cruce ignored my tone. "How is it that the most powerful being in the universe can be so goddamn needy?"

"Do you have to be so vulgar?" I asked.

Cruce exhaled loudly through his nose. "Fuckin' A doodah."

After eating, we went to our first small group gatherings where we learned that the focus of this weekend would be how we could discover God's plan for us. We were given some free time and encouraged to use it to mingle and talk about the Lord. Hank and I meandered toward the sound of a lively discussion in the large central room. I was not all that surprised to discover Skye Book at the epicenter.

"Why would you want to live a long time on earth then?" Skye was asking. "Why not get to heaven as soon as possible? Or better yet just be created in Heaven to begin with."

"Because God has a purpose for each of us here on earth," someone answered.

Skye turned to him. "Do you know what that is?"

"I believe I have found mine," a short skinny cadet answered. "God's purpose for me is to live a good life and lead others to The Way."

"Purposes are made, not found, Eric," Skye said simply as he looked at the skinny fellow.

Eric stared at him.

The cadet who had prayed over our fried chicken flashed Skye a condescending smile. "Do you think you can make your own purpose?"

Skye returned his smile. "If I don't, who will?"

"God."

Skye nodded. "But He already knows how everything will turn out."

Eric shook his head. "He gave us free will."

"You have a choice," the upperclassman put in. "Your whole life could change this weekend."

"God knows the future," I heard Cruce say from beside me, "yet I, a mere mortal lower than whale shit, have the power to change that?"

All eyes turned to Hank. I looked away, as if suddenly distracted by a sound in the adjacent room.

Hank rubbed his chin in thoughtful contemplation. "What you are really saying is that God has a role for me to play, but He already knows exactly how I'm going to play it."

I nudged Hank, hoping to preempt further commentary.

"Unless I have free will," Hank continued, ignoring my ineffectual intervention. "But if that's true, His plan is just wishful thinking against what He already knows will happen."

I looked around, curious how the others were taking this. I could tell the praying cadet was losing his patience.

Hank turned to leave. Catching my eye, perhaps thinking that I should follow him, he rasped softly, "What makes Christians so goddamn arrogant? Why can't they just be meek and let it go at that?"

Later in the evening, I followed the sound of piano music coming from a room where a nice fire roared in a grandiose stone fireplace. I was drawn to the warmth and to the music, which was at once moving and melancholy. This was no ordinary hack sitting at a keyboard belting out

Heart and Soul. Approaching, I realized the notes were coming from a Yamaha grand skillfully played by Skye Book. He was wearing the same pale blue plastic cap I had seen on him at Giuseppe's.

He played with eloquent confidence, as if he alone understood the purpose of each note. I walked to the piano, hoping my approach would not spoil the mood. Standing slightly behind him, I watched spellbound as his long, graceful fingers effortlessly caressed the black and white keys.

The music, which had started softly, was now building to a crescendo that was neither loud nor boisterous. The tune was unfamiliar to me, but even now there are times when I can't get it out of my head. I long to hear it again. But he never wrote it down.

After another minute or so, he stopped and looked at me in recognition. "Criminal Townsend," he said.

I smiled. "Hijacked any more vans?"

He shook his head, turning his attention again to the keys. "Maybe a jet or two."

I nodded solemnly as one does upon receiving a revelation in answer to a lingering question. It must have been the Doolies of Evil Eight that moved the F-104 to the western entrance of Mitchell Hall before the football game against Navy. No great leap was needed to conclude that moving the fighter jet had been Skye's idea.

"How did you pull that off without getting busted?" I asked him.

Skye stopped playing and shrugged his shoulders. "Who's awake at three in the morning except those with evil on their minds?" He lifted his fingers from the keys.

"Don't quit because of me," I said. "It's good. You're good."

Skye shook his head as he closed the fallboard. "God's purpose for me is to go to bed now," he said with a sly grin.

I nodded knowingly. "Interesting discussion with that Eric guy."

"We've had it before." He looked at me. "Salter's my roommate."

My eyes followed him as he pushed the bench away from the piano and stood up.

Gazing down at me, he said, "Later, Townsend."

He glanced behind me as he strode away.

I swiveled to see Cruce sitting silent and alone near a window. His eyes conveyed something I had not seen there before. He nodded and, without a word, turned his attention outside to the drifting snow.

CHAPTER THIRTEEN

With spring approaching, Cruce and I were assigned to room together. In his quest to do all things macho, Hank decided to play on our squadron's intramural rugby team. He was tough for his size, quick on his feet, and there was something almost fanatical about his quest for pain.

One evening after a match he returned to our room awkwardly holding his back. Grimacing in obvious discomfort, he eased himself onto his bed.

"What happened?" I asked.

He closed his eyes and shook his head. "I pulled something."

"Back muscle?"

"Somewhere back there."

"Can you make it to Mitchell Hall?" I smirked. "Should I maybe call an ambulance?"

"No," he said wincingly.

"A coroner?"

He stood up. "Fuck off." He rubbed his back, the pain blanketing his face. "It's sore. I just need to work it out." He tried a few stretches and stopped. "Later." He groaned. "Fucking 39th Squadron! They play for keeps."

"Who hit you?"

"Which time?"

"The time that mattered."

"Do you remember a guy named Evans? At the assault course?"

I considered this. "No."

"Tomi Evans. He was in the running for Meanest Mutha."

"I remember the guy you beat."

"Not him."

The pain in Hank's back did not go away, but he refused to go to the clinic. The next week found him once again on the rugby field.

Hell came the last week in April when, for five days, the upperclassmen indulged in one last concentrated effort to lead us to the brink of physical and mental endurance. It began on a quiet Sunday evening, 15 minutes before taps. Our doors were slammed open, and we immediately came under a barrage of demeaning language espousing multitudinous orders that rivalled those of the Assault Course. We ran in place and made chins and shouted "Yes sirs!" before being sent to bed.

At daybreak the following morning, we were roused to run a lap around the Terrazzo in fatigues and combat boots before returning to the squadron to change into service foxtrot for our academic classes. Between classes, we were expected to return to the squadron for more hazing. Had I opted instead to go to the library to study or to the Chapel to meditate, the hell I was already enduring would certainly have spiraled ever downward like the circles of Dante's Inferno.

The first three days were exhausting for my classmates and me, our only respite coming during the sacred time of evening Call-to-Quarters when the hallways went quiet as we tried to study. By the fourth day, Hell Week began a slow turn toward the comedic when some of the upperclassmen, having lost interest in the intensity of our training, assigned us such duties as guarding the latrines against foreign invasion or inspecting the hallways for "unauthorized communist dust."

On the morning of the final day of Hell Week, we awoke to discover that, despite the addition of the metal chain meant to anchor the F-104 in its place on the grassy quad, the jet had been moved not only off the Terrazzo, but somehow down the Bring Me Men ramp. I remember double-timing to Mitch's for breakfast that morning and seeing the tubular fighter jet backed into a space in the academic faculty parking as if one of the professors had driven it to work.

I nodded to myself, certain that Skye Book had a hand in this ingenious delinquency.

The Friday afternoon run to Cathedral Rock was the culmination of the week signaling the end of our Doolie training. We still faced a triple threat, including the Recognition Parade, before we could wear the Prop and Wings, but after ten months as the lowest form of military academy life, we duly welcomed one last test of our class spirit.

As we double-timed down the Bring Me Men Ramp, I was surprised to see a lone seagull flying solemnly above us. The circling seabird seemed out of place this far from the ocean. I felt an immediate kinship. Soon I would be going home to the beach. I wanted to take him with me. He did not belong here. I was beginning to wonder if I did.

Back in high school, my motivation to join the track team had sprung from visions of myself being no less than legendary. I longed to feel the wind coursing through my hair as I sprinted effortlessly to the front of the race. I aspired to compete, but my failing lay in what it took to win. I did not possess the courage—or perhaps what Melody would later refer to as "spleen"—to push my body beyond that painful threshold where the runner puts everything into a race he knows he cannot win.

We first caught sight of our goal along the paved road that paralleled the athletic fields. When we veered northwest onto a winding dirt road, the Rock seemed to rise and fall like a sturdy ship on a turbulent ocean of earthen mounds. When the run became more uphill, the Third Classmen must have sensed a waning conviction in some of us as they urged us onward in voices more friendly than demanding. I knew my classmates' muscles and sinew must be aching as were mine, exhausted from five days of physical and mental hell. I dug deep within myself, searching for something to turn me away from the point of capitulation.

A memory of the arm test flashed in my head. What came next, softly at first, then rising slowly to a crescendo at the edge of my mind, was the music of horns and timpani and organs. A multitude of pulsating notes, of Bach, of Strauss, of Copland. I felt a resurgence of purpose, of being, of destiny. I thought again of the seagull. He had survived, despite being so far from the home that had nurtured him. I could as well.

The dust disturbed by our boots lifted to form a low gray cloud portending our presence as we shuffled in unison along the path that led to the Rock. With a few hundred yards to go, we made a sharp left turn, putting it directly before us. No longer simply running to the Rock, we were now running at it.

I glanced behind me to see how Hank was doing. The week had been rough on him, but he remained resolute. I knew he was hurting, but no one else seemed aware of his pain, such was his ability to camouflage his weakness. His back was strengthening some, but I had seen him with his shirt off and noted a subtle curvature. He favored it when he thought no one was looking. Right now, he bent slightly forward, but that was no different than the rest of us.

I knew he had seen a civilian doctor who told him the injury might take months to heal, and that he should avoid strenuous physical activity for at least a year. I also knew Hank had no intention of taking the doctor's advice.

"I'm going to graduate from this place," he declared. "No matter what." He made me swear I would tell no one.

As far as I was concerned, if he survived the ravages of the Academy, he would earn the right to graduate as much as, if not more than, those of us less afflicted.

I looked forward again, toward the Rock. I had never been here, which was true for all of us except Lewis Carpenter who sometimes ran to it on those weekends when he could not leave the Academy. Lewis needed a place to run, to get away. Whether that was Denver or C-Springs or the Rock did not matter, as long as he had a place to go. He once told me he hated that it was called Cathedral Rock. He said it was more like a castle, or the skyscrapers he had once seen in Chicago, or maybe it was just a towering stand of eroding sedimentary stone.

It looked nothing of a cathedral to me either, although it did seem spiritual. Here, at last, I was at the end of a part of my life I would never be forced to repeat. I had survived basic training, the Fourth Class system, and now Hell Week. More importantly, I had a revelation that this training, even as it eroded the innocence of my youth, was making me stronger.

When we got to Cathedral Rock, the Doolies from Eighth Squadron were already there. Skye Book loomed large among them. He was trying to scale the Rock to remove a large stone wedged high between the definitive layers. Eric Salter was standing back, clutching the Evil Eight guidon staff in his small hands as he monitored the labor of his classmates.

Our Third Class antagonists, who were rapidly becoming our friends, instructed us to find a big rock to carry back to the squadron. In our zeal for the glory that comes from one-upping worthy adversaries, we sampled several that proved excessively hefty before opting for a less formidable symbol of the weight that in less than twenty-four hours would be lifted from our shoulders.

The walk back to the Cadet Area was much slower than the run to the Rock had been. Transporting the stone required the cooperation of at least two of us at any one time. Despite the effort needed to awkwardly move this stone back to the dorm, my classmates argued over who would have the honor of carrying it. We swapped out several times along the nearly two miles back to Vandenberg, laboring with pride beneath the cumbersome mass. Quince never took a turn. There were plenty of other heroes. I guess that was all right with him.

We marked the stone with our squadron and class, although the Third Classmen said it was not necessary, and we placed it in a prominent place near the CQ desk where it remained for several weeks before quietly disappearing sometime just before semester exams. I would discover this recycled pride a year later when my own fourth class initiates were looking for the perfect stone after their run to the Rock.

CHAPTER FOURTEEN

The Firsties graduated the first Wednesday in June, and we all moved up a grade. By the end of that month, I planned to be skiing on the river back home, reveling in the wind passing through my short hair and, hopefully, admiring Noelle's bikini-clad body as we soaked up the Texas sun in my father's boat.

For now, I sweated with twenty or so other survival trainees in the dry Colorado air, made stale and hot inside the large canvass tent where we sat balanced on one-legged stools with laundry bags over our heads, dangling our arms to our sides.

It was difficult to determine if or when any of the "bad guys" were there in the tent with us, monitoring our compliance. As prisoners of war, we were sure to be punished if they caught any of us removing the bags or resting our arms in our laps. If you fell asleep, you would fall off the stool, and who knew what kind of hell would be dealt to you. As the hours passed, it took more work to breathe. My arms hung heavy; my back ached. My legs threatened to cramp. Suffering into the night, I imagined crucifixion to be something like this.

Peering through a tiny hole in the laundry bag, I was sure I saw daylight. It illuminated a country garden with white latticework fences and yellow flowers. The image reminded me of the thousands of yellow flowers in my grandmother's garden. We often went to Momo's house for lunch after church, and in younger years, Tyson and I would play soldier, hiding from the bad guys in her garden. Momo was the happiest person I have ever met. She had an older brother named Murphy, whom she called Uncle Pete for some reason. He was good at telling funny stories that always made Momo laugh. Uncle Pete came back from France at the end of the First World War a different person, having been much more serious before the year he spent in the trenches watching friends die from artillery and mustard gas. Every day of the sixty years that followed his return home, he looked to find the fun in life.

Momo collected figurines and other dainty things that my dad's youngest sister, Bonnie Jean, sent her from Germany after the Second World War. Pete called it all "bric-a-brac." Momo's favorite was a porcelain dancing lady Bonnie Jean sent shortly before she was killed in a car accident. Momo laughed a lot, except for the year following Bonnie Jean's death when she thought she was dying. Then one spring day, she decided to love life again and planted the yellow flowers.

I heard footsteps. The bag was yanked from my head, and reality uprooted illusion. Before I could look around, the communist roughly lowered the bag on my head again and grabbed my arm, yanking me to my feet. My silent antagonist led me into the night air, and I stumbled, tripping over what I guessed was a tent rope secured on a stake. He grabbed me with his other hand, steadying me before pushing me forward.

I heard the squeak of rusty hinges. The bag was again pulled from my head, and through the darkness I saw the outline of five or six cubicles like make-shift cabinets with plywood doors.

"Get in box, criminal!" he commanded gruffly. He meant to be intimidating, but I detected youthful reticence in a familiar voice—the prayer guy from the Retreat at Farish. He no doubt recognized me as well, but he stayed in character, pushing my head down roughly into the cramped space of the box. My body doubled up as he shoved me inside, my knees at my chin, my feet crossed against my butt. The hinges creaked as he closed the door on me, and I heard the click of a metal latch.

My ankle throbbed from the encounter with the tent stake. I decided to use that as part of my resistance. We were encouraged to make up a cover story to tell the interrogators, a lie to facilitate surviving in a POW camp. Perhaps if I feigned needing medical attention, an opportunity to escape might present itself. I closed my eyes.

The door opened just as I dozed off, and a different communist placed a bag over my head and guided me out of the box into the cool night air.

After a short walk in which I exaggerated my limp, I was forced down into an armless chair and the bag was removed from my head. Seated across a wooden table was a cadet wearing a uniform akin to that of the Viet Cong. Rumor had it that psychology or political science majors made up the bulk of the interrogators. I assumed he was one or the other.

I decided to change my injury ploy and say I was a medic and therefore a non-combatant. I hoped it would be an effective lie.

"Comrade Townsend," my interrogator said in a voice too friendly to be trusted. "You are a medical doctor?" He smiled warmly. "Tell me, comrade, where did you go to medical school?"

I tried to think of one I would be familiar with, at least the area. "The University of Texas," I said.

He nodded. "And where is that school?" He feigned taking notes.

"Austin," I said. "Austin, Texas."

"I see." He watched me silently for what seemed a long time. "So, you have extensive schooling in medicine?"

"Of course."

"Then, Doctor Townsend, you should certainly be able to answer a few simple questions." He paused to flash a wry smile. "If I were to break every bone in your body, how many would that be?"

I subdued a smile of my own. The interrogators were not allowed to hurt us. "You would have to break all 306 of them," I said smugly.

His disingenuous smile devolved into an intimidating snarl. "You are no doctor!" he said, rising from his chair and pointing at me. "You are lying to me, criminal!"

"No, I am a medic," I said defensively.

"You are a dishonorable pig!" He slammed both his hands on the desk. "There is no medical school in Austin of Texas!" He leaned over the desk it until his face was within inches of mine. "And there are only 206 bones in the human body!"

Of all the interrogators I could have faced, I got a pre-med major. "That's wrong!" was all I could think to say. I felt abused. How could a communist know all that?

"Stand up!" he demanded.

"My leg is injured," I said. "I think it's broken."

He pulled away from me and his tone softened. "I am sorry. I will get help." He called to someone outside the tent. A gruff-looking comrade—probably a football player or a member of the hockey team—entered the room.

"Help Doctor Townsend to his feet," the interrogator said to his companion.

The gruff kid said, "Put arm 'round me, criminal."

I did so, and he yanked me out of the chair. It was then I noticed he was holding something. A light from a camera flashed, and my pre-med interrogator said, "See, I have taken your picture!"

The other bad-guy showed me what he was holding—a picture of Nixon with an Adolf Hitler moustache.

"We send this picture to America. Your family will see you being buddy-buddy with your communist comrade while you smile at picture of your Nazi President!"

I was mortified. How could I have been out-maneuvered so quickly?

"Do ten pushups!" my interrogator demanded. "Then sit."

This was the signal for me to try a different story, a new tack to resist giving them information. I was released and my antagonists left the tent.

I completed the pushups and sat in the chair. When my interrogator returned, I pretended to have amnesia. He tried to get me to sign something, but I said I could not remember my name. When he told me to look at the name on my fatigues, I told him I could not be sure if that was even me. This round went much better and taught me that, should I find myself in a tight fix like this, it might be much smarter to play dumb.

I should have taken that lesson more to heart.

I was escorted back to my one-legged stool. Bag-on-head, I looked for the hole with the garden. The light was no longer there. I thought about the idea of near-death experiences. I thought of how evil we believed the communist enemy to be, and what it would be like to spend the rest of your life being tortured. Men can make you burn, scour you with poxes and plagues, make you watch as they maim, torture, and kill those you hold most dear. But the one pure punishment man cannot bestow upon his fellow creature is the capacity to make it last for all eternity. At least death offers an end to the pain.

I turned to thoughts of my father and his love of cameras. When I was old enough to take pictures myself, he taught me to consider how the subject of the picture was influenced by its surroundings—the light, the angles, the background. He called it "composition" because you had to get it right before you took it, and because without it, the picture was non-unique and therefore meaningless. I doubted there was film in the communist interrogator's camera, but the composition seemed permanent just the same.

After some time, I summoned my nerve and lifted the bag slowly above my eyes until I could see my fellow POWs balancing on their one-legged stools, bags over their heads, arms hanging at their sides. Across from me, I caught the eyes of another prisoner. His bag was raised and balanced above his forehead, his hands clasped together and resting on his knees as he leaned forward, looking at me.

As my eyes adjusted, I nodded in recognition.

Neither of us spoke, but Skye Book's brazen defiance of authority emboldened me. He may have been doing this for some time, silently watching the rest of us sitting in torturous obedience. I slumped slightly and glanced around the room. We were the only ones exposing our heads. It must have been funny to the "bad guys"—knowing we were doing their bidding without any of them there to ensure our compliance.

When our eyes met again, Skye wordlessly acknowledged my non-compliance with a broad smile. I was about to speak when I heard footsteps shuffling outside the tent. I quickly pulled the bag down over my face and returned to the upright and rigid position, my arms straight down my sides.

"Piggy Book!" a voice said.

From the sound of the shuffle that followed I knew Skye was on his way to the box and, beyond that, interrogation. I thought it must be extremely painful for someone of Skye's stature to be shoved inside that little plywood container. I composed a warning inside my mind, wishing I could project it to him. 'Lookout for the composition trap!'

The following evening, we were abruptly transferred out of the tent. With the bags still over our heads, we were marched to another place. The air was filled with oriental music from an origin I could not determine. It seemed silly, even campy.

The bags were unceremoniously removed from our heads. Night was falling again, and the bright lights of the compound illuminated the eight-foot chain-link fence topped with barbed wire that glistened like Christmas under the intensity of the floodlights.

We were told to un-blouse our fatigue pants and remove our boot laces, thus making escape more difficult.

The cadet cadre members playing the role of "bad guys"—we were encouraged to call them "gooks"—put us to work making pathways in the dry ground by mounding the loose dirt along the edges lined with small rocks. We made paths to or from every conceivable place from one end of the compound to the other. Invariably, a bad guy would rake his boots across a finished line telling us that it was not straight or one little mound was higher than the other or for any other reason meant to frustrate us. Like Sisyphus, we pushed the stone to the top of the hill only to watch it roll down again.

I began to loathe the incessant music and what it was meant to do to my soul. I tried to think of it as melodies from another culture and nothing more. But the sounds were selected and mixed with the specific purpose of infiltrating the recesses of our minds, calculated to take us to the edge and then pull us back just before we disappeared altogether. It was integral to the dehumanization process.

I felt a sharp poke on my shoulder.

"Criminal! You make prison for fellow criminals who refuse to obey party! Pick four other criminals and come with me!"

I must have hesitated.

"Now criminal! Or you go in box!"

I looked around to see Hank Cruce and Joe Zusman watching me. I nodded in brief recognition at Zusman as he and Hank stopped their work on the trails. I motioned them over. I spotted Philip Quince near them and gestured for him to join us as well. He tried to look away as if he had not seen me, but one of the bad guys grabbed him by the arm.

"You help other criminals," the bad guy ordered.

Reluctantly, Quince stumbled in our direction. We followed the bad guy who took us to a collection of hemp rope and small poles piled near a corner of the fence.

"Make cage for pigs!" the bad guy said loudly.

Steinway and another group of prisoners were working on a similar project nearby. Our bad guy went to the group and told them to use two of the poles to make a cross. "We crucify bad criminals," he said, slapping Steinway. "Go fast! Many bad criminals! But best way to heaven!"

They hastily constructed the cross, lashing it together with rope. When it was completed, the bad guy grabbed Steinway, told him to put the cross on his shoulder, and instructed him to drag the cross around the compound like the stained-glass images I had seen in Noelle's church.

The bad guy looked over at my group with anger in his dark eyes. "You too slow!" he yelled as he strode quickly toward us. "You build good prison! Good to hold dirty pigs!" he said.

The sky was dark now, and the air was growing colder. We were all tired and moving slowly. We had not eaten in a day and had slept only when we could while in the box.

"Spread the poles," I said to Zusman.

The bad guy slapped my back. "No talking!" He glared at us, then smiled his best wicked communist smile before strolling back to join his friends who watched in amusement as they lazed on the benches of a picnic table.

I gestured half-heartedly at the poles, and my group began to lash rope and lumber together for what would be the first side of the wooden cage. I felt a tap on my shoulder. Turning slowly, thinking it was our bad guy friend who would demand we start over, I saw Skye Book's bright blue eyes reflecting the spotlights with an eager intensity.

"Shorter," he said whispering. "And wider."

'What difference could it make?' I thought. I was exhausted and angry. I really did not need the added pain of some perfectionist telling me how to construct a cage. I turned to ignore him.

Book worked the rope, pushing the lashed poles on the ground closer so that the section we made looked more like a train track. He looked at me, obviously intending for me to understand his idea. He glanced behind us to make sure we were not being scrutinized by our captors, then pointed to the nearby eight-foot fence.

Book's eyes took mine to the pieces of wood lashed together. I was suddenly struck by the genius of his idea. I looked involuntarily toward the lounging bad guys, afraid they might see in my eyes what I now understood.

I nodded. As Zusman and Cruce adjusted the ropes, I knelt beside the makeshift ladder.

"Do you have a chit?" I whispered to Book, referring to the piece of paper that allowed escape attempts. Only a few chits had been issued to control the number of escapees. Of course, there would be no such thing in real life, but then in real life the guards would be using real bullets.

"No chit," Book said, glancing at the guards. One was slowly making his way toward us.

"This is a setup," I rasped.

"Maybe." He grimaced. "Does it matter?" He looked at me. "Do you have one?"

I nodded in the affirmative.

Steinway was making another pass near us, his shoulder hunched in the crook of the cross.

'Take the ladder,' Book mouthed inaudibly. He tapped the dry ground to get the attention of Zusman and the others. "Help Townsend," he said softly. They nodded in exhausted obedience as he stood up.

Book strolled to our cross-toting classmate. Steinway fell to his knees as Book transferred the weight to his own shoulders.

I turned my attention to the ladder, trying to look busy as I conjured the nerve necessary to execute Skye Book's bold plan. Suddenly, angry shouts erupted from the center of the camp. I looked up to see that Book had angled the cross on the fence and was trying to shimmy up it, using the cross-member to pull himself higher. Steinway was holding the bottom of the cross to steady it.

"Now!" I whispered loudly.

"What?" Quince gasped.

I grabbed the make-shift ladder. "Raise it! Against the fence!"

Quince looked toward the chaos caused by Book's escape attempt. "We can't do that!" he said. "They'll nail us!!"

"Don't be a chickenshit!" I heard myself say. Zusman and I raised the ladder upright so that it rested on the fence. Quince stood, turned his back on us, and went back to making his dirt path as if he had no idea what we were doing.

"The hell with him," I said. I climbed the three steps of our makeshift ladder and hurled myself into the darkness. Turning back, I could see the bad guys wrestling with Book, pulling him down from the cross.

Zusman dropped to the ground beside me. "Lets' go!"

"The others," I said.

The bad guys were running toward our comrades on the ladder. Cruce was halfway up when two bad guys caught him, pulling the lashed poles to the ground as a cloud of dry dirt billowed around them. Flashing a look of feigned surprise, Quince stood alone from the rest of our classmates.

"Too late," Zusman said.

We ran toward the small hill of tall pine trees that simulated freedom. There was more yelling behind us as we scurried down a shallow gully. I glanced over my shoulder. Our makeshift ladder lay in a heap, and our compatriots were being man-handled by the bad guys. Looking ahead, I saw Zusman was outpacing me as I labored with my loose boots, shuffling more than running to keep them on my feet.

A small shanty appeared among the pines, a dim light glowing through its only window.

"How'd you run so fast?" I asked Zusman as I caught up to him.

He smiled and raised his fatigue pant leg. Rather than the blousing rings that most of us wore, which looked like the elastic ties used in ponytails, his had small hooks. Zusman had unhooked the rings and run them through the eyelets at the top of his boots, re-hooking them to create makeshift laces. It was simple and brilliant.

"Should we knock?" I asked, crouching beside him.

"Just go in."

I looked through the window but could not detect a presence. I crept around to the door and put my ear to it. In the distance, we heard yelling and commands of "Go get them!" More yelling and the sounds of rifles being fired made me flinch, but the noises did not seem to be advancing toward us.

"They know we're here," I said.

Zusman pushed against the door and stepped back into the darkness.

The glow of a single lightbulb formed shadows of a small table and two chairs in the center of the single room's dirt floor. Beyond that, the room was empty. I walked in cautiously with Zusman in close trail.

"Unscrew the bulb!" he said.

I reached for the bulb, then thought of how hot it would be. I started to unbutton my fatigue shirt to use as a kind of hot pad when I noticed a piece of paper taped to the table.

'*You have escaped*,' the note read. '*Take this paper back to the compound. You will not be mistreated.*'

I passed the note to Zusman. "It's what they said would happen when they handed out the chits."

"I don't buy it," Zusman said. "Let's just keep going. Sit it out at Giuseppe's eating pizza and getting drunk on three-two beer." He grinned. "And I could really use a smoke."

"Go OTF? For real?"

Zusman grinned. "Essentially. We're over one fence already. Why not make it official?"

I shook my head. "I'd say yes to that, but then we'd miss out on all this character-buildin'. Besides, I heard that if you give 'em that note they'll give you a donut."

"Wow," Zusman said. "A friggin' donut." His Bronx accent was subtler than I remembered. I'm sure that after a year in the Academy's melting pot my Texas drawl was as well.

He lowered his head so that he seemed to speak through his eyebrows and extended his hands like a balance scale saying, "Drunken stupor. Donut." He handed the note back to me. "Awe, hell." He shrugged his shoulders and looked back toward the compound. "What more can they do to us?"

"We'll be out of here in two days," I said. "With a story."

"Not as good as the one where we got shitfaced in a bar."

In the dark of the moonless night, we slowly worked our way back to the compound, stopping frequently to "catch our breath" or "get our bearings" or indulge in an unsupervised pee. Approaching the compound, we were intercepted by two guards. We showed them the note, and they led us through a tall chain link gate.

As we entered, I noticed a small enclosure bounded on three sides by a tall wooden fence. Inside were two bad guys, one I recognized. Three naked prisoners wearing nothing but laundry bags over their heads leaned against the wooden wall, their hands high on the fence, their bare backsides to the bad guys. Although I could not readily identify any of the butts, I was sure that of the tallest one belonged to Skye Book. I recognized Hank's back and guessed his other nude companion to be Steinway.

One of the interrogators slapped his own arm and yelped, making the hooded prisoners think he was hitting one of them. "Tell us who escape!" he growled, "Or we hurt your friend more!"

"Move, criminals!" a guard yelled at Zusman and me. "Join other happy piggies!" He shoved us into the compound. No donut, no rest, no water. At least we weren't leaning against a wooden fence naked with bags over our heads. Our friends were suffering for a freedom we were not allowed to keep, and guilt was our only reward.

We were "liberated" the next afternoon. Three days later, we were loaded on Air Force buses to be delivered to Saylor Park for the final phase of our training. There remained no hint of the snow that had covered the wintry road the previous February when Hank Cruce and I rode a similar bus along the narrow path to the retreat at Farish. This bus bounced along the dry dusty road for another hour or so before arriving at the tented area where our survival instructors and other cadre would spend the next seven days eating decent food and curling up in warm sleeping bags on cots telling lies about women.

Hank and I were assigned to a campsite with four other survivors: two football players, a guy named Foley who was always hungry, and Walter Oscar Whittaker, a freckled redhead who introduced himself simply as "Whit."

After being searched for food and other contraband, our instructor took the six of us on a short venture to practice our navigation skills and to show us which plants were edible and which would kill us. We were then sent to our campsite with six nylon parachutes for constructing our various shelters along with one live rabbit. Hank named him "Bugs," but as this would be the day's only meal for the six of us, no one considered adopting Bugs as a pet.

It brought to mind the summer my father gave me a rabbit for my twelfth birthday. I wanted a dog, but he said he would see how I did with the rabbit and then decide if I was ready to take care of a more mobile pet.

A friend of mine killed the rabbit when he accidentally dropped a brick on its head. Through the damp fog of my tears I called my friend a murderer. It was the only time I cried over an animal. We parted ways after that, and I stopped asking for a dog.

"Are we supposed to kill it?" Whit asked.

Hank smiled slyly. "We could wait for it to die of old age."

I laughed cynically. "So, how do we...?"

Foley grabbed a stick from the ground and held up the rabbit by its hind legs, gently rubbing the rabbit's back. As the blood rushed to its head, the rabbit began to settle down. Foley swung the stick at the nape of the rabbit's neck. There was no more movement.

I soothed the horror in my mind thinking the rabbit did not know it was about to die. Knowledge of mortality is a curse reserved for man.

We stewed Bugs in two large coffee cans with some plants we had gathered. It tasted okay then, but Bugs got the last laugh. In the next three days, everything we cooked in those cans tasted like bunny rabbit. Even the fish.

On our final full day in camp, the six of us gathered with about 150 other survival students in an open field near the main dirt road. Conserving our energy, we sat and talked lazily as we waited for our next lesson in survival.

"When we get back," Hank said, turning the conversation away from women, "I'm gonna camp out in Arnold Hall and eat pizza and drink beer until I puke."

"To hell with that," I said. "I'm going to the Hungry Farmer!" I thought back to the restaurant where my parents had taken me on our last night together in Colorado Springs. It seemed forever ago now.

A blue truck with a livestock trailer in tow lumbered up the dusty road and stopped near a group of trees. An Air Force captain wearing fatigues jumped from the cab and opened the trailer gate. He directed three cadet volunteers to maneuver a nervous black calf out of the trailer. The calf was having no part of it and resisted the tug of the rope around its neck, knowing instinctively that whatever it was being forced to do could not be good.

I recognized Skye Book among the volunteer calf wranglers.

"Let's go," Hank said as he began a lazy trot toward the road.

Whit and I loped after him.

"What's good to eat at the Hungry Farmer?" Whit asked as we caught up with Hank who had slowed to a walk.

"Everything," I said, keeping my eyes on Skye. "Mountain oysters."

"Mountain oysters?" Whit asked.

"Cow balls," Hank explained.

"Do they make you horny?" Whit asked.

"If you aren't already," I said.

"And I always am," Hank quipped.

Whit looked at Hank as if his priorities were totally out of whack. "Guess I should have seen that coming," he said.

We joined in the struggle. The calf pulled against the rope and braced its hooves in the dust while Skye labored to turn it. Hank pushed against the calf's side, which made it kick at him, barely missing his face with its flailing hooves.

"Don't push him there!" Whit yelled. "Cows kick sideways!" He grabbed the calf's tail and twisted it against its butt which got the desired effect.

After much twisting and pulling and pushing we got the calf across the road and close enough to throw the rope around a tree. Philip Quince strolled over and offered his help, but the work was done now.

The calf tugged against the rope without moving, making it easier for the captain to aim his rifle at the spot right behind the ears. The calf dropped immediately as the gunshot echoed across the valley. We moved in, turning the calf's body until its head was downhill. The captain slit its throat and collected the blood in a bucket. We were hungry and well into survival mode but drinking calf's blood felt a bit much.

Quince seemed to have no problem with it, although I don't think he really swallowed.

When I refused a second shot, Quince rebuked me for my squeamishness before offering the bloody bucket to Skye.

Skye laughed. "Shouldn't you bless it first?"

Quince acted annoyed. "It's just cow's blood. It's not a sacrifice."

"Blood spilled is blood sacrificed," Skye said philosophically as he paused from his work with the other survivors who were butchering the calf as per the captain's instructions. "Unless, of course, it's chickenshit blood." He gazed at Quince a moment longer before returning to his task.

Quince's face flushed crimson as he grabbed the bucket. He went to Josh Steinway who was reclining on the grass with others of his group.

"Hey, Steinway!" Quince yelled. "Want some sacrificial blood?"

Skye turned to me. "Chickenshit."

CHAPTER FIFTEEN

The natural feeling of being home in Texas, of being among all that was most familiar to me, was made foreign by my adopted life in Colorado. I sensed this change as the airliner touched down and the cabin depressurized, exchanging the dry filtered air of flight with the hot humid air of Southeast Texas. For seventeen summers, I had thrived in this atmosphere with a certain indigenous indifference. Now, I felt stifled as my lungs drew in air almost too heavy to breathe.

My town looked much the same. The postmen still walked door to door, the refineries still lit up the night, the churches still filled up on Sunday. And people were still coming to see the house where Jesus had appeared on the screen door.

A revelation came over me. I was no longer a product of my home, but rather a muddled medley of my experiences. I detected a subtle pressure among some I had left behind, almost as restrictive as the discipline of the Academy, demanding I remain minimally modified. But the lives of my friends no longer fit with mine, nor I with theirs.

The summer heat remained oppressive. The economy was still depressed, and any thoughts that threatened the conservative views of the community were suppressed. For many of my high school classmates, the world was different only in that they woke early to go to work rather than to school. All else seemed unchanged, frozen in time.

On my first day home, I drove past the high school, the William F. Rigby Library, city hall, and the old post office, to the river. I stopped at the public boat launch, got out, and stood on the concrete wall that held the river back from the aging moss-laden oaks of the city park. Three roseate spoonbills winged overhead, and I watched their pink forms glide high above the river before descending into the marsh beyond the opposing bank. Facing into the wind, I closed my eyes for a moment and let the warm humid air caress my face.

I looked upriver. A barge sitting low in the water plowed slowly downstream, pushed along by a green and red tugboat. The river rolled behind the tug, the water made turbulent by the powerful engine. The tug's wake was substantial, and my father had warned me some years earlier that if you got caught in all that propeller induced turbulence, it would take you right to the bottom. When I was old enough to take my father's boat out alone, I would follow behind the tugboats, riding the rolling mounds of dirty water like a surfer on a wave. It was thrilling and dangerous, which was why I did it.

I loved this river. It had been my pathway to some of life's greatest pleasures. I spent hours exploring the backwater of the meandering oxbows that branched off the main waterways dominated by huge tankers often christened with foreign names. Sometimes they brought crude oil from various ports to the refineries. Other times, they were loaded with refined oil or gas to be delivered to all corners of a fossil fuel-hungry world.

The river fed into the brackish lake where our father taught Tyson and me how to catch speckled trout and redfish. On our way out, we would dock the boat at old man Bailey's place where he sold us live shrimp at a dollar per hundred. As his wrinkled brown hands transferred the bait from his net to our live well, he often commented that, "These damn little shrimp are too damn little!" But he sold them to us anyway.

This river I grew up on, swam in, skied on, fished in, or just floated along with, was polluted by years of runoff from refineries and roads and oil and gas and outboard motor exhaust. Although the river flowed to the lake and then into the Gulf of Mexico, it never cleared. There were always fresh pollutants. The muck and mud retained the toxins, and the constant traffic of oil freighters and recreational boats, and the rains that carried the filth to the river from the land were perpetual. One wonders, if all sources of pollution ceased to exist, how long it would take for the river to be clean again. What is the half-life of abuse?

My father would not allow us to eat any fish or crabs we caught in the river, but they were okay if we caught them in the lake. He believed the concentration of pollutants in the river became sufficiently diluted by then. The air was probably much more dangerous than the water anyway. Mercury, sulfites, and other chemicals would eventually lead to many of my friends developing leukemia or various other malignancies.

Balanced on the wall, I took in all that was around me. The park looked the same. The concrete boat ramp was still coated with algae, appearing as treacherous as ever. Beyond the dock, seagulls circled a man in a boat who was dumping something overboard. There were cows of unknown origin grazing amid the scrub trees on the far bank.

The river swirled the same brown and gray mix downstream. Yet, I imagined there was not a single drop of water in the river that had been there when I left.

In this, the river and I were brothers. By all outward appearances, I looked about the same. But I was different inside. More importantly, I was new. I was seeing the world in a fresh light. It did not matter whether I looked the same to the world.

After the barge passed, I watched the trunk of an uprooted tree flow much more lazily on its way downriver. Some of the roots rose vertically like sail-less masts of a haunted schooner. There were men launching their boats from trailers to go fishing or skiing or just out for a jaunt, and I hoped they would be able to avoid this danger.

I wondered where the tree and the river had become life mates. Possibly somewhere in the Big Thicket to the north. Perhaps the tree had grown strong along the water's edge, but the river had slowly worn away the clay until the tree could no longer stay rooted. Perhaps a strong wind had finally forced it into the current. It may have held its grip to the land a while longer, but ultimately the river demanded its company.

I imagined all humanity balanced on that fallen tree, drifting slowly past my little town toward the lake and eventually into the Gulf, and from there to the sea. I thought that, flowing downstream, our minds fight against the current in search of something that will allow us to make sense of it all. In this search for meaning, we must accept the inescapable influence of the tributary of our birth. We may try to alter our path, improve our lot, rise above the perceptions of others, but in the end, we started where we started, and nothing can alter that fact. We flow where life will allow. While there are obstacles we can overcome, even shallow areas where we may jump to the left or right, there are also deeply cut channels restricting our course, corralling us between high levees we may never surmount.

And one day, when we reach the delta where time stops and the sun sets, we are deposited with so many others into the eternal sea.

And it is there that we must die.

PART TWO

"A man's character is his fate."

Heraclitus

CHAPTER SIXTEEN

Cadet squadrons were the closest thing to fraternities the Academy had to offer. In August, I was assigned to Ninth Squadron along with Hank Cruce. I was pleased to discover my fellow survivors and Third Classmen, Walter Whittaker and Joseph Zusman, were assigned to "Nooky Niners" as well. Ostensibly, we would all stay together until we graduated, developing a camaraderie that would extend beyond military formality and our cadet years.

Perhaps to define the boundaries of our friendship early on, Zusman confessed to me he held no belief of a god in any form, and that he had forsaken his family's faith as soon as he was far enough away to safely do so. After graduating valedictorian in a class of three hundred students at a prestigious preparatory school in New York, Joseph Zusman embarrassed his family, in fact his entire community, by accepting an appointment to the Academy over full scholarships offered to him by Princeton and Brown. And Yeshiva University.

He was a member of the Cadet Forensic Association, as it was called, which fit in well with his polemic tendencies. There seemed to be no topic, no idea he could not argue against if you were for it, or for if you were not. I never really knew if this was because his convictions ran contrary to the norm, or if he had no real convictions at all.

Zusman smoked like the proverbial chimney when he was contemplating something or working on homework or about to go to bed or getting up in the morning or shaving, which he usually did twice a day. His five o'clock shadow always looked like it was still on Eastern Time.

NOR TOLERATE AMONG US

I had initially taken to calling him "Zeus," but he did not care for it. So I opted for "Zooms." I thought it appropriate because his IQ was stratospheric, and he zoomed through his classes as if he already knew everything there was to learn.

Eric Salter, Skye's one-time roommate, was also assigned to Nooky Niners. Eric was like many cadets I came to know who believed they were special in one way or another. But to question one cadet's exceptionality was to deny your own.

Whit Whittaker was the exception to this self-adulation. He was loyal, trustworthy, intelligent, and brave—he would have made an excellent Golden Retriever—and he was athletically gifted, despite his scarecrow-like build.

Whit seemed detached from the pettiness that often came with being a cadet. He saw the whining of those who hemmed and hawed about being at the Academy as nothing more than privileged blabber. He tried to obey the rules, never seemed to get into real trouble, and he saw the Cadet Honor Code as the loftiest statement of valor ever written.

When we first entered the squadron dormitory room we would share for the next three months, Whit threw a laundry bag full of clothes on the bed farthest from the door. "This okay?" he asked.

"Uh, yeah," I said, tossing my bag on the bed by the sink. "Can't imagine it any other way."

Whit dropped his other bag on the bed and went to the window that ran the width of the far wall. "Nice view."

I glanced outside. Ours was an interior room that looked across the quad to other rooms on the far side. "I think that's the same tree I stared at last year," I said. "The only thing that's changed is the angle. A few more leaves, maybe."

Whit put his hands in his pockets. "You both survived another year."

I untied my duffle and dumped its contents of T-shirts, black and white socks, skivvies, and shoes on my mattress. "What squadron were you in last year?" I asked, turning my back to him as I began folding the shirts.

"Forty-first."

I laughed. "Bullshit." The wing only had forty squadrons.

Whit sighed. "That's the squadron they assign you to if you resign... or get kicked out."

I stopped in mid-fold and eyed him as he turned from the window.

"I hope I can get it right this time," he said, untying his duffle.

"What do you mean 'this time'?" I asked.

He dumped the duffle on the bed. "Guess I never told you."

"What?"

"I was booted for grades," he said matter-of-factly as he plucked clothes from his bag. "After my Doolie year."

I stared at his back. "The whole time we were escaping and evading and corralling sacrificial calves you never thought to mention that?"

Whit shrugged. "It never came up." He grabbed a handful of socks from the bed and strolled to his chest-of-drawers.

"When?" I asked, breaking the silence.

"When?"

"When did they... when did you leave?"

"Last June. I didn't do any summer programs."

"Where'd you go?"

"Bloomington."

"Uh..."

"Indiana," he said.

"And they let you come back?"

"Yeah."

I had always assumed that if you left the Academy, that was it, you were done. "How did you manage that?"

"I worked really hard back at Indiana. I even gave up soccer to concentrate on my grades."

"You play soccer?"

He nodded. "The rules are so simple even I can understand 'em."

I laughed.

"I was recruited by the Academy team's coach," Whit said.

I had no idea the Academy recruited athletes. "They approached you to come to school here? Like normal colleges do?"

"Well, no. I applied for an appointment during my first year at Indiana. The soccer program is kinda new, so I guess I sorta stood out. Coach Wells came to visit me. I think he wanted to make sure I accepted the appointment that he assured me I would get."

I had to think about this for a minute. My own application process had been fraught with doubt. No doubt about my desire to be here, but rather if I would make the cut. Maybe Nicki Delgado had been recruited. It occurred to me that, were it not for his academic shortcomings, he might be here with Whit instead of me.

"My grades sucked," Whit said. "But Coach Wells said there would be plenty of help with my classes."

"What kind of help?"

"Tutoring," he said, looking at me in true understanding of my question. "Not the kind of help that makes sure college football stars stay eligible. Just tutoring."

"Didn't it help?"

"Not enough!" he said laughing and scratching his head through a tuft of thick red hair. "Might never be enough for me."

"What was that like?" I asked. "Going to a regular college?"

He winked at me. "Not what you're thinking. My nose was so deep in the books, the only time I pulled it out was to blow it."

"To make sure you didn't blow it," I joked.

Whit cracked a brief smile. "Yeah."

"And they took you back."

He turned to me and spread his arms. "I re-applied, I was re-accepted, so I re-turned. And here I am, cramming four years of college into six. And hoping it doesn't take longer than that."

"Nino Balducci lives!" I offered a thin smile. "You'll make it."

Whit nodded. "If my friends don't get me kicked out."

I looked at him with feigned indignation in my eyes.

"Not you," he said. "I made... different friends... at Indiana. They said coming back here would be a mistake. Some even threatened to show up some day and stroll down the hallway smoking a joint and yelling 'Hi! We're Whittaker's friends!'" He waived his hands. "They think this place is a life-sucking, character killing hell-hole." He shook his head. "That's pretty much a direct quote." He returned to the bag of clothes on his bed. "They have no idea what this place is about."

"Neither do we," I said.

Whit looked at me. "This place is hands down the best thing that has ever happened to me."

"Yeah," I said. "Well, with two extra years of college, you're probably so far behind that you'll end up ahead."

"I'll be lucky to break even," Whit said. "I'm sticking to the books at all costs."

Five weeks into the fall semester, I could stand it no longer. Whit had been true to his word, living the life of a monk with his nose buried in the books. I did not much care for living that way myself.

"Cruce wants to go to a disco and birddog some babes," I said as I yanked a polo shirt and a pair of slacks from the civilian side of my closet.

Whit kept his head down. "Sounds painfully funny."

I nodded. "The entertainment value alone's worth a trip downtown."

"Too bad I'm gonna miss it," Whit said, adding, "But you should get Zooms to go along. That ought to make for some real fireworks."

I shook my head. "He's at a forensics tournament somewhere." I paused expectantly. "And you don't have any matches this weekend."

"I can't flunk out of here twice," Whit countered. He shook his head. "I'd be lousy company anyway."

I knew he was desperate to stay eligible to play soccer, but I persisted. "Not after pizza and a couple pitchers of beer. It'll do you good to get your mind off classes. Clear your head of this trivial shit."

He dropped his highlighter and rubbed his eyes. "You're killing me."

"Come on," I said. "You can showcase your chick-magnet moves."

Whit exhaled noisily as he flipped the pages he had yet to read. "You guys go ahead. My moves work better if I'm not there."

I laughed again. "You've done nothing but play soccer and study every weekend since the semester started. Keep it up, and you'll go crazy *and* blind." I grabbed my head. "I can't do any more. How can you?"

"The more you do, the more you do more," Whit said.

"I'm worried about you," I said. "You need a break before you go all Charlie Whitman on me."

"Whitman?" Whit asked.

"The guy who went apeshit and started shooting people from the University of Texas Tower."

"Sounds familiar," Whit said.

I had explored the tower when my father took me to Austin to tour the University. I recounted my climb to the observation deck where for 96 minutes Charles Whitman, a fair-haired former marine, terrorized the city with high powered rifles, killing or wounding dozens of locals, tourists, and students before three policemen and a civilian took the stairs to the deck and killed him. The story made a larger impression on me than anything else I remembered about Austin, except that I was now painfully aware there was no medical school there.

"We'll study tomorrow," I said, knowing I did not mean it. "All day if you want."

Whit closed his book in resignation. "You make it sound so good."

We dressed quickly and went to Hank's room. "Cruce!" I yelled, banging on his door. "Let's boogie!"

"Yeah, almost ready!" Hank yelled back.

I opened the door to find Hank combing his hair with great care as he monitored his work in the mirror above the sink. His hairline had migrated considerably rearward since basic training. What remained of his widow's peak now formed a thin tuft above his forehead like an oasis amid a barren desert of sunbaked skin.

"What's that stink?" Whit said.

"Early vintage whorehouse," I said.

Hank turned to face us. He was wearing a tight-fitting shirt with yellow flowers, double-knit brown pants, and blue and brown platform shoes with laces so thick they looked like ribbons. In that one moment, he embodied the essence of so much that was wrong with the Seventies.

"Good god, Cruce," Whit said, laughing. "You're a purple feathered hat short of pimp."

"But I'll get all the women," Hank countered.

"They'll never let you in the Cow Palace dressed like that," I said.

Cruce turned suddenly to stare at me. "We're not going there."

I shook my head. "I wouldn't want you to get jumped by Bubba."

I retreated into the alcove with Whit. When Hank emerged, I turned and strolled down the hallway, noting Cruce's reflection in the mirror behind the CQ desk. The image did not improve. Once in the stairwell, we descended the stairs three abreast, instinctively employing the cadet turn, an unwritten norm that required the cadet on the inside of each turn at the landing to move to the outside while the outermost cadet took the inside lane.

When we exited at ground level, Cruce said, "Hold on to your knickers C-Springs! Here come the three rowdies!"

With Cruce in his body-shirt bobbing between Whit and me in our pullover polos and pressed slacks, I think "rowdy" would have been the least likely moniker granted us.

After catching a ride downtown on the regularly scheduled Air Force bus that conveyed cadets to and from several hot spots in the Springs, we kicked-off our outing at Giuseppe's. We wolfed down thick-crust pizza and 3.2 beer while Hank kept up a running commentary on every girl that ventured in or out of the place. We then took a cab to "Superstar," a dance club that served expensive watered-down drinks without asking for ID. The place was often crammed full of girls of various breeding.

As we entered, Whit leaned over to me and above the din of the disco music said, "If a girl starts to talk to me, remind me to shut up."

"All eyes are on us," Hank said as he led us past the edge of the dance floor.

I shook my head. If anyone was peering in our direction, it was to pinpoint the source of the repellent aroma that was Hank's cologne.

We found an open table near the dance floor and ordered a round of drinks. This was my first real night out since the beginning of the fall semester, and I was determined to have a good time. I told the waitress to bring me a Singapore Sling. Hank and Whit ordered whiskey sours.

As we waited for the drinks, I gazed around the tables and across to the dance floor where couples were moving to Joe Quarterman's *So Much Trouble in My Mind.* I did hope I would meet a girl. A girl from a good, not too ostentatious neighborhood. A girl from a nice family who wore cute dresses and modest shoes. A girl like Noelle. Not someone I was likely to meet in a joint like this.

"There's a looker," I said loudly after the drinks came.

Hank whirled in the direction my eyes indicated.

Whit chuckled. "You being obvious enough there, Hank Boy? He said looker, not hooker."

"Man, the place is loaded with 'em," Hank said bending over his glass and sipping the booze through the stirring straw.

"Which one's first?" I asked.

"What?"

I grinned at Hank. "Who's first on your hit list?"

Hank glanced around. "Which ever one is interested in me."

"How will you know that?"

"You look at 'em and they look back."

"You're gonna stare at every girl until one stares back?" Whit asked.

"Maybe." Hank did not move.

"What a babe!" Whit said, looking over Hank's shoulder. He got the desired reaction as Hank whirled in his chair.

"She's great!" Hank said a bit too exuberantly.

"Great?" Whit whispered hoarsely. "That girl is so sexy I could entertain myself just thinking about her ankles."

"She looks ready to be entertained," Hank said. "Make your move! Faint heart ne'er won fair maiden."

Whit did not budge. "If a girl ever got excited about me, my first thought would be to have her checked for rabies."

"Come on," Hank said. "Go ask if she wants to see you do twenty pushups."

"Show me how it's done," Whit countered.

Hank snorted and downed his drink. "Aw-right you fuckin' weenies!" He pushed back his chair and weaved his way to a nearby table.

Whit and I watched in raptured silence as Hank said something in the girl's ear and then followed her to the dance floor.

"The man's a beast," I said as we watched Hank Boy lay down his boogie.

Hank had his own unique step. He assumed a semi-crouched position and rocked on his heeled shoes. Left right left. Right left right. Like the unbalanced pendulum of a syncopated clock. His afflicted back did not appear to hamper these gyrations.

Two songs later, Hank returned to us sweating and grinning. "Nice girl," he breathed.

"You looked like you were stepping in horseshit," Whit said.

"I danced, goddammit."

Hank took a sip of the fresh drink Whit had ordered for him and turned to me. "You got any grouper down there in Texas, Geno?"

I flinched. "Groupies?"

"Grouper. You know! The fish."

"We've got fish."

"But any grouper?"

"Don't think so. Just trout, mackerel, and redfish. A ling now and then."

"Ling?"

"Cobia."

Cruce went silent for a moment, entertained by his own thoughts. "We catch grouper in Florida. In the Gulf. Great tasting. If I's a fish, I'd wanna be a grouper."

"I always suspected that about you," Whit smirked.

Cruce wiped the sweat from his brow. "Allow me to enlighten you mo-rons." He was talking louder now, slurring his words, and exaggerating his gestures.

"Okay," I said. "Hurry back."

Cruce started to say something then stopped to look at me. "What?"

"I thought you were going to the john."

"No, man. I'm talkin' about the grouper! Listen..." He paused to grab my forearm. "The grouper, man!" He shook my arm, punctuating his words. "When it's young, a grouper is female. When she gets older, she becomes a dude." He released me and took a generous swig of whiskey. "Think about it. While you're young and sexy, you're a female, getting any dude you want. When you get older, you're an experienced male, and you get all the young females." He looked at a group of girls laughing together at a nearby table. "If God really loved us, he'd have made us like the grouper."

I laughed out loud and the girls stopped talking and stared at us.

Hank turned his attention to Whit. "Whit my man, do you believe in God?"

Whit smiled knowingly. "Whenever I start feeling good about myself, there's always something that cuts me down to size. I figure that's God."

Hank leaned back in his chair and took a large swallow of his drink, tossing the straw on the table. "Monkey... shit!" he said loudly. He grabbed my wrist again. "See what I'm sayin', Geno?"

I freed my arm and sought to change the subject. "Hey Hank!" I indicated some girls taking seats near the dance floor. "There's a fresh table of groupers to stare at."

Hank peeked around his shoulder but stopped short of making eye contact. "I can't get up right now," he said.

"Batshit," Whit answered.

"No," Hank said. "I've... I'm..."

"Erected!" Whit said loudly in realization.

"Keep your voice down!" Hank said. "But yeah. Blue steel."

"Now *that's* entertainment!" Whit grinned. "Good thing you're wearing double knit."

I laughed and raised my glass. "To the grouper!" I downed my sweetened gin and gestured to the waitress, spending the last of my pocket cash on three more drinks.

When I awoke Sunday morning, Whit was already at his desk, quietly studying his Physics book and taking notes. The sun was barely above the far side of Vandenberg, bathing our room in a warm glow.

"Sleeping beauty awakes," he said as I made my initial bid to roll off the bed.

I threw back my quilt with the embroidered roadrunner my mother had knitted for me and sat up, nodding slowly. My head felt like it might reach critical mass at any moment. "I thought I heard the obnoxious sound of neurons misfiring."

"Just one of 'em's going so far," Whit said. "But I expect the other one to kick in any minute."

"You're working too hard," I said. "You're gonna blow a gasket."

"The harder you work, the harder you work harder." He rubbed his head dramatically. "I should have known better than to go bar hoppin' with you two delinquents."

I groaned.

"You okay?" he asked.

"I've got the worst hangover in academy history."

"Probably caught it from Cruce. I warned you to use protection."

Pivoting on the bed, I put my bare feet on the waxed floor and rubbed my eyes. "Breakfast?"

"Already been," Whit said, turning back to his work. "After a quick morning run."

I exhaled loudly, shaking my head in wonder. "You know Whit, you just might be the answer to the energy crisis."

I stood up gently, gathered the quilt and the two sheets and flung them into my overhead closet. Being an upperclassman, I no longer slept under the gray blanket, thus avoiding the need to remake the bed every morning.

I pulled on my wrinkled double-knit and traipsed down the vacant hallway to the latrine. The squadron was so quiet that the sound of my bare feet slapping against the hard floor seemed to echo in the alcoves. I stopped at Hank's room, knocked quietly on his door, and stuck in my head. Both he and his roommate were still in bed. Detecting my presence, Hank opened his eyes. When he saw it was me, he closed them again, furrowed his brow, and shook his head.

"Beat it," he said hoarsely.

"I'll bet you did," I answered.

He smiled slightly, keeping his eyes closed. "Twice."

"Such a stud," was all I could think to say. "You interested in a Mitch's breakfast?"

"Don't make me puke."

"Did you get the number of that girl last night?"

"Which one? There were several."

"The one that stared back."

"I think that was her brother."

"What did you think of him?"

"About the same as her." Hank suddenly looked at me, adding quickly, "Just as nasty."

"I'll bet she was a virgin seven times over."

"Yeah, well I'm still on round one." Hank rolled toward the wall.

As I closed his door, Hank sighed. "I shoulda been a grouper."

CHAPTER SEVENTEEN

With the inevitability of the Colorado winter came the certainty of new roommates. In mid-November, I was assigned to room with Eric Salter when Whit moved in with Joe Zusman. The thinking was, I believe, that Zusman would be better for Whit and his ongoing academic struggles. Better than I was anyway.

As bunkmates, Zooms and Whit seemed to get along well enough, but Whit hated for Joe to smoke in their room. Being a reformed ex-smoker himself, Whit tried to curtail this unhealthy habit by either preemptively kicking Joe out whenever he put a cigarette to his lips or vacating the room himself.

I knew very little of Eric Salter beyond the brief encounter at Farish. In the beginning, I saw little of him as he often went directly to the library after the evening meal.

The library was good for studying because you were not distracted by friends barging in uninvited to talk about their day or their weekend plans or their girlfriends or the cadets they disliked. I tried studying there, but I tended to drift off to sleep. I needed the distractions of the dorm to break up the monotony of the books.

Almost every evening, Zusman would open my door and zoom into the room, his breath reeking of rancid smoke, his eyes on fire with some new thought. When Eric was not there, he would stay awhile, keeping me from my studies with whatever thoughts popped into his head. Most of the time, if Eric returned, Zooms would excuse himself to grab a smoke before calling on another distractible classmate.

But sometimes, Zooms would stay just to tweak Salter's nose a bit. He would then excuse himself, leaving Eric with the daunting task of maintaining his Christian bearing in the face of Zooms' strategic offenses.

On Wednesdays, Eric went to a prayer meeting before heading to the library. He had a number of friends in different squadrons who attended these meetings, but he never invited me. Apparently, he had taken Skye to one when they were together in Evil Eight, and that had not gone well.

It was during this time that I began to feel the tug of two diametrically opposed life-views. What I experienced at the Academy played havoc with the earlier naiveté born of my small-town upbringing and my family's faith. It was as if I had understood the world in one way, only to discover the truth did not match my cloistered perceptions.

On a frosty evening in the first week of December, Hank Cruce sat lazily in Eric's empty chair as the two of us hunkered down in my room, preparing for an anticipated physics pop quiz the following morning. In the darkness beyond the room, snowflakes swirled in the turbulent wind like dust amid the light beam of a projector's lens.

We were comparing notes and offering varied opinions of what would be on the test when the door opened and Whit strolled into the room.

"Did Zusman motor in here?" Whit asked.

"Give it time," I said.

"Batshit!" Whit exclaimed in frustration. "He's supposed to help me with the physics thing tomorrow."

Despite the cold, Whit was wearing his usual evening garb of a torn T-shirt and cut-off shorts that exposed his pale, lean limbs. It was difficult to see the exceptional athlete hidden beneath this modest veneer. I had seen him play on two occasions. His soccer uniform seemed to hang from his bones, exaggerating his frail-looking frame, but he was deceptively fast and could change direction so fluidly that he was sometimes impossible to defend.

"Whit!" I said, putting my hands to my face. "You need some sun."

He grinned and threw one leg forward as if modeling on a runway. "Yes, you can definitely tell I am of the Caucasian persuasion."

Cruce said, "I thought soccer players had tan legs."

Whit pointed at the scruffy red hair that adorned his freckled forehead which always reminded me of a connect-the-dots picture.

"Yeah, well with a few more freckles," Cruce said, "your legs might actually look brown."

"And with a few more braincells," Whit countered, "you might actually develop a pulse."

Ignoring the slam, Hank said, "It's getting about time for another trip downtown for the three rowdies."

Whit shook his head and turned to me. "Not any time soon," he said. "And by soon, I mean before graduation."

The door flew open again, and Zooms popped in as if by appointment. "Que pasa, man?" he said as he closed the door. "What's the latest with the babe in Texas?" He never referred to Noelle by name.

"Same ol' same ol'," I said.

"Sorry to hear that." He gazed around, grimacing in disappointment at Cruce's presence before turning to Whit. "I thought you, uh, wanted my help with your physics," he said awkwardly.

"I do," Whit answered. He flopped onto my bed. "I knew you wouldn't show up until I stopped waiting."

"We had a debate meeting," Zooms said.

"And your petty meeting takes precedence over my teetering cadet career?" Whit complained.

"Essentially."

"Guess I should have seen that coming."

Zooms furrowed his brow in feigned interest. "What's the test on?"

"F equals M A," Cruce said from Eric's chair. "We think."

"Or maybe the right-screw rule," Whit offered.

"Right hand rule," Zooms corrected.

"Whatever," Whit said. "If I don't get this stuff down, I'm screwed." He closed his right hand and stuck out his thumb, the memory aid for the rule. "I might as well sit on this and spin, for all the good it'll do me."

"Enough with the 'aw shucks'," Zooms said. "You're smarter than that."

"If I was smart," Whit countered, "I'd be too stupid to know it."

Cruce said, "If the min wasn't good enough, it wouldn't be the min."

Whit nodded. "Thank God for that."

Cruz shook his head. "There's no place for God in physics."

The door opened, and Eric stood at the threshold, his black parka peppered with melting snowflakes. He paused when he realized there were four of us returning his gaze.

"The library too crowded tonight?" I asked, glancing at Zooms whose eyes lit up in anticipation.

"Nah," Eric said. "I need motivational music. Delving into Tommy Jefferson's brain calls for a certain mindset."

"Tommy..." I began.

"President Jefferson to you," Eric said smiling. "You know: '*We hold these truths to be self-evident.*'" He glanced sideways at Cruce and his smile diminished dramatically. "I'm writing a theme paper."

Cruce glanced around as if he had no idea why Eric was hesitating to advance. "Oh. Sorry," he offered, raising his eyebrows and making a noise of sudden realization. He did little to disguise the insincerity of his apology as he rose from Eric's chair and plopped himself on Eric's bed.

Eric unzipped his parka as he walked to his desk. He dropped his books on the corner and rearranged the chair as if Hank had disturbed the feng shui of the entire room before removing the parka and hanging it over the back of the chair. After brushing some microscopic detritus from the seat bottom, he folded himself into the chair with his back to Cruce.

"I'm sorry, really," Cruce repeated.

"No biggie," Eric said without looking at him.

The room went quiet.

Eric opened the bulky American History textbook to a marked page. He flipped the switch on his Panasonic tuner and the background light came on followed by the characteristic "ting" that signaled power up. He placed the headphones over his ears and hit "play" on his Akai cassette deck.

Whit pushed himself off my bed and started toward the door.

"I'll meet you in our room," Zooms said to Whit. "We'll hit everything you need to know." He sighed. "I just want to grab a smoke."

Cruce stood to follow Whit. "Can I get in on that?"

Zooms gazed at the ceiling, nodding slightly. "It's what I live for."

As the door closed, Zooms eyed Salter for a brief moment before turning to me. "I've narrowed it down, Geno."

When I only stared at him, he said, "My major. It's either going to be Psychology or Computer Science."

I nodded. "So, you can't decide if you want to screw with machines or people's minds."

"Essentially." Zooms lowered his head a tad. "I considered a Philosophy major. That would cover all angles. But no such thing is offered here at the Blue Zoo. So..."

"Well, you've still got time," I said.

"I need to start next semester."

"You're that far ahead in your cores?"

Zooms nodded and reached to pull a pack of Winston's from his shirt pocket. He glanced at Eric and changed his mind, wordlessly tucking the pack away.

"You know, Zooms," I said. "You really should give up the smokes. I'd like to see you hang around for a while."

"Shit, Geno," he said, "anyone can quit smoking. It takes a real man to face cancer." He glanced again at Eric.

Eric had raised his headphones and was eying Zooms impatiently.

"Uh, is this report on Jefferson all inclusive?" Zooms asked awkwardly.

Eric paused with the headphones hovering above his head. "What do you mean?"

The florescent light on the wall cast a faint shadow that made Zooms' cheek scar seem more pronounced and his eye sockets even more recessed. "Are you going to mention his rewrite of the Bible?"

Eric lowered the headphones so they encircled his neck. I could just hear the overture to *Jesus Christ Superstar* sounding tinny and distant as he shifted his chair to face Zooms. "Where did you get that?"

Our door opened again, and Eric's friend, Polo, a Second Classman from Tenth squadron, poked his head in. He dropped in from time to time, appearing at the threshold as if he had overheard something Eric and I were discussing that required his immediate attention.

The first time he visited us, I immediately recognized him as the prayer guy from the Farish retreat, the same guy who had stuffed me in a plywood box during survival. I started calling him Marco, and he never corrected me, either because I wasn't the first, or because he liked it.

Zooms had a different name for him.

Marco eyed Zooms warily as he said, "How's it going, Eric?" It was more of a call to arms than a greeting.

"Feeling blessed and highly favored," Eric said with a smile.

The way Zooms returned Marco's gaze made me cringe. A subtle fire was building in those dark eyes.

"We were discussing Thomas Jefferson," Zooms said. "Would you say he was a Christian?"

Marco jerked his head back and smiled. "Of course! That's self-evident!" He laughed at his little joke as he took a seat on the valet.

"Is it," Zooms said.

"Everybody knows that."

I closed my book. I wasn't going to get much studying done for a while.

Zooms lowered his head, looking at Marco from under his brow. "Say nothing of my religion. It is known to my God and myself alone."

"I guess you're entitled to that," Marco offered.

"Those are Jefferson's words," Zooms said. "Not mine."

I considered taking a stab at derailing this conversation, but whenever Zooms got into something, his tenacity for humiliating a debate opponent was like a runaway train.

"Well, he also said that man is endowed by his Creator," Marco countered softly. He lowered his voice as if this show of restraint made him seem more pious and, by association, more convincing.

"That only shows he was a deist," Zusman said. "Our country was founded on the writings of liberals. A lot of our societal morality is despite God."

"What do you mean, despite?" Eric interjected.

The conversation was moments away from going nuclear. I raised my hand. "Guys, I've got a physics test tomorrow," I said desperately.

Marco stared at Zooms as a nuisance whose time it was to leave. "I thought you were Jewish."

Zooms nodded knowingly. "Yeah."

"How can you be Jewish *and* an atheist?"

Zooms threw up his arms. "Oy gevalt!" He grinned, but there was no humor in his eyes. "It's easier than you think." He paused. "And more moral."

Eric glanced at me. "From whence comes morality if not from God?" he said as if quoting a well-known and respected source.

Zooms spread his arms. "From us!" He winked at me and stood. "Societies make the laws. Societies decide what is moral. And when. Nowhere in scripture does it say 'Thou shalt not say fuck.' But a fighter pilot probably won't say it in front of a general's wife at a dining out. It all depends on the circumstances." He brushed past Marco, meeting Eric's eyes once more as he opened the door. "From whence? From thence." He paused. "It just makes sense. That being said, I remove myself hence."

Stepping into the alcove, Zooms turned and bowed his head in modest contrition. "Sorry if I made you wince."

And he was gone.

Marco glared at me. "He likes playing devil's advocate."

"Maybe he would," I said. "If he believed in that sort of thing."

Marco looked to Eric and back to me again. I got the impression he wanted me to leave, so the two of them could talk alone. When I sat unmoving, he slid off the valet and said, "You gentlemen have a blessed night." He opened the door.

"Same to you, brother," Eric answered.

With one last glance at me, Marco walked out of the room.

When we were alone, Eric leveled his gaze on me until I finally said, "What?"

"Don't put too much stock in what Zusman says he believes."

"Marco's right," I said. "He likes to stir the pot."

Salter shook his head. "Like Skye Book. They're of the same ilk."

"Ilk?"

"I don't even know why they're here. They don't seem to fit in with the rest of the wing. I'm surprised they're not gone already." He paused. "And as for Hank Cruce..." He allowed his words to linger like the final sentencing of a criminal.

"We need more than just guys that toe the line," I said simply.

Eric shook his head and put his headphones over his ears, blocking out everything but the Superstar and Tommy Jefferson.

I wanted to believe Eric meant no malevolence when a week before Christmas Break, he posted a simple piece of scripture outside our door:

"No one comes to the Father except by me."

He defended the post as an integral part of his ministry in the wing. At first, I saw it merely as a childish display of conviction, but I later came to understand the deeply imbedded intolerance Eric's actions revealed.

Zusman took it as an affront. The words inflamed my friend at a time when we all should have been soothed by the approach of the holidays.

"How come that bothers you?" I asked Zooms when he made his routine entrance into my room that evening.

"It doesn't bother you?"

"It's just his opinion."

"An opinion based on the belief that he is right and anyone who disagrees is wrong! It's intimidating. 'Toe the narrow line or go to hell!'"

"It's just Salter," I said. "Don't let him get to you."

"It's not just Salter! It's all the proselytizing assholes in this place!"

I was surprised at his manner, which was normally unflappable in the face of such affronts. "I'll ask him to take it down," I said. "He's usually pretty good at turning the other cheek."

Zooms curled his lip. "I tried playing nice already." The disgust in his eyes mirrored the contempt in his voice. "He said it is his right, nay, his moral duty to let the truth be known!"

"That does sound like Salter," I said.

"This can't stand!" Zooms said heatedly. "What if your commander posted that in your fighter squadron? Wouldn't you feel that if you didn't cater to his beliefs, he could make life real tough for you? It would be the same as making a female subordinate... do things to get promoted."

"I don't see it as the same."

"You don't see it as wrong because in your world it's okay."

"Those things aren't okay with me," I said defensively.

"Aren't they?"

I shook my head. "What are you going to do?"

Zooms held my gaze. "Probably nothing," he said finally. "I'll just hold it against him for the rest of his cadet career." He smiled slyly. "Maybe I'll resign in protest."

"No!" I said. "We need you."

Zooms eyed me from under his prominent brow. "Yeah, what the hell," he said, looking away. "He's not worth the sacrifice."

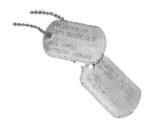

CHAPTER EIGHTEEN

I went home for Christmas obsessed with doubts about my future. It was more of an ache to be normal than it was a fear of being committed to the Air Force. I felt life was passing me by. The more I shared with friends who were at "normal" colleges, the more I began to lament my own situation—with so much restriction in my life, so little relative emphasis on academic pursuit, so little freedom on so many levels. This was my molehill turned mountain. It seemed every day I wore a different set of lenses, and each day I saw the world through eyes jaundiced by my determination to make myself miserable.

Just as Noelle and I were conflicted in our relationship and where we were going, I could not help but notice the signs that indicated my parents were unhappy. The playfulness and pleasure that had typified our Christmas mornings in the past now seemed inauthentic and forced. I looked to shrug it off as a consequence of Tyson and me being older and the lost magic that accompanies the unravelling of youthful myths.

Dad was overly animated at some times, aloof at others. Mom was under the weather with a lingering cough from a bug she said she caught from someone at church. Christmas is never the same when your mother lacks the energy to keep everyone else happy.

There was also something happening at American universities, something that alarmed my parents. They suspected I was having second thoughts about the Academy. Their fear was understandable and not altogether unwarranted. At a more weathered age, now, I understand why they were concerned. The more you know about life, the more there is to fear.

And things were happening a long way from home that were affecting what home was to be. Vietnam was all but over for America though not for Americans. The scars ran wide and deep, and the military was vilified even as it strove to protect the very people that hated it. My classmates and I were seen more as warmongers seeking to perpetuate war rather than as heroes hoping to end it once and for all.

The day after Christmas, Wanda Jackson, the daughter of a locally successful orthodontist, called to invite me to her New Year's Eve party. I accepted, glad to know I had not severed all friendly ties by going to a service academy.

Wanda graduated at the top of her class and accepted a scholarship to a liberal arts college in the Pacific Northwest. Being an only child and spoiled from the moment she emerged from the womb, Wanda was guaranteed to attend any university to which she could get accepted. Her father tried to nudge her toward becoming an orthodontist like himself, but I knew she would likely follow a career that afforded her a more penetrating pathway inside people's heads—psychology or politics— perhaps writing.

I looked forward to taking Noelle to a party of college kids with life views more worldly than her own. But in the days after Christmas, Noelle turned decidedly cold. She called me on the day of Wanda's party to say she could not go, that she needed to "think things out a bit." I suspected another presence in her life and even considered cruising by her house to note any strange cars there. But I refused to pine for lost love.

I went to the party alone. On a whim, I decided to wear my dog tags.

Her friends, a number of whom were home from their first semester of college, exchanged stories of their newly liberated lives. And while I no doubt had the most to tell, some of them politely demurred from hearing the tales of a belligerent. Others treated me with a certain degree of empathy that bordered on pity, as if I had been somehow defrauded into the service of my country.

I wasn't making many new friends. Despite my own misgivings, I felt a primal need to defend the Academy and my presence there. Perhaps being a pressure animal, I pushed against their arguments out of perception rather than principle.

As the midnight hour drew nearer, Wanda snuggled up to me. She had downed a few drinks, an indulgence to which, on this particular night, the orthodontist turned a blind eye. She played with my dog tags amid the hair on my chest, asking, "Doesn't it feel strange wearing these at Christmas?"

I did not answer. I wanted to ask her, ask all our former high school buddies who questioned my reasons for going to the Academy, how they could sit around as though the present was all there was, was all there ever would be. But that seemed a bit harsh for a holiday.

And it was looking like Wanda and I might indulge in an amorous greeting to the new year, so I tried to minimize my burned bridges.

The party was in a room connected to the garage where her father kept his Mercedes. One door led to the pool in the back and another opened to a large overgrown field Wanda's father owned but had not yet decided how to develop. Just before midnight, as several of her friends milled around the pool, some of them pairing up for the New Year's affections, Wanda walked to the far door and coyly wiggled her finger for me to follow.

"I just wanted to ask how things are going in Colorado," she said as I closed the door to the party. "I think I'm the only one who ended up further from home than you did."

I nodded. "I guess we're special that way."

She grinned. "So?"

"It's tough at times," I said, "but I think I'm doing okay."

"Are you sure it's right for you?"

"You mean am I a war-mongering baby-killer yet?"

She shook her head. "I know that's not you." She stood closer and looked up at me. "Why do you want to be in the military?"

"I'm not really sure I do," I answered truthfully, "but I don't have a commitment yet, so I have time to figure it out."

"You have time? Everything you do takes away from that time when you could be doing something important somewhere else."

"It's a good education that I'm not having to pay for." I suspected she was unfamiliar with the concept of being unable to afford something.

141

"You are paying," she said. "With your youth." She raised her hand and touched my forehead with her finger. "And in here."

This was a developing Wanda, a young mind exploring liberated ways to view the world. Being away from home in a free-thinking environment made her ripe for the transformation.

"You need to go to a normal school," she said.

"You talk like my grandmother."

"Really? She sounds smart."

I laughed. "I think so."

"Well, she's right. You need to go where you can open your mind to the problems of the world. Help find solutions that don't require bombs."

I felt my eyes fall involuntarily on her ample chest as she spread her arms wide. "Nixon carpet-bombed the North Vietnamese at Christmas. Then he brainwashed Americans into thinking that was a good thing." She frowned. "Peace on earth, good will toward men." She paused. "It'll be good to be done with him."

This was not the conversation I wanted to be having. I thought to take her hand and go for a walk. I looked south, into the clear night sky where Orion the Hunter was dominant. I put my hands in my pockets.

"I'm not going to let them brainwash me," I said. "I can still do my part in keeping America free."

"For God and country."

"I'm not so sure about God," I said.

"Oh?" she said, looking at me expectantly. "I thought you were deep into the God thing."

"I still believe," I said. "I'm just not so militant now. Have you given up on God?"

"Not completely," she said. "But I don't do Jesus anymore." She looked at me, tilting her head as if a different idea had just surfaced. "Are you worried about my soul?" There was a sudden softness in the shadows around her eyes.

I returned her gaze, trying to look sincere in the darkness. I pulled my hands from my pockets and caressed her shoulders with my palms. "Wanda Jackson, I've always believed you have a good soul."

The impish smile returned to her face. "And I guess you know I had a schoolgirl crush on you, Eugene Oliver Townsend." She lowered her head a bit and gazed up at me from beneath her curly bangs, not moving from my grasp, her arms at her side. As I moved in closer, she raised her lips to meet mine.

From beyond the garage door, a collective commotion indicated the new year was now upon us.

Our kisses grew in intensity, and we melded into the tall dead grass, first on our knees, and then she was on her back. As our kissing became deeper, I found myself wanting to do things I had restrained myself from doing with Noelle. "You're nice," I said.

"Give a girl a chance," she whispered.

I did not know what Wanda may have learned two time zones removed from our little town, but I thought whatever it was might turn out to be fun. Feeling no noble attachments, perhaps I saw less of a need to protect her.

But Wanda wanted to protect Wanda. She let me put my hand on her blouse but stopped me when I tried to unbutton it.

"I like you, Wanda," I said.

"Well, you can't just expect to use me." She closed her eyes.

I could not tell if she wanted me to use her or not. After a few more minutes of kissing, she lifted her head, pushing me away a little. "We'd better go back inside." She got up and brushed herself off.

"Hang on," I said, following her toward the garage.

She did not slow her pace, so I tailed her back through the door into the party room. Once inside, she played her best version of innocent indifference, but the dead grass in her hair gave us both away.

The next afternoon, Noelle called again to say her feelings for me were genuine and that she was willing to wait for me, to see if we were right for each other. While I suspected her own New Year's Eve plans had not panned out, I was glad to be returning to the Academy with the "girl back home" thing more or less intact.

I returned from the Christmas break to discover Zooms had resigned from the Academy with little fanfare. In the end, his tiff with Eric Salter was of no real consequence. Sometime back in November he had received letters from both MIT and Cal Tech accepting him for the spring semester. I think he had been planning to leave all along.

I thought of Zooms often, wondering if he ever found a truth worth arguing for. If only there was some flush of feeling for that eureka moment when you are overwhelmed with the realization that what you are doing is right and true.

But science pulls one way and religion the other. Like tugging on two ends of a rope that only makes the knot in the middle tighter. As Skye would later say, sometimes you have to push on a rope to get things going in a way that will straighten everything out. But with an unrelenting pull on both ends, there can be no meeting of the minds—only actions that make the dialogue more and more adversarial, knotted, and devoid of a willingness to even see if the mess in the middle can be resolved.

Salter may have been right. Joseph Zusman did not belong at the Academy, but for different reasons. The character flaws that haunted too many of us would have been his undoing. So it was that he zoomed out of my life so suddenly that it took time to reconcile what that meant to me. I never even knew which coast he ultimately decided on.

Maybe that was a good thing.

With Zooms gone, Cruce took it upon himself to tweak Eric's nose at every opportunity. He called it "The Zusman Reckoning."

One evening in the middle of January, Hank waltzed into my room without knocking and eyed Eric's empty chair before turning to me.

"Where's Salter?"

I shook my head. "Prayer meeting, I guess. Or the library." Eric and I had been spending less and less time together. Undoubtedly, my associations with Zooms and Hank were no small part of that.

Hank closed the door and leaned against it. "I thought I should apologize."

I turned in my chair. This was a red flag. When did Hank ever apologize?

"About today?" I asked.

Hank nodded solemnly. Another red flag.

Earlier in the day, as Cruce and I were walking back to the Old Dorm, we spotted Eric walking toward the academic area with Marco and Philip Quince, who was making a name for himself in 32nd Squadron.

The "Roadrunners" of the 32nd comprised one of the sixteen cadet squadrons assigned to Sijan Hall, the dormitory named in honor of the Academy's first Medal of Honor winner, Lance Sijan. While meaning no disrespect, it was still referred to as the "New Dorm" by many cadets, despite its construction having been commissioned in 1964.

I once thought myself destined to spend my upperclass years as a Roadrunner. I had adopted the moniker for myself while on the high school track team, which was why my mother made the quilt for me. But Quince was in 32nd Squadron now, which made me glad I was not.

Marco, Eric, and Quince hung together like three bobbing rafts tethered together on a turbulent sea, riding the waves created by those less strident cadets who did not share their exactitude. Anchored together, they weathered the winds of moral leniency, undeterred in their search for errant souls in need of salvation.

"Ah!" Cruce said loudly as they approached. "The holier than thou trinity." We passed like ships maneuvering to avoid a collision when Hank suddenly leaned toward them and mimed the movements of someone casting a net. "Throw out the lifeline, throw out the lifeline, someone is drifting away!" he sang gleefully, his pitch off-key as always.

This encounter was yet another Cruce-induced embarrassment for me. I tried to explain this to him.

"Weak-minded zits," he had said.

The door opened, and Eric walked in, almost knocking Hank over as he did. "Oh! Sorry," he said. He sidled past Hank and went quickly to his desk. I could not but help notice the broad smile on his face.

"That's my line," Hank countered. "I'm the one that's sorry." He paused briefly. "For earlier today."

I almost smiled to myself at the thought that this might be considered an honor violation. But thought crime did not come under the code. Not yet, anyway.

"No problem," Eric said, removing his parka and hanging it on the back of his chair. "No problem at all." He glanced at me and smiled broadly. "In fact, everything's great tonight."

Eric lowered his head slightly and glanced at me.

"Yep, tonight's a good night," Eric repeated.

Hank feigned modest interest as he said, "So, what's up?"

"I'm getting married," Eric said, looking at me for my reaction.

"You're not resigning, too!" I said with some incredulity.

"No, no!" Eric said, laughing and shaking his head. "In another..." He paused to count. "Thirty months? I just signed up for the first slot of our class to get married in the Chapel. Immediately after graduation."

"Immediately?" I said.

"Within hours," Eric answered.

"That seems a little premature to me," Hank said, taking a seat on Eric's bed.

Eric looked at him, his smile never wavering. "You're kidding."

"At the risk of sounding erudite," Hank answered, "I am not."

"You're a what??" I said. I could see where this was going because Hank was always going there. I shook my head ever so slightly.

Hank rubbed his chin as if in deep thought. "That's a long time. You could go through several girls by then."

"Oh, no, not likely," Eric said. "I'm engaged... well, pre-engaged, to the most virtuous woman on God's green earth."

Eric grabbed the framed picture of his girlfriend from the desktop. "Isn't she beautiful?"

Hank reached toward the picture, but Eric pulled it back before he could take it.

"She's very nice," I said, as I always did. A momentary image formed in my head, a summer memory of Noelle.

"She's the perfect lady," Eric said gazing at the photograph. "We are incredibly compatible."

"In bed?" Hank asked. He swirled his hand on the blanketed pillow as he leaned back against the wall.

"Nooooo!" Eric cried. "We're both virgins."

A cynical smirk formed on Hank's lips. "You're sure of that?"

Eric's nod was exaggerated. "Definitely. Will be until our wedding night. I've never been much of a 'wine, women, and song' kind of guy. And she's, well..." Eric inhaled deeply and smiled.

Hank said, "Who loves not women, wine, and song, remains a fool his whole life long."

"What??" Eric asked, still holding his smile.

"Something Martin Luther said."

Eric glanced questioningly at me.

"The Protestant Reformation guy," I offered. My mother had taught me a lot about Luther, but I was unfamiliar with this particular quote.

146

"If you're willing to wait that long," Hank began, "why rush things?"

"We certainly won't want to wait any longer!" Eric said.

A thought came to me, a conversation I once had with my best friend in high school. I told him I wasn't going to make love with my wife on our wedding night because I didn't want her to think that was the only reason I wanted to get married. Sometimes when I look back, it would seem my naiveté knew no bounds.

Hank said, "Interested in my opinion?"

I glanced at him. "I'm interested in you keeping it to yourself."

Hank flashed me the finger. "I was talking to Eric, for fuck's sake."

I forced an awkward laugh. "You know, vulgarity is the crutch of the linguistically crippled asshole dumbshit."

"Fuckin' A doodah."

I detected another Cruce dig close at hand, so I interceded. "You're not going to... date any other girls?" I asked Eric.

"No need," Eric said. "I've found my keeper."

"Two and a half years is a long time," Hank said. "You may experience certain... primordial desires before then."

I really did not want to pile up on Eric, but I could not help but ask something that had been on my mind for some time. "What if you are... incompatible... there?" I said, pointing to his bed. "What kind of lover will you be?"

"Oh!" Eric cried, sounding exhilarated. "I hope I'm the worst lover!"

Hank groaned. "Why would you want to suck at making love?"

I understood. Eric's juvenile elation came from the belief that a total lack of experience was the best testimonial to devoted innocence.

Hank stared at Eric, furrowing his brow as if offering sage advice. "You want to please your wife, don't you? You don't want her thinking, 'Well, at least he's got a good job.' Especially on your wedding night."

"We'll learn together," Eric said with a slight edginess to his voice.

Hank dug in. "Are you sure *she'll* still be a virgin by then?"

Eric turned his back to Hank and returned the picture to its sacred spot on the desk. "What better honor can there be than saving yourself for the one you love? If that isn't honor, what is?"

"If she offers her honor," Hank said, "you should honor her offer. All night you could be on her, off her, on her, off her." He laughed alone.

"Well," I said, exhaling noisily. "I've got to hit the books." I was a bit embarrassed by it all. I hated to see Eric offended, despite his invectives against Zooms. I looked at Cruce in a way I hoped would make him realize it was time to go.

"Oh, yeah," Hank said. "The fucking books." He rose lazily from Eric's bed and headed to the door where he stopped and turned, smiling as if in afterthought. "Speaking of books," he said, looking from me to Eric, "I've got some helpful literature if you decide you need more guidance. Lots of pictures." He lowered his hand and feigned abusing himself before ducking out the door.

Eric stared at me a moment before putting on his head phones.

I could only shake my head.

CHAPTER NINETEEN

As the days that followed the Christmas Break turned into weeks, the Dark Ages descended upon the Academy like a cold muffling veil. With too much time to think, I began to question the stability I had once considered so endemic to my life. My parents no longer seemed interested in each other, and Noelle's stamina for maintaining a long-distance relationship was fading along with the frequency of her correspondence.

My future as a cadet seemed uncertain. The Academy's grip on my freedom of thought was like a vice designed to squeeze out my more liberal notions until only compliance remained. I increasingly agonized over whether I should leave before I incurred a military commitment.

I felt a pang for Noelle, along with a certain emptiness and remorse for New Year's Eve. Wanda would go back to school far away, and I suspected the new year would bring little more than a few soulful letters from her, if that.

I was too young to understand these conflicted feelings. Maybe they came from being far from home. Or from realizing how good my life there had been. Or from imagining a "free" life at a "normal" college. Perhaps it was a form of desperation, a hole I needed to be filled by Noelle. Or at least the idea of her. I imagined the two of us making love for the first time together when the time seemed right. Not waiting for marriage like Eric.

Instead, I lost my virginity in the hills above the Academy. I lost it with a girl who could have meant a lot to me—perhaps even altered my future—if only I had known as much about life then as I think I do now.

On a damp Saturday night in February, I decided to drop everything and set out for Arnold Hall with the explicit purpose of getting as blitzed as drinking 3.2 beer would allow.

I sought out Whit to accompany me, but he declined. Despite his heroic efforts at fending off my regular invitations to debaucherous Saturday nights downtown, his grades had become so dismal that he was placed on Academic Probation. Once again, he was forced to quit the soccer team.

Eric, of course, did not drink. Zooms was gone. I would have conscripted some of my other less-inhibited classmates to join me, but they were in Colorado Springs looking to get laid. That left Hank Cruce.

I knocked on Hank's door and let myself in. The room reeked of Hai Karate, the same odiferous cologne he generously applied whenever he was of a mind to pursue the fairer sex.

"What's up, Geno?" Cruce said. He was leaning against the valet toward the mirror above his sink, brush in hand, experimenting with various combovers for that one resilient tuft of hair that still adorned the top of his bare head. He had shaved the little island on more than one occasion, his self-esteem receding along with his hairline. And each time, he had allowed it to grow out again in defiance of himself. This night, he was combing it all forward and plastering it in place with hair spray. It never looked good, but he thought it did.

"That's my favorite," I said.

Without looking at me, he flicked a few of his thinning locks like a painter lovingly brushing the final strokes of a masterpiece. "It's the luckiest," he answered.

"You're getting lucky these days?"

He glanced at me and smirked. "I'm a killer."

"Okay, killer. I'm off to the Richter for a night of mindless alcoholism. Want to come with?"

"No, dude. I'm going for bear."

"Bare what?" I asked. "Bodkins?"

"Chicks, man!" Cruce often switched into "cool-talk" when he was planning a night on the town.

"Thought I'd ask," I said, about to close his door.

"Hey, wait, man." He put the hairbrush down and made one more sidewise inspection of his work in the mirror before looking at me.

"I'm not signed out for downtown," I said.

"Not a problem. We can hit Lawrence Paul."

"What's going on there?"

"The hockey team, man. It's their annual "Near-the-End" bash. It's the one before the real end of the year bash."

"And you're going to that?"

"Montrose invited me," Cruce said, indicating the sole Nookie Niner on the hockey team. "They beat Colorado College in overtime this week. I doubt they'll turn anyone away."

"Montrose invited you?"

"Well, he told me where it was and when."

"I don't know..." I was beginning the think that drinking alone tonight might not be so bad. "I wasn't invited."

"It's cool, dude. You're with me!" Hank said. "Free beer! Chicks galore!"

"Girls, too?" I said trying to sound sarcastic.

"Hockey jocks are chick magnets! There'll be more than enough."

"If we're going to trek half a mile in the dark, there'd better be."

The Academy made it easy for girls to get on campus. Those who took it upon themselves to attend Academy mixers were an uncommon breed with a broad spectrum of traits. Such a girl might be socially mature, or socially immature and desperate, or motivated by the fact that her cadet got a regular monthly income. Or she might be tired of being burned by college boys who were after only one thing. While most cadets were after that same thing, the acquisition could take decidedly longer due to our limited number of weekend privileges. This dearth tended to slow things down a bit, but it could also facilitate the development of an actual relationship prior to the plunge. Regardless of the circumstances, once a cadet found a girl, he tended to remain loyal to her, knowing what it would take in time and treasure to start over again.

And if she had a car, that could seal the deal.

The evening temperature was quite mild for a winter's night at the Academy's elevation of 7258 feet. Cruce and I took the ramp to the Chapel, then worked our way past the Visitor's Center to the back road that led to the Lawrence Paul pavilion. Hank was wearing his platform shoes with the thick shoelaces and so cursed whenever a heel caught a root.

Once there, we joined a group of non-hockey players who were also crashing the party. Montrose was already very drunk, but he vouched for us. I think he would have vouched for Ho Chi Minh, had he shown up cruising for chicks. Cruce got us two pitchers of 3.2, and I wasted little time in my quest for alcohol-induced oblivion. I was dangerously close to becoming obnoxiously clever when I noticed a girl with a pleasant face and long thick blond hair studying me from a nearby table. She smiled playfully when she caught my eye, and I smiled back. There were three other girls with her, along with two cadets I assumed were hockey players, and Tomi Evans.

"Your buddy is here," I said to Hank.

"Yeah, I saw him," Hank growled. He stretched his back as if trying to make it pop and refilled his plastic cup from the pitcher.

I knew he hated being in the same state with Evans, so being in the same room must have been pure torture.

I looked away nonchalantly but watched from the corner of my eye as the girl engaged in a conversation with one of the jocks. She looked at me briefly while talking to him. She had lively eyes, and her smile was genuine and friendly. I sensed intelligence. Another cadet approached the tableful of girls. He did not sit down but leaned with his hand resting on the back of one of the chairs. After a moment, I realized it was Skye Book and that they were talking to him about the girl who was smiling at me. He laughed, nodded, but walked away without speaking to her and joined Montrose and a group of other players huddled in a corner. He was having a good time. Skye always seemed to be having a good time.

Cruce was also watching Skye. He poked me. "Hey, man, I'm sick of watching Evans pretend he's somebody. Let's split and go to Richter."

I looked at the girl. She raised her eyebrows at me and smiled again. "I think I'll hang" I said. I looked at Hank. "Free beer. Chicks galore."

"Well, I'm outta here," Hank said, standing. He drained the last of his beer and tossed the empty plastic cup on the table. He glanced once more toward the group of jocks in the corner before making his way past a bevy of nice looking girls who entered through the door as he left.

The music changed, and suddenly Three Dog Night was reminding us that Jeremiah was a bullfrog. I looked at the girl who was looking at me and lipped 'Do you want to dance?' She lipped back, 'Yes' as she stood.

I got up and pointed toward the open floor where we merged and started dancing a couple of feet apart.

The song stopped and another fast one started. I opened my arms in a question, and she nodded. We kept dancing. Part way into the song, she danced her way close to me and said, "I'm Vanessa."

I pretended that I could not hear her. "What?"

She put her lips near my ear and repeated slower, "Vanessa!"

"Gene," I said as she turned her head, brushing her curly hair from her ear.

"Hi, Gene!" she said close enough that her hair tickled my cheek. She said it quickly so that it sounded like a health concern and pulled back smiling. She spun a full circle, looked at me and then away at her table. Her friends were evidently watching her. She glanced ever so briefly to the corner occupied by Skye and his friends before turning to me to flash her pleasant smile.

The music went to a Bread song, *If*, and I looked at her and opened my hands. She nodded her answer, and we melded together. The slow dance felt at once awkward and natural. Getting wasted was no longer a priority. I liked dancing with her, but I was also ready to stop and let her return to her friends, if that was necessary to avoid embarrassment.

I whispered into her ear, "Aren't your friends going to miss you?"

"It's okay," Vanessa said. She moved her head back to my shoulder. When the song was over, we unlinked as another fast one started.

"Do you want to sit down?" she asked loudly.

I was ready to turn defensive. If this was a brush off, I would need to act cool and unphased. If she was inviting me to sit down with her, I would need to... act cool and unphased.

"Yeah," I said.

She gestured for me to follow her.

"Is it okay?" I asked. "You're not with any of the players?"

"No," she said. "Just friends."

I sat at the end of her table as far away from the other guys as possible. She may have thought of them as just friends, but I knew cadets. The relative scarcity of girls and of the time we had to meet them meant they had likely crossed over into "possessive mode."

"This is Madge, my roommate," Vanessa said of a rather big-boned girl with straight hair that extended beyond her shoulders and framed a long round face. She sat tall in her seat as she conversed with the two hockey players, one on each side.

I said, "Hi," but Madge either could not hear me or chose not to.

I looked at Vanessa. "What brings you here?"

"We," she indicated her girlfriends, "decided on a night out."

"Here?" I said doubtfully. "At this place?"

"It was a sperm of the moment thing."

"Sperm?"

Vanessa nodded and grinned. "Madge has a car. A baby blue Ford Falcon. It's rusting out and the heater doesn't work, but it's a ride. She calls it The Falcoon."

I nodded at Madge appreciatively, but she remained aloof.

"Where... are you in school in The Springs?" I asked.

"Yes."

"At...?"

"CC. That's where I met these guys." She indicated the other cadets at the table, glancing quickly toward Skye who seemed animated with some funny story. "At the hockey game."

I tried to hide my surprise. Colorado College was antithetical to the Academy on multiple levels that went beyond a mere hockey rivalry.

She extracted a tube of Vaseline from her purse. "Did you go?"

"No. I'm not a fan." I watched her apply the Vaseline to her lips.

"I don't like lipstick," Vanessa said in answer to my unspoken question. "But this dry Colorado air plays havoc on me. So..."

"Where are you from originally?"

"Originally? I was born in Virginia, after nine very cramped months in solitary."

I laughed. "And you just crawled your way out west."

She giggled. "My dad took a job in New Mexico. Raton. Do you know where that is?"

"I've heard of New Mexico," I said smiling. "Wedged between Texas and Arizona." I had a vague memory of going through Raton when my folks drove me to the Academy. "I think I've been through there."

"And you didn't stop?"

"I don't remember."

"But there's so much to see! Trees. And sand. And rocks." Her eyes widened excitedly. "We're famous for our rocks."

"Rocks?"

"You can't beat the New Mexican rocks!"

"Why Colorado College?" I asked.

"I wanted to go to a liberal arts school. My dad's more conservative. Mr. Cardewey and I sort of compromised. CC's not too far from home."

"Cardewey?"

She nodded.

So now I knew her last name. I thought to ask her, as a liberal CC student, what she thought about warriors, but I decided that conversation could wait for another time.

"So... what's special about CC?"

"I like the block plan. And if I decide I don't want to be a teacher after all, I can create my own major."

"You want to be a teacher?"

"I want to be a writer, but you have to start somewhere. Maybe teaching somebody else's brats will give me something to write about."

I gazed around the room. "Do you like hockey?"

"I love hockey!" she said. "The sheer brutality of it all!"

It took me a moment to realize she was being playful.

"The tall blond guy..." I said. "Skye. Is he a good player?"

There was something in her gaze as she focused on Skye, a kind of hopeless longing that almost made me jealous. "He's talented. But there are some better." She looked back to me and lightly touched my hand. "Like the Delich brothers."

I felt a mild flush. "Who are they?"

She gave my hand a playful slap. "You haven't heard of them?"

"Should I have?"

"One plays for Air Force and the other for CC. There must be special genes in that family."

"Oh." I smiled, curious if she was making a joke. "I guess I'm not really your type."

She returned my smile. "Not really." She stood and took my hand. "How about another dance."

CHAPTER TWENTY

Winter's progression toward spring was agonizingly slow, but the progression of my relationship with Vanessa Cardewey was even slower. After Saturday training on the weekends when I could get away, I would hitch a ride downtown, or sometimes she would pick me up at the dorm in Madge's Falcoon, and we would grab something to eat and go to a movie. I didn't have much money, although, as an Air Force cadet basically being paid to go to school, I had more expendable cash than most college kids.

She picked up the check from time to time because she said the "rich bitch"—as she infrequently referred to herself—could afford it. I did not like for her to pay my way, and she knew that, but I still conceded at times. More likely, it was the rich bitch's dad picking up the tab. Either way, I got the feeling she was just trying to keep things friendly.

Sometimes, we ended up going back to her apartment with me clinging to the hope that Madge would not be there. That was often the case because Madge's boyfriend had his own apartment, and she spent the night there whenever they weren't fighting. Madge liked to keep her boyfriend jealous by dating—or at least threatening to date—cadets, especially hockey players. Evidently, her boyfriend hated all of us, whether we played hockey or not, and that played right into her hands. Whatever spats they may have had during the week, I prayed their love life would be on the mend by the time the weekend rolled around.

When we had the place to ourselves, Vanessa would stack her favorite records on the turntable of her state-of-the-art stereo before disappearing into her room to change clothes or shoes or get more Vaseline. I would sit on the floor of the diminutive living area listening to the music while awaiting her return. She adored the rock band *America,* and she played their first album over and over, often singing along. Her favorite song was *I Need You.* There was a scratch in the vinyl that caused a skip at the same place every time. She sang right along, running the words together just like the skip did.

I found her to be intelligent and funny, although a bit standoffish. I could tell she liked me but did not want to rush things. She was my only real connection to the world beyond the gates of the Academy, so I let her set the pace in hopes of future developments.

Vanessa introduced me to the Garden of the Gods the morning after the first time I stayed overnight at her apartment. Madge was on the outs with her boyfriend and therefore not too keen on the idea, but Vanessa vouched for me, insisting I would sleep on the sofa and remain there except to relieve biological urges that involved only myself. We needed to borrow the Falcon for the trip, so Vanessa was more than willing to acquiesce to anything Madge said. I had never spent even a minute in Vanessa's bed. In fact, we were yet to share our first real kiss. So it wasn't like we were negotiating anything away.

In the middle of the night, I awoke to see Vanessa creeping from the apartment's lone bathroom back to her bedroom. When my eyes caught hers, she came to me and asked if the sofa was okay. I confessed it was comfortable enough.

She kissed me on the cheek, and I felt the Vaseline on her lips.

"More," I said, gently holding her shoulders, but she rose away from me and disappeared into her room, closing the door quietly.

Despite my plaints, we left early Sunday morning. Her preparations seemed spiritual, more like we were going to church than to a public park. As we drove west away from her apartment, the sun was low at our backs. Suddenly, the ardor of the "Kissing Camels" radiated before us in a sensuous orange glow.

"That's cool," I said.

Vanessa smiled. "Worth spending the night on the couch?"

"Definitely." I glanced at her. "All of it."

She parked the Falcoon, and we walked silently down the path toward the most prominent outcroppings. As we approached, I thought of how man tends to name beautiful parts of the natural world after something to do with a god or gods. I tried to imagine the first Native Americans coming upon these seemingly sculpted formations erupting out of the crust of the earth, and I wondered if they believed their gods made this place for their pleasure.

Spotting another couple on the pathway a hundred or so feet away, Vanessa slowed. "I hoped to get here before anyone else," she said as we walked between the two largest formations. She arched her back to gaze at the peaks. I consciously looked away, averting my eyes from her chest.

"This is my sanctuary," she said inhaling deeply. "I come here and think of the world and what it is and what it could be for us if we would only learn to take care of it."

Pulling my sunglasses from my shirt pocket, I put them on and tilted my head, taking in the majestic rise of red rock. The sun low in the east seemed to set the rocks on fire, but I noticed heavy clouds over the mountains that were coming our way. "It does look like two camels kissing," I said. "They have lips."

"But it's a closed-lip kiss, see?" Vanessa said. She poked my shoulder. "No tongues."

"Maybe it's their first, and they just never stopped." I grinned slyly at Vanessa. "The one on the left looks like she might be wearing Vaseline."

Vanessa grabbed my hand, and I could feel her warmth through the mittens. I made a mental note to thank Madge for the use of the Falcoon.

We followed the pathway leading to the heart of the garden.

"Madge seems kind of stiff," I said.

Vanessa laughed. "She's okay."

I nodded. "She did loan us her car."

Vanessa held her smile. "She takes care of me. She gave me a whistle for when I take out the garbage at night. I've told her I don't need it, that I'll scream if I'm being raped. And I'll scream twice if I'm not enjoying it." She laughed to herself.

"She doesn't seem to like me."

Vanessa smiled and squeezed my hand. "Being on the outs with her boyfriend tends to make her grumpy."

"So I noticed," I said, thinking that was only one of many things.

The rising sun cast a welcoming glow on a bench near the sign dedicating the place to the free pleasure of the public. Two climbers were busy making preparations to scale the biggest rock. I tried to imagine what that would be like, standing on the apex in the rising sun.

"It seems manmade," I said. "Like an amusement park for the eyes."

Vanessa held her gaze. "Man could never craft anything like this."

"A garden worthy of God," I said, propping my foot on the bench. "I guess that's how come they think of it as belonging to the gods."

She looked at me. "It's not like this is Olympus or something. Two explorers thought it would be a good location for a beer garden. Hence the name."

"Hence?"

She gave my shoulder a close-fisted tap.

"So," I said, feigning pain. "A beer garden... for the gods."

"Yeah."

"They could have one hell of a big party," I said, gazing around us.

Vanessa looked down the trail and then to the dust at our feet. "What does that really mean? Big. To an ant, a rut in a road must look like two mountain ranges separated by a huge valley." She looked at me warmly. "I'm not sure God cares one way or the other." She paused a moment. "Why would She?"

"She?"

"You think there's a cosmic penis dangling out there somewhere?"

I laughed at her blasphemy. "I guess He wouldn't have much use for one. Unless He actually turns out to be Thor."

"So, why be He?"

I had never really thought about Him, or rather It, this way before. "Because we say, 'Our Father in heaven.'"

"What makes fathers better than mothers?"

"Okay then," I said, feeling bold, "does your God have a vagina?"

"She doesn't need one. She has a temperament, like Mother Nature. And you don't screw with Mother Nature!"

I smiled. "Cecil B. DeMille's God had a pretty ballsy voice."

Vanessa shook her head and gently pulled me away from the bench. "Maybe She was just menstruating."

"God on Her period." I nudged her arm. "Doesn't seem much like heaven to me."

She released my hand and started down the path, then turned for me to follow.

I caught up and sneaked my hand again into hers. I was afraid I might have embarrassed her. She gave me a light squeeze.

"How about Father Christmas?" I offered to lighten the mood.

She rolled her eyes. "You notice they gave him a wife."

"An immortal being with nothing to do 51 weeks out of the year," I said. "He needed a distraction."

She released my hand and slapped at it. "Is that all women are? A distraction?"

"You know I don't think that," I said.

Vanessa smiled warmly as I reclaimed her hand.

"That's the Three Graces," she said pointing to a rock formation with her free hand.

"It's cool," I said, taking in the tall grouping of red pillars. "What are they?"

She considered the red rocks. "The Three Graces?"

"Yeah. Wives of the Three Stooges? Opposites attract, you know."

"Very funny."

"Do you know what they are?"

She took off a mitten and put her hand on the sandstone. "I'm not sure. Chastity, maybe? Or fidelity? Selflessness. I don't know." She almost slipped as she worked her way up the vertical rocks. "I've never been very graceful," she said with a quick laugh.

The clouds obscured the sun, casting a shadow on the Graces. I followed her as she turned slightly and backed her way in, wedging herself between two of the sandstone pillars. I put away my sunglasses and moved in closer. The air was colder now, but there was warmth in her eyes as she looked at me in questioning anticipation.

I kissed her for the first time, feeling the softness of her lips protected by a thin layer of Vaseline.

"I hope this one isn't chastity," I said, working my arms around her. Vanessa's eyes glowed as her cheeks flushed. "It better be!"

I pulled her closer and kissed her again. Her lips were soft and sweet, and they parted just enough.

It started to snow as we walked back to the car. I stopped, and she turned toward me. Some flakes settled gently on her long lashes as she blinked them at me. I liked the way the snowflakes looked in her hair. I thought I might be falling for her, but I brushed that idea aside. Most girls look special with snow in their hair. She raised up on her tiptoes and kissed me with open, inquiring eyes.

We walked hand in hand back to the car and drove south out of the garden toward Manitou Springs by way of the Balanced Rock. Wind and time had worn away the bottom of the sandstone. The bulky rock seemed destined to tumble over at any moment.

Vanessa said she had heard it was cemented in place to maintain the illusion of balance for the tourists. It seemed phony to me, but I decided that, in more ways than one, rocks are no different than people.

CHAPTER TWENTY-ONE

Vanessa left Colorado in late April to spend most of that spring and summer in Santa Fe working for her uncle at his restaurants. I had a growing feeling she might not return to Colorado in the fall. I decided to apply to Texas A&M. I convinced myself I wasn't reacting to Vanessa or Noelle or anything else. I just wanted to see if I would be accepted.

The war in Vietnam was ending. I could resign before the beginning of the fall semester without incurring a commitment and without the threat of being drafted. I was not sure what I was going to do, but the time when I would have to do it was bearing down on me. I was feeling pressure from all sides, and at every turn I felt the deck stacking against me.

My standing in the class military order of merit began to suffer as I struggled to resist being brainwashed as Wanda Jackson had warned. I wanted to fly fighters, but I did not want to kill people. I wanted to be the intelligent, compassionate fighter pilot who was not a "veins-in-the-teeth" killer, but who nonetheless understood the possibility of taking life in defense of his country.

My GPA had fallen as well, as indeed a form letter from the superintendent to my parents declared would probably happen, due in part to the relative lack of intensity compared to that endured in the Doolie year. While I craved instructors who would shape my mind without trying to control it, my grades suffered mostly because I feared spending too much time in the books would cost me my 20/20 eyesight, my ticket to pilot training.

I was one screwed up dude.

Tyson sensed a change. He knew I was actively contemplating my options. In a rare letter to me, he confided that it seemed the only thing keeping our parents spirits up was their mutual pride in having a son at the Air Force Academy.

After the Firsties graduated and we all moved up again, I spent the first three weeks of the summer at the Academy teaching Third Classmen how to survive in hostile territory, and the last three teaching basic cadets how to survive the assault course. In the three weeks between those two assignments, I went to Texas, unsure of what awaited me there.

No one told me about my mother's sickness until I got home. Mom did not want to talk about it, and Dad did not want to talk about anything else. He sought to bandage the pain by renewing his vow to stay with my mother for the rest of his life.

I think Mom knew Dad's time of penance would be much shorter than he anticipated.

Dad's guilt carried over to me. Earlier, when I insisted she knit that roadrunner afghan for me, I had no idea she was getting sick. I began to think of this woven security blanket as my "guilt quilt."

"You've been home," I said to Tyson, stating the painfully obvious. "How is... everything?"

Tyson seemed bright and hopeful, but I sensed doubt brewing beneath the surface. "If there's anything good that has come from this, it's that they've gone from fighting all the time to cuddling just about as much."

"What were they fighting about?" I asked.

Tyson scratched his head. "I think Dad did something he shouldn't have."

I nodded. Tyson, having turned thirteen in April, was still too young to understand much that was implied, although he seemed to have matured quite a bit in the past seven months. "When did they find out that it was more than... that it was..." I stopped myself, unable to say it.

Tyson squinted, furrowing his young brow. "I don't know. They told me about it after school let out for the summer."

"So," I said, "I've been out of the loop for more than a month."

Tyson nodded. "Mom started acting different in April."

"Different? How?"

"I don't know... sitting alone reading things when Dad wasn't here. I guess she had to because he rarely leaves her side when he's home. And she's started writing in a journal."

I looked at him. "Have you seen what she's writing?"

He frowned at me. "No."

I grimaced.

Tyson said, "The doctors think she has a good chance to survive."

I felt weak all over as it hit me. A "chance" to "survive."

"You mean there's a chance she will not?" I asked without thinking.

I detected a tear developing in Tyson's eye. "It's cancer. I guess it could go either way."

In the three weeks I was home, Tyson and I went water-skiing on the river as often as the guilt of indulging in such pleasure seeking would allow. The search for smooth water became our ritual, the roar of the engine our apology for avoiding painful conversation.

My first date with Noelle had been on this river. I still remember the smile she flashed me when, after only three tries, she got up on a slalom without having to kick a second ski. I longed to rekindle that knowing smile meant only for me.

Her correspondence in the spring had dwindled considerably, the time between letters noticeably extended. When she had written, she had done so on the scented stationery that delightfully contaminated the drawer in my desk where I stashed her letters. There seemed to be a cadence to her communications, whether by post or by phone, engineered to orchestrate my pheromonal flow.

I invited Noelle to join us on the river for the Fourth of July, and she accepted with more enthusiasm than I had anticipated. That felt good.

Tyson was also pleased, despite his feigned indifference. He insisted on piloting the boat, relenting command only when it was his turn on the skis. And he scowled at me when I called him "squirt."

He was becoming a skilled boat-hand, being careful to keep us from rough water and the dangerous areas near the shoreline. He was also becoming an accomplished skier, to the extent that I felt conflicted in my big brother urges to either offer him no challenges at all or to cut the boat so tightly that he was sure to wipeout.

When Noelle donned the ski vest, I noticed it was a snugger fit than the previous summer. Her first run ended with a magnificent wipeout when she tried to jump a wave. She grinned broadly as I offered my hand to her while Tyson snagged at the floating ski with the boat hook. As she pulled herself up on the gunwale, I reached behind her and palmed her butt, lifting her unceremoniously into the boat.

Tyson's interest in the maneuver seemed a bit more pointed than in the past. Smiling with brotherly pride, I tapped his shoulder and said, "Get the ski." Things were beginning to flow in him as well.

I took the helm for Tyson's second chance to showcase his skills while Noelle, standing with her back to the wind, served as observer. Even then, some 75 feet behind the boat, Tyson seemed determined to monopolize her attention, weaving like a fearless daredevil in and out of the wake. I wheeled the boat a bit tightly once or twice, sending him flying awkwardly as the waves rolled the skis beneath him. But he regained his balance as he usually did.

I stole glances at Noelle. She looked cute in her pink bikini, matching flip-flops, and pink mirrored sunglasses. I think she was as much aware of how good she looked as I was. The wind blew her long hair so that it curled seductively around her cheeks and neck and bikini top. She would brush it back, look at me, and smile. And I felt very good.

She was a high school graduate now, and her senior year had been good to her. And, by extension, to me. Still, I could not ignore the melancholy reminder that, while this healthy growth was opening a fresh chapter to her life, and perhaps to mine as well, the growth in my mother's breast was killing her.

That evening, Noelle and I made plans to see a new movie. As we drove out of her neighborhood, she said, "Do you really want to go?"

"Go?"

"To watch a silly show?"

I glanced at her. "You think it's silly?"

Her lips were pursed in suppression of a knowing grin. "A VW Beetle with a mind of its own?"

I nodded. "What do you want to do?"

She squeezed my hand. "Sarah Jane?" She tilted her head as she looked at me.

I forced a smile and fluttered my eyebrows without taking my eyes off the road.

Sarah Jane was the nickname for a backroad that ran between the refinery and the river. Despite the lights from the plant, a long stretch of the meandering road was cast in the dark shadows of the trees, especially on a moonless night like this. It harbored a legend about a young girl, Sarah Jane Brown, who fell off the road's bridge on just such a night and drowned in the canal. Some said she was pushed by a jealous lover. Others maintained she got lost in the fog trying to find her way home after her lover abandoned her on the road. Regardless of the particulars of her demise, everyone agreed she haunted the road, walking along it in a flowing silk gown and wailing her lover's name.

It had rained recently, and even in the dark I could see the ruts to the side of the road made by the cars of people who had stopped to fish illegally in the holding ponds or hunt squirrels in the heavily wooded area owned by the refinery. Or to park, as we were about to do. The road was so narrow that people seldom used it for any other purpose.

I pulled off the asphalt, turned off the car and the lights and looked at Noelle. She lowered her eyes in her seductively bashful way, turning her face up and closing her eyes completely when we started to kiss. Her mouth was insistent, which made me a bit uncomfortable, but I matched her amorous murmurs with a couple of my own.

I had said nothing to her of what was going on inside my family's house. I fought to cram the image of my mother's face as far into the dark recesses of my mind as I could.

She moaned as I cupped one of her breasts in my palm. I kissed her neck—she always liked that—and slowly worked my way down to her neckline, a new move for me in total disobedience of her father's tacit rule. I felt Noelle's hand under my chin, so I pulled away. What I thought was a gesture to draw the line was her unbuttoning her dress.

She parted the top, exposing a pink bra with a little bow in the middle. My heart started to pound in a confused rhythm of arousal and concern. My body was ready physically in a way that the rest of me was not. Still, I placed my hand on her thigh and started to work my way up. Noelle offered no resistance. Whatever happened next was up to me.

I whispered in her ear, "Noelle."

I unbuttoned the rest of the dress and parted it, revealing her bare stomach and panties. She moved in a way that made me think she wanted me to remove her underwear.

"God, you feel so good," I said. I pulled away slightly. "But I can't lose my virginity on Sarah Jane in my mother's Impala."

She opened her eyes wide and stared at me. "Don't you want me?"

"Yes, I want you." I was sure I did. "But I also want to protect you."

"From what?"

"From... your emotions." This idea had been drilled into my head by both my parents, even before I reached puberty.

"My emotions? What about yours."

"Mine, too. We're not ready."

"I don't need to be protected," she whispered. "I'm ready." She touched me. It was the first time she had ever done so. "Seems you are, too." She moaned softly. "We've waited so long."

The car was becoming hot and steamy, the humid Texas air was beginning to make me sweat. For some reason, I thought of Hank Cruce and how he would find it inconceivable that I could turn down such an invitation. Thoughts of Cruce were replaced with visions of my mother. "I have a lot on my mind, now," I said.

Noelle sat up and looked at me in disbelief. Shaking her head, she began to button her dress. "Then we might as well go to the movie."

"No," I said, staying her hand. "I like being with you here."

"Why stay here?"

"To be together. To talk. To... kiss." I put my hand on her neck and caressed her cheek.

"If we stay here, we'll either do it or be frustrated that we didn't." She dropped her hands into her lap and shook back her hair. "Don't you like me?" she asked. The tacit follow up being, 'How could you not?'

"I like you a lot," I said. "More than a lot."

"But not enough to..."

"Enough not to."

"Oh." She flashed a warm smile. "I see." Her breathing was becoming more regular. She retrieved a brush from her purse and began to gently stroke her hair. After a couple of pulls, she stopped and looked at me. "You know, Gene. You just might be a keeper." She turned the rearview mirror to survey her progress. "I am proud of you. How many girls have an Air Force cadet for their guy?"

She took my left wrist, twisting it to look at my watch which caused my fingers to brush against her chest. I turned on the map light to help.

"Oh! Too bright!" she protested.

I turned it back off.

"We'll miss about ten minutes," she said. "But I can fill you in."

I looked at her. "You've already seen it?"

"That's why I suggested it. I know your parents usually ask what it was about and all that."

I couldn't concentrate on the movie. I started thinking about Vanessa, imagining how she might be spending her summer. And I realized I might be making a mistake in sending a virgin Noelle off to A&M where I knew there were plenty of guys willing to do what I was not yet ready to.

CHAPTER TWENTY-TWO

I returned to the Academy to spend the last three weeks of my cadet summer as an assault course instructor while I contemplated my future. In late July, I had received my acceptance papers to Texas A&M. In just a few more weeks, I could join Noelle at a "regular" college. Having no interest in joining the Corps, upon graduation I would have to search for gainful employment like everyone else.

There were two letters in my mailbox postmarked from Santa Fe. On the back of one envelope, Vanessa had drawn a red puckered mouth and written 'Sealed with Vaseline on the lips.' On the other she had sketched a free hand version of the Three Graces. I am sure it was not her intention, but her rendition appeared borderline vulgar. I knew it was supposed to be the Three Graces because under the drawing she wrote 'I know what they are now.'

She said she was using the generous tips from rich vacationers to attend summer theatre productions. She told me of a place she had recently visited called Glorieta Pass. She wrote that it was hard to imagine the pretty little gap as the backdrop for the bloody battle that altered the western version of the Civil War. Her reverence for such things was uplifting.

She ended both letters saying she was looking forward to seeing me again in September.

My Academy class would graduate into a time of peace, at least for America. The bitter war that had divided the country—and played a role in my decision to attend a military academy—was over. The highest class attrition from the Academy occurred at this time, when young men were no longer being conscripted into service.

To make up for this, the Academy accepted a higher number of appointments to the Doolie class that entered my Second Class year. They would become known as the LCWB—the Last Class With Balls. Following them, gender specific appointments to the military academies would be a thing of the past. No longer would Fourth Classmen be called squats or wads or smacks or anything else so derogatory. We would be compelled to clean up our collective act.

The evening Call-to-Quarters announcing the beginning of the academic fall semester also signaled to all Second Classmen who had not signed resignation papers that they were now committed. One minute, you were free. In the next, whether you stayed at the Academy or not, you owed Uncle Sam two years.

It is interesting to think this all-or-nothing decision of a lifetime hinged on the harsh blaring of a faux bugle. But that obnoxious noise carried little fanfare for me.

I had undergone a shift from the hurt and confusion that dominated my mood at the beginning of that summer. I was further renewed by the unwavering strength of my mother's convictions. The sickest among us was the least fearful of the future. I promised her I would stay at the Academy and do my best to make the most of it. Doing it for someone else seemed to make the decision easier.

Hank Cruce could have easily justified yanking the plug on the whole academy experiment. His back was not getting better. The muscles seemed to be pulling in odd directions, but he never let anyone know just how much pain he was in. Those of us who knew what he was battling tacitly agreed that it was between him and the Air Force.

Had I been given such an excuse, I think I would have taken it.

Hank burst into my room just as the klaxon sounded. The look on his face suggested he half-expected me to be gone. "Did you pull the trigger?" he asked.

I held his gaze for a moment or two, heightening the suspense.

He laughed. "You dipshit! You chickened out!"

"No, I didn't," I countered. "I'm here to stay."

"That's what I mean."

"So," I said. "We'll be dipshits together."

Hank nodded. "What's the latest with the cock-tease?"

"Nothing new to report," I said coolly. Hank knew I did not like him referring to Noelle, or any other woman, with such derogation, but his manner seemed beyond his control.

"Fuckin' pity," he said, leaving as quickly as he had entered.

I walked down the hallway to Whit's room, hoping there was nothing new to report there.

The fear of being booted had motivated Whit to prioritize academics over anything else. The soccer coach would be very sorry to lose him.

When I asked him how his summer had gone, he groaned. "I spent part of it retaking physics."

"That sucks."

"Yeah, but then I got to do second Beast, which wasn't so bad."

"I didn't know you were out there!"

He shrugged by way of apology. "I went into town every chance I got. My carrot for finally passing physics. This semester will be hard. Who knows when I'll see daylight again?"

I spread my hands. "The harder you work, the harder you work harder, I guess."

Whit smiled in appreciation. "You've paid attention, my son."

I nodded. "So, where were you in the Valley?"

Whit smiled. "It was great duty. I was at the firing range, teaching Basics the basics of getting your gun off."

"Hey, I thought..."

"Yeah, I know. 'This is my weapon. This is my gun. This is for shooting. This is for fun.'"

"Did you have any?"

"What?"

"Fun."

He grunted. "My whole summer was what you could call asexual."

I nodded. "Are you one of those guys that can pop two balloons by splitting a bullet on an ax blade?"

Whit snickered a bit. "Well, we get one shot at it. If we fail—and we almost always do—we use rat shot."

"Rat shot?"

"Like a mini shotgun shell you fire from a pistol."

"That... doesn't seem honest," I said cautiously.

Whit held his hands up defensively. "We never say *what* we're loaded with. Just that we are trying to hit the ax so the bullet splits. Which is true."

"A very slick truth," I said.

He shook his head. "We've all made that shot before, splitting a real bullet. We just can't do it every time."

"Then why do it at all?"

"The awe factor. The Basics are in awe of us, so they listen to what we say when we're training them."

"That's awe-fully fun, I guess."

CHAPTER TWENTY-THREE

I made a date with Vanessa for our second home football game. She drove alone to the stadium in the new red Mustang her dad bought her. Once there, she waited in the stands while 1ˢᵗ Group, which included Nifty Niners—as we jokingly referred to ourselves now—paraded onto the field for the Star-Spangled Banner. Football was one of the few things that made the Academy almost like any other college campus in the fall. The clear, dry air, the excitement of the contest, the civilian girls who came to the games to meet cadets.

The afternoon was warm, the autumn air clear, dry, and refreshing. The wind was blowing as it usually did from the south. I felt a kinship with the players who would soon run where we marched, zigging and zagging wildly where we squared corners, calling plays and colorfully cursing on this same grass where we stood in stoic silence.

Once dismissed, the ten squadrons broke ranks and ran to the cadet section on the northeast end of the field. Zigging and zagging, we clambered to find seats in the stands among the rest of the wing.

I escorted Vanessa to the end zone where civilians were allowed to sit with cadets. We sat with Whit and a girl he had met a week earlier who was selling football programs for the express purpose of meeting a cadet so she would not have to spend the rest of her life selling programs. Whit was an easy target.

After the game, we went to The Hungry Farmer. I tried to convince Whit and his girl to join us, but Whit said they were going to Arnold Hall for pizza and beer. Whit was on academic probation, making even his weekend options very limited.

Vanessa insisted on splitting the dinner bill which was okay with me. I think she was mostly interested in showing off her new "Pony." The Mustang lacked the horsepower of previous models, but it was sexy enough. I was sure she was not paying for it, so I felt little guilt in allowing her to help with the tab.

At dinner, she told me she was working on a big project. I thought perhaps she was referring to me, until she drove me back to the Cadet Area, bypassing her apartment. It was still early.

"I'm sorry," she said, as we cuddled in the Pony amid the shadows of Vandenburg Hall.

I was disappointed. "That's okay." There would be neither hanky nor panky this night. "What's your project?"

"It's for a psychology class."

"You're not going to be a teacher anymore?"

"It's child psychology."

"Are you working with children?"

"Quite a bit actually," she said with a sly grin. "On many levels."

I leaned away and cocked my head. I was sensitive to being considered immature. While I thought many cadets were just that, I did not think I fell under that headline.

Vanessa giggled. "I don't mean you!"

I forced a smile. "What about next weekend?"

She nodded. "Are you free?"

"That's a relative term," I mused. "There's no home football game or weekend-killing inspections."

She leaned close to me and looked into my eyes, her own flickering brightly. "You want to go camping?"

"Sure." I tried not to act surprised. "Where?"

"I'm wide open."

I pointed west to the mountains. "How about up there? There's a trail."

She kissed me, her lips lingering in a way that felt good. "I'll call you," she said.

"I'll be waiting."

Around midday the following Saturday, Madge dropped off Vanessa at the bottom of Vandenberg Hall. Her long hair was nicely groomed, and, with the exception of her pants and hiking boots, she looked more like a lady going to the opera than a girl heading into the hills.

I was geared up with Whit's sleeping bag and backpack, in which I had loaded what I considered to be the essentials—two blankets, a canteen of water, three bags of potato chips, and some potted meat.

She kissed my cheek. "Sorry I'm late."

"Where's the Pony?" I asked.

She crossed her eyes. "Don't ask." She shouldered her backpack. "I couldn't park overnight here anyway."

I nodded. "I guess not."

She allowed her thick curls to flow over her shoulders until we were beyond the Lawrence Paul Pavilion, at which point she paused to corral them into a bushy ponytail. She smiled warmly at me as I watched her hands stroke her hair behind her head before finally applying the elastic band she held in her teeth. She raised and lowered her arms several times, fluffing and pulling until she had it the way she wanted it.

We followed the steeper path until I thought we were beyond the level where most cadets looking for a weekend hike would go. I gathered dry wood and made a small fire. As it came to life, I tore off green boughs from the abundance of pine trees surrounding us and arranged them on level ground before placing our sleeping bags over them. Survival training had been good for something.

When we had finished eating her premade sandwiches, we sat atop the sleeping bags staring at the dwindling fire as the night descended quietly on us.

In an effort to loosen up a situation that was dangerously close to becoming awkward, I asked, "You really can't talk about the Pony?"

Vanessa rolled her eyes and stared at the fire for a moment or two before saying, "It got totaled."

I jerked my head in genuine surprise and gently held her arm. "You seem okay."

She forced a smile. "I wasn't driving."

I released her arm. "Who was?"

"I let some guys from the hockey team borrow it." She glanced at me. "Last night."

I briefly considered the implications before saying, "From CC?"

"No." She looked into the fire. "Cadets."

I wanted to ask if she meant Skye, but I figured she would tell me what she wanted me to know. Had there been a serious accident involving cadets, I was sure I would have heard about it. "Are they okay?"

"They weren't in it, either. Nobody was."

I laughed. "Did it just run off on its own and crash into a mountain somewhere?"

"Sort of." She grabbed a stick and poked at the fire. "I guess..." She paused, "...whoever was driving wasn't completely familiar with the particulars of a stick shift. He put it in neutral and didn't set the parking brake. They were at a party at somebody's house west of Manitou. When the party was over, the car was gone. They thought it had been stolen and were about to report it when someone spotted my Pony a quarter of a mile down the hill in a bunch of trees."

"And that totaled it?"

Vanessa sighed. "As is my luck." She surprised me by resting her head on my shoulder. I felt stiff as I tried to act cool.

"So, it can't be recovered?" I asked awkwardly.

She shook her head. "That's what totaled means." She paused. "Well, it could be, but it would cost more than getting another car." She raised her head. "Which my father is not going to do. I told him I was driving. I can just imagine what he'd say if I told him the truth."

"I'm sorry," I said. And I really was. I silently mourned the freedom I had imagined the Pony would give us. Give me.

"I don't think my dad would be so mad if I was a guy. You guys get away with so much more."

I laughed. "I always thought it was the other way around. Girls can talk their way out of anything."

"I don't think so."

"Daddy's little princess? Blinking those baby blues?"

"I don't think so," she repeated. "Girls have to be so careful, but boys will be boys."

"I guess it depends on which you are." I thought to put my arm around her but hesitated. "What if you could be both?"

Vanessa laughed and inched closer to me. "What do you mean?"

I told her Cruce's story about the grouper.

When I finished, she smiled and said, "Did I ever show you my fish imitation?"

Before I could answer, she pulled a pair of large reading glasses from her backpack and placed them at the end of her nose. She sucked in her cheeks, crossed her eyes, and made swimming motions with her hands near her face. It was cute.

"A grouper with Vaseline on the lips," I said.

She laughed and playfully puckered her lips. I wanted to feel those lips on mine, to kiss her, to touch her. To caress her bare skin. But I felt the guilt tugging at me.

The last few times I had seen her before she left for Sante Fe, our relationship had become somewhat more physical. After talking and listening to records for a while, she would dim the lights, saying bright lights bothered her eyes. The evening would then digress into a wrestling match where I tried to touch more of her and she resisted, sometimes pretending to give me a karate chop accompanied by a cute "Hi-yah!" to keep my wandering hands in check. I always respected her limits, but we still played the game.

Back in high school, my best friend taught me to write "J'taime" on the notes we wrote to girls we liked. It took some of the awkwardness out of our teenage affections because we weren't really saying "I love you." It just sounded cool in French, misspelled as it was, and required some sort of response from them without really putting us on the hook of committing to all that "I love you" means, or at least should.

Vanessa seemed so open, but I could not say "I love you" because she would know it was not true. And I could not say, "Je t'aime" because what had sounded cool in high school would seem prosaic in the granite hills above the Academy.

Now, as she silently stared into the fire, I studied her profile. When she did not return my gaze, I leaned over to kiss her. I thought she might react stiffly or reject me all together, knowing that the usual impediments were gone.

Vanessa turned and tilted her head. Her lips were parted and soft. We sat kissing for a long time before I gently guided her into a more prone position. She pulled a blanket over us both and rolled onto her back. There was no wrestling match. No awkward conversation to break the mood. No playful karate chops. Vanessa's yielding moan in response to my touch was anything but "no." I slowly undressed her beneath the blanket, and she helped by raising her arms and hips when necessary. I had seen the poster in her apartment that declared 'Small breasted women have big hearts.' I assumed it had been hung there by Madge.

Almost everything we did that night was new to me. I had never felt her bare legs before. They were smooth and must have been quite recently shaved. The only time she said "no" was when I made a move to peel off the blanket as I kissed her belly. I thought what I had in mind was a gesture of love or at least lovemaking, but mostly I wanted to see her completely uncovered.

Vanessa opened her eyes and looked at me. "Gene, I'm not protected."

For a brief moment, the image of a young naked girl strangled to death by a tie flashed into my mind. I rolled away.

She was silent for a short while. "It doesn't mean I don't want you."

I nodded and kissed her cheek.

"I just want to be safe," she said.

I think she felt she had let me know where things were and if we continued, I was fully aware of the possible consequences and was willing to accept them.

It happened so easily that I wondered if she had been here before. She moaned and moved with me in a way that seemed to confirm a higher level of experience. I felt no resistance as I had believed there would be when crossing the line for the first time. I thought it was supposed to hurt.

After a time, I could tell Vanessa was in a good place. I had plateaued, and with my physical and mental distractions, I was never going to reach the summit. I started to get a headache.

I kissed her and rolled on my back. She turned to me, and I felt her damp arousal when she put her leg over mine.

"That was my first time," I said, fishing for a confession.

"Mine too," she said, her eyes closed.

"I thought it was supposed to hurt."

She opened her eyes and looked up at me. "It did hurt."

"I went right in," I said.

"That was when it hurt. But after a while, it started to feel good. Especially right before we stopped."

"I'm sorry." I felt myself getting defensive. "Do you know what an orgasm is supposed to feel like?" I asked.

"Sure," she said. She looked at me and smiled. "I have a bicycle with a skinny seat." She laughed. "Do you?"

"Own a bicycle with a skinny seat?"

Vanessa laughed softly. "Don't avoid the question."

"I have never been with a girl before," I said.

She smiled and stroked my chest. "But haven't you... uh...?"

"I've tried a few times," I said.

"A few times?"

I did not care to get into my masturbatory history. "It's not my thing."

I felt pressure on my bladder. I grabbed my jeans and, moving my legs from hers, began putting them on under the blanket. "I need to... take a short walk." I stood and walked up the path. My head was throbbing. When I was done, I walked slowly back to our camp. The fire was reduced to glowing embers. Vanessa was sitting up with a blanket over her legs. She was wearing a T-shirt with kittens on it and applying the everpresent Vaseline to her lips. I slipped back under the covers with her. The T-shirt was all she had on, and I contemplated how I could take my jeans off again without seeming too forward.

"Pretty uncomfortable without skivvies," I said, removing my jeans.

We lay back again, holding each other close. She did not touch me. She never touched me the entire night. I closed my eyes.

I did not sleep right away. I was thinking about what had just happened. For years, I had tried to imagine what it would be like, and always I made love for the first time on a fragrant bed with the girl that was perfect for me in mind and body. That was what I had waited for. That was my fantasy.

Vanessa had much of what I wanted, but not all. She was considerate and cute, an intelligent girl with broad hips, something Cruz referred to as "Colorado women's hip disease." She was the only girl I really knew in Colorado, and I would have liked her quite a lot even if she had not been. But I did not think I could marry her, and I really hoped I would not have to.

I woke to discover that it was morning and Vanessa was not with me. I dressed quickly, taking advantage of the solitude. I was thinking I should go looking for her when she appeared from the trees with a roll of toilet paper under her arm. Another provision I had neglected to pack. I needed to do what she had obviously just done, but I hated confessing to such primitive bodily functions.

"Good morning!" she said brightly. She rubbed some Vaseline on her lips and put the tube in her pocket as she watched me.

"Want some breakfast?" I asked.

"Sure," she said. "What have you got?"

"Potato chips."

"Good thing I brought eggs," she said. She flipped the toilet paper at me. "I'll fix them." She tossed our remaining deadwood on the coals and stoked the fire to life.

I felt myself blush crimson. I turned and silently started off into the woods.

"There's a little stream that way," she called after me.

I drank plenty of water from little streams during survival training, often without using the iodine pills. Some people like peeing in a stream. Or worse. At the Academy, we were constantly reminded how the stuff flows downhill. I believed in the sanctity of the stream, but I always made sure no one was peeing in it before taking a drink. Some people like the idea that the stream is taking their trash away from them, never realizing someone else upstream may be doing the same to them.

Our walk down the hill was relatively quiet. When we got to the Cadet Area, I accompanied her to the street level of Vandenberg Hall. I told her I needed to catch up on my studies, and she said she would be okay. Madge had agreed to come pick her up and was due there shortly, assuming the Falcoon had not broken down somewhere.

CHAPTER TWENTY-FOUR

Two weeks would pass before I could see Vanessa again. In that time, I thought about everything that had happened. I was not in love with her, but she was my connection with what I thought of as a real college, of the real world. And I did like her a good bit.

She called me on one of the squadron pay phones to ask if I wanted to go to Fargo's Pizza Company with some of Madge's friends.

On a beautiful fall afternoon, I caught a ride to Colorado College. I was looking forward to seeing Vanessa again, although I felt some trepidation thinking about what she might want to say to me.

The Falcoon was crowded, so I sat in the backseat with her on my lap, which allowed us our own private conversation while the others talked about themselves.

"I missed you," she whispered.

"I missed you, too. How have things been?"

"Funny," she said.

It would have been easy to read so much into that one word. I wondered if she was about to lower the boom.

"Funny?" I repeated.

"I started my period."

I had outfoxed the devil, but I nodded as if I had expected nothing else. "That's good," I said.

"But I got sick."

"A cold?"

"No. I threw up a lot. I heard that happens to girls after their first time. Sometimes." She kissed my cheek which I am sure made me blush, but in the dark car no one could tell.

I had to ask the question that threatened to bruise my ego. "Did you enjoy it?"

She laughed. "Getting sick?" She put her soft Vaseline moistened lips to my ear. "You felt good," she said. "It felt right."

"Did you..." I wanted to say 'come,' but it seemed too vulgar. "...have an orgasm?"

"I think I almost did," she whispered. "Did you?"

I was sure she knew I had not. "No," I said. Then I lied. "I still don't know what that feels like."

"You didn't go back to your room and...?" She let her question hang in the space between her mouth and my ear like a bridge between our sexuality. She had bled and gotten sick, and I was supposed to have relieved myself of the tension.

"I want the real thing or nothing at all," I said simply.

She leaned against me. "Should we try again?"

I could feel myself getting aroused. "I don't know. We took a pretty big chance." I felt so cavalier.

At Fargo's, she indulged me, sharing my favorite pizza—the Big Red, with freshly cut tomatoes on Canadian bacon. I knew she was not particularly fond of it, but she voiced no complaints as she removed the tomatoes from her slices. We laughed with her friends. They took me back to the Academy before midnight, and I kissed her once more.

We made a date for the following Saturday to watch a Colorado College football game. She assured me I would find it more entertaining than academy football. I looked forward to spending the weekend on a real college campus, complete with red and yellow leaves on the ground and the cerebral atmosphere I was sure infused all liberal arts institutions.

And I wanted to discuss the possibility of "trying again."

Waiting at the usual place, I caught a ride with a Firstie driving a red Corvette. Having bummed rides for three years themselves, most Firsties were more than willing to give an underclassman a ride into town. This car still had that new-car smell, and I think he picked me up to show it off as much as anything else. I don't recall him telling me his name, and he talked mostly about his car and what a "chick magnet" a Vette was and how I should consider getting one myself when the time came.

He went out of his way to drop me near the Colorado College football field. His pleasant demeanor sullied when I asked if he was going to see his girlfriend this weekend. He said he hadn't decided yet. I don't think there was one.

Vanessa must have seen me get out of the car because she tapped me on the shoulder as the Stingray drove off. I wondered if watching someone step out of such a hot car meant anything to a self-proclaimed "rich-bitch."

"Hi," I said. "Sorry I'm late. I had to wait for my chauffeur."

"Such a wit," she replied.

"I've been working on my salutations."

She smiled. "You're improving."

"I'm considering adding a hand gesture. Has the game started?"

"The first quarter's almost over," she said. "Maybe half-over. So maybe the first eighth, or maybe they're in the last three sixteenths." She shrugged. "I never watch the clock."

There were no ticket sales, so I followed Vanessa directly to the only side of the field with bleachers. We sat near a group of girls, evidently friends of hers. We were just far enough away to allow a private conversation yet close enough that she could turn from time to time to say something witty to them. Madge was not among them.

While the girls joked among themselves, I watched the game in relative silence. The Colorado College team was winning with a very unorthodox offense. What they lacked in size they made up for in speed and intelligence, much like the Academy team.

The quarterback never took the snap under center. He crouched in the backfield with one or two other backs beside him, and you could never tell who the center was going to snap the ball to. Sometimes another player would go in motion and intercept the snap before it got to the quarterback. The other team seldom guessed correctly. It was fun to watch brains win out over brawn.

When the players took a time out, Vanessa said, "Football must be the most unethical game there is, don't you think?"

"Really?"

She smiled and nodded. "They try to hide the truth. 'I got the fumble! I caught the ball! I was over the goal line!'"

"If you aren't cheating you aren't trying," I said.

She smiled mischievously at me. "Is it considered an honor violation if a cadet tries to say he caught a pass when he knows he didn't?"

I smiled back. "If a cadet says he caught it, he caught it."

The sun emerged from the clouds, bathing the stadium in a warm fall glow. Vanessa donned a pair of sunglasses she pulled from her jacket.

I turned to look at her. She was staring through the dark lenses at some distant point beyond the field of play.

"So why are we here?" I asked. "If you hate football so much."

She glanced at her friends who seemed to be keeping an eye on us. "I don't hate it. I just like other sports more."

"Like hockey," I said. "All that brutality."

"But honest brutality!" She laughed. "It's more ethical."

"Hockey?" I said. "Ethical?"

She nodded. "The puck either goes in the net or it doesn't. The red light doesn't lie."

As the players returned to the field I asked, "What's the most ethical game?"

She furrowed her brow before saying, "Golf."

"I've played golf," I said. "I can't remember a single round where I didn't improve my lie or take a gimme putt or something."

"Okay, professional golf. It's almost impossible to cheat."

I nodded. "Too many people watching."

She edged closer. "When people don't feel well, why do they say they're not up to par? Shouldn't it be they're not feeling *down* to par?"

I laughed.

After a moment, Vanessa said, "Ever heard of the Ring of Gyges?"

"The what?"

"Ring of Gyges. The ring makes you invisible. The idea is that the true test of character is how you would act if no one can see what you are doing." She paused. "I read about it in philosophy."

"I wouldn't masturbate in public," I said. "Even if I was invisible."

She turned her head and smiled at me. "You've done that now?"

I could feel myself flush. "Haven't you?"

186

She looked away without answering, but the crooked smile on her faced broadened.

Halftime came quickly. I think the officials used a running clock.

Vanessa said, "This is the part I wanted you to see."

A dozen or so CC students dressed in street clothes entered the field from one endzone as the announcer introduced them over the public address system. "And now, ladies and gentlemen! For your Halftime entertainment pleasure, the world renowned Marching Tiger Cub Band!"

There was one tuba, one clarinet, a trombone or two, two drummers—one on bass drum—and some trumpets or coronets. Maybe a flute. They took the field in a line abreast formation.

"The Cubs begin their award-winning program with the incredible straight-line formation!" the announcer said. "One cannot help but notice the dexterity! The flaw-filled grace! The stunning fluidity with which they shuffle in unison!"

When they reached the fifty-yard line, they turned toward the stands.

"The Cubs now transition into their world-famous pencil formation! Such indelible talent. Oh, I tell you, these Cubs are sharp! Note their seamless progression into the challenging circle formation! What radius! I mean radiance. You may want to cover your ears as they blast out the school fight song!"

The band formed a circle and stopped to play a few bars directly at the crowd of maybe fifty students before transitioning to the "anthill" formation where they exited the field all running in different directions.

"What do you think?" Vanessa asked.

"I think they've got their priorities straight."

As we waited for the second half to begin, I decided to broach the subject of another camping trip or something else along that line.

"I've been thinking about that," Vanessa said.

"And what are your thoughts?"

"Maybe you were right. Maybe we shouldn't do that again."

"Go camping?"

"No. What happened when we did... it should be more than just a casual thing."

I wondered if she was toying with me. "I didn't think it was casual."

"Maybe you got what you wanted." She removed her glasses and glanced away.

"If that was all, would I still want to spend time with you...?" I glanced around. "...and your friends?"

She looked at me. "Are you saying there is more?"

I thought I had Vanessa figured out, at least some of her. But this was something new. I felt the red flag unfurling. I did not think I was in love with her, but it would be easy for her to finesse my guilt.

"It was my first time to ever... make love," I said. "And it seemed to just happen. I thought for you as well."

She put her sunglasses back on. "My mother did not raise me to be a loose woman."

I turned to look at the players on the field below us. I, too, was being outflanked and outwitted. I wondered how many other cadets had endured this exact same thing.

"I'm the one who could get pregnant," Vanessa said to my silence.

"Were you scared you were?" I asked.

"Yes," she said. "I was afraid I had morning sickness." Her mood turned decidedly somber. This was not the same Vanessa who had whispered in my ear in the backseat of the Falcoon.

"I would protect you from that," I said defensively. "From... getting in trouble. I am a gentleman. I would never force myself on you. I think you know that." I was sure my hesitance that night had been a testament to my intentions. "Do you really think I am just using you? For sex?"

"To you, it may be sex. For me, it is making love."

Why were we in a semantics battle?

"Gene," she said, her voice suddenly softer, even reassuring. "I really like you. You're a diamond in the rough. I just don't want to be hurt."

"I don't want to hurt you," I said almost too quickly. I didn't want to be hurt, either. And our idea of what hurt was not the same at this point.

She looped her arm through mine. "I think we could work," she cooed softly. "I would feel better about... making love... if I felt there was something more there. A commitment."

The price for having a steady girlfriend and a ride downtown was getting steep. It seemed I had gone from watching a game to being actively involved in one.

As if on cue, Vanessa's friends stood and ventured down the empty bench seats to where we were sitting. I looked up at them as they descended, thinking our intimate conversation was suspended, at least for the present time.

"So, you're Vanessa's cadet," one of them said.

I looked at Vanessa, then at her friends. "I'm Gene," I said, trying to decide if I should offer my hand. I was heavily outnumbered, and such a gesture would have been nothing more than awkward.

"Hi, Gene," said another. "Oh, that's funny! Hygiene!" She laughed. "Do you keep yourself clean, Hi–Gene?" She laughed again.

"No, I'm a dirty boy," I answered somewhat flippantly.

"Does the Academy allow you to get dirty?" another joked.

"They encourage it," I said.

"And they take care of you when you do."

I looked at the girl but said nothing.

"I mean, they may ride you hard in the hills up there..." she pointed toward the Rockies. "But if you get in trouble out here... in the free world... they cover for you, don't they? I mean, I've heard they have lawyers that can, like, get a cadet out of anything."

My social ineptitude deprived me of an effective response. I looked at Vanessa. Her friends were gathered around her in what could only be called an offensive formation. "That wouldn't be my style," I said finally.

"I'm glad to hear you are an honorable man."

"Most of us are," I said defensively. Maybe this girl had been burned by a less-than-honorable cadet somewhere in the past. I turned to watch the game, hoping to put an end to this ambush.

"Good," she said to my silence. She hugged Vanessa playfully. "Because this girl is important to us!" She smiled as if to reassure me that the worst of this little tribunal was over.

"She's important to me, too," I said, trying to convince myself as much as them.

Halfway through the fourth quarter, I told Vanessa I needed to head back to study. I thought about excusing myself with the cadet non-lie that I was on the Alpha Roster. It sounded very official, very important, like you had a serious duty you had to get back to the Academy to perform.

She may have heard that one already. All cadets were on the Alpha Roster. It was the list of cadet names.

Walking away from the stadium, I gazed around the campus with a jaundiced eye. The trees, the buildings, the students. Everything I had loved about being on a real college campus suddenly seemed like a lie. This was hostile territory, and I was being forced into survival mode.

I was ready to walk to Giuseppe's and grab a pizza and drink a lot of beer. I didn't care if Vanessa or any of her friends decided to go there and caught me in my falsehood.

A Firstie from my squadron stopped his Porsche 914 as I started to cross the road.

"Need a ride?' he asked, opening the passenger door. The Guess Who was singing *No Time* on his radio.

"Thanks," I said, sliding into the getaway car.

CHAPTER TWENTY-FIVE

Perhaps Vanessa's sudden shift in attitude was just a desperate counterpunch to the remoteness of the cadet, his ability to blend back in with the other cadets in the mountains, untouchable, selectively unapproachable. Having no phones in our rooms made incoming calls easy to ignore. And we were always busy, so it was always easy to be too busy.

The Academy was a monastery when we needed it to be, our own Ring of Gyges when we chose to be invisible to the outside world.

Funny to think we had so many opportunities for social interaction—mixers, squadron parties, formal galas in our fitted and pressed mess dress. How was it that so many of us were teetering on the edge of social ineptitude?

I returned to my room a confused but changed man. I was staring out my window, trying to make sense of what had just happened when Whit ambled in with his usual 'I hope I'm not bothering you' look on his face.

"What's up?" I said.

He was either unaffected by my mood or oblivious to it. "Geno, you're not going to believe what happened!"

"You were sodomized by aliens."

The expression on his face did not change. "I mean this afternoon."

"You don't want to talk about the alien thing?"

"There was nothing queer about it," he said.

"Sodomy's okay then?"

"Sodomy don't bodda me but boo foo do!"

I could not help but laugh, and my afternoon with Vanessa and her friends became a few degrees less threatening to my manhood. "Did you and Program Chick finally do the dirty?"

Whit ignored my question. "I went flying at the Aero Club."

I nodded. The Academy's airstrip had become Whit's best means of escape. Being on academic probation severely limited the number of Off Duty Privileges he was allowed to take. But he could rent a plane for eight dollars an hour and fly over Colorado Springs or the Garden of the Gods or the Rocky Mountains without ever having to sign out since he technically never left the Academy grounds.

"I took the Beech Sundowner out to check on potential camping sites around Stanley reservoir," Whit continued. "I decided to fly over Pikes Peak."

"Is that legal?"

"I don't know. It's over 14,000 feet. Hypoxia starts at ten grand. So maybe not."

"Did you?"

"Get hypoxic?"

"No. Fly over the Peak."

He crossed his eyes. "I can't remember..."

"Come on."

He smiled. "Yeah. I rocked my wings at some tourists and they waved back."

Whit once told me he was going to do a touch-and-go on the Terrazzo after we graduated. He liked the way it rhymed. He had it planned right down to the where, when, and how.

I shook my head. "How much do you weigh?"

"What? Around 160 I guess. Why?"

"Because half of that must be brass balls."

Whit closed one eye. "I yam what I yam and that's all that I yam."

I forced a light smile at his Popeye imitation.

"But that's not the exciting part," he continued.

"There's an exciting part?"

"I almost died."

"You what??" He had my attention.

"I flew into the mountains south of Eagle Peak. The aspens are changing color. I pulled the power back and glided into an incredible valley full of them. It was so beautiful. I was creaming in my pants. I didn't know where I was going, but I was getting there like a scalded-ass ape! Then I looked around and realized I was in the proverbial box canyon, mountains all the way around." He smirked. "I could have sworn I heard God laughing."

"And you couldn't just climb out?"

"Let's just say the Sundowner doesn't quite have the horsepower of a fighter."

"It must have something or you wouldn't be here to tell the tale."

"Well, I realized my only chance was to start circling in a gradual climb until I could get out again. Halfway through the turn, I saw another valley, so I started toward it, climbing all the time. From there I could see another valley appearing, so I just kept climbing and looking for valleys." He flashed me a knowing smile. "There's gotta be a lesson in there somewhere."

I shrugged my shoulders. "I guess."

"The more you see, the more you see more." He grinned. "You should go flying with me sometime."

"Not if I've learned my lesson." I turned slightly away to the window. "I kinda got boxed into a corner myself today," I said. "One I didn't see coming."

"Really? What a coinkeedink."

I nodded and told him about my afternoon with Vanessa and her cadre of friends.

When I was finished whining, he said, "Sounds like Vanessa's trying to finesse ya."

I groaned. "What a wit." Vanessa's words.

"Yeah, I'm a real intellect," Whit said. "But really, you should talk to her."

"I'm not sure I trust her anymore."

"Don't leave her hanging. Popeye says, 'Honesky is the besk polisky.'"

Not always, I thought.

Two weeks later, I received a letter from Vanessa. She wrote that she had been thinking about all we had done together and about how compatible we were and how she liked me more than a little. She did not ask why I had not called or done anything to get in touch. There were no accusations.

She also told me she was mobile again. Her father had given in and used the insurance money to buy her another car, a used Plymouth Valiant with push-button transmission. It seemed punitive.

I was not sure what Vanessa really wanted from me, but I thought that whatever it was, I was not ready to give it. I put off answering her letter. After a while, the idea of calling her seemed awkward. The first thing I would have to give her was an apology.

From time to time I got notes from the CQ that 'A Vanessa Cardewey called,' but I never acted on any of them and the calls eventually stopped.

CHAPTER TWENTY-SIX

That Christmas my family was in high spirits, optimistic of the future we would share. Mom was showing a positive response to the chemo. There was more open love in our family than there had been for some time.

Mom surprised me by coming to the airport with Tyson and my father. She seemed so much stronger. She was not wearing her wig, and her hair was growing out. It reminded me of my first haircut during basic training and how I would examine my head every day, noting any evidence of growth.

I considered Mom's remission as God's Christmas present.

When I asked Mom why she had not shared the good news of her progress, her answer bordered on superstition, like tempting the Evil Eye. Her brave battle with cancer and my father's subsequent determination to be a better man and husband rekindled their relationship more than couples therapy or cheap talk about the value of commitment ever could have.

Tyson was doing better in school, due in no small part to his belief that our mother was well and destined to live a long, fruitful life. It was all coming together again.

Noelle had a Christmas present for me as well. As the sun was setting on my third day at home, she pulled into our driveway in her dad's Ford Country Squire station wagon. After the compulsory but brief repartee with my parents in our kitchen, she put her hand under my arm and led me out of the house. Settling myself on the passenger's side, I noticed all the back seats were down.

"Lots of space," I said. "Looks like you could almost fit a sheet of plywood back there."

Noelle backed out of the driveway. "Maybe," she said, looking at me with an impish smile. "But why would you want to?"

She drove us directly to the seawall, which consisted of rocks, gravel, and compacted sludge that separated the lake from the island created by engineers when they dug the intracoastal waterway. A thin gravel road ran the length of it. Short turnoffs were spaced along the way, almost like intimate driveways designed for privacy away from the other parked cars. In the past we had only frequented the place near the end of a date, which afforded little time to get into trouble.

"No dinner?" I asked. "Or movie?"

"Movie maybe." She waggled her hand. "Dinner?" She smiled playfully. "Depends on your appetite."

The night was warm, and although it was officially winter, when we opened our doors to move to the back, the mosquitoes were immediately upon us. We dove back into the front seat and slammed the doors as if choreographed. The next several minutes were spent frenetically slapping at the bloodthirsty pests bouncing against the windshield and windows.

When it appeared our tormentors were vanquished, I looked in the back. "We'll have to crawl over," I said.

Noelle lowered her head slightly, eyeing me from beneath her bangs. "I'm game," she said. She reached below the steering wheel and took off her shoes.

I followed suit with my own as she squirmed over the seat, her short dress billowing to reveal baby blue panties. She rolled over, elbowing her way rearward as I struggled awkwardly over the head restraints.

I spotted a mosquito flitting against a side window and stopped to swat at it, missing several times before finding success.

"I bet that's not the last one," I said as I edged next to Noelle.

Her hand at my back urged me closer. "We must be brave."

We began to kiss and touch while Bruce Springsteen sang *Born to Run* on the car radio.

As our passion grew, Noelle was open, even insistent to my touch. Her desire coupled with my own quickly fogged the windows. I unzipped the front of her dress and spread it open as if unwrapping a delicate gift. The moon glowed through the hatch window, painting a bluish haze on her exposed body. When I tried to release the hasp of her bra, it pinched her skin.

"Ow!" She pushed my hand away. "I'll get it." She reached around and the bra came loose.

She closed her eyes and arched her back, raising her hips as I slid her panties below her knees. She bent her legs and used her feet to take them completely off.

Without speaking, I moved onto her as if we had done this many times before. It was then I felt the mosquito on my butt.

"Aiee!" I slapped but missed. I got luckier when it tried for an encore on my leg.

I waited and watched the windows, poised for another attack. After a few minutes, I said, "Must have been the last one."

"I'm sure it was," Noelle said, pulling me down again.

As I kissed her, there was a buzzing near my ear. I slapped at the noise. "Dammit!" I said.

"What?"

I pushed away and brushed my ear. "Blood-suckers!"

Noelle propped herself on her elbows, eyeing me in the moonlight as I maneuvered to scratch the growing welt on my behind.

"Well, this isn't quite as romantic as we expected it to be, is it?" she said.

I nodded and gazed at her well-formed athletic body. It was the most I had ever seen of her at one time. I felt myself becoming aroused again. "You are beautiful," I said.

She leaned forward to brush a lock of my hair then kissed me softly. "I'm sorry we've had to wait so long."

"Some of that has been me," I said. "I just wasn't ready to take a chance on becoming a daddy."

"You wouldn't. Not yet, anyway." She pulled me close to her, like a mother comforting a child. "I'm due any day now."

She seemed more schooled about things like that than in the past.

"Do you know what it's supposed to feel like?" I asked. "Will it hurt?"

"It may a little," she said shyly. "Have you... had orgasms before?" Her voice sounded almost clinical. "You know... to relieve the back pressure." She touched me briefly.

"I've had sex before," I said, feeling strangely liberated.

She pulled away and stared into my eyes, her brow creased in disapproval. "You're not a virgin?"

"No. But just barely."

"What do you... I always thought you were waiting for me."

I was certain it would be better for her this way. I tried to tell her as much.

She cut me off. "I wasn't worried about how good you are," she said, her voice tinged with sarcasm.

"You seem more experienced yourself," I said defensively.

"Maybe a little," she said. "But there are three times as many guys as girls at A&M."

"What does that have to do with anything?"

"I just mean it's not hard to find boys there. And..."

"You found one."

"For a little while." She frowned at me. "But there are no girls at the Academy."

It seemed she had come to view the Academy as a cloister where cadets pined away for the girl back home, waiting for that magic moment when she finally opened up and said yes.

"Does this temporary guy have a name?" I asked.

She avoided my eyes as she nodded. "Nick. Delgado."

I was stunned. It seemed that, while Nicki Delgado did not have what it took to get into the Academy, he had enough to get into my girl.

I pictured them together in the back of his El Camino. "You gave up your virginity to a quarterback?" I asked with excessive indignance.

She shook her head. "I'm still a virgin."

I must have misunderstood. "You're... still a virgin?"

"Yes." She paused. "Well, Nick... the guy... he sort of put it in a couple of times."

"But there was no movement?"

"Some."

"But it was not finished. No... orgasm."

"Well, yeah, there was that... for him. But not inside." She suddenly turned away and moved her wristwatch into the moonlight.

I thought to ask her what she thought being a virgin meant, but I was afraid I would laugh at her answer.

"The movie starts in fifteen minutes," she said frowning at the watch. She fumbled behind herself for her panties. "We should go."

We dressed in hurried silence and climbed one by one over the seat. The motor faltered when she turned the key.

"Oh, crap!" she said. She punched off the radio and tried again.

The instrument panel dimmed as she turned the key without effect. "Crap!"

"Turn off the lights," I said.

Noelle pushed in the switch and turned the key. There was just enough juice to start the big V-8.

"Thank God!" she sighed, looking at me.

I nodded as I envisioned her father coming to our rescue on this dark stretch of rock and gravel. I knew his rules. I also knew he had a shotgun. In the hands of a pious Catholic, the only question would have been whether the gun was there to ensure a wedding or facilitate a funeral.

Noelle put the Ford in gear and drove us to the theater and away from our side road of unconsummated love.

And she had been right—she was due. It lasted the rest of my break.

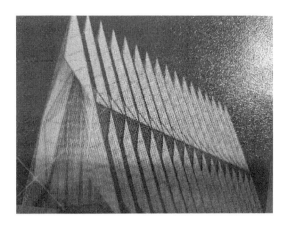

CHAPTER TWENTY-SEVEN

I was sure Hank Cruce would appreciate the awkward humor behind my latest Noelle story. Returning from the holidays, I expected his first stop to be my room, perhaps to complain about some girl who had wronged him. But two days passed without a visit. Toward the middle of the week, I waltzed into his room, preempting his typical greeting with one of my own.

"Cruce, you miserable waste of sperm, how the hell are ya?"

He was reading from a leatherbound book. "Ah. Gene," he said looking up from his desk.

"So you do remember me. Did you have a holly jolly Chrissmyth?"

He closed the book and eyed me questioningly. "It was... different."

When he offered no further explanation, I prompted him. "How different?"

He turned his gaze out the dark window. I could hear the Colorado night wind howling mournfully on the far side. We would get two feet of snow by the end of the storm.

"It's fu... it's hard to explain," he began.

"What's her name?"

He seemed to be in a kind of fog. "It was snowing..." he began.

"A night just like this one," I said. "Always a good way to start a bullshit story. Did she lose her virginity? Or did you lose yours... again."

He looked at me in a way that shut down my wisecracking.

"I got... pretty drunk New Year's Eve," he began again.

I thought to say, 'Standard,' but I opted out of making any more flippant remarks.

"I went to a party. It seemed half of us there were getting obliterated while the other half were staying sober. I was trying too hard with a couple of chicks... girls. I wasn't very discreet. One of them suggested I find another party."

"Well, we learn over time who our friends are," I said. He usually did not care what impression he made on people.

Hank eyed me, squinting the way he did whenever he was really trying to explain something. "I had nowhere else to go, so I decided to walk home. There was fresh snow on the road. At least I knew I was too drunk to drive."

"In the snow," I added.

"I was... plastered," he said, shaking his head.

"Obviously."

"Well, after a few minutes, the cold sobered me enough to turn around and head back to my car. I was crossing the road—in the middle of it—when these bright headlights came bearing down on me. The lady driving said her hand was pressing against the horn as hard as her foot was against the brake, but I never heard anything."

I ran my eyes up and down his body. "Are you okay?!"

Hank stared at the shiny waxed floor. "The headlights blinded me. I had no idea how close the car was until I felt it nudge my leg. I was frozen in space and time."

"That sounds pretty fucking melodramatic," I said.

"You weren't there."

"No," I said. "Sorry." I motioned for him to go on.

Cruce looked out the window. "My mind seemed to shift into high gear, as if coming out of a stupor. I guess I realized how close I had come. Anyway, this blonde lady comes running out of the car and slips and almost busts her ass in the ice and snow. I just sat down beside a mailbox on the curb and put my head in my hands. The whole world was spinning. I tried to think where I was and what had brought me to this place." He paused to look at me. "She seemed really nervous. I think she was afraid I was going to sue or something. I could smell the booze on her breath, and I'm sure she could smell it all over me."

Hank looked away into the darkness. "It was crazy, Gene. *She* was crazy. She started in about how her husband was stepping out on her, and how she had gone to a bar to get even..." He looked down again. "I could have died and she was going on about her scumbag husband. She said she was not normally like this, then asked if I was okay. I told her I was not hurt, just..." Cruce frowned. "She thought I must be in shock, and maybe I was. I didn't want to go to the emergency room on New Year's Eve, so I let her take me back to her brother's house."

This was sounding more and more like a typical Cruce story where he ended up bragging about some sexual exploit.

"So, was she a real blonde?" I asked.

Hank fixed his eyes on me. "I am a sinner, Gene," he said simply.

I laughed awkwardly. "You're just now coming to that? I could have told you months... hell, years ago!"

"It never occurred to me." He paused. "Well, it occurred to me, it just didn't matter."

"But it does now."

"I should be dead." He exhaled sharply and looked away.

"If you were supposed to be dead, you would be," I said. "And I'd have your stereo."

Hank smiled, his green eyes flashing a look of thanks. "Darlene—the lady—left after a while, but Timothy—her brother—and I talked well into the New Year. It was—"

Taps began over the PA.

"I gotta go," I said, turning to leave. "But next time we're out, the first pitcher's on me."

In the following days and weeks, I observed a strange metamorphosis overcome my friend. He seemed to bounce between contentment and misery, without spending much time in the middle. What he was becoming was so far removed from what he had been that I thought it impossible for him to continue in this new direction. He was bound to backslide at some point.

One day it hit me that he was distancing himself from the Hank of his past. And I was part of that past. I was a remnant of a former life he wished desperately to forget.

When we did talk, he insisted I call him by his middle name, Francis, which I found taxing. Evidently, "Hank" reminded him of how close he had come to dying drunk on a snow-covered road. Not that I cared to talk to him that much anymore. I was rather fond of the old Hank, but I hardly knew this new guy. Our brief conversations seemed forced. The path of least resistance was simply to move on.

Ironically, I was the one who missed the mark. The person most responsible for my college corruption was now redeemed or reborn or whatever it was that caused such men to abandon the profane in their evolution from fun-loving rogues into sanctimonious prigs.

We never shared another pitcher.

CHAPTER TWENTY-EIGHT

Three weeks later, I received a "Dear John" from Noelle, this time enumerating in some detail why she wanted a break. The letter read like a report written to expose the flaws in a project that needed correcting before any real progress could be made. It angered me because her intention, above all else, seemed to be to get a rise out of me. I read it twice before putting it away in my desk drawer. I wanted to hit back, but I also wanted to deny her the satisfaction of knowing she had struck paydirt. I decided to wait to see what she did next.

But several weeks passed without either a letter or a phone call. I imagined her lying in the shallow bed of Nicki's El Camino on one of the backroads of College Station, or maybe with some other new guy who would make it easier for her to ditch me. Permanently this time. Maybe a normal college guy to help her see life in a whole new liberating light.

My fantasy, and only consolation, was that she would realize too late just how she had lost a keeper right at the boat.

By mid-February, the Academy was again entrenched in the Dark Ages. We went days at a time without seeing direct sunlight. The snow was so heavy and came so constantly that academics were cancelled for two days along with all other activities. No one there could remember the weather being so inclement as to result in the cessation of classes.

Just before it all came to a screeching halt, I received two letters. One was from Noelle, the other from Tyson.

I opened Noelle's letter first. Rather than writing that she had reconsidered our relationship and wanted to give it another shot—which was the letter I anticipated—it was more of a confirmation reminder. I had not answered her "Dear John," which took her aback. She asked if I had received her previous "correspondence," as she put it. She was nice enough to apologize if I had not, but she wished nonetheless to assure me she was moving on, that our "swinging the bat" relationship—one of her less endearing euphemisms—was at an end.

I ripped the letter in two and threw it in my desk drawer with the other one. I grabbed her framed picture from my desktop and thought to chunk it, glass and all, into the trash. Calmer judgment prevailed, and I put it face down in the drawer atop the shredded letters.

I opened Tyson's handwritten envelope.

Our mother was sick again. I could feel Tyson's pain through his words and the way the letter was crumpled, the writing erratic. I decided to call home the following evening, but the snow and ice came and the pay phones stopped working.

I was alone in my mind. I sat for a day in the squadron TV room staring at the walls, feeling sorry for myself.

By Sunday, the guys with the shovels and bulldozers had removed most of the snow, and the phones came on. I called home.

Mom answered.

"Mom?" I choked. "Mom... it's Gene."

"Hello, Gene," she answered in her clear soft tone. "It's good to hear your voice. How are you?"

"Those should be my words," I said.

"What?"

"How are you? How do you... feel?"

"Oh." She paused. "I'm okay. Tired. A little under the weather."

I heard a distant cough. "Mom."

"I'm here." She coughed lightly again, this time closer to the mouthpiece. "I'm back in chemo."

I cannot remember what we said after that, except for her repeated reminders of how much she loved me.

I began to miss Vanessa, regretting my decision to ignore her calls. The ring dance was a few months away, and I had no prospects for a date. One of the biggest events of my cadet career, and I was going to have to attend stag. In the two states I now called home, Vanessa was the only girl I felt I could talk to. I decided to use that as my opener.

"Hello?" I heard a familiar friendly voice say.

"Vanessa?"

"Yes?"

"It's Gene. I've missed talking to you. How are you?"

Her answer was an extended silence.

"Fine," she said finally. "I've been fine. How are you?"

"I'm okay," I said. "As okay as you can be at the Blue Zoo."

She laughed, but it seemed forced. "I know," she said.

"You do?"

"I do," she answered in a voice intended to pique my curiosity.

"How was your Christmas in beautiful downtown Raton?"

"It was good," she said. "A welcome break."

"Yeah," I said. "So, what's going on? Anything big? At school?"

"Well, I'm engaged," she said. "That's probably the biggest thing."

I was stunned, but I tried to recover as one who could never be surprised by anything. "Well, congrats. Who's the lucky longhair?"

"A Firstie in 10th Squadron," she said.

"A cadet?" I asked. It seemed so unlikely.

"His name is Douglas Polo. You might know him."

"I don't think so," I said. "This place is small but it's still big enough to not know everyone."

"I guess so," she said. "He knows you."

"He does?"

"He's a friend of Eric Salter. He said you and he have had some interesting conversations."

"Oh, him," I said blankly. "I call him Marco."

"You do? Why?" She was silent for a moment. "Oh. I guess that makes sense."

"I never meant anything by it."

There was a pause.

"So," I said as much to myself as to her, "Vanessa Cardewey is engaged."

"We're getting married shortly after graduation."

"Oh."

"Gene, what made you call?" she asked.

"We haven't talked in a while. I just wanted to see how you were."

"Is that all?"

"Sure," I lied.

"Nothing else?"

I made up something on the fly. "My squadron's having a party soon. I promised the guys I'd talk to you, that you might know some unattached girls who would want to come." That was half-true. We were planning a party for the week before Spring Break, but I had made no such promise.

"I know some unattached girls," she said. "But I don't know if any of them would be able to come."

"That's okay," I said too quickly.

"But I'll ask around."

"Okay," I said.

"I'd call to let you know, but you never seem to get my messages."

"You've left messages?"

"A couple," she said. "Several. Back in October? November maybe? You know what it's like trying to call a cadet."

"I do." I thought back to that Saturday watching the football game... the last time I had seen or spoken to her. I felt a tinge of guilt.

"There it is," she said.

"Well, I'm sorry about that. About not... about your messages."

"Forget it." I thought I heard a faint sigh. "If I can scrounge up any interested parties, I'll give you a call."

"Okay."

She snickered. "Be sure to check your messages."

"I will. It was good to talk to you, Vanessa."

"Have a good life, Gene."

I hung up the phone and went into the stairwell. The wind was howling from another storm that threatened to cover the Cadet Area in frost. I went to the glass wall, sat in the corner, and cried.

CHAPTER TWENTY-NINE

I called home again the next day before evening Call-to-Quarters. Tyson answered.

"How's Mom really?" I asked.

Tyson's voice was soft. I sensed that our mother was close by. "She's weak," he said. "She's strong inside, but it takes all she has to move from the bed to a chair."

"Do I need to come home?"

"You can do that?"

"I can try if I need to."

"Save it. We're okay now."

There was a certain reservation in his voice, a hopeless acceptance that grew with each phone call until two days before the beginning of Spring Break, when he called to tell me our mother had passed away.

The following day, I flew away from the cloistered cocoon of the Academy to join the world of genuine grief and anger.

On the flight home, sitting numbly by the window, I tried to appear disaffected by life. The flight attendants could see something was wrong, I think, but they did not presume to enter my world.

I imagined my mother meeting God in heaven, and God explaining to her why He needed her more than we did. Then I imagined myself dying and coming face to face with something I was struggling to believe in anymore. Would God forgive me? Would Mom put in a good word for me?

When the plane touched down and the cabin depressurized, the thick humid air filled my lungs, adding more weight to my depression.

My father's older sister, Millie, picked me up at the airport and drove me home. The crux of her questions and comments seemed aimed at determining if I was all right. I don't know what anyone means when they ask that.

The lavender pink Formosa azaleas were in full blush. An errant spring storm had drenched the area, and the ditches between the byways and lawns were clogged with standing water. As we drove to my house, the sun shone briefly through a light drizzle. "The devil is beating his wife," Millie said. "He must be unhappy."

I did not think that was true. I was sure the devil was quite pleased.

In their early years, my father called my mother Kitten, because he said she had nine lives. This was reassuring to him, I think. My diminutive mother was a mountain of grit. She survived a burst appendix in her youth that nearly killed her, and a bout with pneumonia when I was born. She was unharmed in the freak accident that instantly killed my grandparents. Nothing could shake her faith.

It seemed to me that God had tried to call Mom home on several occasions. When she survived one trial, He would give her another. He kept trying until He got it right. Some church people said Mom must have done something wrong to suffer so. Loathsome people.

When we were dressed and ready, Millie, Dad, Tyson, and I piled silently into the blue Impala. It seemed strange driving Mom's car to the church for her funeral.

Tyson's hair was slicked back from excessively applied Vaseline hair tonic, and Dad still had a piece of tissue clinging to his cheek where he had cut himself shaving. He gently removed it as we walked the long passageway past the Fellowship Hall.

It was a solid building. My family had once camped on the second floor for a night, waiting out Hurricane Carla. I remember how secure I felt then, that everything would be okay because the church was safe.

We entered the sanctuary from a side door and went to our place in the front pew. As we settled in, I was surprised to see Noelle coming up the aisle. She made sure she caught my eye, gazing soulfully at me as she took a seat near the front and across the aisle from us. She mouthed, 'I'm so sorry' and with her eyes let me know that she wanted to talk when we could.

The organist composed mournful music as the church filled with those who knew and loved my mother. Momo sat between her two remaining children, my father on her left, Millie on the aisle. As I gazed upon Momo's wrinkled, sad face, I realized how much she had aged since my childhood years.

After the preacher's opening remarks—none of which I can recall—the choir sang "It Is Well with My Soul." I closed my eyes to hold in the tears. My soul was anything but well.

Aunt Millie gave a stirring eulogy filled with memories of the past and promises of a glorious and everlasting future. Then we rose to sing *Trust and Obey*, my mother's favorite hymn. I recalled hearing her humming or singing parts of it in her sweet soprano voice as she dusted our house or cooked our meals. "Trust and obey, for there's no other way to be happy in Jesus than to trust and obey." I could think of very few times when my mother was not happy. Or at least content.

But as I stood in close-lipped silence listening to this mantra, I reflected on what I thought was really being said. "Trust and obey what other men aver without proof. If you do that, you will always be happy."

Or at least content.

There was a time when I sought to reconcile the beliefs of my youth with the reality of the world. I came to understand that searching for the truth behind your faith is a double-edged sword. "Seek and ye shall find" may open doors you would rather have remained locked, delivering you into the hands of apostasy. The more you know, the more you must either confess the truth or buttress your faith against a raging sea of doubt.

When the graveside service was over, Noelle came to me and took my hand. She smelled too sweet for a funeral.

"I'm so sorry, Gene," she said, peering intensely into my eyes. When I said nothing, she closed her eyes and clasped me in a lingering hug. "I'm sorry about the letters."

Under the circumstances, her words seemed odd. Was she sorry about writing them? Or just sorry about the timing. Did she care how it made me feel? I thought she might say she was sorry for hurting me, but I think she wasn't sure if she had, and that might bother her as much as anything.

My father's response to my mother's death can only be described as devastated relief. During the post-mortem rites and rituals to which we as human beings seem to be addicted, he swayed between tearful grief and detached reflection when he would go within himself, often unresponsive to my attempts at spoken comfort. When he got into one of these trances of memory and acceptance, I could only coax him back to the present through physical touch—a shaking of his shoulder, a finger to his arm, a hand to his head. He would begin to cry silently and look at me like a convicted sinner searching for a redemptive face among a hoard of devils. It was at once heart-wrenching and pitiful.

Tyson wanted to cry more than he did, but he must have recognized how much our father was clinging to his strength. He did his crying in the dark after Dad fell asleep.

My own thoughts turned cynical. I found it difficult to forgive God for breaking my family's heart. While I was certain He existed—I still felt His presence—I did not much care for Him. I saw God not as a force against evil, but rather the architect of it.

Tyson put it best when he said, "God should have tried harder when He was making the universe. He could have created a world of happiness. Instead, He made cancer."

The day after the funeral, I drove Dad and Tyson to the cemetery. The rain had stopped and the skies were clearing. Damp mounded clay and flowers and memories were all that remained of Olivia Townsend. The cemetery was close to the river park, so we went there before going home. The tugboats chugged up and down the river as if nothing about this day was different from any other.

When we got back to the house, the Stanquist's Country Squire was parked on the street. Noelle was alone, and when she saw us, she got out and followed us through the garage. After a quick greeting, Dad and Tyson went inside to change clothes. In happier times, Dad would have light-heartedly reminded us to "Take off your pretty clothing and hang them up," as if enunciating every syllable of every word of instruction was the only way to ensure we did just that. This afternoon, what remained of my family trudged to the back of the house in pitiable silence. I had seen their rooms earlier. Both beds were neatly made.

I invited Noelle in and escorted her to the living room.

She fluffed her knee-length A-line dress and sat nervously in my mother's favorite Queen Anne wingback chair, her hands—fingernails displaying fresh red polish—clasped tightly in her lap, her sculpted hair set as if awaiting a tiara, her ankles crossed daintily as she must have seen royalty do. I sat across from her on the green love seat.

She looked at me, her eyes set in sympathy and sadness, obviously wanting to speak but unsure where to begin.

"Thanks for coming to Mom's..." My voice drifted off.

"Oh. Of course. I loved your mother." She brushed a curl from her forehead that dropped right back in place when she returned her hand to her lap. She squinted slightly and leaned forward. "Are you okay?"

I sighed heavily, raised my eyes to the ceiling, and closed my mouth when I realized I was breathing through it. "Are we being honest?"

"Yes. We always are, aren't we?"

"A little too much, sometimes," I answered without looking at her.

She lowered her eyes to her hands. "I know. I'm sorry." She looked at me and her long lashes flashed twice. "I'm so sorry."

"Water," I said.

"What?"

"Under the bridge."

"Oh." She did seem sincerely penitent. "I get so very confused sometimes." She spoke like a little girl.

"We all do." I forced a smile of forgiveness. "Are you on Spring Break?"

"Not really," she confessed.

"You skipped school?"

She lowered her head, keeping her eyes on mine. "Yes."

I nodded. "How did you get home?"

"I caught a ride."

I looked out the front window that illuminated Mom's piano. "That wouldn't have been in a maroon and white El Camino?" I asked.

She pretended to bite her lower lip as I returned my gaze to her. "I don't think his girlfriend would have cared much for that."

"So, that's..."

She nodded. "Months ago."

She pivoted as she fixed the curl again and leaned back, resting her arms on those of the chair. "Are you still going to the Ring Dance?" she asked, casually looking around the room.

"Yes." Did she think I would not because she was not going with me?

"Oh. Okay." She inhaled sharply. I knew she wanted to ask it, and she did. "With a date?"

"I hope." I decided to be noncommittal to see what she did with it.

"Is she from C-Springs?" She called it that because she had heard me say it.

"She might be."

"What do you mean?"

"I haven't asked her yet."

"Oh." She paused. "Is it... her?"

"There's nobody," I confessed. "I still haven't met many girls there."

"Well. One was all it took."

I let that pass. I guess we had both been hurt. "I may be going stag."

"Oh?" She looked away as if pondering something, and for a minute I thought she was going to ask me to my own Ring Dance. She leaned toward me again.

"It's okay," I said. "I won't be the only one."

Tyson came into the room, and Noelle moved back suddenly as if we had been caught in an intimate exchange.

Glancing at Noelle and then to me, Tyson said, "Dad gave me money for groceries. I need a lift."

"Are you cooking now?" I asked.

The question seemed to make Tyson both proud and sad. "Yeah. For a while."

I looked at Noelle, thinking we might want to continue this conversation. "When are you going back?"

"Two days. When my dad can take me."

"I could drive you then," I blurted almost without thinking.

Her face brightened. "Could you? You know it's three hours. Each way."

I looked at Tyson. "Would you be okay if I did that?"

He shrugged off his disappointment. "I have school anyway."

"Just there and back," I said. "The same day."

Noelle raised her eyebrows but looked away with a sly smile saying nothing.

When I left the following Sunday to return to the Academy, Noelle was my date for the Ring Dance.

Back in the squadron, I was approached by friends and those who wished to be doers of good deeds. Whit, despite his own concerns of flunking out for a second time, was the most attentive and least invasive. He neither tried to comfort me with words nor hinder me with advice.

When I confessed I had a lot to think about, he smiled and said, "The more you think, the more you think more."

I returned his smile. "I guess I should have seen that coming."

Salter's approach was different. "God is there for you," he avowed. "He knows what is best. Truly, everything that God created is good."

"I don't think cancer is good," I said.

"No, but God's will is. God reached your mother and she is with Him. Now God wants to reach you."

"I don't know," I said, trying to ebb my growing ire. "I'm not sure I want him to if the next step involves dying." We were standing in the hallway near the alcove for my room. I knew cadets were studying beyond the doors.

Salter flinched but stuck to his sermon. "Let these words soothe your spirit," he said. "'It is well with my soul.'"

My head jerked as the words echoed in my mind. I thought of Zooms and his willful apostasy. In that moment, something released within me, like a weight ascending from my shoulders, and I felt a freedom of words unknown to me before.

"I am trying to sooth my spirit," I said, raising my voice. "I truly want to be calm." I squinted my eyes and glared at Salter. "But it is you that denies me peace. You think I'm a heretic, one who can only know the truth by embracing your faith."

Salter's eyes widened as he retreated from the fury of my onslaught. "I've never said..."

"It's what you believe, isn't it?"

"How can you..."

"Where do you get the audacity to declare you know the truth and anyone who thinks differently is wrong?"

Salter stared wide-eyed at me for a moment before saying, "I'm sorry about your mother. I know it hurts."

I detected no sincerity. "Yes," I said. "That is the truth."

He wheeled and walked away.

I felt a presence behind me and turned to see Cruce standing in the open doorway of his room.

"Sorry," I said for lack of anything better.

"It's okay, Gene."

"Something he said reminded me of the funeral."

A certain rivalry had developed between Cruce and Salter in the time after Hank became Francis. Eric refused to believe Cruce had changed as much as he professed. Cruce, on the other hand, decided there was no one more suited to spread the Word than himself.

"Salter is not the only one with a wing ministry," he once told me. "His is not the only way. I've lived the other side. I've had to overcome more. I see it more clearly."

"I really am sorry about your mother," Cruce said now, touching my arm.

"Thanks." I turned toward my door.

"Remember—*Whether in pretense or in truth, Christ is proclaimed; and in that I rejoice.*"

I turned back to him. "So, a lie is okay if it makes me feel better."

Cruce's eyes were soft as he lowered his voice. "That's not what he meant."

"How can you know?"

"I feel it."

"Yeah," I said, turning away again. "You've been a great comfort."

"*It is not me, but the Spirit.*"

CHAPTER THIRTY

The Stanquists were so pleased to have their daughter invited to attend a seminal event at the Academy that they turned the whole affair into a family vacation, bringing her to Colorado for me. After hearing this disappointing news, I cancelled the room I had reserved for Noelle at the Howard Johnson's along with all other imaginings of three intimate days and nights with just the two of us.

When I went to the Stanquists' hotel to get her, she was alone.

"Where are your folks?" I asked as she invited me into their suite.

She closed the door and kissed my cheek. "They know how important this is to you, and they didn't want it to be like prom. You know, where they remind you how precious I am and all that."

I did not think it necessary. The time had long since passed when I could be intimidated by anything like that. "I'm sorry I missed them."

"They'll be here tonight. But probably asleep."

"So, we are not going to be alone."

She lowered her eyes and drew in her lips. "Not like that." She stepped back and brushed her hand on the sleeve of my white jacket. "You look very nice in your cadet tuxedo."

"Summer mess dress," I said.

"Well, it looks very formal."

"It's as formal as the Air Force gets."

She looked and smelled enchanting. Her dress was a long sleeveless white empire-style with a delicately plunging neckline that stopped just short of risqué. Her mother must have spent hours on her hair because it was piled high in a blonde beehive with every strand in place. I could not see them, but I knew the shoes she was wearing were heeled because they brought her lips closer to mine. I kissed them.

"Not your color," she said as she wiped the red from my mouth. "Let me get more lipstick, and then we can go."

We drove the short distance on Garden of the Gods Road to The Hungry Farmer in my new blue Datsun 280Z. Noelle's dress gave her a little trouble getting in and out of the low-riding sports car, but I could tell she was almost as excited about my new purchase as I was. She sat slightly slumped in her seat to keep her hair from touching the roof.

For dinner, I decided to forgo the mountain oysters. We both ordered the "shot out of season, so don't blab it around" duck. They poured the coffee their special way, but not for us. I was concerned about all the white we were wearing.

When we got to Arnold Hall, I immediately began to search for Whit. He was still dating Program Chick, but he rarely saw her, spending most of his current academy life in the books. Forced to quit all his extra-curricular activities—the soccer team, the aero club, the pistol team—what he had left, he said, were the books he loathed and the girl he loved.

Noelle and I caught up with them standing in line for pictures in front of a huge replication of our senior class ring.

"Whit! You scoundrel!" I greeted him trying to defray the awkward situation of being at once formal and friendly.

"Geno. This is Tina."

At long last, Program Chick had a name. I took her hand and kissed it. "This is Noelle," I said as Tina withdrew her hand.

Whit took Noelle's hand and shook it gently. He smiled. "So, you are Noelle."

She looked at me. I am sure she wondered how much of us I had shared.

"How are things?" I asked Whit.

He took Tina's hand in his and shrugged. "Okay." He leaned to me so only I could hear. "I gotta do summer school again."

"Really?"

He nodded and leaned back. "Guess I should have seen that coming," he said above the music.

I had only recently learned what Whit had hidden for some time. He was dyslexic. While he confessed this to me in a moment of academic frustration, he never once offered it, or anything else for that matter, as an excuse for the way things turned out.

"You'll be all right," I said.

"Or done for."

"Maybe you'll be Tail-end Charlie."

Every class had a Tail-end Charlie, the lowest in the graduation order. Traditionally, each graduating cadet gave him a silver dollar. I heard rumors of cadets who tried to tweak their grade point average negatively, hoping to win the race for what would be around eight hundred and fifty dollars. It was a dangerous balancing act. Miss it by one to the good, and you graduated with only a diploma. Miss it in the other direction, and you did not graduate, period.

"He'll be fine," Tina said, patting his hand and forming a smile that made Whit blush.

Whit shook his head. "I can see my epitaph now." He raised his free hand as if framing half a picture. "Here lies Whittaker the Cadet. He was fast neat average friendly good good."

I laughed as Whit and Tina walked hand-in-hand to the front of the giant ring for their picture. After Noelle and I posed, I looked for Whit, but Tina had spirited him away.

Noelle and I laughed and danced and generally had a good time. When we were not dancing, we conversed lightly as I looked around the room for other cadets I had come to know over the last three years.

I saw Eric and his fiancé enjoying a slow dance. They were holding each other quite close. I chuckled to myself thinking they needed to be careful there.

I spotted Francis Cruce hanging with some of our classmates who were attending stag. His brand new Laguna Blue Porsche 914 had failed to land him a date. The car was strange and ugly. But it was also exotic and looked like something a spy or a lady's man would drive. I wasn't sure Frank tried all that hard to find a date. Or perhaps Eric Salter was right when he observed that, "no girl wants to be seen in what is just an ugly, underpowered Volkswagen."

When Noelle excused herself to the powder room, I decided to talk to Cruce. After all, we had been through a lot together and, despite our parting of the ways on spiritual grounds, we were still classmates, and he looked like he could use a friend.

Sidling up to him, I said, "So, Frank... uh, Francis... did your girl stand you up?"

Cruce looked at me as if I had fired a silver bullet into his heart. "She couldn't come."

In our former days, I would have jokingly asked if he needed help making that happen, but that ship had sailed. "Sorry," I said. "You can dance with Noelle if you like. I'm sure she won't mind."

Frank looked at me. "That's okay. My... affliction's acting up a bit tonight anyway." He shrugged his shoulders and looked out over the dance floor. "What do you think this will be like next year?" he asked.

"Next year? Who gives a shit." I looked at him.

"The girls will be here then. The first class with females. I bet some of them will be at our graduation ball." He swept his hand around the room. "Dates of our classmates. Cadets dating cadets."

"Maybe," I said.

"I can't believe they are actually going to let girls in the Academy."

I just nodded.

Cruce continued. "They'll never be able to do what guys can."

"In some ways, I guess that's true," I said.

"And we're lowering our physical standards just to accommodate them. You remember what we had to do to pass the PFT the first time."

"Yeah," I said. "7 drop, 7 hop..."

"Well, I heard the first time the Doolies do the PFT next year, all they have to do is try."

"Really?"

"This place is going to hell."

"It'll be an awakening," I said. "We'll find out who we really are." I laughed. "Maybe it'll be our own road to de-mask-us. Get it?"

"Stupid."

"Thanks."

"Not you. The idea." Frank's eyes softened. "I'm sorry about your mother."

I nodded.

"I'm sorry if what I said hurt," Cruce said.

I nodded again. On this night, I wanted thoughts of my mother to be as obscure as possible.

220

"Regardless of what you think, I believe you will see her again and forever. Your father will, too."

"Will that matter?"

"Of course it will."

"I mean, is there sex in heaven?"

Frank laughed. "I guess we won't be making babies." He looked around the dance floor. "Sexual orientation won't matter. Just soulmates dancing together forever."

I looked at him with new understanding. He was still gazing out over the crowd of slow-dancing lovers.

"If it won't matter then," he said, "it makes you wonder why it matters so much now."

In that moment, I realized the affliction he sometimes talked about had less to do with his crooked back than with something more innate. I offered my friend my hand. "Here's to the grouper."

Frank took my hand and forced a smile. "To the grouper."

I turned to leave.

"Geno," he said. "I hope you find what you're looking for."

"A Road to Damascus like yours?"

"I wasn't going there," Frank said, his eyes widening. "I wasn't going anywhere."

I began to feel melancholy. It started when I spotted Vanessa across the floor. It seemed she was not getting married after all. I was a bit surprised to see her dancing with Skye, although there did seem to be a certain symmetry in the idea. She was having a good time, or at least appeared to be. I think she may have indulged in a bootlegged bottle.

I did not feel guilty for having lost my virginity with Vanessa, or that she lost hers to me. My guilt arose instead from my weakness and apparent inability to treat her honestly, to be a true human being able to face my own insecurities head on.

I wanted to talk to her, if only for a moment. But this night was not one for apologies.

I was looking for Noelle when Vanessa caught my eye, or I caught hers. Either way, neither of us crossed the floor. She mouthed something to me, something like 'Hi,' but I could not be sure. I mouthed 'Would you like to dance?' She looked around and mouthed back 'Yes.'

I took the first step in her direction and felt the gentle but firm hand of Noelle on my arm. I turned to her, unaware of what she might have seen. She said nothing but smiled and took my hand. I glanced over my shoulder. Vanessa's back was to me. Skye was making her laugh.

Later that evening, I caught another glimpse of Vanessa outside Arnold Hall. She was petting the marble statue of Pegasus that the Italian Air Force had given to the Academy. There was a tradition that went with the statue. If a girl touched it or kissed it and Pegasus flew away, she was a woman of true virtue. I watched as Skye helped Vanessa climb onto the pure white marble stallion, her dress billowing as she flung her leg over the statue's back. She threw back her head and rode him like a bronco buster. Pegasus never moved.

I wish I could have said something to her then. The fact that I did not would haunt me much of my adult life. What if I had? Everything that followed that evening would have been voided by an alternative path. She was so good and so easy to get along with and so intelligent and so fresh and so fun. It always bothered me that I treated her the way I did after that one weekend at the college.

Sometime after the dance, Eric Salter told me she and Polo had called off their wedding. "Postponed," Eric said. But I knew he meant cancelled.

I could not help but wonder if the breakup had something to do with me, however indirectly. Polo may have discovered that Vanessa was impure and been unable to live with that. Or perhaps it was Skye. I thought he was a much better choice for her than Polo anyway. Regardless of the reason, I was certain that, on that one night, I had experienced my final fleeting glance of Vanessa Cardewey.

I could not know the role she would play in the drama that would soon consume my world.

PART THREE

"The aim is to balance the terror of being alive with the wonder of being alive."

Carlos Castaneda

CHAPTER THIRTY-ONE

I have such marvelous music-induced memories of driving in my 280Z as that last summer began. I can still smell the vinyl new-car fragrance, feel the power beneath my foot, hear the music from my cassette player blasting my "driving music" into my head, taste the incredible freedom of leaving the Cadet Area in my own car as I watched the Chapel and all around it grow smaller in my rearview mirror.

I can still see the Z's long metallic blue hood in front of me, feel the black tires hugging the road, recall the thrill of speed-shifting on the snaking Colorado mountain roads. After three years of limited mobility, it was an incredible feeling to know I could go anywhere I wanted as long as I returned to sign in on time.

And it did not matter from which echelon of society cadets were spawned, we all emerged as equals. We all made the same amount of money, we all had the same opportunities, and we were all able to afford almost any car we wanted thanks to the generous terms provided by banks wishing to retain their clientele when we became officers. A whole new world opened up to us. We felt we had earned it.

I would spend the first three weeks of my final summer at the Academy teaching survival techniques to Third Classmen, after which I would leave Colorado for six glorious weeks. I would spend three weeks at Altus, Oklahoma, as part of the program called "Third Lieutenant." After that came summer leave.

Whit, on the other hand, was to be at the Academy for most of the summer, retaking the classes he had flunked the previous semester. I dropped in on him when I could. I felt more like a family member visiting an inmate at a state prison than a friend popping by his room to tempt him into a beer break.

On my way home, I stopped in College Station, spending a few days looking around the campus and a few nights playing around with Noelle in her apartment. I played tourist, aware that, in another life, this could have been my alma mater. I even tagged along to some of Noelle's classes. She had decided to take summer school to graduate early. We talked of a future together that seemed almost inevitable.

When I got home, Tyson took me aside to update me on our father's unsettled life. On the good days, Dad would talk of how wonderful our mother had been. On the bad days, he would sit at the kitchen table, assaulting worn out memories with shot after shot of Evan Williams in a quest for forgetful, or perhaps forgiving, oblivion. Tyson sat with him sometimes. But sometimes, it was too much for my little brother to bare.

It rained every day with no sign of letting up. After a week, I decided I had seen enough and packed my brown suitcase. I thought to spend another night or two with Noelle before meandering through Texas on my return to Colorado. I briefly considered stopping in Raton. I had Vanessa's address, although I had no idea if she would be there.

The evening before the day I planned to leave, I strode into the kitchen, intent on heading out into the night alone. My father looked up from his cups, his hand on his head, his pale eyes beginning their evening shift to bloodshot. I knew in the morning he would appear amazingly recovered, but he was wearing it hard now. I was at the door, the guilt searing my hand as I touched the knob. I lowered my head and turned toward the man who had once been my hero.

"Dad... can I bring you anything?" I asked.

"I've got what I need."

"You should eat."

I tried again to leave but could not bring myself to turn the knob. I pulled a chair away from the table and sat across from him. He did not offer me a drink, although he knew I was adept at downing a few.

Dad spoke first. "Are you ready for the war, Gene?"

I blinked in surprise. "There is no war," I said. "Luckily." I meant it to sound reassuring, that his oldest son was not in eminent danger of the perils of battle.

"That's what you do up there in Colorado, right? Get ready for war?"

"I suppose that's true."

He seemed oblivious to my response. "You're never ready for it." His eyes were focused on a distant past that was far too close. I nodded and listened in silence.

He spoke of LSTs, the landing craft for tanks and armored vehicles made famous during the invasions of Normandy and southern France. Sometimes his eyes seemed dull and withdrawn as he spoke. And then they would dart about as if watching one scene after another flash by so rapidly that he could not keep up.

He was a gunner's mate, having joined the Navy to avoid being drafted into the infantry. His boat was assigned to land at Utah, but because of the tides or someone's navigational error, they ended up at Omaha Beach.

"It had to be done," he said, his hand cupped over his curly black hair, speckled prematurely gray from life. "We knew it did. Like the bomb, it had to be done. The Nazi's weren't going to surrender just because we showed up with a tremendous show of force. No. You have to prove you mean it. And that's when boys die. We sacrificed our guys like burnt offerings, hoping we had more soldiers than they had bullets. When... we opened the outer doors and tried to get them out as fast as possible. The Nazi's tried to kill everyone. On the threshold of hell... what I saw float by... going back and taking more... lambs to the slaughter... the sea was bleeding... how could God...?"

It was a rational assessment veiled in madness. I felt my mother's death, and all that preceded, and all that followed, was pushing him into the breach. I needed to back away before being capsized by his wake and taken to the bottom to drown with him.

But he continued unabated.

"How do you get a bunch of teenagers to murder another bunch of teenagers?" he asked suddenly, looking at me as if I was the one with the answers. Before I could speak, he said, "You make them hate. You call the bad guys krauts and chinks... or gooks... Huns... wops or... kikes. They become less than human beings. There will always be war as long as old men can fill the hearts of young men with fear and hate and intolerance." He shook his head. "I know. If only it was that simple."

He poured himself another shot.

"I may be drunk, but I am not stupid," he said. "There has to be a place where we draw the line... a line that we defend. We got into World War One because Wilson said the right is more precious than peace. But winning does not prove you were right." He stared into my eyes, an inebriated soul in search of a savior. "I'll tell you something right now, son. War is evil. And evil only begets evil. Even after the peace."

My father glanced around the house he had designed in what now seemed another life.

"It's still a good house you made, Dad," I said.

He nodded. "It's not what you make that defines you. It is what you value."

Lifting his glass, he threw the bourbon to the back of his throat and ran his hand across his lips. "The Higgins boat may have won the war, but it also made Higgins rich. Wars would never be fought if no one profited from them."

He poured himself a tall one. "I wish I had never sent you to that place."

"What??" I said, somewhat shocked. "The Academy?"

He nodded. "I know I pushed you. I wish I could have kept you right here."

A lingering silence followed as I processed what he was saying. It is easy to be regretful after the damage is done. I recalled when Whit had once said, 'You can wish in one hand and spit in the other and see which fills up first.'

"Were you going somewhere?" Dad asked, breaking the quiet that was everywhere except my head.

"Not really," I said.

"Not going out with your girl?"

I shook my head. "Noelle's at school. I'll see her on my way back."

He raised his eyebrows. "That's good. I like her."

"Yeah, well..."

"I think she's good for you."

"Yeah."

He jerked his head. "Go ahead and go."

"Dad," I said.

He turned to me. "Yes son."

"You asked if I am ready for the war, if that's what we do at the Academy."

He nodded.

"I went to the Academy because I was excited about the idea. I stayed because you and Mom wanted me to."

"Look..." he began.

I put my hand on his shoulder. "I'm there now because I want to believe it's better to try to change things from the inside than it is to bitch about it from the outside." I paused, gazing into his tired, bloodshot eyes. "I learned that from you."

His smile was sad but sincere. "Maybe... in a way."

He reached for the bottle.

I thought to intervene. But he stood, walked to the cupboard and shoved the bottle away with a degree of finality that told me he might be done for the night. It seemed a valiant gesture, but I knew it meant nothing. It would start again tomorrow. At least I would not be there to see it.

The drive back to Colorado was less exhilarating than the trip home had been. Immersed in my thoughts, I drove more slowly, played less music, and more softly when I did.

I was backsliding. I had not stopped believing in God altogether. I just had little faith in Him. I was angry. The world He created seemed so prone to turning happiness into misery and hope into despair. I could not imagine watching my loved ones suffer through this world while I sat in the glorious sanctuary of Heaven in the presence of a God who knows every horrible thing that is going to happen but is unable or unwilling to stop it. I desperately needed Him to convince me this was the best way things could be.

When I got to Raton, I did not stop. I did not even slow down. It wasn't that I didn't think it would be interesting to surprise Vanessa. I simply did not feel worthy.

CHAPTER THIRTY-TWO

I cannot rush ahead, if I am to reveal the truth, but it should be understood that everything could have been so different. Unless you believe in fate. In which case, everything was predetermined, and nothing would have altered the future. I cannot pretend to understand God's plan. But I think I know the purpose of fate.

Life is the setup. Fate is the punch line.

I returned to the Academy to the jarring news that I had been reassigned to 8th Squadron. Why I was touched by what became a sweeping wing shakeup I never really knew. Perhaps it was the result of my run-in with Salter. Maybe the powers-that-were thought I needed a fresh start.

Thinking back to my impression of the spirit of Evil Eight when I was a Doolie, a distinct image came to mind. I recalled awakening one wintry morning to discover the planetarium covered by a huge black tarp with a white "8" painted on it, making the dome look like a giant 8 ball lodged in the snow. That display of esprit de corps would have been weeks in the planning. Skye was no doubt a central spark to that spirit.

Each squadron claims a unique, honored past. A past to be built upon and treasured as a means of furthering the sacred concept of camaraderie. It is, after all, the past that gives us something to hold dear, to rally around, and claim as a continuation of ourselves. But it seems that in striving to perpetuate a memorable past, Evil Eight was having too good a time at it.

Unable to salvage the good name of the 8th Squadron in its previous form, the powers that were in Harmon Hall decided to dismantle it completely, leaving nothing that resembled its former spirit. When the dust settled, all that remained of this proud heritage was one First Classman, Lewis Carpenter, and one Second Classman, a guy named Mattie LaForce—who, along with a dozen or so of his classmates, would ultimately form a sub-group in the squadron that referred to themselves as Bad Company.

Lewis and Mattie were left in place to provide a sense of continuity. The remaining members were spread among the other thirty-nine squadrons as if doing so would somehow dilute whatever poison festered inside the eight ball. Cadets from other squadrons were reassigned to the 8th, and the moniker of "Evil Eight" was replaced with the relatively benign "Eagle Eight."

Despite all this, the displaced cadets never let it die. Especially Skye Book. As part of the upheaval, he was removed from 40th Squadron—Ali Baba and the Forty Thieves—and reassigned to his old Doolie squadron, effectively, and I think unintentionally, bringing the prodigal 8th back home. He was delighted.

As he would often remind me, "Evil lives!"

Whit was also relocated. Permanently this time. The stress of the summer academic classes had taken their toll. From what I could gather—as there seemed to be a collage of fiction and fact—something in him snapped, driving him to unload five rounds of rat shot through his opened dorm window in the direction of the Chapel. There was no damage done, but they kicked him out anyway. When the officers running the summer program figured out the shots had come from his room, Whit told them he had "meant no harm to the Chapel, but just wanted to get its attention."

I looked for Whit's heroic return, thinking perhaps as a last act of defiance he would do his promised touch and go on the Terrazzo.

But all that remained of Whit was his beloved Popeye glass, which he presented to me on his last day as a standing reminder that "Honesky is the besk polisky."

The newly appointed Air Officer Commanding of Eagle Eight, Major Harvey Wainwright, scheduled one-on-one meetings with each of the newly arriving Firsties. When my time came, I reported to him as if to the executioner.

"Cadet Townsend, sit down," he said as he returned my salute.

"Yes, sir."

"Are you settled in?"

It was no doubt the same question he had use to start each conversation with all the new Firsties.

"Just about, sir."

"Got your new Eagle patches sewn on?"

"Just about," I answered, adding, "Yes, sir."

Wainwright nodded and folded his hands. "Look, I was sorry to hear about your mother."

"Thank you." This surprised me.

"I know that is hard. I lost close friends in combat. Ones that were like family to me."

I nodded.

He rested his eyes on me. "But it didn't make me lose sight of my obligation. You must not let it make you lose sight of yours."

"My obligation, sir?"

"To the Academy. To your country."

"Yes, sir."

"I think all of us here... all that choose to serve our country... do so because we have a red, white, and blue circle around our heart." He encircled his chest as he spoke. "We love this country more than anything. We are willing to give our lives for it. Because of that red, white, and blue circle, we are willing to sacrifice whatever it takes to make sure this remains the greatest nation in the world."

"Yes, sir."

"It's what motivates us to do whatever it takes in our career to get back in the cockpit again, to fly that fighter into combat." He glanced out his office window at a distant horizon and then looked at me. "I hear you had a little run in with Cadet Salter at your old squadron."

It occurred to me that the only way he could be aware of anything that occurred between Eric and me was to be told by one of the parties involved. And I had said nothing.

"Water under the bridge," I said.

Wainwright leaned back in his chair, steepling his hands. "Good."

I did not answer.

"You know," he said. "Part of being a good Air Force officer is having a strong faith in God." I got the impression this was an ad lib, a distinct departure from the script he had used with the other Firsties. "As you rise in rank, it will become more and more important in your social standing."

"Shouldn't religion be a separate thing?" I asked.

He lowered his head, looking at me from beneath his eyebrows the way Zooms often had. "You want to take God out of everything?" His voice bordered on threatening.

"No, sir..."

"If we take God out of everything, He will no longer protect us. If we deny God, He will deny us."

I did not argue.

"When people are getting shot at and fear they are dying... even atheists cry out to God. There's a reason for that." He looked out the window again as if contemplating the eternal. "Your soul knows it to be true, even if you don't."

I nodded in agreement. I just wanted to get out of that room.

"You'll see that for yourself." Major Wainwright turned to look at me. When I said nothing, he said, "Okay?"

"Yes, sir." Somehow, I did not think it was.

"Okay." His look was dismissive. "Welcome to the squadron."

"Thank you, sir." I saluted, did an about-face and left his office hoping never to be in there again.

I now regretted my decision to stay at the Academy. It seemed all my reasons for staying were being dashed against the rocks. My final year should have been one of the finest of my life, but it was now looking like little more than something to be gotten on with, a burden to be borne, survived, and endured, to be finished with as little fanfare as possible.

As expected, Wainwright appointed my old roommate, Lewis Carpenter, to be the first cadet squadron commander of Eagle Eight. He would command the squadron until the end of the fall "go-around," whereupon Wainwright would assign the job to another Firstie he deemed worthy. Due to his high military standing, I assumed in all likelihood that would be Skye.

Lewis picked his own staff, which included me as Athletic Officer. The job was about as far away from a military job as you could get.

When time allowed, I went to Lewis to thank him.

"Of course," he said. "I know how seriously you take your sports."

I thought this interesting coming from a track star who once wrote an essay for his English class on how to run the quarter mile.

"Probably the only thing here that I do," I said.

He smiled. "Maybe that will change."

I nodded and looked away. "Are you going to make DG?"

Lewis inhaled deeply. "I've got a shot if I can keep the grades up. It's a long race. This job's gonna dig into my study time."

"You'll make it," I said. I had no idea how close he was to the top. Distinguished Graduates usually made up less than eight percent of the class.

He glanced at me and smirked. "You'll be in your old buddy Philip Quince's flight. Not my call, but you'll be okay. You're on my staff. You report to me."

I nodded again, waiting for the other shoe to fall. I had almost forgotten Quince was also reassigned to Eagle Eight, along with his bosom buddy, Dusty Durskan.

"We have an odd number of Firsties, so I'm putting you in a room by yourself."

"Oh." I was relieved. I really did not care, as long as I was not going to room with Quince.

Lewis must have read my mind. He looked toward the window, breaking a thin smile.

"How are your folks?" I asked. "Still in North Dakota?"

He shuffled some papers on his desk. "Yep."

"Pretty cold in winter."

"They're happy."

I realized he needed me to leave. Squadron commanders always had something they needed to be doing. I turned to go.

"Did you hear about Newell?" he asked without looking up.

"Newell?" I said. "No."

Lewis Carpenter's eyes met mine. "He was jumped by four Black enlisted guys while walking to his car after a night at the Officers' Club."

"What happened? Is he all right?"

"He's never going to fly again, from what I hear."

"He... survived."

"Yes."

I looked at Lewis. "Does that seem... poetic to you?"

He shook his head slowly. "Justice is never served by violence."
I nodded, noting the sincerity in his voice. I turned again to leave.
"Did I ever tell you about the town where I was born?" he asked.
I stopped. "It wasn't Minot?"
He turned to me. "Ever hear of Shubuta? In Mississippi?"
"No."
"That's where my family's from originally. My father got us out of there as soon as he could, enlisting in the Army."

"I can understand. I have no desire to live in Mississippi." It sounded more close-minded than I intended. I declined from adding 'Which is why I'll probably be assigned to pilot training at Columbus.' I winced for effect.

"My father had a friend there," Lewis continued as if I had not spoken. "When they were teenagers, some white guys accused my dad's friend and another Black boy of raping a white girl. A mob broke into the jail where they were being held. They overpowered the guard—which may not have been that difficult—and they took the two boys to the bridge just outside Shubuta."

Lewis looked at me in search of my reaction as he said, "They hung them both from the bridge." He paused. "They were fourteen."

I closed my eyes, as if trying to blind myself to the horror. "It's good your folks got you out of there," I said weakly.

"You can't fix everything," Lewis said. "Sometimes running is your only option." He sat at his desk. "I don't know why I needed to tell you that, Gene. Maybe it's because you treated me as an equal when we were roommates, which was not what I was expecting when I first heard your accent."

"But I ain't got no accent!" I protested.

Lewis smiled. "Get out of here."

"Yessir." I snapped a quick comic salute. "Thanks for the job."

In some ways, Skye's induction into his new squadron was baptism by fire. He was assigned to room with Dusty Durskan for the fall, perhaps to remind him that Eight was no longer Evil. Looking back on it, it seemed more like corralling a bull with a steer in hopes of calming the bull.

Dusty was possibly the most anal guy I ever met. His desk was always perfectly organized, nothing out of place, his bookshelf arranged as if for a portrait. Even his civilian dress was meticulously maintained with pressed collars and pants—never jeans—and penny loafers with no pennies.

He was a small, tightly wound guy who seemed on the verge of snapping at any moment, and when he walked, he hunched his shoulders as if in preemptive defense against a hostile world. His favorite quote was that of Patton, *"A piece of spaghetti or a military unit can only be led from the front end."* From this, he developed the Durskan corollary, 'You can't push on a rope.'

Skye began stopping by my room for brief visits on his way back from hockey practice to see how I was faring in a room by myself, or to ask if I was interested in going into C-Springs for a beer that weekend, or just to distract me from my schoolwork as Zooms had done. Perhaps he considered me a fellow refugee adrift in the same boat. He may have thought I was lonely, although I was quite content with my setup.

Sometimes, he would bring his most valued treasure—a hand-crafted Spanish classical guitar—and serenade me with something new he had written or was working on. He never asked me what I thought of it. He just played.

Skye always seemed to be watching me, assessing my character. Or perhaps I was just a respite from Dusty. Whenever I mentioned that possibility, Skye would just shrug his shoulders and smile that warm smile. But I could see something in his eyes, a hint that things were not going well.

On one of our earliest trips to the Springs, while working on our second pitcher of Coors, I casually mentioned that my father had never once offered to buy me a beer.

Skye immediately looked at his watch. "Thirteen minutes," he said, looking at me with that all-knowing half-smile.

"Thirteen minutes?"

"I was thinking it might be closer to twenty, like last time."

"What would?"

"How long it would be after the beer came before you started talking about your dad."

"Oh." I took a long drink of Coors and refilled my glass. "I'm that predictable." I tried not to look offended.

"It's okay," he said. "It's the same reason I don't like to talk about my old man."

"Why you... don't talk about him?"

"The older I get, the more I realize I really don't know him. How can you talk intelligently about something you know so little about?"

"You think I talk about my dad because I don't understand him? Maybe it's because I know too much about him."

He shook his head. "It's not about him."

"It's not?"

"You're just trying to come to terms with how you feel."

I felt a bit miffed. "Is that why you never talk about your roommate?"

"Dusty? Why should I talk about him?"

"To come to terms with it."

Skye had nodded solemnly. "So why should your dad buy you a beer?"

"Forget it!" I said. "He just hasn't bought me a beer. That's all. Don't read anything into it."

CHAPTER THIRTY-THREE

Senior Father's Weekend was scheduled to coincide with the Navy game. On this cool and beautiful Saturday morning in mid-October, the parade field bleachers—normally sparingly spotted with dignitaries and tourists—were crowded to overflowing as fathers gathered from all over America to sit or stand and watch their magnificent sons display their knack for walking to music together in a straight line.

Somehow, watching a military formation on the march always makes the observer feel good about himself. Most cadets do not enjoy it in the same way.

Bedecked in my parade uniform, I stood at attention in the rear of the Eagle Eight formation on the Terrazzo, holding my wheel cap at my side for yet another pre-parade haircut inspection. I was consumed in a fog of condescension and self-pity, barely conscious of my surroundings. My father had said he would be there, but I knew he would not. I anticipated passing this weekend wallowing in my disappointment.

Skye stood stiffly beside me as Quince inspected his head. Their difference in stature made it difficult for Quince to see above Skye's temples. Quince lingered as if wrestling with an assessment of what he saw before finally saying, "You should get a haircut. Your hair is within regulations, but it doesn't look like it at first sight." He moved further along the line.

"Then what's the point of regulations?" Skye whispered.

I nodded slightly, returning to thoughts of my own injustices.

The sudden animation of my squadron mates stirred me from my musings, and I turned my head in the direction they were pointing. Emerging from over the mountains to the south of Eagle Peak, a fighter jet was turning toward the Cadet Area. We were accustomed to occasional noon meal fly-bys of T-33s and other fighter trainers flown by Air Force pilots, but we watched this jet with the exhilaration only military cadets can feel when they realize something special is about to happen. The excitement crescendo-ed as we realized this guy was continuing below the crest of the mountains.

The fighter, a Navy F-8, angled lower and lower as it neared us. The jet disappeared between the Chapel and the mountains for a moment before reappearing abeam the Terrazzo, left wing up giving us a once in a lifetime view of the top of the craft—the wings, the cockpit, the cocky pilot who lit the afterburner as the jet roared past us. Cadets on both sides of the Terrazzo broke ranks, erupting in spontaneous yelling and whooping as the jet continued north, its afterburner glowing orange against the blue sky.

We learned sometime later that the pilot, Lieutenant Commander Bell, call sign "Taco," was questioned by the senior Navy exchange officer overseeing all Navy instructors assigned to the Air Force Academy. Taco explained that he was merely showing the cadet wing how Navy pilots fly.

It took some time for the cadet commanders to restore discipline to the Wing, calling us to attention several times before we acquiesced. Finally, we began to march squadron by squadron down the Bring Me Men ramp for this first Cadet Wing parade that included female cadets.

A year earlier, President Ford signed Public Law 94-106 by which the military academies were directed to provide "for the orderly and expeditious admission of women to the academies, consistent with the needs of the services." Along with the law came certain semantic changes. When referenced in official documents, cadets would no longer be "sons" but rather "children." And we were no longer "men" but would instead be referred to as "members."

Pictures of civilian girls no longer appeared in the Contrails calendar, and we no longer had "squadron sweethearts," which I found interesting as, back home, Rigby High School was still unashamedly crowning Homecoming Queens but not Homecoming Kings.

It was good that women were allowed at the academies. It properly reflected the feminine potential and the progress of American culture. And male cadets needed that social interaction. The bad came from the way it was done. Rather than admit to differences between the sexes, the Academy tried to make all things equal, even as the administrators made things unequal.

It would take some time for a code of ethics and morals against sexual harassment, assault, gender bias, and mistreatment to take effect. This was not just the Academy's fault. It was, is, cultural. The Academy didn't need Title IX, it needed something more stringent. But saying girls should not attend the Academy because they might be abused is like saying soldiers should not fight in wars because they might be killed. The idea is to know young soldiers will die in war and try to minimize that; and realize that, by the very nature of the military structure, young women will be mistreated at military institutions, and try to minimize that.

That summer, a social dance was added as part of basic cadet training. I remember seeing snapshots of it in the Contrails calendar and other places, complete with Air Force officers "getting their groove on" with enlisted personnel. In one picture, two basics dressed in fatigues slow dance, their sad expressive eyes glazed with that faraway look of lost love. The caption for this moving scene was the ever so subtly misquoted line from John Dryden's poem that declared "None but the brave deserve the fair." If women were to be treated on an equal plane with men, which of these was "the fair?"

As we marched in formation down the "Bring Me Men" ramp, the irony of it struck me. Perhaps the "Bring Me Men" ramp was not as yet affected because nowhere in the poem did it say "Bring me members."

After emerging from the ramp, we continued down another concrete incline and onto the parade field where we stopped and stood solemn and still while the wing commander and his staff performed a series of formalities that excluded most of us.

Finally, the command signaling the beginning of the end came as the wing commander ordered us to "Pass... in... review!" The sound of underclassmen rattling their rifles in thankful appreciation could undoubtedly be heard by the fathers in the stands.

Skye whispered loudly, "Piss... in... your shoes!"

Standing to his left, Dusty admonished him with a quick "Wheesht!" that sounded more like steam escaping.

As we waited our turn to pass in review, Skye began to whistle with the military music played by the Air Force band.

This prompted another "Wheesht!" from Dusty who furrowed his brow for emphasis.

Skye smiled but stopped.

Joshua Steinway, now the First Group Commander, called the first ten squadrons to attention. Steinway had done very well. In the running to be the cadet wing commander, an unsubstantiated rumor had it that someone in the hierarchy determined the Academy was not ready for a Jewish wing commander. It made me wonder if the women would fare any better.

On Lewis Carpenter's command, the Eaglets, as some of us were calling ourselves, made the right turn that would take us to the far end of the parade field where we made two left turns to pass by the reviewing stand before continuing to the ramp and ultimately the Cadet Area.

When we regained the Terrazzo and were dismissed, Dusty turned to Skye with a look of silent admonition, as would a mother to a child. Skye returned Dusty's cross stare with a smile and a wink as he patted my back. "Lunch," he said.

We went to Mitchell Hall for the noon meal and afterward walked back to the dorm to change into our Service Alpha uniforms for the game.

Once inside, Skye asked, "Is your father picking you up?"

"He's not here," I said.

"Oh?" Skye looked at me in a way that portrayed both pity and opportunity. "My father's not coming either. To the game, anyway. I'm meeting him later."

Part of the full immersion of females into what had been an all-male school included allowing Fourth Class girls to try out for and become cheerleaders. While we were instructed to treat female cadets like every other cadet, Doolie males had never been afforded that equal opportunity. Even at Texas A&M, where girls have been a part of the University since 1963 and part of the Corps starting in 1974, "Yell Leaders" are still only men. But the powers that were thought it important to make women an integral part of all aspects of cadet life right away. And some of the guy cheerleaders were more than willing to help that along, dating some of the girls, and giving them special privileges. Administrative officials denied this was happening. But we knew it was.

The vast majority of the wing supported the USAFA football team. Even Skye, although he had fun with the Academy cheers. "Lets' truck south!" for Skye became "Let's suck trout!" He altered the "Air Force!" "Napalm!" cheering exchange to "Air Farce!" "No plan!"

We argued who we thought was playing this week's version of "Bed Check Charlie." He was always an anonymous cadet of medium build who dressed in World War One fighter pilot regalia, complete with dark goggles and a flowing scarf. He was usually down at field level with the cheerleaders, offering his own manor of team spirit.

At halftime, Skye pulled an orange out of his coat pocket and began to peel it. "Want a slice?" he asked me.

"Nah, I'm good," I said.

"This is a really good orange, Geno."

"You haven't even tasted it yet."

"Doesn't matter. It's a special orange."

"What is it?"

"A Nebraska orange," he said with a stealthy smile. He pulled the peeled orange apart and handed me several plump sections. "See how you like that."

I plopped a section into my mouth. "Something extra," I said.

"Vodka."

"What?"

"It's a chewable screwdriver."

I swallowed and put another section in my mouth. "How?"

"Syringes. From a pre-med class."

"Are they... used?"

He eyed me with amusement. "Not as far as you know."

"Come on!"

"They're clean."

"Cool idea," I said. I began to feel the effects of the first sections.

"Slow down," he said. "I've only got two."

By the start of the second half, our enjoyment of the game had risen to a whole new level.

Several of Bad Company's affiliates were sitting near us. To them, it must have appeared our good mood was due to an alternative influence, perhaps involving cannabis, as I was aware they covertly indulged in from time to time.

Quince and Dusty knew nothing of this, but they thought little of Bad Company just the same. They were forced to hold their disdain in check, however, as these same Second Classmen were among the highest in the squadron military order of merit. At least half of them were on the Commandant's list, and several, including Mattie, were also on the Dean's list, which made them part of that elite group of cadets called "supies," those on the Superintendent's List. What irked Quince most I think was his inability to bend them to his will.

Looking around, I saw Tomi Evans, also a new Eagle Eight Firstie, eying us with his smirky smile. It occurred to me he might have an idea of what we were doing.

The Tomi, as I called him, personified what Skye dubbed "Colorado cool." Tomi saw himself first and foremost as a ski bum from the greatest land in the world, the slopes of the Rocky Mountains, specifically, Gypsum, Colorado, which he called home. His father was a big man in that town, a Real Estate developer and, apparently, the only human, male or female, that Tomi held in high esteem.

From his refusal to ski with anybody who could not spend the entire day on the black diamond runs to the unique one-handed way he laced his $200 Danner Mountain Trail Boots, Tomi wanted everyone else to be aware of his exceptional self. Each interaction with Tomi was a furthering of one's Tomi education as he revealed that he was living just a little better than they.

Tomi drove a light blue Datsun 280Z 2+2 but bragged that he also kept an International Scout back home in Gypsum. "For four wheeling and skiing," he said. The longer chassis of the 2+2 gave the car a sexy European appeal, but that was a different kind of sexy from what Tomi had in mind. When I asked why he paid the extra money for the 2+2, he raised his eyebrows and said, "The backseat. It may be tight, but it's always ready." He never asked a girl if she wanted to have sex. He simply suggested they get naked.

Skye christened him "Fattafred." He did seem a bit overweight for a cadet.

I nudged Skye and tilted my head.

"What?" Skye asked taking another bite of the orange.

"Fattafred watches," I said.

Turning around again, I almost bumped my hat against Tomi's. He had moved near us with such stealth that I did not know he was there until he was.

Tomi smiled his half-smile accompanied by his half-opened eyes. "Got a slice for me?"

"Depends," I said preemptively. I was sure Skye did not care to share anything with The Tomi. "Who're you pulling for?"

Again Tomi flashed his casual smile. "What do you mean?"

"Aren't you going into the Navy after graduation?"

Tomi held his smile. "Maybe. But I'm all Falcons until then."

Skye pulled a third orange out of his pocket and tossed it to Tomi.

"You guys going to the post-game thing at Howard Johnson's?" Tomi asked as he pealed the orange. "All the squadron seniors' dads will be there."

"My dad couldn't make it this weekend," I said.

Tomi smirked. "Don't let that stop you. Dusty Durskan could be your dad. He's got some experience with that." His eyes widened knowingly.

"Oh, yeah?"

Tomi turned to Skye who shook his head.

"Your dad's not here either?" Tomi asked.

"He's in town, but he wants to see us alone."

Tomi pressed him. "Who's 'us'?"

Skye eyed him for a moment but said nothing.

Tomi put a slice of his orange in his mouth, and his face registered surprise. "Good orange," he said.

"What about Dusty?" I asked.

Tomi grinned slyly. "Let's just say he hasn't always been careful."

Skye glanced at us before redirecting his attention to the game.

After a moment of silence, Tomi said, "He has a kid back home."

I stopped chewing. "Kid?"

"Yeah. A little Dusty spermy must have sneaked through."

"I thought having a kid was against academy regs," I said.

"Being married is. Nobody knows about the kid." Tomi eyed us with a look that said, 'And you won't tell anyone, either.'

"You know," Skye said.

Tomi smiled his condescending smile. "I'm guessing you did, too."

Skye was noncommittal.

I looked at Tomi. "You know this for a fact?"

"Maybe it's just a rumor." The look on his face belied his words.

"How come he didn't just get her to have an abortion? Kill any chance of a scandal," I said.

Skye suddenly turned stern eyes on me. "You don't think having an abortion is scandalous?"

I shook my head. "Less, I think." I was feeling the vodka.

Skye looked squarely at me. "I'm glad my mother didn't abort me."

I wanted to ask if that had been a possibility but thought better of it.

After another minute, Tomi smiled and left us.

"The Navy should be a good match for him," I said, watching him climb the few steps back to his friends. "A girl in every port." Lowering my voice, I leaned toward Skye. "So that's why Dusty always seems one tick away from losing it."

Skye barely nodded.

I popped the last slice of orange in my mouth. "You said you only had two of these."

"Two good ones," Skye corrected.

"There wasn't anything in The Tomi's?"

Skye shook his head. "Nope."

I looked toward Tomi's group. Quince and Dusty stood behind him. Quince seemed to be watching us.

"That's brilliant," I said.

By the time the game was over my buzz had gone into remission. Navy was defeated and the Doolies were excited at the prospect of being at rest for the next several days.

As we walked to the parking lot, Skye casually suggested I go to dinner with him and his father.

I was caught off guard. "I thought the 'us' was you and Vanessa."

"Why would you think that?"

I shrugged, attempting to look disinterested. "I saw you together at the ring dance."

Skye smiled wryly, offering no further clarification.

I contemplated ways to opt out. I was curious, but I was also concerned about hovering at the fringe of a father and son evening. The whole idea seemed awkward.

"I have an Astro GR Monday," I said. "I think I'll go back to my room and hit the books."

Skye nodded and laughed. "Yeah I'll buy tickets to that!"

"I'm sellin' 'em!" I countered.

"Well, I want front row center."

"You got 'em."

Skye eyed me with a knowing grin. "You'll end up drunk at The Richter."

"Hopefully," I confessed. "Eventually."

His countenance reflected a subtle mood swing. "I'd really like you to come with me tonight." There was the hint of pleading in his eyes, like a lost puppy hoping to be let in from the rain.

"Didn't you say he wants to see you alone?"

"We're supposed to meet him at the Broadmoor at seven."

"You already told him I'm coming?"

"Yeah."

"The Broadmoor." I shook my head. "Out of my league."

"Dad will cover you." He paused. "You'll need a coat and tie, though. Civilian type."

I nodded in surrender. "I'll need a drink more than anything."

CHAPTER THIRTY-FOUR

As we drove toward Cheyenne Mountain in Skye's Alfa Romeo, we were still juiced about what the Navy fighter pilot had done. We argued the consequences of his clear commitment to "shine his ass" in front of God and everybody. Skye maintained that such a display of flying skills and pure bravado called for nothing less than a citation of excellence. Although the pilot had become an instant hero to the cadet wing, I was a bit more pessimistic of his chances.

After a few miles of contemplative silence, I decided to broach a new subject. "How did you find out about Dusty?" I asked. "Did he fess up?"

Skye smiled as he watched the road. "You mean about Little Dupert's Little Dupert?" He glanced at me. "I've known for a while."

I replayed our conversation with Tomi Evans in my mind. After a brief silence, I asked, "Was there a chance you could have been aborted? I mean, it wasn't even legal back then, was it?"

He looked toward the mountains. "It's just a philosophical thought."

"Okay," I said. "Then philosophically speaking, you would never have known. I mean, it's not like you'd be in heaven looking down on the earth saying 'I hope I get to go to that party.'"

"I guess not. But my parents would have known they cancelled my invitation." He looked at me briefly. "If a human is conceived, mistake or not, that human should not be denied its one shot at life."

I turned my head and gazed unfocused out the window.

Skye breathed in deeply. "I respect Dusty for having the balls to do it his way."

When we got to the Broadmoor, Skye called his father's room from the concierge's desk.

"We've got about ten minutes," he said, motioning me to follow him into the bar. He ordered a Macallan for both of us. I was not a Scotch drinker, preferring beer or the harder drinks that were made softer by adding a Coke or some other sugary adjunct. But I did not wish to appear unsophisticated. It was smoother than I anticipated. And much more expensive.

As I took another sip of the Scotch, I noticed by way of the large wall mirror beyond the counter that Skye was looking behind me. I turned to see a tall figure poised in the shadows at the entrance. The man moved, and, as he approached, his silhouette melded into the form of a strikingly handsome, well-proportioned man of perhaps fifty years. His hair was jet black, his chin square, his nose Romanesque, his eyes as dark as his hair.

Skye brushed passed me and took his father's outstretched hand.

"Good evening, Vincent," the man said. "You are looking well."

"Thank you, Father. It's good to see you." Their eyes locked noncommittally.

The fact that Mr. Book called his son by his first name caught me by surprise. As I watched this proper exchange of perfunctory pleasantries, I saw something come over Skye that was new to me. He was taller than his father, yet he ducked his head as a young pony might in the presence of a stallion.

Skye motioned me forward. "This is Gene."

Skye's father reached out his hand. "Gene..." he said with a quick side-glance at his son.

"Townsend," I said. "We're classmates," I added awkwardly.

Skye flinched almost unnoticeably, having evidently made a social faux pas in failing to introduce me by my full name.

"Good to meet you, Gene," Mr. Book said. "Harold Book. You'll be joining us?"

"Well, I had thought that..."

"He will," Skye interrupted. "Would you like a drink, father?"

Mr. Book looked questioningly at him. "Oh. Yes. You're twenty-one now. Happy birthday."

"Thank you, Father."

Skye's father nodded. "Bourbon then," he said. "Our table is ready. Have it sent there."

Skye went to the bar, made the order, and the two of us followed Harold Book into the Penrose Room. Never in my life had I seen such opulence. Despite my best coat and tie, I was out of my element in ways I could not begin to imagine.

I spoke as little as possible, fearing anything I said would appear trite or inappropriate—not that I thought I was outclassed intellectually, although I am sure I was. But when rich people talk, they seldom wish to hear from those that are not, except perhaps as a form of entertainment.

As we spooned our soup, Mr. Book asked, "Was it a good game?"

"We won," Skye said. "We beat Navy."

"Yes, I know."

"Any game we win is a good game."

"Congratulations," Harold Book said.

Silence reclaimed the table. Watching them interact as father and adult son, I began to understand Skye's insistence that I come along.

Mr. Book finished his soup, tipping the bowl away from himself for the last spoonful. He placed the cloth napkin to his lips and wiped once. "Have you taken the MCAT yet?"

Skye put down his spoon and wiped his mouth. "No, sir."

"You should take it soon."

"I'm not interested in being a doctor."

Mr. Book looked at me briefly before turning again to his son. "What are you interested in?"

"I want to be a fighter pilot."

"A soldier." Discomfort shadowed Harold's dark eyes.

"A fighter pilot is not just a soldier," Skye countered.

"There's not much call for fighter pilots outside the military is there? Assuming you come out of it alive." Their eyes locked as something passed between them.

"I don't plan to get out," Skye said. "Not for a while, anyway. It's a good career and..."

"That can't be all you want to do with your life."

"It is for now."

Harold looked at me. "Gene, are you planning to be a career military man?"

I wiped my lips and chin where I thought I had dripped some soup and placed the napkin again in my lap. "All I'm thinking about right now is graduating and getting my wings," I said. I took a drink from my water glass. When I placed it back on the table, a waiter immediately filled it to an inch from the top. "I won't know about a career in the military," I said as I leaned away from the waiter, "until I've spent some time there."

Mr. Book looked at Skye. "Son, you know your mother and I supported your appointment to the Academy. But it's only a steppingstone for greater things. You need to plan ahead for a career that translates to the real world."

I was intrigued by his word choice, expressing the same sentiment most cadets felt about the world beyond the Academy.

Two waiters arrived with the main course. Mr. Book watched them place our lobster and steaks before us as if evaluating their degree of competence. When they backed away, he cut into his steak and looked at Skye as he moved the severed piece to his mouth with his fork still in his left hand, Continental style. "What are you interested in, Vincent?"

"History," Skye said without looking up.

"History?" Mr. Book grounded his fork. "You can't expect to wander aimlessly until your future magically appears. You need a goal. If you don't take aim, you will certainly miss. As Ruskin says *Living without an aim is like sailing without a compass.*"

I looked up to see Harold Book staring at me as if evaluating a psychotic. I thought perhaps he was tacitly suggesting I excuse myself, which I was ready to do when Skye said, "*An aim in life is the only fortune worth finding.*" He paused. "Robert Louis Stephenson."

It suddenly hit me why Skye held such a proclivity for quotes. It was part of his breeding.

"Are you going to be a distinguished graduate?" Harold asked.

Skye's shoulders fell ever so slightly. "No, sir. I'll never get the MOMs."

"Your Military Order of Merit," Harold said knowingly. "Why?"

Skye glanced at me. "The new squadron. I'll probably fall off the Supe's List after Christmas."

"You'll have to try harder."

"It's not so simple."

"Maybe you should give up hockey."

"Our first game's next weekend. I can't quit now."
"You need to concentrate on your studies and your military."
"I'm not giving up hockey." Skye clenched his fist but immediately opened his hand and placed it on the table under his father's watchful eye.

Harold Book brushed the air with his hand. "You don't need it."
"You have no idea what that place is like." Skye worked to control his frustration. "I need something that keeps me going, keeps me alive." He paused and looked at me.

I was becoming genuinely uncomfortable. Mr. Book suddenly seemed to consider my presence more significant than he had previously determined. He went back to his meal. I glanced at Skye who was staring at his lobster with disinterest.

"I know you would never purposefully dishonor the family," Mr. Book said at last. "But you shouldn't be happy with just being content. The world abhors mediocrity."

Skye's father glanced at me. He grabbed the wine bottle from the bucket and emptied it into my glass. As the evening progressed, this courtesy became a trend. He ordered more wine, and I drank more.

Through a pulsating fog of conscious oblivion, I caught snippets of their conversation. For the first time in over three years, I entertained thoughts of the man who had appointed me to the Academy. The one time I met with Congressman Rigby, he appeared to me then as Skye's father did now, a common breed battling to be relevant. But there was more to it than that.

I sensed the evening was drawing to a close when I heard Mr. Book say, "I could get you a room." He glanced at me like a nuisance to be discarded. "Or two."

I was reeling with a euphoric numbness that facilitated my growing desire to be neither present nor accounted for. I held no desire to see Mr. Harold Book in the morning.

"Thanks, Dad," Skye said, rising from his seat. "But we have to get back. We're on the Alpha Roster."

It was getting cold when we left the Broadmoor, but Skye insisted we put the Alfa's top down. We drove north in silence, the night air cold on our faces, the heater's air warm on our legs. We meandered toward the

Academy on back roads Skye seemed to know well but which were unfamiliar to me. After a time, he looked at me and smiled.

"So."

"So what?" I asked.

Skye laughed. "Exactly!"

I was enjoying the chilling wind in my shortly cropped hair, wishing it was longer. I closed my eyes, thinking I might fall asleep.

Skye said, "Is it as high as Pikes Peak or by bus."

I opened my eyes and looked at him. "What??"

"Your thoughts on my father."

I glanced at my watch. "Wow!" I said jokingly. "Twelve minutes."

Skye laughed and looked at me. "Yeah, I know."

"I'm too wasted to talk about this now," I complained, closing my eyes again.

"You've got to talk to me," he said. "When we get to the dorm, I've got to go back to that hole I share with Little Dupert. He's not much for insightful conversation."

"Yeah, we've never had much to say to each other," I said. I paused before adding, "Luckily." I looked away, but I felt Skye's smile on me.

"We all have our trials."

"I suppose."

He went silent for a moment before asking, "So what about it?"

"What about what?" I looked at Skye.

With the wind blowing his blond hair as it was now, he looked like a bust hewn from the finest granite with the classic features of a square jaw, a noble nose, a high handsome brow, but with the typically dignified frown replaced by a comical smirk. He turned his attention briefly from the road to peer at me with those laughing blue eyes that masked thoughts much deeper than I could ever know.

"Ah," I said. "Daddy."

"Yeah." He returned his attention to the dimly lit road, steering the Alfa around a tight curve without slowing.

I put my hand reflexively against the passenger door. "I think he's very proud of you."

Skye stared straight ahead, concentrating on our path as the headlights cut through the darkness.

"He calls you by your first name."

Skye inhaled deeply. "He's not one for nicknames."

"He does come across a bit reserved," I said, hoping I was not overstepping my bounds.

"Yep."

My head was spinning from the alcohol and sharp curves. It seemed we were not following the road so much as avoiding the edge.

"I'll be the first Book to graduate with a real degree," Skye said.

That caught me by surprise. I had assumed Harold Book carried Ivy League credentials.

"Could have fooled me," I said.

"It's all show." Skye glanced at me. "We're what you would call 'nouveau riche.' My father dropped out of college when he discovered he had a certain... proclivity for making money."

I nodded my understanding. "A self-made man."

I waited for him to say something else, but he remained silent, staring at the road as if hypnotized by the asphalt.

"He seemed edgy tonight," I offered.

Skye blinked. "Meaning?"

"Meaning I think he's proud of you but afraid you could blow it."

Silence.

"But you must also be proud of him," I said. "He's obviously worked hard for everything he's got, and he's made something of himself. And your family. My father works at a plant."

"A what?"

"A refinery. Like half the people in my hometown."

"What does he do?"

I thought of the years my father spent working the graveyard shift. I felt obliged to paint him in the best possible light.

"He's a supervisor. He used the GI Bill to get his degree from the local university when it was still just a community college. So I guess my family is what you would call 'educated blue collar.'" I paused to look at Skye's profile. "At least your dad came to see you."

Skye shook his head in dismissal. "He's in town for a convention. It just happened to work out that way."

"Maybe he made sure it did."

"Maybe."

"I don't even know if my dad will come for graduation."

"Really? Why?"

I refrained from blurting out 'Because he's a fucking alcoholic!' "He's still pretty messed up about my mother," I said. "He gripes about war a lot." I paused. "That's unfair. He reminisces about... the horrors of it."

Skye nodded without comment, but his face turned momentarily sour.

"Mom died of cancer. Last spring," I said. I paused and looked away from him to the shadows and darkness beyond the edge of the road. "It seems to have opened a flood of... lamentations." For some reason, the word flowed easily off my drunken lips.

Skye left me alone with my thoughts for a mile or so.

"I think my dad still feels guilty," I offered finally. I certainly did.

"Last I heard, cancer isn't contagious."

"Yeah, but he's still alive."

Skye nodded again, his head bobbing up and down as if in a trance.

"There was a time when I thought he was infallible," I said.

Slowing only slightly for a tight curve, Skye said, "My father is the strongest man I have ever known."

"So, you do like him."

"I like him, but I don't want to be like him." His smile seemed forced. "Some parents aren't satisfied with raising their kids to be better people. They want them to be just like they are. They decide their life is the right life, and so their children should follow in their footsteps. It's the worst kind of incest."

"But your dad wants you to be a doctor."

"I'm not talking about careers."

"What are you talking about?"

"That's a discussion for another time."

"What a fucking tease!"

"Yep," Skye said smiling. "I suppose so."

We should have hit the sack when we got back to the Cadet Area. Instead, we went to Arnold Hall and drank 3.2 beer in the Richter Lounge until they chased us out. Beating Navy was always a reason to celebrate, although I admit I would have drowned my thoughts with equal enthusiasm had we lost. My debauchery had nothing to do with a game.

Had my mother never developed cancer, I think my dad would have been proud to spend this weekend with me. But Mom was taken from us, along with so much else. It is almost impossible to imagine the way things could have been.

I thought back to survival training, when I peeked from beneath my bag to see Skye staring at me from across the tent, his arms crossed casually on his solid thighs. That vision defined the whole situation pretty well. I was precariously balanced on a one-legged stool while Skye sat astride a life anchored soundly on three pillars—his gritty determination, his ability to find humor in anything, and his relentless belief in the concept of honor. That one night with Skye's father helped me understand what had fashioned those legs. But there was more. Had this domineering and obsessive older man been the sole force in his life, the organism that was Skye Book would have been a far easier study.

—

CHAPTER THIRTY-FIVE

arly the next morning, Skye banged on my door, waking me from
a booze-induced coma as he barged into my room.
"Go away! You flea-bitten sociopath!" I muttered.

Skye ignored my protests, turning on the sidewall lights. "Show some respect for your new roommate."

I groaned. "Up your nose with a rubber hose." I shook my head, trying to force my brain to wedge its way back into reality. "You're not with Dusty anymore?"

Skye smiled. "Does a chicken have lips?"

"So you're not with Dusty anymore."

"Now you're getting it. As of..." He glanced at his watch. "...twenty seven minutes ago, I'm stuck with you." He moved to the window and threw open my curtains. "Bitchin' day!"

I buried my face in my pillow. "Did Little Dupert file for divorce?"

"Let's just say we have irreconcilable differences."

"You came home drunk and tried to hump his scrawny as."

Skye grabbed Whit's memento from my bookshelf. "Up your ass with a Popeye glass!"

"Ouch," I said, rolling just enough to see his face.

"Yeah, ouch." He returned the glass to the shelf, gently nudging it back into place like the cherished artifact I considered it to be.

"It was by mutual request," he said, thoughtfully eying Whit's gift.

"A very sudden mutual request."

"Naw. He's known since... yesterday. Probably after the parade."

I looked up from the bed. "You think I'll be any better?"

"Does a worm do pushups in the grass?"

I smirked. "I don't know. Ask Quince." I eyed him a moment before rolling away. "Wake me when you're moved in."

He pulled my guilt quilt from me, leaving my hands grasping at air. I curled toward the wall in useless defiance.

"*Obedience and a sense of humor are virtues of the soldier.*" He kicked the headboard. "So move your sorry ass!"

I sat up. "I could use a shower."

Skye sniffed the air in exaggerated disgust. "What you need we don't have time for. In the hall in 20 minutes, wad!" He was gone before I could invoke a response.

We put the top down on the Alfa and drove to Wade's. Now that we were Firsties, going into town for breakfast seemed as easy as taking a walk.

"Are we meeting your dad?" I asked.

"Nope."

"Did he leave?"

"I don't know. He'll probably have a fine seven-course Broadmoor breakfast and then head north. Or maybe east. Could go west. Who knows?"

At Wade's, we bought a paper and read about the game while we waited for our pancakes. When they arrived, I doctored mine with syrup until they were completely drenched.

Skye frowned. "What a waste."

"What?"

"These are perfect! All they need is butter!" He smeared the melting butter on the hotcakes with his fork, his right hand at his forehead feigning disgust with my method. "Next time, I'll drop you off at the sign of the golden haunches."

"The what?"

"McDonald's."

"No wonder Little Dupert sent you packing."

After breakfast, I was anxious though not excited to get back to the dorm to delve into my Sunday studies.

"Ever been to Eagle Peak?" Skye asked as we drove west through the South Gate.

"Not really," I said. Several times I had eyed it from the valley below, thinking I should make the hike. Inevitably, I would make an excuse to myself about the absence of time.

"We should go," Skye said.

"Sure." I looked at him in realization. "You don't mean today."

"Does a snake have hips?"

"I don't have the time. I need to..."

"You have the time if you make the time. And there's no time for making the time like the present time."

I did not care to follow in Whit's footsteps. Not as far as getting kicked out anyway. "I really need to study. Last night didn't help."

"Look," Skye said, "you can grab life by the balls. Or you can spend your life making excuses, promising yourself you'll do it some other time. When you never do, you'll either resent yourself or make up more excuses."

"I'm borderline in Astro, and I have a Graded Review tomorrow."

"Carpe diem!" He tilted his head as if breathing in the entire world and closed his eyes.

I knew there was no argument I could make that would spare me. I looked toward the Peak. "Maybe there's a cross-legged Astro guru with all the answers sitting up there."

It was beautiful. The air was as clear as the blue autumn sky, and the smell of pine and granite invigorated us as we lumbered up the trail. We stopped near a vertical wall of rock to take a drink from our canteens.

"I used to come out here when I was a Doolie," Skye said. "On weekends when I couldn't sign out. I'd don my USAFA T-shirt and fatigue pants and head up." He looked at me. "More rewarding than donning Service Bravo and heading into the Springs to get drunk on three-two beer."

"Probably," I said.

Skye tilted his head back, gulping the water. "This place," he said, indicating the rocks. "Salter and I tried to scale that wall."

I looked at the ragged rocks jutting from the sheer wall. "Did you make it to the top?"

He shook his head. "Chickened out. It didn't seem such a cool idea when we were clinging to the edge fifteen feet above the ground." He touched the wall.

"You're not thinking about doing it now?"

"Nope. It's as bad an idea now as it was then." He pushed away and brushed his hands. "But it wasn't too long after BCT, and we believed we were bulletproof." He laughed for my benefit.

"What?"

"It was funny. And a little scary. I managed to lower myself back down, but Eric couldn't. He froze, unable to go up or down. He yelled that his arms were giving out. I didn't want to go back up, but he just clung there, breathing hard into the rocks and saying, 'God has a plan for me. God has a plan for me.' It was pathetic, really."

"He obviously made it down," I said.

Skye nodded. "I climbed back up and got him to put his boots on my shoulders to work our way lower. When we were almost down, he pushed away from me and the wall. I grabbed him to break his fall, but his foot hit a rock." Skye pointed. "That one."

I nodded, eying a nasty looking piece of granite erupting from the loose gravel.

"His combat boots kept it from being worse." Skye paused. "It was the beginning of the end for Eric and me."

"Is that the deal?" I asked. "He never forgave you for saving him but not his ankle?"

Skye looked at me, then again at the rock. "This was just the tip of the iceberg."

I tried to picture Eric in my mind. I could see his boyish face cringing in fear as he clung to the edge of the mountain, unable to go any higher or backtrack to solid ground. That must not have sat well with him, owing Skye because he wasn't strong enough on his own.

Skye took another drink of water before securing his canteen on his web belt. "We better keep going. This takes a while."

"Shit," I said. I had lost my Dean's List star the previous semester. I silently lamented what flunking Astro would do to my already dismal graduation order of merit.

Much of the last part of the climb was steep, even on what appeared to be a well-worn path. The wispy air fluttered the leaves lightly from different directions. As we neared the peak, the wind became stronger, making our ascent challenging, almost treacherous. It was just past noon when we reached the ledge. Skye walked out onto it. I followed but stopped short of where he stood. The drop was sheer for a hundred feet or more, disappearing into a thicket of trees. I did not want to admit it, but the whole thing made me uneasy. At least the wind had died down.

"Isn't this fantastic, Geno?"

"Yeah," I said with less conviction.

"When I look out there," Skye said, "I feel like I can see my future waiting on the edge of the horizon."

The rest of the mountain obscured our view to the west. "What about behind us?"

"Nothing to see there." He pointed east out over the plains. "That's where the sun rises. The undiscovered country."

"Hamlet," I said. "He was talking about death."

Skye looked to the mountains behind me and shook his head. "Death is a certainty. We all discover it sooner or later. But life. That's the real mystery." He turned again with his back to me. "From here, you can look past the Academy and know there is more to life than these four years of wading through all their piddly-ass bullshit."

He took another step too near the edge for my comfort. I backed away as if the gravity of my body could pull him into a similar retreat.

Skye inhaled deeply. "It'll all be over before you know it."

"Thank God," I said. "A few more months and we're out of here."

"No," he said, turning to me. "I mean all of this. This world." He looked again to the east. "But whatever the next frontier might be, this seems a good place to start."

I nodded noncommittally, although he could not see me.

Standing his ground, he was silent and still. Suddenly, he threw his arms above his head, his hands clinched in triumphant fists. "I am fuck!" he yelled to the wind. "Fuck of the mountain!"

He pivoted. "Come on, Geno! Get over here! Have a look at what the meek are supposed to inherit."

I took a deep breath and moved a step closer to the edge.

Huddled in the nether regions below us, the Cadet Area seemed diminutive, surreal and empty, an abandoned fortress glistening in the October sun. To the east, well beyond the aluminum and concrete and the green of the athletic fields, I could just make out the Black Forest, and beyond that the Kansas-like topography many Coloradans make little claim to when describing their beautiful state. Looking north I could see Jack's Valley, Cathedral Rock, and the place where I imagined the SERE compound to be. I was getting the sky's eye view of my academy career. I remember thinking that, despite this breathtaking panorama, I looked forward to the time when I would be done with all of it.

"The meek will never inherit anything that the strong don't give them," I said finally.

Skye lowered his gaze and laughed. He pointed at the Chapel. "They're down there, worshiping inside an aluminum wedge." He turned his gaze upward to the blue October sky. "And here we are." He spread his arms again. "Those people may think they can find the truth by sitting meekly in some manmade blight every Sunday. But up here, among the rocks and trees, we're closer to it than they'll ever be."

I thought back to my church in Texas. I sculpted a mental mélange of metal folding chairs and tables on the linoleum in the Fellowship Hall, the uncomfortable singing of hymns during Sunday School, the singsong recitation of responsive readings in the sanctuary. How awkward it all seemed now. I thought of the people I knew there. Working hard hours in a refinery. Bleeding purple and white on Friday night. Going to church Sunday morning. They needed to really believe, to have faith. Life was just too hard without it.

"Your friend who shot the Chapel had the right idea," Skye said with conviction. "He took it head-on."

"He didn't shoot the Chapel," I said perhaps a bit too pointedly. "Just in the general direction. With rat shot. No harm. No foul."

Skye lowered his arms. "And they booted him."

I turned and looked west into the mountains. "They don't know what they lost." A breath of wind whistled through the pines. I looked over my shoulder at Skye. "If we're closer to the truth, where is it?"

"That's the point," Skye said. "There's no such thing."

I shook my head slightly. "What do you mean?"

"Truth is nothing more than an idea. An idea that exists only because of man and his bullshit. Take away the bullshit and the world simply is."

"Is what?"

"Just is."

"But there are truths," I countered. "We used to think the world was flat, but then we discovered the truth."

"Right, but the world wasn't telling the flat-earth lie. Men were. You see?" Skye turned, staring intensely into my eyes. "Without man, there are no lies. And without lies, there is nothing true or false."

"There's deception," I said. "A snake that looks like a stick." I looked around the ground behind us, suddenly very aware that there could be a rattler waiting in ambush. I had killed a few in the past.

"A snake doesn't think," he said. "It just does what nature has designed it to do. Nothing more. Truth exists only because man exists. Truth comes from the same place that lies do."

"Opposites," I said. "Like darkness and light."

"Not really opposites," he countered. "You can say darkness is the absence of light, but you can't think of light as the absence of darkness."

I looked at Skye as it hit me. "So... a lie is the absence of truth, but truth is not the absence of a lie."

Skye nodded thoughtfully. "That's the truth." He laughed.

We were quiet for a time, enjoying the view and the air and the trees. Then Skye said, "I had a meeting with the AOC."

"Wainwright? What about?" I felt a sudden excitement. Was Skye going to be our Winter Squadron Commander?

"He called me in to talk about my 'attitude.'" Skye made finger quotation marks.

"Oh," I said disappointed. "What about it?"

"Wainwright said he was—what were his words—saddened by my lack of interest. He knew I had high MOM's before I came to the squadron, but he's disappointed I have not shown the military enthusiasm my ranking would 'suggest.'" Skye looked at me and smirked. "He told me I need to get on board, be a part of the solution rather than the problem."

"He's a snake in the grass," I said. "You need to be careful."

Skye seemed to drift toward some inner idea that was too painful to express. After a brief silence, he looked to me as if waking from a nightmare.

He suddenly reached around under his coat and pulled out a revolver. "Well, we don't need to worry about snakes." He pointed the gun at the ground near my feet.

I flinched. "What the hell?! Is that thing loaded?"

"Oh yeah." He grinned at me. "Don't Texas boys carry?"

"Rifles on gunracks in trucks," I said. "What is that?"

"This," he said, holding it like a trophy, "is a three-fifty-seven Magnum. Double action."

"Why is it up here? With us?"

Skye shrugged his shoulders. "Wolves?"

I glanced around. "There aren't any wolves out here," I said without conviction."

He laughed. "Snakes, then. Sex crazed women."

He tucked it securely away again.

I was getting antsy on a number of levels. I turned and started in the direction of the path.

"Wait a second," Skye called to me. He pulled a Kodak Instamatic from his jacket and offered it to me. "I need a memory," he said.

I inspected the camera as he walked to the edge, turned to face me, and thrust his arm toward the cadet area below. "Make it a good one," he said.

I composed two pictures of Skye that day. One through the viewfinder, and the other in my mind. Looking back, they seemed at once harmonious and conflicted.

I handed the camera to Skye and turned again toward the path.

"Don't you want one?" Skye asked.

"No," I said. "You're proof enough I was here."

I started down.

Skye caught up with me. "You want to know what I think, Geno?" Before I could answer, he said, "I think it's all about buying into it. It's all about getting on board. People want you to get on board with their version of the truth." He stopped and took one more look out over the plains to the east. "*By their fruits you will know them.*" He looked at me. "There is some wisdom in the big book," he said. "Once you get past all the smiting."

On the way down the hill I tried to reconcile everything, but all I could think about was my failing Astro grade. I started walking faster.

"What's your hurry?" Skye asked, catching up with me.

"Astro GR, remember?"

"If the min wasn't good enough, it wouldn't be the min," Skye said, intoning the cadet adage I had first heard from Hank Cruce. He looked up at the clear blue sky. "Hey! That could be God's mantra! 'Good enough!' Eagles have better eyes than ours. And wings. We make babies out of the same hole we piss from. And what was He thinking with the platypus?"

"Maybe He should have tried harder," I said, remembering Tyson's words. "Or maybe he just ran out of time."

"Or ideas." Skye gazed across the edge of the flat area that opened in front of us. "Let me ask you one of life's most persistent questions." He gave me his most intense look. "Are you ready to be serious?"

I sighed. "I guess so."

"You better be sure."

"I'm sure," I said, a bit frustrated.

"Okay. Answer me this." He paused for effect. "What's the difference in a duck?"

"What??"

He suddenly took off running through some small bits of brush. It reminded me of Tyson racing up the hill to the "lookout" in what now seemed an eternity ago. An image came to my mind of a ghost dancing lightly in the wind as Skye spread his arms, moving them rhythmically up and down. Whether for balance or pleasure, I could not be sure. Either way, he seemed to be in perfect communion with all that was around him.

I longed to feel so free.

CHAPTER THIRTY-SIX

O ne of the most challenging aspects of rooming with Skye was learning to tolerate the quirks that so often accompany those of exceptional character. When he woke in the morning, he dropped to the floor and cranked out thirty pushups before doing anything else. He would then throw the curtains open, whether the sun was out or not, and declare it another glorious day. In the evening, after we shut off the lights, he would sit cross-legged on his bed wearing that blue plastic-bag hat of his, silhouetted against the dark, gently strumming his beloved Spanish guitar.

There were a few mornings when the curtains did not fly open, followed by nights when there was no music. It happened only a handful of times, but he never talked about it. I welcomed the break because I knew it would all come back in full force. As it always had.

I was humbled that such a person would consider me his friend. But good character can be a liability. There will always be those who, being unable to match that character, conspire to destroy it.

The brewing envy and frustration that would ultimately consume Philip Quince bubbled to the surface in mid-December, a time when we all should have been content to concern ourselves with important things, like semester exams and Christmas leave.

Quince wanted more than anything to be an Air Force general. He saw himself as a leader, all the while possessing few leadership skills. He possessed neither charisma nor empathy nor the personal insight to recognize these flaws in himself. He would never have been the one to grab the guidon and rally the troops to follow him into the breach. He was much more suited to manning a desk and ensuring the paperwork was in order. The most important lesson I learned from watching Philip Quince was that to be a successful coward, you must be a clever one.

With the promise of the Winter Holidays approaching, Major Wainwright devised a way to spread his word among the cadets in his care. He announced that the Squadron Assembly Room would be open one evening for an informal discussion, a "free chat," for the Doolies.

Our proselytizing AOC worked to make this gathering seem a unique opportunity for the Fourth Classmen to talk freely and openly about their first Christmas back home. He made it clear he expected all Doolies to take part, essentially making this "free chat" a mandatory formation. Upperclassmen were encouraged to attend, and Skye took him up on his offer, as did several of the members of Bad Company. I went along to offer cover.

Taking a seat at the front of the gathering, Wainwright started it off.

"I think you will enjoy your leave most if you remember the reason for the season," he began. "If you think on that, you will feel better, more fulfilled when you return in January. You will be stronger and more able to cope with beginning your second semester." He glanced around the room, his eyes coming to rest on Skye. "I know there are some of you who probably don't feel this way. But if you open your heart, you will find the truth." He stood and nodded at Quince whom he had recently appointed as the winter squadron commander of Eagle Eight. "This is meant to be informal. So, I will leave it to you gentlemen..." He glanced around and smiled. "And ladies... to continue."

Wainwright left the Squadron Assembly Room, closing the door behind him.

Quince turned to the Fourth Classmen, seated together like schooling young fish. There were five females among them, transforming this collection of impressionable freshmen into a churning gulf of uncharted waters. "This is a wonderful time of year," Quince began, making eye contact with the most attentive among them. "So much celebrating. Just don't overdo it, eh?!" He winked like one sharing secrets with his closest friends.

The Doolies laughed nervously.

Dusty Durskan joined in. "I don't know if all of you attend church... when we were Doolies, it was mandatory..."

"For a short while," Skye put in.

Dusty glanced at him. "Yes, for a while." He turned away from Skye. "Sometimes, this place can be hard on you when you're a long way from home. My faith has helped me overcome some of the... less joyous aspects." He smiled.

"What a pal," Skye whispered to me.

"Enjoy the tree and the lights and even the Christmas cheer," Quince enjoined. "Just remember whose birth it is really all about..."

"And as you perform your pagan rituals," Skye interrupted, the corners of his mouth curling into a sly grin, "just remember the reason for the season is different for different people."

"Pagan rituals, sir?" a Doolie said. A nervous laugh followed.

Skye nodded. "The decorated tree," he said. "The lights, the gifts... Yule logs... that's all historically Pagan."

The Fourth Classmen hung on to every word, no doubt intrigued by how free the chat was becoming.

Skye smiled warmly, a sure sign of impending mischief. He glanced around at the impressionable Doolies. "This festive time of year reminds us that we can all work to make the world a better place," he said. "Whatever your personal beliefs."

"You are free to believe what you want," Quince said, shaking his head at Skye. "For me, I'm throwing in with Jesus." He looked around the room. Some of the Doolies were nodding in agreement while others appeared non-committal.

The electronic bugle tolled the Call-to-Quarters, and the Doolies had to be released without any of them having chatted freely. As they filed silently out of the room, Quince rose and eyed Skye with an intimidating glare.

"Why don't we continue this in my room?" Quince said. It seemed more a threat than an invitation.

"Sure," Skye said with a broad smile. He winked at me as we stood.

I followed the small processional to Quince and Dusty's room. Once inside, Quince closed the door as Dusty turned on Skye.

"What was the point of that?" Dusty snapped.

"Of what?" Skye asked in feigned innocence.

"The pagans thing" Quince answered for Dusty.

"Honesty," Skye said simply.

"Yes," Quince said, trying to curb his ire. "Honestly, tell us."

"No. I said honesty." Skye took a step in Quince's direction. "That was supposed to be a free chat, wasn't it?"

Quince exhaled sharply and sat in the chair at his desk, turning to face the rest of us like a king holding court. "That doesn't make you free to degrade the chain of command."

"Oh," Skye said. "How was this a chain of command thing?"

"You disrespected authority in front of the underclassmen."

"Are you that authority?" Skye asked.

Quince glared at him. "We all are. We have to stick together as a class. Otherwise, this new squadron of ours is doomed."

"So it wasn't a free chat after all," Skye said.

"Free doesn't mean there are no guidelines."

"We have to lead from the front," Dusty said. "You can't push on a rope." There it was, his favorite quip. He looked at Quince and shook his head as if saying 'What's the point.'

Skye turned and strolled to the vanity where he hoisted himself to sit next to the sink with his back to the mirror, his hands flat to secure his balance, his legs dangling above the floor. From his perch, he asked, "Have you done much sailing, Dusty?"

Dusty jerked his head. "Sailing? Not in Iowa."

"One of the first things I learned about sailing," Skye said, "is that if you get a knot in your rope, the worst thing you can do is pull on it. Sometimes, you not only *can* push on a rope, you *have* to."

"That's not what I mean."

"Then your analogy is meaningless." Skye looked as if he meant to laugh but changed his mind.

Dusty was almost shaking, his frustration obvious. He pointed angrily at the Chapel looming large in the window, its colorful display of stained glass glowing in the December night. "That says it all. That's what the Doolies needed to hear tonight. Not some BS about pagans and rituals."

Skye smiled. "There's a Jewish synagogue in there, too." He paused. "Look, Dusty, you can cling to that old rugged cross, believe whatever you want. I really don't care. Just show everybody else the same courtesy."

Avoiding his eyes, Dusty shook his head. "I don't understand why you are here." He sat in his chair at the desk across from Quince.

Skye followed him with his eyes and said, "Knock knock."

Quince looked around from Skye to Dusty. "Knock knock?"

"Who's there?" Skye said.

Dusty grimaced. "Funny."

"It is," Skye said. "Argo."

"Argo?"

Skye closed one eye like Popeye. "Arrrr go fuck yourself."

Quince closed his lips so tightly they went ashen.

Skye shrugged. "A man has the right to make a fool of himself."

Quince nodded in agreement at Skye's personal assessment.

A broad grin grew on Skye's face as he added, "But you shouldn't use up that privilege in one sitting."

"You need to be careful," Quince said menacingly. "You're still a cadet under the chain of command."

"And I plan to graduate and fly fighters in defense of my country," Skye said. "That doesn't require me to profess blind faith in something simply because it is your wish." He lowered himself from the vanity and looked around the room. "I've got studying to do." He turned away, adding, "Merry Christmas." At the door, he stopped and ran his fingers along the empty wooden gun rack then rubbed them together as if removing dust from them. He looked back a moment and then was gone.

I caught up with him in our room. "You're one brave dude," I said.

Skye looked at me with the same grin he had flashed at Quince.

"You don't have to be brave to face stupid."

"It can sure come in handy when you are dealing with crazy."

He sat at his desk. "Hey," he said, "I was talking with my sister..."

"You have a sister?" I interrupted, yet again taken by his knack for seamlessly changing the subject.

He nodded. "She's coming here."

"To the Academy?"

"To the Springs. To go to Colorado College."

"Does she play hockey?"

"What? No." Skye laughed. "She's not a fan. Too much violence, she says. Guess we'll have to get past that."

"So she's not a jock."

"She's just a young girl."

"How young?"

"She turns 19 in February. The only reason my folks agreed to let her apply to CC is because I'm here."

"She must be pretty smart."

Skye nodded. "She's halfway through her second year at Western Nebraska. My parents, uh... well, she wants to get her degree from CC."

"And you're telling me this because..."

"You're my best friend."

I was so struck by this confession that I momentarily forgot the other one about his sister. I felt at once flattered and defensive.

I looked at him in sudden understanding. "And you don't want anyone else to know."

He smiled, pointed at me, and said, "Is the chickenshit catholic?"

"I still think you'd better watch it with those two," I said. It bothered me that Skye did not consider insulting Dusty and Quince a big deal. I offered a more pragmatic approach. "We're out of here in six months, and they'll be gone from our lives. Don't let them ruin our senior year."

Skye shrugged his shoulders and pointed beyond his door. "Those wimps are in charge because they give the system the least amount of grief. They're... onboard. The real Air Force will eat them alive."

I should have anticipated the blowback from Skye's confrontation with Quince and his minion. Both of us started getting written up more. We regularly got Form 10s—or as Quince and Durskan insisted, "Forms 10"—for discrepancies they discovered while inspecting us and our room. Our shoes needed shining. There was dust found on our desks. The mirror was smudged. Our hair was too long. It was little things, but those things added up as we accumulated demerits, edging us nearer and nearer toward Conduct Probation.

Finally, they separated us, putting me in a room with a guy named Nathan Friendly, whom I knew little about. Skye moved in with Lewis Carpenter who was almost never there. After handing over the squadron to Quince, he divided his time between academics and indoor track while serving as our squadron's honor representative.

Skye seemed to be in denial of the situation, or at least brazenly defiant of it. I, on the other hand, became overly cautious about what I said and did, a restraint that bordered on paranoia. It was like having four fouls in basketball. You have to be careful to avoid the final foul that will take you out of the game.

CHAPTER THIRTY-SEVEN

I went home that final winter to discover that you really can't go back. What remained of my family was there, the house was still standing, my room was as I had left it. But there was nothing of the past to revive and nothing to claim for the future. It was only where I was from, a place on the map for Doolies to memorize along with my name.

My father had taken his drinking to a whole new level. Millie finally got him to rehab, but only after he was too weak to resist. Tyson helped her get him in her car and to the hospital two days before I arrived home. When I went to see him, he was so jaundiced, his eyes so yellow, that I was certain he would not see the new year.

For years my father had been my hero. Now I was being exposed to flaws I never would have known, I think, had my mother survived.

But something happened. He knew he was in trouble. He saw his sons standing before him, one he was sure wanted to save him and one he was afraid he had lost, and he decided to turn it all around. From what could easily have been his deathbed, he told us he had to fight this one on his own, and that, win or lose, he was willing to do so.

Dad spent Christmas in a hospital room hooked up to monitors and intravenous tubes. He weakly insisted we leave him alone with that which alone could save him—his willpower and a room full of VA doctors. Ignoring his protestations, Momo stayed with him, refusing to allow another of her children to die before her.

"Our Dad is a war hero," Tyson said one night when I must have seemed a bit overzealous in my criticisms of the man.

"Believe whatever you need to," I said.

"This is not something I just believe," Tyson said. "He jumped into the bloody water at Normandy to save a soldier who was drowning. The guy died in his arms." He gazed at me. "Just like mom."

"How do you know?"

A tear formed in Tyson's eye. "One of the VA specialists recognized him from the Navy. He was there. He saw the whole thing."

Dad was released New Year's Day. The remainder of my Christmas leave I spent at home with Tyson and Millie, taking turns sleeping at night on a rollaway near his bed. I wanted to ask him about the war and the dying soldier, but I feared he was still too fragile to think about such things. Or maybe I was.

I knew Noelle was contemplating my future and her place in it, that she was weighing things in the balance in an effort to keep her own. She knew I would have a job and travel the world, maybe live in Europe, and that Vietnam was behind us. Her summer classes had served to catch her up to me. She would graduate in the spring.

The Friday before I left to drive back to Colorado for my last semester as a cadet, I tried to tell her what I thought to be the truth.

"Do you really believe we could be happy after all our ups and downs?" I asked. "Marriages can't survive breakups like we've had."

"No one's happy all the time," she answered. "We've shared so much. We can make something good, a strong family. And that will make us happy."

I did not think so. To me, it all seemed a bit too calculated. But I had nothing to lose in seeing what happened between then and the first Wednesday in June.

What I *do* know is that I had grown calloused, determined never again to become as vulnerable as I had once been.

Never again would I allow a girl to matter that much to me, even as I was resigned to taking a wife someday. Even then, I would never relent completely. I would never allow myself to lose control, to be so caught up in love that I forgot everything except the moment. What Noelle had done to me, and what I imagined Vanessa had as well, cut too deep.

Of course, I was far from innocent. I had wounded Vanessa, perhaps just as deeply. I wondered if it was ever possible for love to become a cure rather than a curse, a salve rather than a sore.

The day I left to return to Colorado, Dad was on his feet again. He promised he was done with the drinking. Millie promised as well. I wanted to believe them both.

I signed in from Christmas leave Sunday evening thirty minutes before Call-to-Quarters. Nathan was already in our room, talking to Tomi Evans.

"Townsend," The Tomi said as I walked in and plopped on my bed.

"Que pasa." I lay on my stomach and buried my head in my pillow. I was tired from the drive and my thoughts and was not in the mood for socializing. I hoped Tomi would get the hint.

He did not.

"How was Texas? Still suck?"

I did not look up. "Not as much as this place."

As often as not, our conversations devolved into Tomi espousing the superiority of Colorado over Texas. Although Colorado was becoming like a second home to me, I still considered myself one hundred percent Texan, especially when Tomi and I got into it. While I did not hail from those regions that produced cowboys or ranchers or even the "Texas Two Step," I embraced the braggadocio of being born and bred in the Lone Star State.

I raised my head and squinted at Tomi. "How come you're so obsessed with Texas?" I asked as my head fell to the pillow again. "Did your family get kicked out?"

"Nope," he said. "Most are from Ohio, originally. A few came from Tennessee. But they've been in Colorado for generations."

"My great grandparents were from Tennessee," I said as I rolled over on my back.

"Don't tell me... Davy Crockett."

"No."

"I thought every Texan claimed kin to Davy Crockett. He must have been a real man with the ladies."

"No kin of mine."

"Hm."

"But my great grandfather fought with him at the Alamo."

"Really?'

"No." I looked at Tomi. "Did you know Colorado was once part of Texas?"

"Not where I'm from."

"Exactly where you're from," I countered. "Your great granddaddy might have been a Texas redneck and you not even know it."

"I doubt that."

"Could be," I said. "At one time, Texas went all the way into Wyoming." Lying on my back, I stretched my arms above my head, touching my hands together. "I've seen the map."

"That must have been before the Coloradans kicked their asses out."

I dropped my arms and rolled away from him, burrowing my head in the pillow.

"I'm planning a squadron ski trip," Tomi said to my back.

"Cool."

"For Spring Break. For anybody not going anywhere else."

"I'm going!" Nathan said.

"I didn't know you could ski," I said into the pillow.

"Tomi says there'll be chicks. Snow bunnies!"

I lifted my head toward Tomi. "Where?"

"Vail. I can get great rates for a hotel my dad owns. By great, I mean free. It's an early graduation present. But rooms are limited. First come first served." He smiled slyly, looking at Nathan. "Or is that first served, first come?"

Nathan laughed as he usually did at whatever Tomi said.

"Do you have plans for the break?" Tomi asked me.

"Too far ahead to think about," I answered.

"Don't wait too long," Tomi said as he walked toward the door. "Free rooms and babes. Sounds better than drinking Shiners with shitkickers."

I grunted and buried my head in the pillow.

Fifteen minutes before taps, Skye waltzed into my room carrying a Jerry Jeff Walker album, *Ridin' High,* under his arm and singing the chorus to "Pissin' in the Wind." He was wearing that well-worn newsboy-style hat I had first seen on him over three years earlier, that evening when we managed to avoid a fight with the four Colorado rednecks outside of Giuseppe's.

After two months as roommates, he had finally explained the origins of the hat. He said his Gram had woven it using plastic bread bags. "She made this the same way she makes hooked rugs." He had smiled warmly. "Guess that makes Gram a hooker!"

Skye stopped singing when he saw Nathan in the room with me.

"You busy?" Skye asked. He looked directly at me, avoiding Nathan's blank gaze.

"Sure," I answered wearily. "Piaget can wait."

"Pee -on... who?"

"Never mind." I closed the Developmental Psychology textbook.

Skye looked at Nathan, then at me. "Outside," he directed.

I scraped the floor noisily as I backed my chair away from my desk.

"Hey!" Nathan admonished. "The wax job!"

I ignored him and followed Skye into the alcove. I closed the door and thumbed in the direction of the room. "Did you know Friendly is Bed Check Charlie?"

Skye eyed the door. "He is?"

I nodded. "Sometimes he just gets up from his desk and puts on the whole regalia."

"That's kinda batshit," Skye said.

I smiled. "Sometimes he puts on camouflage face makeup."

"Weird."

"Then he disappears completely in the room."

Skye seemed unaffected. He glanced around the hallway. "Let's go to the stairwell."

I followed him down the hall and past the CQ desk where Tim Deaux was busy typing up his report. He only nodded at us.

In the stairwell, the howling night wind foretold the coming of the dark ages.

Once he was sure we were alone, Skye said, "Forgive the cloak and dagger."

I smiled. "Are you in trouble? Should we be wearing camouflage?"

He grinned. "Could be. I never know."

"So..."

"Are you still with Noelle?" Skye asked.

I nodded. "More or less. It's honor offer, honor offer," I said. Skye just stared at me, so I added, "The possibility of an encore June Week visit has turned her more on than off."

Skye smiled briefly. "Do I hear wedding bells?"

NOR TOLERATE AMONG US

"Is this a pep talk?" I asked.

He looked toward the stairwell door then back at me. "My sister's flying in from Nebraska this weekend." He paused.

"Okay."

"I won't be here."

"The Army match," I said after a moment.

"Right." He put his upper lip over his lower one, which always preceded his asking a favor of me. "This is the kind of thing I could only ask my best friend to do."

"You want me to cancel my weekend plans and pick up your sister."

"You have plans?"

"I plan to get in my car and drive out the South Gate. It's a bit less concrete after that."

He laughed. "So. You're available."

I sighed. "Pete Field?"

"I wouldn't want you to have to drive all the way to Denver."

"You already had this planned."

He shrugged his shoulders and did the thing with his lip. "It's just a commuter flight."

"That *is* something you could only ask a friend to do," I said.

"Best friend," he corrected. "Saturday afternoon. 2 o'clock."

"And do what with her?"

"Take her to her dorm."

"Which is where?"

"I've got a map of the campus. I'll get it to you if I remember. But she knows."

"And then what?"

"Make sure she gets settled in."

"And?"

"You're done. Free to pursue a life of debauchery." He looked at me. "Just not with my sister."

"That's all you want of me?"

"Yeah." He paused. "No."

"What then?"

"Look," Skye said. "That college is full of liberal arts types just aching to teach my little sister all about free love. And this place..." he spread his arms toward the dorm rooms beyond the stairwell walls. "This place is full of tow-headed hard knots like Fattafred who would like nothing more than..." He eyed me.

"Can't you handle that?"

"I will when I can. But I'll be busy—out of town most weekends—until hockey season is over."

"So," I said. "The third degree about Noelle. You want me to date your sister because I'm already involved, however stupid that sounds."

"Not date," he said, throwing up his hands. "I want you to keep her busy so she doesn't have time to date. At least until she gets more settled."

I put my hand to my chin and stroked it. "That's quite an offer. How many languages does she speak?"

"What?"

"I heard of a girl at CC who speaks seven languages. She can say 'Argo screw yourself' in all seven."

"You're a real joker, Geno."

"What about my social life?"

"What about it?"

"I mean, what does she look like?"

"What does that matter?"

I feigned deep thought. "Well, if I'm going to be seen with her..."

"Don't be so shallow."

"You think she'll like me?" I asked somewhat teasingly.

Skye shrugged his shoulders. "I really don't care. Just take care of her for a few weeks." He looked at me with a rare intensity. "I can trust you, right?"

"I suppose."

"I'd rather have her with you than with one of these horny Tomi-type bastards."

"I'm not sure how to take that. Sort of makes me the steer that keeps the bulls from getting nervy."

He smiled. "I know you won't screw me."

'Or your sister,' I thought. "If she turns out to be a pain in the ass, I reserve the right to bail."

CHAPTER THIRTY-EIGHT

Shortly after noon the following Saturday, I signed out on a weekend pass. Even as I did, I laughed inwardly at my own impudence in imagining that taking care of Skye's sister would require so much flexibility.

Skye had not shown me a picture of her. He kept "forgetting." He told me her name—Melody—and that she was about five-seven with black hair and brown eyes. I was to meet her at baggage claim for the commuter flight from Scott's Bluff. I took a few wrong turns on my way to Peterson Field, having never been there before, and when I finally parked the Z and went running into the terminal, I was more than fashionably late. I hurried directly to Baggage Claim, hoping her flight had been delayed which would mask my own incompetence.

There were only two passengers there when I arrived, both with long hair, both obviously female. One was in a black dress much too short for the Colorado winter weather. The other sported a thick green ski jacket over blue Levi's. I opted for the colorful one, thinking her taste in clothes fit the image I preferred.

I tapped her shoulder softly.

She turned to me. Her high forehead and bright smile were so evocative of Skye's handsome traits that I knew immediately I had guessed right.

"Melody Book?" I asked trying to appear neither formal nor casual.

"Yeah." She held her smile and nodded. "Gene?"

"Gene," I said. I caught my breath. "Yeah. Gene. I'm Gene."

NOR TOLERATE AMONG US

"You sure?" Her smile broadened.

"I'm Skye's friend Gene," I said.

"Okay, Skye's friend Gene." She stuck out her hand. "I'm Skye's sister Melody."

I took her hand.

"Just Gene?" she asked. "Or is there more?"

"Gene... Oliver Townsend," I said awkwardly. "You can call me anything but Oliver. It was my grandfather's name."

"And you don't like it?"

"I tolerate it."

She smiled. "Gene is short for Eugene?"

I nodded.

"Well, Eugene," she said. "Shall we go get Skye's sister's luggage?"

Thinking back, it seems everything there was to know about Melody Book was somehow revealed at this first meeting.

She was not wearing makeup—she seldom did—which made the softer features of her face even more appealing. She seemed oblivious to her allure. Everything about her was real and true and she needed no artificial embellishment. You could look into her soul and find nothing wanting.

Melody had two large suitcases. I lifted them both, realizing immediately I had overreached on the macho thing.

"You must have half of Nebraska in here." I turned toward the exit.

"I'll take one," she said.

"No, I've got it," I insisted.

"Where's your car?" she asked.

"Further away than it seemed when I got here."

"This is... give me a bag."

I determined the soft-sided bag was lighter and put that one down. The difference was actually negligible, from what I could tell.

She grabbed the bag with both hands, bouncing it off her knees as she followed me across the parking lot to the Z.

"Guess I should have brought the other car," I said.

Melody dropped her suitcase and assessed the situation. "I thought everybody from Texas drove trucks."

So, Skye had told her something about me. I wondered why he had avoided telling me more about her.

"Gas guzzlers," I answered, lowering her other bag to the ground. "I like it," she said, eying the Z as I unlocked the hatch. "It fits you." "It does?" I was pleased she thought so.

"Not like that showy thing Skye drives."

"You don't like the Alfa?"

She shook her head. "Especially since he didn't pay for it."

"He didn't?" This was news to me.

"Daddy got it for him. A reward for six semesters on the Superintendent's List." She tilted her head. "You didn't know?"

An image of Vanessa popped briefly into my head. "So you don't like the car because your brother earned it but didn't pay for it."

She smiled at me. "I don't like the idea of him thinking he owes anybody anything."

"He could have declined."

"Have you met my father?"

"Yes."

"Then you see."

I tried to maneuver the bulky bags to allow the hatch to be closed, but nothing I did worked. After watching my failed efforts with some amusement, Melody opened the soft-sided bag and began removing various pieces of clothing. Among them were bras and panties and some night clothes, but she seemed completely unabashed as she wadded them up and shoved them into whatever space was available, even throwing some forward into the passenger's seat.

"I'll get those in a minute," she said.

We compressed the soft bag enough to get the hatch closed and navigated out of the parking lot toward Interstate 25.

"How did my brother talk you into this?" Melody asked.

It was my turn to smile. "He owes me," I said. "I've bailed him out of jail once or twice."

"Really?!"

"Sure, or rather, no."

She smiled warmly. "Then why?"

"He trusts me, I guess."

"For something other than punctuality."

"Sorry about that," I said. "There was a six-car pile-up on the interstate, and I stopped to help a little old lady save some baby puppies."

She eyed me with amusement. It was then I noticed the small scar under her left eye. She had a very pleasant face, but the scar looked like a single tear that could not be wiped away.

"Cute little Benji-like puppies," I added.

"You're lying."

"It's not lying if it can't possibly be true," I said.

I was in a good mood that evening when I returned to my room. Even the new Form 10 waiting on my desk could not alter my mood. 'Dust on bookshelf,' it said. Four demerits. I ran my finger along the shelf. Nothing. I laughed to myself as I imagined them writing me up for the dust and then cleaning it up for me. What considerate gentlemen they were, this petulantly petty team of Dusty Durskan and Philip Quince.

CHAPTER THIRTY-NINE

Rivalries are an unavoidable staple of life, whether we admit it or not. It probably goes back to the caveman days, with one clan vying against another when there was not enough food or shelter or companionship to go around.

For the Air Force Academy to have strong rivalries with Annapolis and West Point was to be expected. But, by all measure, the Air Force versus Colorado College hockey games were seismic events, made even more so this particular winter, when two great hockey-playing brothers were slated to skate against each other at the Broadmoor World Arena.

Recent events had transformed my indifference into an avid, if somewhat amateurish interest. When Skye suggested I bring Melody to the game, I readily agreed.

Skye and Melody had seen little of each other since her arrival in Colorado, although he had taken her out for her nineteenth birthday at the beginning of February. I had visited Melody a few times at CC where we would spend a brief part of an afternoon talking about nothing important, as if we both feared knowing too much about each other.

On this night, as I navigated the route I had last taken with Skye before the winter snows began, Melody's usual light-hearted banter failed to hide pensive undertones. Sudden uncomfortable lapses in our conversation arose when she seemed to drift with the falling snow.

She was an inexperienced, impressionable young small-town Nebraska girl on her first real adventure away from home. She was so full of life, so open to anything new. Perhaps she thought to contain her enthusiasm, lest she go so far out on the limb as to be unable to return to the relative safety of the tree. If so, her fears were aligned with mine. I had made a tacit agreement with Skye that I would not get involved with his sister. But from the first moment I heard Melody's laugh, I was hooked.

As we approached the parking area, she asked, "Do you think Skye will score tonight?"

"I don't know. Doesn't he play mostly defense?"

"Who says you can't score just because you're defensive?" She gave me a whimsical smile.

I was unsure what to say. Was she making an innocent observation? Or was she toying with me? "I think you can score on defense," I said. "If your stroke is powerful enough."

"Really?"

"I mean, if no one's guarding the net."

"I see."

"Like on a power play."

"A power play," she repeated.

I looked at her for a moment then peered searchingly out the windshield. "Let's just find a place to park."

"Don't get defensive."

"What?"

"There's one!" she said, pointing while watching me.

"It looks pretty tight," I said.

"I think you can squeeze in."

After we parked, I locked the Z as Melody zipped up her green ski jacket, and we walked briskly toward the arena. She slipped a bit on the ice, and I reached to steady her, perhaps being a bit too helpful. I really did not mean to get so close to her chest. When she regained her balance, she gazed at me with a look that both asked and answered the unstated question in my mind.

We found two seats close to the ice but above the protective Plexiglas that was there to keep members of the audience from losing teeth to a wayward puck. I never liked being at ice-level. It was like watching a match through foggy glasses. You might be closer to the action, even safer, but it was harder to tell what was really happening.

The arena was warm, and we did not need our coats. Melody removed hers to reveal a soft white mohair sweater that accentuated her femininity in all the right ways. She smiled sheepishly at me when I noticed.

Air Force came out onto the ice, and the Tiger fans booed while the rather large contingent of cadets stood and yelled wildly. Many were in uniform, making their presence even more conspicuous. Melody yelled with the cadets, specifically at Skye, trying several times to get his attention as he warmed-up.

I gazed around the arena and spotted Tomi Evans sitting near the Air Force bench. I hoped he would not see us.

A few rows above him sat Dusty Durskan and Quince, both wearing Service Bravo. I think Quince only felt comfortable when he was in his uniform. There was a girl next to him who whispered something in his ear. She looked in my direction, and Vanessa Cardewey's eyes met mine. Quince looked at her and then at me and we all turned our attention to the arena below us.

I had thought that, should Quince ever find a girlfriend, she would be very much like him—insecure, unfriendly, predisposed to a judgmental take on the world, unyielding in the face of diversity. Yet there he was, sitting with Vanessa.

When the Colorado College Tigers took the ice, a larger crowd erupted in cheers. Melody was among them.

"Turncoat," I sneered.

"What?"

"Pick a side."

"Nope."

"Who are you pulling for?"

"All of them."

"You can't do that."

"Why not?"

I shrugged my shoulders and smiled. "I'm sure there's a reason."

"Nobody knows who I'm really pulling for."

"I guess that's true," I said. "You could shriek your head off in here and no one would care. Do the same thing walking down the streets of C-Springs and they'll put you away for life."

"I'll try that sometime." She nudged me. "Will you bail me out?"

"Nope."

She was the epitome of exuberance throughout the first period. When the teams left the ice for the break, I offered to get her something to drink, but she was not thirsty.

"Have you seen many hockey matches before?" I asked.

"In Nebraska?" She laughed as if I should know better.

"Oh."

"This is my first."

"It is?"

She smiled at me. "Yep."

"I guess I don't know much about Nebraska."

"I guess not." She eyed me warmly. "Skye never played hockey before his second year here."

"You're kidding!" I said in disbelief.

"Honest."

"He sure took to it."

Melody smiled. "Is that a Texas phrase?"

"Shore is, ma'am."

When the teams came out for the second period, I noticed that Skye was searching the crowd. He had not spotted us and must have been curious to see if we were actually there.

Midway through the period, a CC player took a shot on goal that flew wildly off the outside of the goal cage. The puck careened toward us, and Melody ducked her head into my chest as I knocked it down. We stood to search for the puck, but it seemed to have fallen into the lower seats.

"This is why I like to be above the glass," I said.

"Yeah!" Melody said. "That was exciting!"

"Really?"

"Yes!"

"More exciting than Nebraska?"

"Anything's more exciting than Nebraska."

"I don't believe that."

Skye looked in our direction, having followed the flightpath of the puck. I saw him raise his head ever so slightly when he spotted first me and then his sister. So we all knew where we were.

"He found us," I said as Melody waved.

"Yeah. He'll play better now."

"I thought he was doing pretty good."

"He has to play better than good if we're gonna beat these guys."

"Ah," I said, "so now you're with us."

"You need all the help you can get."

As the teams left the ice at the end of the second period, we sat without talking for a minute or two.

"I've always wanted to head up that way," I said after the gap in conversation seemed excessive. I looked out over the ice. "Up north to Wyoming. South Dakota. Maybe Nebraska. I'd like to see Rushmore. It's up there somewhere, right?"

"Why don't you?"

"Someday, when I have time, I will," I said. "After graduation maybe."

"If you don't go to Texas."

I felt myself flush. "Maybe."

"You shouldn't put things off for someday. Nobody knows their expiration date."

I looked at her. "You're right. I'll probably never see it."

I felt a tap on my shoulder. I turned to see The Tomi flashing his 'I'm so cool' smile at me.

"Townsend," he said. "Didn't think you'd be here." He turned his gaze on Melody.

"Gotta support the team," I said.

"I'm Tomi," he said to Melody when it became awkwardly obvious that I was not going to introduce him. He stuck out his hand.

Melody took it briefly. "I'm the girl with Gene," she said.

"Okay." Tomi's grin broadened. "Enjoying the game?"

"Very exciting," she said.

"Yeah," Tomi said. "The brothers are putting on a hell of a show."

As I listened to this exchange, I saw something pass between Tomi and Melody. It was as if she read him and knew immediately why he was there. I guess she could tell Tomi and I were nothing beyond classmates, that he would not have bothered to come talk to me if she had not been there, that Tomi was an opportunist, and that she was the opportunity.

She turned her attention to the ice as the teams skated into position for the faceoff to begin the third period.

Tomi peered beneath our seats, then reached down and recovered the puck we had been unable to find. He played with it for a minute before offering it to Melody. "A token of our first meeting," Tomi said. "Happy Valentine's Day." He flashed his squinty-eyed grin.

Melody's lips formed a fleeting smile. "Yeah. I guess it is." She looked at me before taking the puck. "We were looking for that. Thanks." She returned her attention to the game.

Tomi pressed on. "You go to CC?"

Melody looked at me then at Tomi. "Oh, you mean me?"

I chuckled.

Tomi only smiled.

Melody turned her gaze to the players. "I do now."

When she said nothing more, Tomi seemed to get the idea. "Take care of our puck," he said. "Maybe we'll see each other again." He raised his eyebrows at me and winked at Melody.

When he was out of earshot, I said by way of apology, "The Tomi."

She nodded. "You're not friends."

"Hard to tell," I said, surprised at her insight. "He does want everyone to like him."

The crowd of cadets around us were suddenly very animated. Looking to the ice, I saw Skye skating hell-bent for leather toward our end of the rink. He controlled the puck, outmaneuvering the Colorado College defensive players as he neared their goal. He sliced the ice in a quick change of direction that sent a CC defender careening into the Plexiglass. With a quick flick of his wrist, he sent the puck past the goalie and into the net.

We roared to life, jumping to our feet as the red light confirmed the goal. Melody grabbed my arm with both hands and squeezed almost until it hurt. I gazed into her laughing eyes and felt myself drawn into them for a brief beautiful moment.

I looked beyond her into the crowd. Vanessa was standing on a bleacher seat, clapping and yelling as Skye took a victory lap near the center of the ice.

Quince remained seated. He seemed childishly disinterested, almost disappointed.

Despite this brief surge of momentum for the Academy team, they could not overcome the relentless assault of the Colorado College players. The match was a heartbreaking loss, the Colorado College Delich brother getting the better of us in the waning minutes of the game.

On the way out of the arena, a voice behind us called Melody's name. We turned to see her roommate, Julie O'Terry, working her way toward us through the dissipating crowd.

"Julie O," Melody said smiling.

"Exciting game, huh!" Julie said enthusiastically. She turned to me and pouted playfully. "So sorry."

"They're tough," I said. "But we almost put it to 'em."

A guy with long straight hair draping to his shoulders sidled up next to Julie.

"I didn't know gals from Wyoming knew anything about hockey," I said, glancing at the long-haired guy.

Julie O smirked. "At least as much as saddle-sore dudes from Texas."

The long-haired guy laughed at that.

"Next time is at Air Force," Melody put in. "They'll get 'em then."

Julie drew back in mock surprise. "I guess you have to pull for your brother, don't you?"

"Whenever I can."

The long-haired guy put his hand on Julie's back.

"This is Kevin," Julie said as if in afterthought. She tilted her head my way, raising her eyebrows. "Gene."

"Kevin," I said, putting out my hand.

He took my offered hand limply and dropped it quickly without a word or a smile. I suspected this dude did not much care for baby-killers.

"We're heading back to the campus," Julie said, turning toward Melody but keeping her gaze on me. "Do you need a ride?"

"I don't know." Melody looked at me. "Do I?"

"Up to you," I said. I felt like the odd man out.

"We're okay," Melody said, eying me slyly. "Gene's taking me to A&W to celebrate."

"Oh, yeah?" I said.

"How exciting," Julie said blandly. She grasped Kevin's limp hand and they walked away.

"A&W?" I said jokingly to Melody.

"Sure! It's Valentine's Day! Special occasion."

At A&W, I ordered two root beer floats that a roller-skating carhop brought to the Z.

After we had said everything there was to say about Skye's first goal of the season, Melody said, "Any plans for Spring Break?"

"I'm not sure," I said. "I haven't really thought about it."

"Come on," she said. "Cadets live for the next break. You probably started thinking about it right after Christmas."

"Skye's mentioned taking a blowout trip to Acapulco," I said.

"Really? Is that what you want to do?"

"Even if I could afford to go, I wouldn't," I said. "Sitting on pristine beaches quaffing sweet coconut drinks while waiting to ogle the next bikini-clad perfect 10 that strolls by just doesn't seem all that exciting to me."

"You're going home to your Texas girlfriend, then."

I felt embarrassed. "Probably."

She nodded solemnly.

"Unless," I added.

"Unless?"

"Unless she decides for like the hundredth time to have a relationship meltdown." I put air quotes around relationship. I looked at Melody. Her eyes were receptive to everything I said, every move my hands made, every wrinkle in my brow. "Do you ever talk about your relationship with your boyfriend?" I asked.

"No," she said. "I think it's dumb to talk about a relationship with the person you're having it with. You're either in it or you aren't. If the relationship needs that kind of attention, it's probably clinically dead already."

I had hoped the answer to my question would reveal her current status in the boyfriend department. It did not, so I said, "Maybe this... thing with Noelle has been dying a slow lingering death, only electro-shocked back from the brink whenever I go home."

"Don't you have the guts to pull the plug?"

I thought about that for a moment. "I don't know."

"Are you afraid there won't be anyone to fill the void?"

"What do you mean?"

"You figure it out. I'm not into analyzing relationships."

I tried to ignore the possibility that she was flirting with me. As always, my promise to Skye hovered over me like a predator ready to strike should I dare to venture beyond the protection of my platonic cave.

We were quiet for a while, slurping our floats slowly to avoid brain freeze. "What are *your* plans for Spring Break?" I asked.

"I was hoping Skye would drive me to Nebraska to visit our Gram so I can talk to my boyfriend about our relationship."

I felt my heart plunge to my stomach. "Really?"

She nodded. "Except for the part about the boyfriend."

About a week later, as if on cue, I received a letter from Noelle thanking me for my belated Valentine's Day card and to say she and a girlfriend were planning to spend their spring break travelling around Europe on a Eurail pass, a pre-graduation present from her parents. Her letter implicitly discouraged any thoughts I might entertain about joining them. I had neither the money nor the inclination for it anyway.

CHAPTER FORTY

"**D**ecision time!" Skye said as he sailed into my room in the middle of the following week.

I threw down my pencil and put my head in my hands.

"Time to expand your horizons, Geno! See the world! What happens here is not... life! It's not even the Air Force!"

"I don't want to go to Alcapulco."

"Al–capulco?!" Skye said, emphasizing my mispronunciation.

"Wherever."

"So, you're going home to Noelle?"

I shook my head, grabbed Whit's Popeye glass, and trudged to the sink. "She's going to Europe with a friend," I said, filling the glass while avoiding his gaze. "She still wants to come for graduation, though." I paused. "I'm thinking of asking her if she wants to marry me," I said unconvincingly.

Skye smirked in obvious disbelief. "That's some bizarre thing you've got going on there." He paused and rubbed his chin thoughtfully. "You're not going to Texas?"

"After graduation will be soon enough," I said. The guilt hit me. I should have been at least considering going home to see my father. And Tyson. I just thought I needed to be away, to do something with my last break from the Academy that didn't involve the tainted environment back home.

"So, no plans."

I drained the glass. "Evans is organizing a ski party."

Skye put his upper lip over his lower lip before saying, "CC's Spring Break is the same week as ours. Melody wants to go home."

"She told me," I said.

"You mean she's asked you already?"

I took a step rearward, ready to make a run for it. "Asked me what?"

"For a ride."

"No," I said, shaking my head. "She may have mentioned she wants to visit your grandmother." I put the glass on my bookshelf and sat at my desk with my back to him.

"And she needs a ride."

"Not from me she doesn't." I pushed my chair from the desk and turned to face him. I don't know why I was acting so disinterested.

"Look, Geno," Skye said in his 'I know what's best for you' voice. "You'll just sit in this place and brood." He spread his hands, indicating the room. "Get out and see the world!" He put his hand on my shoulder. "You'd be doing me a big favor."

"How's so?"

Skye lowered his head in mock humiliation. "Somehow, my parents got the idea Melody and I were coming home together."

"I see," I said sarcastically.

"What?" He took his hand from my shoulder. "What do you see?"

"I see you sunning on the beaches of Mexico while I trudge through the corn fields of Nebraska with your sister." I looked at him. "That didn't come out right..."

He gasped in dismay and lightly slapped my forehead. "There's more to Nebraska than just corn!"

"Really."

"There's wheat, alfalfa, soybeans... Trees even! Hell, we invented Arbor Day!"

"Well that changes everything."

"Ever been to the Black Hills?"

"Why would I?"

"It's beautiful. Except for that place called Rushmore."

"Your home's near Mount Rushmore?"

"No, but Gram's is. That's where Melody wants to go first."

"First?"

Tomi Evans stuck his head in the room. "Greetings mortals."

"The Tomi," I said. "How was your weekend?"

"Vidi Vici Veni," he said.

"What?"

"I saw, I conquered, I came."

"Another virgin bites the dust," I said.

"This one was no virgin."

"A shallow conquest then," Skye said.

"Hey, a win's a win," Evans said. "Deep down, they all want it. Some just take more convincing than others."

"Sounds like true lust to me," I said.

"What the fuck over!" Tomi said. "A man's always gotta be ready. If guys were only ready every 28 days the human race would go extinct." He smiled, adding, "I can't help it if I want to love women."

"You want to possess them," Skye said. "Trophies on a shelf."

"Possession is nine tenths of the law."

Skye narrowed his gaze. "I can't help feeling sorry for you."

"What do you know about it?" Tomi asked. "How many girls have you slept with?"

Skye looked at me. "None."

"None?" Tomi laughed. "Oh, well then I guess I lose." He frowned at Skye. "You do... like women, don't you?"

I studied Skye's face, uncertain what would be revealed.

Skye eyed Tomi. "I'm partial to them."

"Well, I'm more than partial," Tomi answered. "I've got a hunger. And if you've got a hunger for women, I say bon appetitty!" Tomi laughed and scratched his head. "So why the fuck did I come in here? Oh, yeah. Last chance to sign up for the Spring Break ski trip. My dad's covering the rooms for the weekend! All you pay for is lift tickets. There's gonna be bitchin' powder!" He looked pityingly at Skye. "Maybe you'll get laid."

"Pass," Skye said. "The only thing I'll be bitchin' about is my skin getting burned on the beaches of Al–capulco." He glanced at me.

I nodded.

Tomi turned to me.

"I can't do it, either," I said. "I'm heading north, to the Black Hills."

Tomi smirked. "The back hills?"

"The Black Hills. Rushmore. I want to see all that stuff." I was now championing an idea I had been dead set against five minutes earlier.

"Townsend, I had no idea you were such a tourist."

"I won't be a tourist. A local is taking me."

"Who's that?"

"Skye's sister."

Tomi looked at Skye like he had never known him before. "You have a sister? Why didn't you tell me?!"

There was no laughter in Skye's eyes. "I think that's obvious."

"Hey, I'm careful. I'm always careful." Tomi looked at me. "Is that the babe you were with at the hockey game?"

I nodded slightly and said, "So, go Vici Venzi yourself in Vail."

Skye rubbed his chin and squinted at The Tomi. "A guy named Evans was the governor of Colorado during the Civil War." He paused. "You wouldn't happen to be related to him, would you?"

"Could be, I guess," Tomi said, grinning. "Was he good-looking?"

Skye did not smile. "Ever hear of the Sand Creek Massacre?"

Tomi shook his head. "Was that a hockey party?"

Skye sat back. "It happened in the flat nothingness of Colorado you ski bums don't claim." He looked at Tomi like a tiger sizing up its prey.

Tomi held Skye's gaze. Neither moved.

After a moment, Tomi blinked his eyes and smiled. He glanced at me. "So, that's two no's for the ski trip." He retreated toward the door saying, "When the sister gets bored, send her my way."

"Hey Tomi," Skye said to his back. "Do you walk to school or carry your lunch."

This was yet another one of Skye's playfully nonsensical invectives, meant in this case, I think, as a subtle insult.

Tomi paused momentarily but did not look back. He shook his head and walked away, leaving the door open as he threw up his middle finger. We could hear him down the hall singing, "...*the Rocky Mountain way is better than the way we had...*"

I turned to Skye. "What do you expect from a guy who wants to fly F-14s in the Navy?"

Skye nodded. "That should work for him. He's always been a 'launch and leave' kind of guy." He gazed at me thoughtfully. "So."

"So? What?"

"Can you take Melody home?"

"Home to her boyfriend?"

"No such thing."

"What's in it for me?"

"My eternal gratitude."

I sighed in resignation. "Who could ask for anything more."

CHAPTER FORTY-ONE

After dropping Skye off at Peterson Field in the wee hours of the morning, I picked up Melody at her dorm, and we headed north on Interstate 25. We decided to take Julie O'Terry up on her invitation to spend a night at her parents' house in Douglas, Wyoming. Nixon's 55 mile per hour speed limit made getting anywhere take a lot longer than it had before.

I decided I would drive the entire way because it was my car and because I was the man and because I needed something to do with my hands and my mind. Melody was good at keeping a conversation going. She knew when to ask questions, when to be quiet, and when to offer an observation of her own.

We saw a sign for an A&W in Cheyenne and decided to stop there for lunch. To fill the time while we ate, I told her about my first memory of Skye and the arms-out endurance test. Melody listened without interruption, apparently fascinated at hearing a story about her older brother.

"It seemed he would rather die than let his arms drop. He kept them up longer than he had to." I glanced at her. "It just hit me," I said. "He's never once talked about it."

"That is just like him and not like him at all."

"How so?" I asked, although I thought I knew the answer. You saw of Skye what he wanted you to see.

"He flaunts his victories sometimes. But usually he waits for you to bring it up."

"It wasn't the kind of thing you would go around bragging about, anyway," I said. "It was just something we did. He was the last one to hold his arms straight out and level. That's all."

"How did you do?" she asked, looking at me with a smile so big I could easily detect it out of the corner of my eye.

I looked at her then took a sip of root beer. "I wouldn't want to flaunt it."

"Come on!"

"I was in the running."

"Runner up?'

"Not that close."

We got back on the highway heading north. Melody was silent for a while, so we drifted along, watching the scenery, the incredibly flat nothing that is southern Wyoming. There were rocks and barbed wire fences and every now and then mounds sticking out of the ground, like piles of grassy dirt that Melody called Mother Earth's goose bumps. The clouds above us were like puffs of nothing, coming and going with no real purpose other than to break up the blue-gray film over the plains.

"Did you want to win?" Melody asked.

"What?"

"Did you want to win the contest? To be better than Skye?"

"I didn't know who he was."

"But you wanted to win."

"I didn't care," I lied.

I don't think she bought that for a second.

"I remember him talking about Jack's Valley," Melody said. "The 'meanest mother' and all that."

"The pugil sticks."

"He didn't like that."

"It wasn't so bad." I had no idea why I was making everything sound so blasé. "Then he told you about the assault course?"

"Not much. Just that he thought it was... kind of..."

"Brutal?"

"No. Pointless." She looked at me. "I mean, he understood why they wanted you guys to yell 'Kill!' while running through a maze of dirt and barbed wire. But beyond that...?"

"It was just a game," I said. "A mind game. You toughed it out and kept going. It made you feel like you could take whatever they dished out. It certainly didn't make you think you were ready to retake Omaha Beach."

She nodded, looked out the window at nothing then turned her attention back to me. "So, how did you guys meet?"

I stared straight ahead as the memory came back to me. "We were pretending we were on patrol in the woods." I related the story of the vans and how Skye had covered for me in what might otherwise have been perceived as an egregious lie. "We weren't under the honor code, yet."

"And now you are, and you can't lie."

"Not supposed to."

"Doesn't it only apply within a certain distance of the place?"

"No, that's Annapolis."

"Oh." I could feel her eyes on me. "So, I've got a tough question for you."

"What's that?"

"What do you think of me?"

I looked at her for a brief moment. "That's not really a tough one."

She did not give me the chance to continue. "How do you handle the tough ones?"

I studied the road as it passed under the Z. "Me personally?"

"Yes."

"I lie."

"Really?"

"No."

"So you just did."

"You got me."

She twisted toward me in her seat. "What if a C-Springs chick asks if you love her? What do you say?"

I thought I felt her fingers just brush against my arm. My cheeks suddenly felt on fire. "Something that resembles the truth but isn't," I offered.

"Isn't that the definition of a lie?"

"No. There's a big difference between telling a lie and avoiding the truth. C-Springs girls rarely ask the really tough questions anyway. Maybe they're afraid of the truth."

When we crossed Chugwater Creek, I asked her if she was thirsty, or anything else.

She said she was doing fine, so we pressed on.

"Are you sure you don't need me to show you how to drive this car?" she asked.

"What do you mean?"

"I mean we're out here in the middle of nothingness, and you're barely doing 60."

"I'm keeping you safe."

She looked around. "From what?"

I pressed the pedal and got us up to 70. "Do you have to go to the bathroom?"

She shook her head.

"Then why the sudden urgency?"

"There's a big difference between urgency and excitement," she said.

We were on yet another long straight stretch, so I looked at her. She was flushed a little, but she was not blushing. Her eyes met mine, and I thought I saw desire. But it could just as easily have been that she wished she had said "yes" to stopping back in Chugwater. I checked the road. It was still there, still straight.

"How about some music," I said.

"Sure."

I opened the lid of the center console and fished out one of my favorite mixed tapes I had labeled "Driving Music."

"See if you like this." I handed her the case.

Melody pushed the cassette into the player I had installed on the passenger's side of the car. It was a beautiful player, and I had taken great care in splicing the speaker wires into those of the car radio.

As the first song played, Melody asked, "What's that?"

"*Woman of a Thousand Years*," I said.

"Oh."

She was obviously unfamiliar with it. I felt empowered, like I was about to introduce her to a whole new world. Until the second song.

"I know this one!" She began to sing along with Jefferson Airplane. "*Have you seen the stars tonight? Would you like to go up for a stroll and keep me company?*" She smiled at me brightly.

"I'm impressed," I said, hiding my childish disappointment.

She looked forward through the windshield, either unaware or unconcerned with how she was gracing me with her presence and the beauty of her voice. "*Any place you can think of, we could be.*" She glanced at me out of the corner of her eye as she sang.

She was not obnoxious, as some people can be. She seemed to understand when to sing along and when to just listen. I imagined that she was having a good time and that we had more in common than just her brother.

About a half hour out of Douglas, we passed a big lake that was more likely a reservoir. I wanted to go back and look at it, maybe walk around a bit, but she said Julie was waiting for us, so we kept going.

When we found Julie's house and pulled into the driveway, Melody wordlessly opened the car door and went running into the house, leaving Julie and me staring awkwardly at each other.

"So. Julie O," I said. "How's your spring break so far?"

Julie's eyes were dark. At times they seemed to be almost completely devoid of color. I got the feeling she did not think much of me. She rolled her eyes and groaned. "I'm nineteen years old. And I'm spending my only week off from school in historic Douglas, Wyoming."

"Historic? Really?"

"I think so. Why else would it be here?"

I looked around. "The scenery?"

Julie tilted her head and looked at me. It seemed awkward.

"How's... Kevin?" I asked. "Wasn't that your dude's name? Is he coming to see you?"

She opened her mouth to speak but closed it again when Melody reappeared.

"So," Melody said in obvious relief as she grasped Julie in a brief hug, "show us what brings all the tourists here."

Julie gave out a fake laugh and said, "I'll show you the number one attraction that keeps bringing 'em back!" She nudged my arm.

"Okay," I said.

"Then I'll show you the other one."

After putting our bags in the house, we piled into Mr. O'Terry's Chevrolet pickup, sitting three across on the bench seat with no seatbelts, and drove into town. Parking wasn't hard to come by because there wasn't much traffic. We slid out of the seat, and Melody and I followed Julie into the middle of what looked like the main downtown street. We crossed to a median guarded by an eight-foot-tall statue of a jackrabbit with antlers.

"Here it is!" Julie said waving her hands in exaggerated fanfare.

"Here what is?" I asked. "What the hell..." I remembered Melody saying Julie's father was very religious. "I mean, what is that?"

"A jackalope," Melody said with obvious pride at her own insight.

"*The* jackalope," Julie corrected. "Douglas Wyoming's claim to fame. Two local guys were the first to shoot and mount one."

"They can't be real," I said, unsure whether I was playing along or looking stupid.

"Of course they are!" Julie said.

Melody looked at me. "No they're not."

Julie glanced at her. "Have you ever seen one?"

Melody shrugged. "No."

"Then how do you know?"

"Okay." Melody laughed. "They're real." She looked at me. "Must be in the same family as unicorns."

"You can go to the courthouse Monday and buy a jackalope hunting license, if you don't believe me," Julie said.

"We'll be in Nebraska Monday," I said.

"Your loss. They're good eatin'."

"Right."

"I love this guy!" Melody said. "He's so cute." She stepped up onto the pedestal next to the fallacious statue and hugged it.

"One of a kind," I said, thinking more of Melody than the statue. I smiled to myself. Surely there could be no Pegasus-like legends relating to this thing.

Like a good tourist, I had my camera ready. I didn't have time for composition, so I pointed it quickly and snapped off a shot.

"When's jackalope hunting season open?" I asked.

"The same day it closes," Julie said. "June 31st."

"Oh," I said. Then, "Oh," again, when it hit me.

We walked away from the jackalope and up onto a small, raised area in the nearby park where the statue of a sleek brown horse graced the well-kept lawn. "Let me guess," I said as we walked toward it across the grass. "A jackamule."

"This is serious," Julie said. "Show some respect."

I fell to one knee. "Forgive me dear Jackamule! For I am but an ignorant wayfarer and know not of thy fame."

"Come on, get up," Melody said.

"No, let him stay there," Julie said. "He's right about the ignorant part."

I got up and read the plaque. "Sir Barton. Star Shoot. Lady Sterling. There's three of them down there?"

"Stacked on top of each other," Julie said. She stretched out her arms. "Land's at a premium in Wyoming."

"That must have been one deep hole," Melody said.

Julie sighed playfully. "It's only Sir Barton."

I studied the life-sized statue. "Nice horse."

"Read the rest," Julie commanded.

"First triple crown winner," I said, reading the plaque. "From Kentucky? What's he doing here?"

"A Douglas guy bought him, for stud, I think. But he died before he could get going good."

"Then let's move on," I said, "before whatever got him rubs off."

"Wait just a bit," Julie protested. She climbed up onto the pedestal and hugged the horse much as Melody had done with the jackalope, enhancing the image by wrapping her leg around one of the statue's front legs. She looked at me, expecting me to take her picture.

As I fumbled for the camera, Melody turned to me and said, "Don't worry, you've still got it." She reddened suddenly.

I took a quick picture of Julie, then pointed the camera at Melody and snapped off another one. Both would come out blurry.

We walked quickly back to the truck.

"One more stop," Julie said.

Melody and I groaned in unison.

"I'm sorry, Julie O," I said. "It's been a long day, and I'm really Douglas-ed out."

Melody smiled. "I'm hungry. Is there a place in town that serves fresh jackalope?"

"There's Dee's Tavern," Julie said. "Their specialty is chicken-fried unidentified. Maybe it's jackalope, maybe not."

"What's the Wyoming drinking age?" I asked.

"Relax, cowboy," Julie said. "We're going for the burgers, not the booze." She smiled impishly. "We've got church tonight."

Julie's church was modest with a small but undoubtedly loyal congregation. Church on Saturday evening struck me as odd, but Julie explained that her church did this regularly to allow people who chose to work on Sunday the freedom to do so.

After the service, Julie drove us in the pickup back to Dee's Tavern, insisting we get the full cultural experience. I ordered beer for Julie and myself. Melody declined to partake, finding the evening more entertaining watching Julie try to match me drink for drink. No one there seemed to know Julie, which was good for both of us since she was underage. Around midnight, we piled into the cab of the truck with Melody at the wheel while Julie pretended to sleep on my shoulder.

Melody shared the bed in Julie's room, and they put me in the room of Julie's older brother. When I asked about taking his room from him, Julie said he was out. They expected him back any day now, although not this night.

I was just settling in when there was a knock on the door. I made sure I was covered then said, "Come in." I wasn't sure what Melody was thinking, but having had a little too much to drink, I was curious.

The door creaked opened, and Julie peeked her head in. "Are you decent?" she asked.

"Always."

She took a step inside, leaving the door ajar. "Do you need anything, cowboy?"

That was the second time she had called me that. Having spent the better part of the last four years in Colorado, it could not have been my accent. "I'm good, I think."

She was wearing a light robe over a night gown that seemed a bit too flimsy for this chilly Wyoming night. "There's cold water in the fridge," she said, indicating the kitchen. "And sandwich meat if you get hungry."

"Thanks."

Julie seemed hesitant to leave. "Okay," she said. "If you need me..." She pointed to the door of the Jack and Jill bathroom that connected her brother's room to hers.

"Till tomorrow," I said.

She looked at the clock on the wall above my head. "Too late."

I glanced at my watch and nodded.

"Sweet dreams, cowboy," she said.

I went to the bathroom once around 4AM. After getting back in bed, I heard the door open on the other side and saw the light creep underneath the door of my room. After the light went off again, I sensed someone was standing on the far side of the threshold. Maybe the knob started to turn, maybe it didn't. After a while I fell back asleep.

CHAPTER FORTY-TWO

I n the morning, I dressed without showering and went downstairs. Julie and Melody were talking in the kitchen. The atmosphere seemed kind of tense for a Sunday morning. They looked guiltily at me when I wandered in.

"There you are, sleepy head," Melody said.

I massaged my temples. "I thought it was just for burgers."

Julie smiled. "You can repent next time you're in church." She gazed at me, her eyes widening slightly. "So, what do you want to see today?"

I looked at Melody. "Uh, we were hoping to get to her grandmother's house in time for brunch."

Julie looked at her watch. "That's a pipe dream, now. Chandron's what... two hours plus from here."

"Linner, then," I said.

"What?"

"The meal between lunch and dinner."

Julie looked plaintively from Melody to me. "Can't you stay a while longer? My folks left this morning and won't be back until Wednesday."

"Where'd they go?"

"Montana. The doc's been wanting to go to Little Bighorn. This was the only time he could get away."

"Your dad's a doctor?" I asked.

Julie glanced at me. "Use to be. He retired early."

"Why Little Bighorn?"

"He wants to find my great grandfather's marker," Julie said. "He was killed there."

I detected a subtle change in Melody's cheery manner. "At the battlefield?" she asked.

"Yeah. The doc's a big history buff."

I looked at her. "Why didn't you go?"

"It's 250 miles! Each way! I'd be a babbling idiot! Staying in Douglas was the lesser of two boredoms."

Melody laughed. "You didn't seem bored last night."

Julie glanced at me. "I wasn't."

"Is your brother home?" I asked, glancing around. "Or did he go with your folks?"

Julie eyed Melody and lowered her gaze. "I don't know where he is." She sighed. "We haven't seen him in four years." She looked again at Melody. "One more night? Just the three of us."

"It's hard to resist another day in Wyoming," Melody said, eying me secretively. She stood and pushed her chair to the table. "But we gotta go. Gram is expecting us." She smiled. "Maybe next time."

Julie curled her lips together as if trying to avoid saying something more. I thought she might be on the verge of inviting herself to go with us. Luckily, my two-seater made that impossible.

"You're coming back this way?" Julie asked in anticipation. Standing next to Melody, she looked petite, almost childlike.

"Uh, I don't think so," I said.

"We'll be heading back to Colorado via my parents' house," Melody said, glancing at me. The usual brightness of her face seemed forced.

Julie sighed. "I'll be bored out of my gourd. Maybe I'll head back early. At least I won't have to get drunk alone." She suddenly stood on her tiptoes and kissed me on my cheek. "Ya'll be careful," she said.

On the road, Melody began to relax, her natural smile becoming more prevalent the further east we traveled.

After a while, the conversation turned to Julie, as I had anticipated it would. "What do you think of her?" Melody asked.

"I think she's painfully aware that she's in for a dull time in Douglas." I glanced at Melody. "Why did you tell her we were driving back to the Springs together? I thought your mother was taking you."

Melody turned her gaze out the passenger-side window. "I don't know."

I nodded to myself.

She looked at me and touched my arm. "So, what did you think?"

"Of what? Julie?"

"I think she likes you."

"She hates me." I did not believe that, and I don't think Melody did either. "Besides, she's not my type." I really wanted to know what Julie thought of me, but I did not want to hear it from Melody.

Melody clasped her hands in her lap. "What is your type?"

"Women who drink too much." I laughed and glanced at her. "But right now, I'd rather be with you."

"You would?" she asked expectantly.

"Yeah. We're friends. There's no stress."

She sighed softly. "And I'm Skye's sister."

"I suppose. Sure."

She looked away from me out the side window. "Tomi Evans called me last week."

I jerked my head and stared at her. I was curious how The Tomi got her number, but then he was a very resourceful cadet.

"He wanted to know if I was interested in some ski trip he was planning." She looked back to me. "Something about free rooms."

I turned my attention to the road ahead. After an extended silence, I said, "You need to be careful of that... of guys like The Tomi."

"Are you my guardian angel?"

"No..."

"So let it go and trust me to decide for myself."

I felt blindsided. I could not imagine what had suddenly brought on this hostility from a girl I considered practically incapable of such feelings. But when I glanced at her, taking my eyes off the road for a moment, I realized she was smiling as if she had just delivered the punchline of a sour joke.

"I can leave you alone if you like," I said, trying to imitate her mood. "I just thought we always have a good... uncomplicated... time together."

"There are lots of ways to have a good time."

I kept my eyes on the road. Not for us, I thought.

The house was a small wood-paneled one-and-a-half-story structure with a picket fence that enclosed a little flower garden in the front and a

NOR TOLERATE AMONG US

narrow graveled driveway that led to a carport in the rear. A figure with graying hair and stocky limbs was bent over, working in the dirt. She was dressed in heavy clothes and thick gloves and wearing a wide-brimmed straw hat. Realizing who was emerging from the strange sports car in her driveway, the old woman took off her gloves and called out, "Mastinca!"

Melody ran to her as she emerged from the open gate. Their warm greeting made me wish I could have known my mother's parents. There was a bond between these two generations that was foreign to me. It felt awkward being outside of this brief loving scene. They released each other, and Melody led Gram toward me. I walked to them not knowing whether to hug the old lady or just smile. She extended her hand to me, something I had not expected, and clasped mine firmly.

She then put her other hand on top of mine and said, "I hope your trip was a good one." Her hands were calloused and strong. There was nothing feeble about her voice. Her manner was one of comfort born of eight decades of intelligent, soulful living. On her lean round face, deep wrinkles remembered hard times and good, frowns that had come and gone, smiles that remained. Her dark eyes were piercing, but not rudely so, and though she was obviously sizing me up, I knew right away she accepted me into her world because I was with her Melody.

"Are you hungry?" she asked.

"I could eat," I said rather awkwardly.

Melody said, "I'm starving!" She winked at me. "Anything but jackalope."

I cracked a smile, hoping Gram did not take that to mean I was not taking care of her grandchild. "Yeah. Too chewy."

Gram wrinkled her old brow but said only, "Good."

"I'm Eugene Townsend," I said. For some reason, the formality seemed important to me.

"Yes, I know. Gene." Gram guided us through the gate up to the porch of the house and into the front room she called the parlor.

"What's for linner?" Melody asked.

"What's... what?" Gram said.

"Gene's word for a meal between lunch and dinner." Melody smiled at me. I felt at once warm and nervous.

"Runza," Gram said.

"Runza!" Melody nearly screamed. "One of my favorites!"

"Of course, mastinca," Gram said.

Melody looked at me excitedly. "You'll see."

Following Gram into the house, I leaned to Melody and whispered, "What did she call you?"

Melody smiled. "Bunny rabbit."

The aroma coming from the back kitchen was somewhat familiar. After a moment, I realized what I recognized was baking bread and cabbage. Gram opened the oven briefly, took a quick sniff then closed the door and turned the heat up. "Five minutes," she said.

"Too long!" Melody complained happily.

While we waited, Melody explained. "It's a German sandwich, basically. A yeasty pocket of dough with cabbage in it. Sometimes onions..." She looked at Gram who nodded. "Yep, onions in these, and meat..."

"Beef," Gram said.

"You're going to love it!"

Melody and I sat at a fold-out table in the parlor while Gram put a plate with a large runza in front of each of us. I could see why it was a Melody favorite.

I surveyed the front room as we ate. Every wall was suffused with framed art or hand-made artifacts or a combination of both. Two oaken bookshelves displayed numerous collectibles, artifacts, and relics, each a testimonial to a long and interesting life.

There was a worn Bible with many tagged pages sitting on a stand between two winged-back chairs. A collection of framed photographs covered the mantel beyond the chairs. An upright piano graced one corner of the room beneath a mixed collection of paintings. Some were landscapes, others were portraits. I recognized Skye's handsome physique in one.

"Are you a painter?" I asked Gram.

She looked thoughtfully toward the wall. "Sometimes," she said. "When I am inspired."

"She's more than a painter," Melody said. "She's an artist."

Gram shook her head. "I am not yet that."

"I think you are," I said.

"Are you a critic?"

I felt myself blush. "No, ma'am." I returned my gaze to the wall.

Gram nodded and looked at Melody. "You are going to the bluffs from here?" she asked. It was a question and a statement.

"Yes," Melody said. "But we're going to the Black Hills first."

Gram eyed me.

"We'd like to spend a night or two here," Melody said. "If it's okay."

"I want you here as long as you want to stay," Gram said.

"Great!" Melody touched her arm.

Gram nodded quietly, her expressive eyes fixed on mine. After a moment, she turned to Melody. "It is a shame you could not get your brother to come with you."

"Skye went to Acapulco with some old squadron mates," I said.

Melody nodded. "A reunion of some sort."

"I see," Gram said, and I could tell from the way she said those two simple words that she was seeing a lot more than I was.

"Evil lives," I said.

"What is that?" Gram asked.

"It's a cadet thing, Gram," Melody offered. She glanced at me with a soft yet stern look I could not interpret.

Gram's nod was almost imperceptible. "In this world, there are few things more resilient."

I glanced at Melody. There was no embarrassment or surprise in her eyes, no recoil from the unusual. For her, the depth of Gram's character was normal and expected, rather than as it was for me—exceptional and a bit unnerving.

"But good will prevail," I said glancing at the aged Bible.

Gram looked at me. Her eyes portrayed both a question and the answer. "What makes you think so?"

I felt uncomfortable for a moment. "Well, because of God."

Gram threw a wrinkled smile at me and said, "Which one?"

"Well," I answered, feeling a bit confused, "whatever you call Him, there can only be one."

"Why is that?"

"Because otherwise, He couldn't be in control."

Gram said, "And yet evil lives."

After the meal, I volunteered to help clean up, but Gram said she would rather visit for a while. The dishes could wait. She made herself

318

comfortable in one of the winged-back chairs near a stack of books that rose from the floor behind her. "Play something for us," Gram said to Melody.

I looked at Melody expecting to see embarrassment in one form or another, but she only nodded and said, "I'll need to wash up first."

I followed Melody with my eyes as she disappeared through the kitchen. There were no hallways in this house. I wondered what rooms I would have to traverse to find the bathroom.

"Are you a player?" Gram asked when we were alone.

"I'm sorry?" I realized I had been caught watching Melody.

Gram gazed at me evenly. "The piano. Do you have any training?"

"A little," I said, glancing down at the black and white keys. "But I'm really out of practice."

Melody returned from the back and sat at the piano bench before Gram could coerce me onto it. Without hesitation, Melody began a piece I recognized, Ravel's "Pavane for a Dead Princess." She played from memory, closing her eyes, lost in the music of the spheres.

As the music filled the room, I turned to see Gram swaying in her chair, her eyes closed, her lips slightly parted. My mind retreated to the time I first heard Skye play at the winter retreat. Perhaps his entire family inclined toward the arts. Skye had even shared a couple of his poems with me, although he had been very particular in what he let me read and what he did not. I leaned against the piano as Melody worked through her repertoire. Thanks to my mother's insistence that I develop a degree of musical training, I recognized almost everything she played.

I was comfortable enough sitting at the keys of a piano, but I was not accomplished. My piano teacher was the elderly wife of a retired minister of our church. Sometimes my mother would drop me off early at the little house the old couple called the "Welcome Inn." I would then run around back to the termite riddled shack the old man used as his woodshop where he made little pine stools for the kids of the church. I was much more interested in apprenticing for him than I was in mastering the piano.

On those times when the old man was not there, I would trudge back slowly to the house to sit in the parlor in bored agony, listening to the ear-torturing banging of another student. But if the old man was there, he would smile a quick smile before putting me to work cutting or nailing or sanding, depending upon where we were in the process.

As good Christians, neither of us would have called it Zen. But that was what it was.

As I wandered slowly around Gram's parlor, I embraced the mood. I stopped to admire the collection of bric-a-brac that exposed a different value system from that of my youth. There was a photo of a young man in uniform I assumed to be Harold. Skye had never mentioned his father's military service.

In a place of prominence on the wooden mantel above the fireplace was a small, framed picture of a young girl perhaps four years old. She was on her knees. Her hands were pressed together as if the photographer had caught her in the middle of a clap. Her eyes were shut, though not tightly, her angelic face turned upward with a radiant glow on her cheeks and forehead. Dark straight hair trailed downward along the back of her tilted neck. Her lips were tightly closed, but her forehead was absent the telltale wrinkle that often accompanies an overly earnest prayer.

"That is Melody," Gram said.

I nodded to Melody as she lifted her hands from the keys. "Looking into the sun?" I asked.

Gram shook her head. "She is praying."

I smiled, returning my attention to the photograph. "For rain?"

"For the soul of a dead spider," Melody said simply.

"Oh," I said. "Did you kill it?"

"No. It lived in a corner of the window in my room."

"It lived in your room?"

"She insisted we all attend the funeral," Gram interjected. "We put on our best clothes as she dug a little grave and made a cross out of Popsicle sticks."

"Were such last rites customary?" I asked jokingly. "You must have been very busy."

Melody smiled sweetly. "My... brother explained the problems I would face if I insisted on conducting a service every time I came upon a dead creature." She glanced at Gram then back at me. "But this was special." She paused and turned to the picture. "The spider weaves the dream net."

I was tempted to pick up the photograph. I put my hands in my pockets, saying, "I would have opened the back door, given the bug a decent throwing out, said a few choice words like, 'And stay out!' and been done with it."

"Not if you had the heart of a precocious four-year old," Gram said.

I looked at Melody who was blushing again. I smiled. "I guess not."

321

CHAPTER FORTY-THREE

Immersed in a macabre nightmare of crying rabbits, I felt a presence and opened my eyes to see Melody backlit by a distant light as she appraised me from beyond the bedroom door. She was already dressed, her long black hair braided in matching pigtails with yellow ribbons securing the ends. I glanced at my watch. Half past six. On a morning such as this at the Academy with nothing pressing militarily, I usually slept in until at least nine.

I pushed myself up a bit. "What time do you want to leave?"

She glanced at my bare chest then looked above my eyes at my hair and smiled. "As soon as you can tame that cowlick."

I detected the smell of bacon mixed with a faint whiff of the floral perfume Melody wore on occasion. Or maybe it was just soap.

"Okay," I said. I grabbed the covers and threw them off my legs as she closed the door. I heard her giggle something to Gram when I ducked into the bathroom. We had a long way to go, and we could not stay overnight anywhere along the way.

Gram greeted me when I lumbered into the kitchen. "Afternoon, Longhorn."

"I'm normally up by now," I answered hoarsely.

"Uh huh," Melody said.

"During the week."

"Okay."

Gram pointed to a chair. I sat as she flipped three eggs on my plate, adding a generous side of bacon. "I hope over easy is alright," she said.

I nodded as I took a bite. 'I hope you like them spicy' would have been more revealing. I reached for the orange juice.

In deference to my waking stupor, we ate in silence until Gram asked, "What do you think you will see today?"

"The Black Hills," Melody said.

"And Rushmore," I added.

Gram said nothing, but there was a glint of disapproval in her eyes. "You may as well see it while you are here."

"It," I said.

"That scar on the mountain."

"Rushmore is a scar?"

Gram just nodded. "When will you be back?"

"Before sunset," Melody interjected.

Gram had stopped eating and was watching my every move. "Do you have enough gas in your car?"

"Gas? Sure," I said. "We will."

"Before you leave town."

"Yes, Gram," Melody answered for me.

We stopped for a quick top-off at Buffalo Bill's Garage and Fill-up. Bill was covered in grime and denim, and he wore an oil smudged red bandana around his furrowed brow that ineffectively corralled his long dark hair behind his ears. When he approached us, my first impression was that of a man I would never have to be—one that worked from dawn to dusk to make enough money to survive another day. The wrinkled black circles under his eyes illuminated the blended effects of heavy drinking and a hard life. He smelled of perpetual sweat and axel grease.

The air of familiarity in his greeting to Melody caught me off guard. "Hello, Beautiful," he said as she got out of the Z. He feigned a hug which Melody laughingly rejected at arm's length. He eyed me with more skepticism than suspicion. "Bill," he said extending his hand to me before quickly pulling it back. "Sorry."

"Gene," I replied. "Townsend."

He turned to Melody. "You heading home?"

Melody shook her head. "We're going north."

"Not to..." he stopped and looked quizzically at me.

"The Black Hills," she said.

His nod implied relief. "You are going to play tourist at the scar." His look was hard but his voice was softly subdued.

"Uh, yeah," Melody answered.

"Bring me back a stone." Bill looked beyond me to the Z, caressing it with his eyes before bringing them to bare on me again. They seemed to tacitly ask something to the effect of 'How is it that a young punk like you has a car like that?'

With the Z topped-off, Melody waved to Bill, who refused to allow me to pay for the gas, and we were on our way north.

"What did he mean about bringing him back a stone?" I asked.

"Oh, he's crazy!" Melody laughed. "He doesn't like Rushmore. He thinks it can be taken down one stone at a time."

"He called it a scar. Like Gram."

She stared straight ahead. "He's fullblood Lakota. He believes the white man stole the Black Hills from his people and then carved out Rushmore to rub it in."

"And Gram?"

She glanced at me and nodded. "About the same."

We were silent for a while, each of us enjoying the dawning of a beautiful crisp day that declared spring to be on its way. The sun was low behind us for a while which made navigating this unfamiliar road easier for me than it might have been. It was very flat and would have been boring were I not seeing it for the first time. It reminded me of New Mexico. I thought briefly of Vanessa but shook it off.

Parts of the road seemed a bad place to have car trouble, which prompted me to check the engine gages more often than was necessary. I was impressed Melody had thought to bring a jug of drinking water, thinking that, even if we didn't need it to survive, the Z's radiator might. I mentally registered the locations of the houses and other bastions of civilization we passed, noting the mileage in case I had to double back or hike to one for help.

After a while, Melody asked, "What do you know of Rushmore?"

"Not much," I admitted. "I didn't know there would be a test."

"I thought you were excited to see it."

"I am." I was a bit embarrassed for lack of a better answer.

"Can you name the presidents?"

"Of course," I said. I glanced at her. "Four of them, right?"

"Yep."

I feigned deep thought. "George..." I began.

"Okay..."

"John, Paul, and Ringo."

Melody laughed. "It *would* be cool to have a president named Ringo." She smiled at me, and I felt good. "But nope."

"Washington," I said looking at her. "George Washington. Father of our country."

"Uh-huh."

"Lincoln... Jefferson..."

"Yeah. Good."

"And... I'm not sure of the fourth."

"Roosevelt."

"Yeah! Teddy Roosevelt. My favorite."

"Oh? Why?"

"Because of all the national parks and monuments. That must be why he's on it."

"Not really."

"Are you sure?"

"Pretty sure."

"Uh oh. Have I insulted a Roosevelt descendent?"

"No... pretty much the opposite."

"You're a Democrat?"

She laughed. "Unaffiliated in that department."

"You seem unaffiliated in a lot of areas," I joked.

She looked out the window. "Conflicted might be a better way to describe it." She pointed ahead. "That's them."

"The big guys?" I looked in the direction she indicated.

"The Black Hills."

On the horizon, I could just make out the rising terrain that promised a welcome change to the flat plains that melded with our path in a way that made the road seem superfluous.

"Okay," I said. "So you don't like Teddy. Why not?"

"I didn't say that." She looked out the side window. "The Black Hills are sacred," she said finally.

"To Indians, I bet."

"To the Lakota."

"Like Bill," I said.

She nodded. "You know them as Sioux."

"Oh. Are they a branch or something of the Sioux?"

She nodded. "The reservation is about 15 miles that way." She pointed out the passenger window in the direction that had held her attention during our quiet times. "South of the Badlands. What Roosevelt deemed a 'grim fairyland.'"

"Really." I glanced to the east. "I've never been on one," I said. "Except for high school."

"You went to a reservation in high school?"

"I went to school on one."

Melody looked at me with surprise and even a bit of delight in her eyes. "You're...?"

I laughed and shook my head. "Our mascot was an Indian. We called the campus The Reservation."

She looked out the window. "Oh."

"Yeah. Our fight song is called Cherokee, and at football pep rallies, if the team has won the previous Friday, the captain of the team presents the Indian Spirit with a scalp."

"Indian spirit?"

"Sort of a human mascot. He does Indian dances to keep up the spirit of the team."

We were crossing the Cheyenne River, which in comparison to my river back home seemed little more than a creek to me. Melody became very still, as if in a reverent trance.

When we turned left toward the hills, the road was more winding, practically doubling back at times. We were almost upon the monument before I spotted it around a bend in the road, maybe a half mile away. Then it was gone again.

Thinking back, I'm not sure what I was expecting, really, but it was not what is there. I had not anticipated such an ostentatious presentation, with walkways and pillars and flags, although I suppose I should have. After all, these were *the* Presidents of the United States.

"I expected it to be bigger," I said.

"It's bigger than it appears," Melody answered.

"It probably seems huge if you're standing on one of their noses." I paused. "Are they bleached white?"

"That's just the granite."

"So the hills aren't really black."

"Most things aren't. They're just darker than what's around them."

"The faces are whiter than the rock they came out of," I said.

"Sort of interesting, isn't it?" Melody said. "White faces carved out of black hills."

I shaded my eyes. "It's really cool. How could anyone do that?"

"That's a question a lot of people have."

I nodded in understanding. "I know there are people who don't like the idea of carving up mountains to make heads of presidents," I said. "But really, who would even come out here just to see rocks and trees?"

She did not answer.

I put a coin in the viewer binoculars and looked through them, curious if it was worth a quarter.

Melody said, "Before it was Mount Rushmore it was called The Six Grandfathers."

I continued looking through the pay binoculars. "Who called it that? The Indians?"

"Yes."

"So, Six Grandfathers became four Founding Fathers."

Again Melody said nothing. Even when I was not looking, I could feel her eyes on me.

"And Rushmore is the sculptor?" I asked.

"Nope. The guy's name was Borglum." The name rolled off her tongue like a curse.

I released the binoculars. My time was up. "Then who was this guy Rushmore?"

"Some lawyer from back east. He liked to hunt here, and the prospectors didn't care, so they started calling it Mount Rushmore."

"He didn't discover it?"

"Didn't discover it or climb it or anything. He just happened to be in the right place at the right time."

"Before or after all this?"

"Before."

"Nothing more than that?"

"Nothing more than that."

Melody squinted. "There's an old Lakota proverb that says we do not inherit the land from our fathers, we borrow it from our sons." She swiveled her head, sweeping the panorama of hills with her outstretched hand. "So you could say all this belongs—belonged—to the sons of the Lakota." She looked away from the presidents. "To them, the Black Hills are like a cathedral to a Catholic." She brushed a tuft of long black hair from her face, corralling the wayward strands behind her ear.

"Nature is as close as we can get to God," I said. I sounded more like Skye. Or Vanessa.

Melody nodded. "Imagine how you would feel if that was taken from you." She paused, as if weighing what to say next. "Let's get closer."

We walked the boardwalk and stood in silence on the deck directly beneath the faces. I had not expected all the rocky debris. The dynamited granite lay beneath the heads like wood chips on the floor of the old preacher's workshop behind the Welcome Inn. An image formed in my mind of the sculpted eyes staring out day and night, rain or shine, unaltered, aloof and unaffected, uncaring whether people were there or not, unwaveringly focused on an eternity somewhere beyond the hills.

"What do you think?" Melody asked after a time.

"Very impressive," I said. "Why does Gram call it a scar?"

"She's Lakota."

I must have seemed quite oblivious. "You mean your grandmother is an Indian... I mean Native American?"

"Fullblood Oglala."

"Does she think she... does she consider herself..."

"An American?"

"Also. Yes."

"Her parents moved off the reservation around the turn of the century... sometime after the massacre at Wounded Knee. She was still very young when they died."

It hit me. "That means..."

Melody looked at me with her innocent, knowing smile. "Only one quarter," she said in answer to my unfinished question. "My mother's mixed, but mostly German."

"And so Skye is..." I looked at her. I thought of Skye's blue eyes and blond hair.

"It's okay."

"You and Skye have Indian blood."

"Yes. The white people who adopted Gram wanted to give her an Indian sounding name, so they called her Knowing Book. Kind of odd, but she liked it. She's always been an avid reader. My father never knew his father, so of course neither did I. But according to Gram, he was a handsome, intelligent, blue-eyed Scottish immigrant. He died in a construction accident two months before my father was born. Gram doesn't talk about him much. She never took his name."

"I wish you hadn't let me be so loose with my talk about Indians," I said. "I never..."

"It's okay," she said. She took my hand. It felt warm and soft and forgiving. She looked back at the four presidents. "Seen enough?"

"I guess so. What do you have in mind now?"

"Something else."

My heart skipped a beat, but I could not imagine that she was making a pass at me. "What?" I asked weakly.

"A different scar."

I took one more look at the stone countenances of the emotionless presidents. "I had no idea Lincoln wore his hair in a flattop," I said.

Back in the Z, I followed her directions along the winding road through the heart of the Black Hills. After a half hour, she said, "It should be about here." She turned to look at me with her gentle eyes. "Gene?"

"Yes?"

"Please don't..." She hesitated. "Don't tell Julie."

"Sure." When she said nothing more, I asked, "Can I know why?"

"Her father wasn't going to Little Big Horn just for the history."

"He doesn't like Indians," I said in understanding. "I mean Native Americans."

"Indian is okay. Some prefer it."

I nodded awkwardly.

"Julie let it slip one night," Melody said. "When she'd had a few too many." She looked at me. "There was something in the news recently about Indian sterilization. Did you see it?"

Embarrassed, I mumbled I had not.

"The Indian Health Service performed over three thousand sterilizations of Indian women. I think the doctor... Julie's dad was mixed up in it. That's how he ended up in Douglas."

I thought about the implications. "Sort of like witness protection?"
Melody stared at me. "I think he was more than a witness."
I nodded solemnly.
She looked out the window. "There it is."
"What is?"
"The road. I think this is it."
A rocky hill in the distance reminded me of a dog's face emerging above the land, with a snout and a hollow cave that looked like an eye. Driving on the gravel road, I did my best to shift gears in our conversation. "Is this natural?" I asked. "Did nature do that?"
"Nope," she said.
"What is it?"
"The better question is 'What is it going to be?'"
"Okay. Let's say I asked that."
"Crazy Horse."
"A crazy horse?"
"*The* Crazy Horse. The great warrior of the Lakota. He fought at Little Big Horn."
"Did he kill Custer?"
"Nobody knows how Custer died exactly. And nobody knows what Crazy Horse looked like because he never allowed his picture to be taken. And even after the army killed him, they forgot to take a photo."
We stopped at a small building and parked. A few people were milling around. From their dress, I could not tell if they were tourists or workers.
Melody pointed to a marble carving at the entrance. "That's what it's going to look like. Crazy Horse astride his pony and pointing south."
A resounding explosion pulsed through the air, shaking the building and rattling the windows. A cloud of rocks and pale dust expanded skyward off the hill.
"What was that?" I said loudly, taking a step back.
"Art," she said. She smiled at me. "They're blasting parts of the mountain away."
"Art can be so violent sometimes," I joked. I examined the marble carving and then looked toward the hill, trying to imagine how it would look when it was completed. "How long have they been working on it?"

"Since after World War II." She indicated a marker below the carving. "That's the guy."

I read the name. Ziolkowski. "Is he American?"

Melody eyed me with a knowing smile. "As much as you and me."

I felt embarrassed, realizing what she might have thought I meant. I nodded toward the mountain. "When will it be finished?"

"Who knows if it ever will be. Rushmore never was. And it had government funding."

"Rushmore's not finished?"

"They were supposed to have hands and coats." She laughed. "And better haircuts."

"So, they're still working on Rushmore?"

"Nope. They're done. The war stopped it."

"But Crazy Horse was started after the war?"

She nodded and put money in a container. "Ziolkowski refuses to take financial aid from the government."

I gazed again at what might someday be the face of someone nobody would be able to identify as the actual guy. "So why isn't this just another scar?"

"Those who believe the Black Hills should remain unaltered call it just that. Others consider it a fitting answer to Rushmore."

I looked into her soft brown eyes. "Thank you for this," I said.

She smiled brightly and touched my cheek for an all too brief moment.

We sat and listened for a while, hoping for another explosion of art. But none came.

"Are you hungry?" she asked.

I looked at my watch, realizing how late in the day it had suddenly become. "I could eat a horse," I said. "I mean..."

She laughed. "So could I. I'll guide you."

We walked back to the Z and drove south.

"You want to eat in a town called Custer?" I asked when I saw the welcome signs.

"There's an okay café here," Melody said pointing where I needed to turn.

We parked in front of a place sporting a wild west façade that appeared to be relatively new. "Looks deserted," I said.

"You should see it in August, when the bikers get here." She touched my hand. "Just don't tell Gram."

"Does she have something against bikers?"

Melody smiled coyly and opened the passenger door, swinging her legs out of the car. She glanced back at me over her shoulder. "It's just that I'd hate for you to get scalped in your sleep."

We pulled up to Gram's house just before sunset. Gram was bent at the waist, working her garden in the cool of the twilight. She seemed busy, but Melody whispered before opening the car door that she was out there waiting for us.

"Sorry we're a bit late," I said. I involuntarily placed my hand on my head and scratched my scalp.

Gram was pleasant enough, but she kept to her work. "I thought you could be trusted, Longhorn."

I was not completely sure whether that was meant as a compliment or subtle chastisement.

Gram indicated the open spot near the garden path. "I'm going to put the gaura here this year," she said.

Melody turned to me with a broad smile. "I love gaura!"

"I've never heard of that," I said.

"There's really not that much to it," Melody said. "Just a kind of low-lying plant with long thin stalks and little pale pink flowers on the end. You might not even notice it until the stalks come up. It's also called Indian Feather." She turned to Gram. "It's not native here, but Gram has the magic touch."

"Oh," I said. I looked at Gram.

"The bees love them," Melody continued. "Dozens come at a time. When they nectar on them, the weight of the bees makes the stems bend. It looks like the gaura is dancing."

Gram straightened herself and dusted her hands on her apron. "It is a dance that makes them both happy." She turned to me. "The stem bends, but the bee trusts it not to break." She paused, studying me. "And the gaura trusts the bee to take only what it needs."

We ate dinner in the kitchen. Afterwards, when we moved into the parlor, Gram turned on a floor lamp and made herself comfortable in the winged-back chair closest to the fireplace.

As I joined Melody on the small sofa, Gram said, "Tell me, Longhorn, what did you see today?"

I crossed my legs in the "figure 4" to give the appearance I was not sitting too close to Melody. "The Black Hills and Crazy Horse," I said, hoping to acceptably portray the order of importance.

Gram indicated a painting hanging on the far wall, a framed landscape in gray tones of what looked like connected columns of bare rock. "Do you recognize that?" she asked me.

I squinted in exaggerated concentration before glancing at Melody. "I don't... think so."

"That's Rushmore. Before it was Rushmore," Gram said.

"Oh! The Six Grandfathers!" I said, proud to have remembered.

Gram smiled as she looked at Melody in understanding.

"Yes," I said. "We went there. But I forgot to ask who they were."

Gram eyed me. "The Six Grandfathers are the six sacred directions."

"Six?" I said. "North, south, east, west..."

"And above and below," Melody said.

I nodded, pausing to admire the painting again before looking at Gram. "Did you paint that?"

"Yes," she said. "From memory."

I nodded solemnly.

"Is that all you saw today?" Gram asked.

I considered how Gram might want that question answered, but she was looking intently at Melody. "You stayed off the reservation."

"We'll go tomorrow," Melody answered, returning her gaze.

I tried to hide the fact that this was news to me.

"No," Gram said simply. "Not Wounded Knee."

"Yes, Gram," Melody countered. "Gene should see it."

Gram turned her stern gaze on me.

I felt trapped. "We don't have to see..."

"Yes, we do!" Melody said, cutting me off. "You've come this far."

"You know what your father thinks about that," Gram said flatly. "The trial..."

"That was in Fargo, Gram. Far away."

"The people are still disturbed." Gram looked sternly at Melody. "The *wanagi* are still there. Of the girl. The men."

I looked questioningly at Melody who was nodding, but her face showed disbelief.

"Souls," Melody said for my benefit. "The Oglala believe after you die, your *wanagi* stays behind, enticing family and friends to follow."

"You understand some of it," Gram said.

"Most of it," Melody countered. "I have paid attention."

Gram's countenance softened, but her words still carried an edge. "If you go," she said, concentrating her gaze on me, "you must be ready to understand. If you are not, it will mean nothing."

"I'm not even sure what is there," I said, trying to defuse the subject.

"The memorial is sacred," Gram said. "But there are no pleasant memories. Men, women, and children buried like the Holocaust, like My Lai. Like after a plague. You must have reverence in your spirit or you will come away from it as empty as when you arrived." She paused and the intensity returned to her face. "Perhaps if you learn of mankind's recurring cruelty, you will develop a sense of duty."

"I'm not cut out to be an activist," I said.

"A single altered mind is like a pebble in the ocean," Gram said solemnly. "It's a matter of perspective. The intolerant ripple flows just as broadly as the enlightened one."

She leaned back, eying me with interest. "There is a story of a young Indian boy," she began. "One day he went to the tribal elder and said, 'I feel good and evil fighting inside me.' The elder said, 'There are two wolves within you, one good, one evil. They fight for dominion over your spirit.' And the young boy asked, 'Which one will win?' The elder looked at him and answered, 'The one you feed.'" Gram looked at me in silence.

I nodded. "I was taught the devil tries to pull you away from being good." I paused. "I guess that's the same thing."

She sat up straight in her chair. "You got that from a book that says there must be something evil lurking outside of you. Something you cannot control. But it's what you let inside that matters."

The intensity in her eyes made me flinch.

I nodded as solemnly as I could. "So, how do I distinguish between the wolves?"

"You start by realizing you are not the only one feeding them."

CHAPTER FORTY-FOUR

G ram pulled me aside the following morning as I was packing the Z. While Melody was inside the house making snacks for our trip, Gram took advantage of her brief absence to air her concerns.

She said Melody had expressed activist propensities at a very early age. The transfer to Colorado College had transpired in part out of consideration for her safety. The hope was that spending time with Skye would quell her more militant ambitions.

"You must protect our Melody," Gram said taking both my hands in hers. "Think nothing more of the memorial."

I promised Gram I would not allow anyone to put Melody in danger. Especially herself.

Once on the road, I planned to drive west and south to Scotts Bluff by way of Fort Robinson, but Melody was not going to be told what she could or could not do. Less than a mile from Gram's house, she instructed me to turn north.

"We're going," she said firmly.

"Why?"

"Because if you take anything with you from my world, it must be the thing most people ignore."

I put the gas to the Z, and we sped down the lonely two-lane road. I was losing control. I was vulnerable. I had never felt more on edge. The road was an endless ribbon of concrete and asphalt that conjured feelings of impending doom leading nowhere good.

"Why are you so determined to go to Wounded Knee?" I asked.

"I've never been."

"What?!"

"My father has broken all ties with the fullbloods. He's done everything he can to mask his Native heritage."

"Has that put Gram and your father... at odds?"

Melody gazed out the passenger side window. The rain was starting. "It's been seven years since they've had anything to say to each other."

"What will we do if your father finds out I brought you here? That won't make him think much of me."

"We'll explain I insisted."

"And then what?"

"And then we'll see."

I lowered my head in resignation.

We entered Pine Ridge from the south. I was ill-prepared for the raw imagery, the desolation and poverty that scorched my mind and flayed my naiveté. We were, after all, three quarters of the way through the twentieth century. We were harvesting millions of acres of wheat. We were the most powerful industrial nation on Earth. We had driven dune buggies and golf balls on the moon.

"Go right here," Melody said.

My heart sank. I don't know why I anticipated tepees rather than shanties, romance rather than wretchedness.

"Left here, I think," Melody suggested after several minutes passed.

Dark billowing clouds were forming as I stopped the Z on the gravel road near the front of the monument. Owing to Gram and Melody's renderings of this hallowed ground, I had envisioned something along the lines of the entrance to Mount Rushmore, with loudspeakers and a place to buy refreshments.

Nothing I saw here inspired awe. Modest columns of red bricks and cinder blocks painted white anchored the thin metal archway that memorialized the gravesite. The mass grave itself was little more than a raised concrete rectangle forming a long thin border around an area of dirt and sparse grass. It seemed barren and make-shift, like someone's cluttered backyard.

I was surprised to see several crosses, including the small one at the top of the arch. The intermingling of Christian faith and Lakota spirituality seemed to devalue both.

I followed Melody, matching her thoughtful reverence with my own less pious version. She stopped under the arch. Standing next to her, I formulated questions to make me appear caring and insightful, but I did not ask them, deferring to her solemnity.

I tried to imagine what had occurred here eighty years earlier. Closing my eyes, I could just see the men, women, and children as they fell, their bodies riddled with lead, the surprise and terror they must have felt, babies still suckling from the breasts of their dead mothers. The one large hole dug in the frozen earth to hide the evil and swallow its memory.

"Sitting Bull warned the Sioux not to take spoils from the white men they killed," Melody said. "But they ignored him. Some believe that explains all the bad things that have happened to the Lakota."

I turned to watch the gathering storm clouds threatening to shorten our stay. I silently welcomed their approach.

Coming toward us over the shallow hill were two dark men shouldering rifles. Long straight hair emerged from their cowboy hats.

"I think we should get going," I said, starting toward the car.

"Why?" Melody asked. She followed my gaze to the approaching men. "We've done nothing wrong."

"Neither had they," I said, indicating the grave.

"Let's see what they want."

"It can't be anything good."

If they meant us harm, I knew it was already too late. Even if we ran for the Z, they could cut us off, or gun us down in the car.

Neither of us spoke as the two men drew within a few steps and stopped. I was ever more aware why both Skye and Gram had urged me to watch over this youngest Book.

"You should not be here," one of the men said sternly.

"Yes, we should," I heard Melody say. She pointed to the mass grave. "I have as much blood in there as you do."

"Then you know why you should not be here now."

Melody did not move. "If not now, when?"

The one looked at the other then back at Melody. "You're a brave little rabbit. What does your man say?"

I felt the adrenaline flowing through my veins like liquid electricity. I started thinking of the options my training had given me: 'Give him the money!' 'Go for the balls!' 'Use his weight against him.' 'Run!'

"I'm here because she wants me here," I said.

He looked expectantly beyond us, his eyes searching the darkening horizon. "Okay," he said finally. "You have been here. You have seen the sorrow." He glanced at Melody and nodded. "Perhaps even felt the pain. Now it is time for you to get in your fancy car and go home."

"When we're ready," Melody said.

I was ready. I moved closer to her. She had an advantage. A woman standing her ground seemed gutsy. Me doing so might only be seen as stupid. Still, the thought occurred to me that she would not be a bad person to spend my last minutes with. I flashed a determined if not defiant scowl.

The two men looked at each other. "Please go," the quiet one said.

Melody nodded, her head bowed slightly. She put her hand on my elbow and turned toward the Z. As we walked down the little hill, I tried to imagine what getting shot in the back would feel like, and how it would be to watch someone you loved shot dead beside you. I tried to imagine how it would feel to have your land stolen, your family and your culture annihilated by people who believed God was on their side. To be lied to and betrayed. How could you ever explain that to your children and still have them see the world as a good place?

When I started the Z, the two men were still looking at us. One lowered his rifle from his shoulder, cradling it in his arms as if it was his most valuable possession.

Melody tucked her arm under mine and leaned her head against my neck. Her hands were trembling. "You were very brave," she said softly.

I looked away from the scene. Fighting back the tears, I put the car in gear and pulled away as slowly as I dared.

CHAPTER FORTY-FIVE

When we arrived at Scotts Bluff, I was surprised but not disappointed to learn that Mr. Book was away on business. Melody's mother, Sophie, was amiable, though at times awkwardly proper. She did let her guard down a couple of times, and I almost came to enjoy her company. In those brief moments, I could see a bit of Melody in her, and of her in Melody.

But then she would revert back to the nouveau riche wife and mother, and the façade made her difficult to reach.

Her house was clean, almost sterile. I felt sure she did not do the dusting. Curio cabinets in the living room displayed neatly placed Hummel figurines, each granted its own space so there was no crowding, which the little figurines, had they been real, would no doubt have appreciated. The pastel-colored lamp shades were ensconced in protective plastic, and the chairs and sofas in her family room were covered with afghan blankets to minimize wear and tear.

Sophie told us Harold would be back from Lincoln in a day or two. I hoped to be on the road to Colorado before he returned. Sophie said she was still planning to take Melody back to college after the break, to swap out clothes and other things. She was nice about it, but I think she did not much care for the idea of Melody and me returning to Colorado Springs alone with several days to kill before school started while Skye was still in Mexico.

She did encourage us to see the sites and have a good time while I was there, even as she made little remarks meant to keep me at arm's length. I went out of my way to prove I entertained no nefarious notions for her daughter, but she must have seen more than I was willing to admit.

"Is there anything to do out here?" I asked Melody jokingly when we were alone. "Or is Scott's Bluff the Douglas of Nebraska?"

"There are treasures," she said smiling and gesturing toward my car. "If you know where to look."

"I like your attire," I said as we slid into the Z. "Why do girls always look so good in boots?"

She just smiled and motioned for me to drive.

Under Melody's direction, I maneuvered the Z out of town and west toward the bluffs before turning south again. We crossed over the North Platte and under a railroad bridge. To me, it all looked rather sparse, hardly a place where one could expect to find something special.

After another minute or so, she said, "There."

An ancient red barn in need of paint rose from the prairie grass. A long, equally ancient wooden fence encircled a barren area behind the barn. There was very little else.

We parked beside the fence, and I followed her exuberant steps inside the building that smelled of hay and manure and moldy wood. A man wearing coveralls and holding a rake appeared from an empty stall.

"I thought I heard a car," he said, leaning against the rake.

"Cliff!" Melody cried as she ran to him with little consideration of the "land mines" she might encounter. "I've missed you!" She hugged him.

Cliff returned her affection. "I've missed you, too, little bunny."

Melody leaned away from the man while still in his grasp. "When are you going to drop that? I'm almost twenty!"

He shook his head. "You're barely nineteen."

I watched Melody kiss his rather dirty cheek, making me wonder whether she would now need to find soap and water or something more stringent. It occurred to me that I would not mind a kiss on my own cheek. For starters, anyway.

"He's missed you, too," Cliff said.

A blush of jealousy overcame me, and I felt obliged to shake it free before I was discovered. Even so, I realized someone like Melody Book must have a beau waiting for her back home.

Cliff seemed to notice my presence for the first time.

"This is Gene," Melody said. "A budding hippophile."

I thought to protest, but as I had no clue what I would be protesting, I hesitated. Finally I said, "You can't prove that."

Melody glanced at Cliff then back at me. She released her grip on his waist. "It means 'a lover of horses.'" She turned to Cliff. "Where is he?"

"I moved him closer to the door," he said, pointing toward the far end of the barn.

I followed Melody as she paced rapidly along the line Cliff had indicated. She broke into a trot when the long nose of a red rabicano stallion appeared beyond the last stall gate.

"Fireball!" she practically screamed. She clasped his neck and kissed his nose.

Fireball nodded and snorted his pleasure.

Melody caressed the horse's neck with one hand while she patted its withers with the other, repeatedly cooing his name. Finally, she turned to me. "This is my treasure." Fireball moved his head as if nodding in agreement. Melody laughed. "I've missed you so much."

I was beginning to feel like an intruder. Then Melody turned to me and said, "You want to go for a ride?"

"On him?" I asked.

"No. You can ride Harold's horse." She pointed to the opposite stall where an older-looking roan mare was eating from a pile of fresh straw. Either out of boredom or jealousy, "Harold's horse" ignored the exuberance of Fireball's reunion with Melody.

"I'm really not much of a cowboy," I said, glancing at her riding boots then down at my sneakers. My experience was sparse. I had gotten the first infection of my life from a skin abrasion on my ankle when I stupidly wore short pants to ride a neighbor's swaybacked gelding.

Melody touched my arm reassuringly and said, "That's May Belle. She used to be quite a dickens, but she's gentle as a lamb now."

"A dickens," I repeated.

"She's the rascal that gave me this," Melody said, touching the tear-shaped scar under her left eye. "Tried to brush me off under a tree limb." She patted May Belle. "But we've reconciled, haven't we girl?"

I turned to scrutinize May Belle for a moment, then turned my head back to Melody, bumping my chin against her head in the process. I had not realized she was that close. She did not flinch, but looked up, her glistening eyes searching mine. "Think you can handle her?"

"We'll see," I said.

Melody saddled both horses, instructing me as she did so, as if she thought riding together could become a common occurrence.

She patted May Belle. "You be good."

We mounted outside the barn, and Melody cooed Fireball into a gallop toward the bluffs. I noted the white flairs in his tail that gave the impression of a pale fuse leading to his muscular rump. I clucked to May Belle who broke into a reluctant trot.

We followed Melody and Fireball to a small ridge overlooking a group of houses under construction near the manicured green fairways of a golf course.

"That's Monument Shadows," Melody said as I pulled up beside her. "Brand new." She pointed to an expansive frame with no siding. "That's the eyesore Harold is building."

I nodded and stood in the stirrups for a better view like I had seen cowboys do. Silently admiring the future home, I considered the stark contrast between the opulence of Harold and Sophie Book and the much more modest lifestyle of Gram.

Melody gazed scornfully on the skeletal framework of the future Book home. "Big, isn't it," she said. There was no pride in her voice.

"Yeah."

"Skye's going into the Air Force, and I'm at CC. But he's still building... that thing."

"Maybe he's thinking grandkids," I offered.

Melody reigned Fireball to the left, heeling him into a gallop toward the bluffs. Before I could react, May Belle followed suit with me grasping tightly on her reins. I don't think May Belle put much stock in my skills. The animal is always the most mindful of how you sit a horse.

Suddenly, May Belle turned away from Fireball and went into a full gallop toward the distant barn. I yanked on the reins to turn her. She obliged, but not without protest. I pointed her toward the receding image of Fireball and Melody, satisfied that I had laid a certain dubious claim to the question of authority. With Fireball yet in full gallop, Melody swiveled her body to find me. She pulled up, setting her horse to a fast walk as May Belle and I approached more or less as one.

"Thought I might have lost you there," Melody said with a grin.

I would have sworn May Belle flapped her lips in disdain.

"We're getting to understand each other," I said. "She's kind of a willful horse."

"She's not willful." Melody rubbed May Belle on the underside of her long nose. "She's just a free spirit."

"A dickens," I said.

Melody nodded, pulled her hand away and pointed to the white hills to the west. "That's Saddle Rock."

I turned May Belle so we could both see the unusual formation sculpted through untold eons of wind and water erosion. The peak held an unusual, stark shape that looked more to be the work of man than of Nature.

"It reminds me of Crazy Horse," I said.

May Belle snorted her impatience.

Melody angled her head as if seeing it for the first time. "I guess it kind of could." She smiled at me, which kindled a warm flow through my chest, the needed antidote to the chill I was feeling from the ride.

"This is a treasure," I said. "I wasn't expecting anything like this."

"I guess there's lots of things in the world people never see. Makes you wonder how anybody can be sure the world is what they think it is."

I considered the insightfulness of this idea coming from a nineteen-year young girl, how quickly people are willing to say what is true and what is not with so little actual experience to draw from.

She clucked Fireball into a walk and May Belle and I followed close abreast. "This was on the Oregon Trail," she said. "The bluffs got their name from a guy who died here."

"How did he die?"

"The tale says he was left for dead in one spot, but when they came looking for him the following spring, what remained of him was a long way from where they had last seen him."

Melody looked to the sun dipping low beyond the bluffs. "We'd better head back." She turned to me.

I briefly admired the sunrays glowing on Melody's pleasant face. "Should we run 'em back?"

Melody inspected May Belle whose head was getting lower with the sun. "Better not. May Belle's got a strong heart, but she's never had much spleen."

"Spleen?" I said.

"It provides the red blood cell reserve a horse needs to run far and fast. It can be four feet long in a thoroughbred." She made a circle with her gloved fingertips. "And that big around."

"It takes a spleen horse to run a long race," I joked.

"Yeah." She glanced at me. "You have to have the guts for it."

After dinner, Melody guided me upstairs to the guest suite. Her room was just across the hall, which surprised me. I had anticipated we would be separated not only by intimidation but by floors as well. She went into her room, and I stood at the door, leaning against the threshold. The decor was noticeably absent the proliferation of cuddly teddy bears and other cutesy things I associated with a teenage girl's room.

The walls were accentuated with pictures of horses and outdoor scenes, mostly mountains and canyons. A pellet rifle leaned in one corner beneath a well-worn bridle suspended on a hook. A stack of record albums accompanied a Magnavox stereo cabinet wedged between a mahogany chest of drawers and her closet door.

"It's all right," she said, noting my hesitation. "You can come in."

I nodded and entered, leaving the door open.

"Close the door," Melody said. "Mom doesn't like my music." She went to the Magnavox and opened the cabinet's sliding door, pulling more records from storage there.

Several books crowded her nightstand, most of them nonfiction, although I thought I spotted a Harlequin novel or two among them.

I recognized the record she unsheathed. She placed the LP on the turntable, and "Wildfire" began as she perused the back of the album. She joined in the chorus, with her eyes closed, and I felt intensely jealous of Michael Murphy.

I noticed a small round netting decorated with feathers hanging in the window. Melody looked up from her reverie with Michael, following my gaze.

"That's my Dreamcatcher," she said. "Harold gave it to me. A long time ago."

I nodded. "It does look like a spiderweb." I thought of the picture of her as a four year old giving last rites to her eight-legged roommate.

She went to the window. "Indians don't believe nightmares can come from inside someone who is not evil." I followed her eyes as she gazed around the room. "Dreams float around in the air, trying to get in your head while you sleep. The Dreamcatcher allows the good dreams to pass through, but traps the bad dreams in the web, where they perish at dawn."

"Were you having bad dreams?" I asked.

She climbed on her bed and knelt at the head, taking a framed portrait of a young man in uniform from the shelf above the pillows. She gazed at the picture for a moment then handed it to me as she sat cross-legged in the middle of the down comforter.

I recognized it as the same picture I had seen at Gram's house and assumed it to be of Howard in his formative youth. He looked a lot like Skye.

"That's Harold Junior," Melody said. "At the end of boot camp."

I glanced at her. "You have another brother?"

"Harold is... was the oldest. Now the youngest."

I furrowed my brow. "Youngest?"

"He was killed in Vietnam. At least, we think he was. Technically, he's MIA." She looked at the picture over my shoulder. "He was eighteen."

"Oh." I looked at the stern young face again. "I'm so sorry."

She took back the picture. "I think the hardest thing in this world is to love someone and not know where they are."

I nodded my agreement. "Is that why Skye went to the Academy?"

"Sort of. Harold did not want him to be drafted. You should have seen what it was like around here when Skye got accepted. You'd have thought he was elected president."

"Did that bother you?"

She smiled warmly. "No. I was excited."

"Excited?"

She looked around and laughed. "This used to be his room."

Melody returned the picture to the shelf, adjusting it to match the silhouette marked in the dust. She swiped her finger through the light dust layer. "The maid doesn't come in here."

"Dust doesn't bother me," I said. "In fact, I look forward to it being an acceptable part of my life again."

She nodded, but her mind was somewhere else. "I know you think my mother is... kinda stiff... proper. I wish you could have known her before my brother went to war. She was so lively, the opposite of my father. Now, I think she's afraid of... more tragedy. It's almost like she's holding her breath."

I felt a sudden revelation. I had seen Gram's influence in both personality and intelligence right away, but I had found it puzzling how two children reared in the Book household could have turned out like Skye and Melody. My understanding ran a little deeper now.

She pushed her hair back and gazed at me. "Do you really have to go tomorrow?"

I shrugged. "I should try to get some studying in. Whether or not I graduate in June remains to be seen, no thanks to Skye."

"He can be a bad influence."

"Not really," I said. "I'm just lazy."

Her smile was warm, her gaze hopeful.

I thought I heard Sophie at the bottom of the stairs. "Well, I should get some sleep. Long drive tomorrow." I could not tell her that as much as I wanted to spend more time with her, I wished at least as much to avoid spending time with her father.

A cloud seemed to form over her face. "I'm going to be very bored."

I looked at her, expecting some form of a cute pout. But that was not Melody Book.

Michael Murphy was singing "Wild Bird."

"You've still got Michael."

She momentarily crossed her eyes. "I just like his music."

I felt a twinge in my chest. "See you in the morning."

"And back in Colorado," she said.

"Sure," I agreed, doing my best to sound flippant.

I slept poorly.

CHAPTER FORTY-SIX

I rose early the following morning. I had heard Harold's return in the middle of the night. I decided to forgo taking a shower for expedience sake. I hoped to be gone before he got up. I made the bed and shoved the rest of my clothes into my brown Samsonite. My thoughts turned briefly to Skye and Acapulco. My life by comparison seemed quite banal. Prior to this week, whatever wear this four-year-old suitcase exhibited had occurred only on trips between Colorado and Texas.

There was not much light in the house, and I tried to creep quietly downstairs.

"In here," Melody said softly as I walked past the entryway connecting the kitchen to the hallway. I placed the suitcase on the hardwood floor and followed her voice. Standing barefoot at the coffee maker, she looked over her shoulder as I walked in. She wore a short silky nightgown under an open robe.

"What do you take in your coffee?" she asked, turning to face me.

"I don't really drink coffee," I said.

My eyes were drawn to her shapely legs and the curve of her hips. I had never really noticed her figure before.

She returned to her work. "Cream and sweetener with a smidge of coffee in it then."

"The real stuff," I said. "Not saccharin."

I watched her head bob in assent.

"Have you got something I can take with me?"

She turned again to face me. I tried to keep my eyes on hers. She smiled slightly, pulled her robe together and tied it in place as she padded to a large cupboard.

"We have paper cups. Are you in that much of a hurry?"

"I think your folks would like some time alone with you."

She rolled her eyes. "They're still in bed."

Good, I thought. "It's a five hour drive plus stops."

"You could go this afternoon. Or even tomorrow."

"It's time," I said.

Melody nodded, took a large paper cup from a stack in the cupboard, and quickly closed the door. Her nearly perpetual smile dissipated as she returned to the coffee maker. "Julie's going back early, too," she said matter-of-factly.

I reached to touch her shoulder but thought better of it. I wanted to turn her around and kiss her. "So what," I said.

"Well..."

"I told you. She's not my type."

She shrugged her shoulders.

"Let's go for an A&W burger and float when you get back," I said.

"Okay." She did not look at me. "When?"

"Soon."

She forced a smile as she handed me my heavily-doctored coffee. "I'll check my schedule." She turned. "Oh!" She brushed by me and started up the stairs. "I've got something for you."

The sweet aroma of her hair still lingered when she returned and handed me a cassette tape. She had written "For You-Gene" on the case.

"Cute," I said.

"I thought so."

"What is it?" I asked.

"Just play it."

I tried to look confused.

She moved in to hug me, and I placed my open palm lightly on the small of her back. She squeezed tightly for a moment and pulled away.

I drove south, avoiding Wyoming altogether. There were no boundaries, and it all seemed much the same. It was not the same with me. I thought briefly of Noelle's European adventure. I hoped she was being safe, but that was about the extent of it.

I looked at Melody's tape several times without playing it, thinking I needed to concentrate on where I was going. The truth is, I was afraid of what might be there, her voice declaring something I wanted to hear but knew I could do nothing about. My mind created scenarios of commitment and secrecy in varying degrees. I imagined Melody agonizing late into the night as she fashioned her confessional.

The road cut through white sedimentary bluffs that emerged from the grassy plains like chalky islands amid a sea of dead grass. The scenery was what I was coming to expect of this land, and yet it was extraordinary. I felt special for being allowed to find beauty among the obscure and the ordinary. Surely if people valued this natural landscape, they would want to live among it. But for many miles I saw little indication of civilization. I imagined myself a Native riding bareback through the dust and brush, as free as any man could claim to be. I felt my horse beneath me, my woman on hers riding line abreast with equal vision for a future unencumbered by the demands of others. A wide-open sky, an unfettered existence—no commitments to a government, no taxes to pay, no ideologies to embrace.

The gray ribbon of the road revealed new treasures before me as I sped with little concern for the law that sought to reign me in. The white stripes and solid yellow lines seemed meaningless. I drove for many miles without coming across another vehicle going in either direction. On long flat stretches, I took the very middle of the road, bracketing the pale stripes with my wheels. The road was mine, but only if I followed it. No alternative paths were offered. But that was okay with me. It was all part of my new world.

I suddenly realized I could see Noelle's presence in none of it.

I loaded Melody's tape in the player.

It was music, a string of songs starting with "Wildfire" and moving on in a mix from there. I was disappointed and yet relieved that Melody had not recorded some dreamy professions of love.

I began to think about what I had seen and heard and done with and because of her. Perhaps, at long last, I had stumbled upon something I could believe in, something that was real.

I looked at the speedometer and saw I was doing well over eighty. I wished then that the Z was a convertible like Skye's Alfa. I imagined my hair longer and flowing in the breeze created by the power of my steel steed. I was ready to disagree with Skye, to say there is a truth beyond mankind, perhaps in need of an alternative definition, but a truth nonetheless that ignores man or at least discounts him.

But it seems every time we think we have found the truth that will guide us through our lives, we forget that we are still human. We are given to frailty and shortcomings and all the other flaws that have been bred into us from the beginning of life.

It occurred to me that, without mankind, there also was no such thing as honor because, in nature, there is no opposite to it. But man concocts codes of honor.

"And then we break them," I said out loud.

I thought of the cadet honor code: we will not lie, steal, or cheat... And yet, the white man had lied to the Indian, stolen his land and his identity, and cheated him out of everything else. All the while believing he had every right to do so.

Therein lies the wolf, I thought, and the evil that comes when you decide you alone are in the right.

Back in Colorado, I stopped at A&W for a burger and a root beer before going to the apartment Skye shared with other members of the hockey team. I had not cleared this with Skye beforehand, but I had his car keys, and therefore the key to the apartment, and I was fairly certain none of the other hockey-playing tenants were in town.

I found a bottle of bourbon in a cabinet that sported a framed picture of several hockey team members and cadet fans posing together after the win against Army. There was another of some of the same guys huddled around two dirt bikes and a Harley, which I found interesting. Cadets were not allowed to own motorcycles until the last month before graduation. I was surprised to see a smiling Francis Cruce standing close to Skye.

It rained on and off for the next three days, and there was little to do but drink and study. I did more of one and less of the other, vowing to clean the sheets and replenish the booze when the weather cleared.

I left the apartment only a couple of times. I briefly contemplated calling on Julie O, just to see if she had really come back from Wyoming early, but I could not get excited about the idea. I could think of nothing we might have in common, nor did I care to go searching for any possibility. There was simply no there there.

Instead, I wondered around the new Citadel Mall in search of fast food and distractions. Through a store window, I spotted a faux gold necklace that got my attention—a simple starfish hanging from a cheap chain. It wasn't very expensive, so I decided to buy it and maybe give it to Melody. Or maybe I would just tuck it away for something or someone in the future.

I bought another bottle of bourbon before returning to Matilda's.

While I remained playfully dependent on the booze to placate my bouts of self-pity, my father was now three months sober. I knew I needed to be stronger, to feel worthy of a man so wounded by love that he sought to drown the pain of not having it before deciding to make it the priority of his life. It was a lesson I was yet to learn.

I felt the downhill run coming. I found myself in a contemplative mood on the Sunday morning that heralded the end of Spring Break. Little more than two months remained of my cadet career. I was about to become an Air Force officer, free of the oppressive rules and regulations of the Academy, a captive of new rules and a new life. I would go to Arizona to learn how to fly the Air Force way.

Skye returned from Mexico with sun-bleached hair and a healthy tan. He regaled me with stories of his listless days on the beaches of Acapulco, the different bars he had frequented, the fishing trip where he landed his first sailfish. He laughed when I asked him about the girls on the beach, and his eyes widened in exaggerated delight.

"Beautiful, Geno! Everywhere!"

"Anyone special?"

Skye exhaled audibly. "It was like fishing. To hook one was to chance losing the opportunity to land all the rest."

"You're obviously not going to tell me if you got any tail," I said. "So, regale me with the tale of your fish."

"Incredible! Biggest fish I've ever seen! I fought him almost an hour."

"Was he a fine fish? A brave fish? A noble fish?"

He looked at me from his desk chair.

"Hemingway," I said. "Sort of."

"Whatever. When we got him to the boat, he was exhausted."

"Could have been a her," I said.

"Not this one."

"What did you do with him?"

"Got a picture, then we let him go."

"We."

"The guys running the boat." He paused in memory. "One of them jumped in and pull him around by his beak until he could swim again."

"His bill," I said.

"What?"

"Not a beak, it's a bill."

Skye nodded and looked out the window. "It was inspiring. He fought as if his life depended on it."

"I'm sure he believed it did."

"Fish don't believe in anything but God and their country," Skye said.

We exchanged grins at the academy joke.

Skye went on to talk about the dolphins. I found it a little annoying that he felt he needed to tell me about experiencing things for the first time that I grew up doing in Texas. But his water was bluer, his fish bigger, his beach prettier. In some ways, it reminded me of The Tomi.

"I crashed a few days at Matilda's," I said. "I hope that's okay."

Hearing me use the code name he had concocted for the illegal apartment, he eyed me evenly. "Did you wash the sheets?"

I nodded. "And cleaned the tub. And I restocked the booze."

"That's all right." He paused. "The tub?"

"I soaked one night."

"Alone?"

I grinned. "Your sheets are unspoiled."

"How was Nebraska?" Skye asked.

"I had a good time. Learned a lot." I paused. "How come you didn't tell me you're... Native American?"

His smile vanished as his eyes met mine. "It never came up." He shrugged. "I'm not full blood anyway. Don't hold it against me."

"Why would you being a Native American bother me?"

"I mean not telling you. I knew you'd find out if you hung around my sister long enough."

I nodded. "She shared a lot."

Skye eyed me questioningly.

"You never told me about your brother either," I said.

Skye returned my gaze for what seemed a long moment before looking out the window again. "Why would I want to burden you with that?"

"You didn't trust me?"

"Trust you?"

"To understand."

"It's not a fun thing to talk about." He seemed irritated. Or hurt.

I nodded. "Maybe this way was better. Hearing it from Melody."

Skye lowered his head. "She was young when he left. So innocent. She expected him to come back. Sometimes I think she still does."

"She said he was killed."

Skye looked at me. "Maybe she's finally accepted it."

"And you?"

"What?"

"Have you accepted it?"

His shoulders sagged ever so slightly as he turned his eyes from my gaze. "Pretty much."

So we both carried that scar. At least I had been able to say a kind of goodbye to my mother. I had closure.

Skye looked at me and his countenance lightened. "You're not telling me something."

"Like what?"

His lips formed a faint grin. "You were in my sister's room."

I felt my eyes widen and glanced away. "What makes you..."

"The picture of my brother that Melody keeps. It's the only one in the house."

"She told me it had been your room."

"Yeah." He looked away. "What did you guys do?"

I gave an abbreviated version of our exploits, capping it off with riding May Belle, but omitting some details, like Wounded Knee.

"That's it?"

"Pretty much," I said. "I left the morning your father got back." I looked at Skye and smiled. "There's nothing going on between me and your sister."

Skye nodded. "So, what did you think of Rushmore?"

"It makes me angry to think of white Americans stealing the land of Native ones," I offered.

Skye nodded. "That was not right." He paused. "But then the Lakota took the Black Hills from the Cheyenne."

This was news to me. "It makes more sense now," I said. "The way you went after Evans.

"That pompous ass?" Skye scoffed. "It wouldn't matter what my blood had in it. He makes it hot."

"I noticed he's not the only one."

He shook his head dismissively and glanced at me. "I may have made a few enemies here."

I was glad to hear him acknowledge that. I shrugged. "Who gives a crap? Two more months and we can blow this shithole."

Skye grinned. "Now there's a pleasant picture."

PART FOUR

"We can endure neither our vices nor the remedies for them."

Livy

CHAPTER FORTY-SEVEN

I nursed a certain tacit resentment in thinking my last two months as a Firstie could be made less than glorious by my association with Skye. I wanted to coast, to be but a speck on the wall, to shrink into an anonymous heap that was of no consequence to anyone. In short, I no longer wished to be esteemed. I just wanted to make it out alive.

Skye was quite the opposite. As our remaining cadet days counted down, he sought fresh and insightful ways to tweak the noses of his nemeses. It seemed a bit petty to me, although I shared his distaste for a handful of our classmates who had risen in the ranks on the backs of those they tried to keep down.

But graduation was the great equalizer. In two months we would all be peers once again, sliding from the top of the heap to the lowliest commissioned rank, the second lieutenant. The butter-bar. The whale shit of officers' ranks.

On Friday, I met Melody outside her dorm and we drove to A&W. She seemed as pleased to be with me as I was with her. Our exchanges were impulsive, lighthearted, and playful. Melody, especially, was in rare form—joking and teasing and finding a humorous meaning in everything we said.

When the conversation lagged for a moment, she asked, "Why are you being so boring?"

"Just trying to keep up," I said. "You're setting quite a pace."

She laughed. "No spleen!" She took a sip of her root beer float.

"I've got spleen coming out the..."

She turned in her seat and popped my shoulder, making me spill a little of my drink.

"Root beer abuse!" I said. It was silly, but we were in a mood.

"What are we going to do tonight?" Melody asked.

"We're doing it."

She looked at me and frowned. "This can't be all there is to life!"

I wiped some mustard from my mouth. "Well, the hockey team is putting on a big soiree."

Melody turned away a little. "Yeah, I know. The pool at Skye's..."

"We call it Matilda's." I looked at her. "You know about his... about that?"

She eyed me knowingly.

"Cadets aren't allowed to have apartments," I said.

"I hear a lot of them don't need to," Melody said. "There's plenty with girlfriends."

I nodded. Several of my classmates helped pay for apartments with the lease in their girlfriend's name. It was a way around the technicality.

"So," I said. "We could check that out if you want."

Melody shook her head. "I've been barred from that drunk fest." She looked at me. "It's okay. I'd be bored anyway. But if that's your idea of fun, you should go."

"Hanging around a bunch of plastered hockey players sure won't be dull," I said. "You never know what kind of amusement they'll come up with." I paused and looked at her. "It's the last big bash before June Week. It'll probably go on all weekend."

"You go and have fun. I'll find other amusements on my own."

I felt a flush of anger. I did not wish to be manipulated by a girl I was not even technically dating. But the only response that came to mind was hurtful, so I said nothing.

Melody turned in her seat to look at me. "Look, I know you're trying to be loyal to my brother. You want to go to his final fling, but you're afraid of turning me loose on a Friday night."

I was afraid of turning her loose. But it was not for fear of letting Skye down. I was thinking about Evans, and those of his ilk.

"What kind of amusements?" I asked.

"What?"

"You said you'd find other amusements." I glanced at her. "What do you have in mind?"

Her look was one of feigned shock. "A bit personal, isn't it cadet?"

"I don't mean to be nosy," I said, although I truly did.

"No?"

"No."

We were silent for a time before I asked, "Would you... make other plans if I went to the hockey thing alone?"

She frowned and looked out the window. "Maybe."

"With Tomi Evans?" I was fishing.

"Would that bother you?"

"Yeah. He's the kind Skye told me to keep you away from."

She laughed and looked at me. "This is quite the conspiracy."

"It's not a conspiracy."

"What would you call it, then?"

"Okay. It's a conspiracy. But a well-meaning conspiracy."

She turned her gaze outside to a couple laughing and eating burgers on one of the benches. "He'll probably be at the party, anyway."

I glanced at her. "So that's why..." All I could think of was The Tomi and his 2+2 with the tight backseat that was always ready.

She laughed as she turned to look at me. "Don't worry about it. My virtue remains intact." I detected a subtle "come hither" look that I fought to ignore.

"I don't know if Skye ever told you," Melody said, "but I didn't have much experience with guys before I left Scotts Bluff for college."

My skin tingled. What was I about to learn?

"We don't have to talk—" I began.

"I wasn't what you would call attractive in high school," she continued.

My surprise was genuine. "That's... I don't believe that." She must have known she turned her fair share of heads. "You're a... well, you're not bad to look at."

"Oh, thanks," she said sarcastically and punched my arm again. "Anyway, I was younger than my classmates. I didn't have a real date until my senior year. By then, it was almost too late."

I frowned. "Too late?"

"After my brother... well, after he left, I became quite the tomboy. My hair was short. I liked to ride horses. I preferred a hike in the hills over a slow dance at the prom. It came as sort of an... inconvenient shock when I suddenly started getting the looks and phone calls that had been absent before then."

"You weren't interested?"

"I was a late bloomer, I guess. I missed those years where a girl learns how to use her looks to get what she wants." Her eyes flickered down to her chest before she raised them to rest on mine. "I knew what guys were paying attention to. What brains and personality had been unable to avail, physical attributes could."

"My mother must have been an early bloomer," I offered. "She's only twenty years older than me."

"Really?"

"Yeah. My folks were high school sweethearts. I was born less than a year after they were married."

"But they were married... before..."

I smirked. "I'm sure she was a virgin."

Melody laughed lightly. "That was probably more of the norm then. Now, there's pressure from all sides. Your family telling you to wait. That you have to be careful. You want to be good, but you don't want your friends to think you're square." She looked at me. "My parents approached it from an economic standpoint. Very clinical."

Then she said, "I had friends in high school who lost it in the back seats of cars. They talked like they had experienced something special, but if you watched them afterward, you could tell it wasn't the same."

I was caught off guard. "You know you're pretty amusing yourself," I blurted. "For someone who doesn't know much about... whatever it is we're talking about."

"I am?"

"Yeah. Sure. You can be fun." I sought to lighten the conversation.

She smiled playfully at me. "But that's not what I'd call fun, anyway."

"You don't think... love can be fun?"

She inhaled deeply. "I don't put love and fun in the same category." She glanced at me. "Julie thinks it's fun, though. That seems to be enough for her."

I turned in my seat to face her. "I have no interest in Julie O. And to your unspoken question, I haven't seen her since Wyoming."

"I saw the way she was acting with you," Melody said. "And she's available."

My headshake was exaggerated. "My hair's too short."

"I think she'd overlook that. You have other assets."

"Well, forget it," I said dismissively. "She's not my type."

"Who is?" Her eyes were gently searching mine.

I thought to kiss her, but I feared the embarrassment of rejection from having over-read her intentions. I looked away. "I have something for you," I said.

"Oh?" She gazed at me in wide-eyed curiosity.

"It's just a..." I fished out the necklace from my jeans pocket. "It's a friendship thing," I said awkwardly, handing her the chain with the gilded starfish. "To remind you of the guy from the Texas Gulf Coast."

Melody took the medallion and turned it over in her hands in genuine admiration.

"No big deal," I said. "I just saw it and thought of you."

She smiled and placed it over her head, brushing her long dark hair from her neck as she lowered it to her chest. "I'll always wear it."

"I wouldn't carry it that far."

She leaned to me and gave my cheek a lingering open-eyed peck. "We do have fun don't we?"

"But you know we can't have too much," I said, feeling flushed.

"To much what? Fun?"

"Certain kinds of fun."

Melody turned to look at the space behind the seats. "You're right." She smiled impishly. "You don't even have a backseat."

After A&W, we cruised along Academy Boulevard for a while before turning back toward CC. There was more in our silence than could have filled an evening's worth of words.

"Hey," I said, trying to sound upbeat as we approached her dorm. "Tomorrow's supposed to be a beautiful day. Why don't we take a hike?"

I sensed her eyes on me. "Okay. Where?"

I looked west. "In the mountains. Behind the Academy."

"Sounds like fun. I'm well equipped for that."

I nodded. "Oh, shit!" I glanced at her. "I mean shoot. We have a parade tomorrow. The earliest I could pick you up is probably around one. That might be too late to make it back by sunset."

Melody nodded. "What time will you be done with your shit?"

I laughed freely. "The parade should be over by 11:30 or so." I stopped at the entrance to her dorm, and we sat with the Z idling.

"So," I said. "What do you want to do?"

"Take a hike," she said, flashing a whimsical smile. "A girl I know is dating a Firstie. She likes watching you guys march."

"How boring."

"I'll catch a ride with her and meet you after," she said.

I tried to look unaffected. "That'll work. Where?"

"The Chapel?"

"Okay."

She cocked her head. "So, the hockey team is having a bash tonight even though you all have to be back for a parade tomorrow."

"Yeah."

"That should keep you out of trouble." She pinched my arm.

I thought to squeeze her leg but changed my mind.

"Will a bunch of hungover hockey jocks be able to keep step with the rest of the cadets?" she asked.

"We'll see," I said. "Theirs is a different drummer."

"Yep."

"Who's the girl?" I asked.

"The girl?"

"Giving you the ride tomorrow."

"Oh. Her name's Vanessa Cardewey."

I flinched.

Melody's gaze rested on my lips for a moment before she looked into my eyes. "Do you know her?"

I nodded slowly. "I think she and Skye were an item for a while."

"I doubt that," Melody said with certainty. "I bet he knows her, though. She has an apartment near... Matilda's." She smiled knowingly. "But I think her boyfriend is paying for it."

I suspected it more likely that the rich bitch's dad was footing the bill.

CHAPTER FORTY-EIGHT

Self-serving despondency crept over me as I watched Melody walk away to her dormitory. I idled away slowly, contemplating a return to her room where I would invite her to join me for an evening drive into the mountains. Meandering along the backroads, I spotted a liquor store where I stopped to buy a pint of Southern Comfort. I was disappointed to discover the joint did not offer a cadet discount.

I drove around in search of a place where I could see the Rockies illuminated by the moon. I stopped on the edge of a quiet neighborhood, killed the engine and opened the pint. The liquor was sweet, and I settled back to think about the last four years and my time at the Academy, and how it was all coming to a close, about Melody and Skye and Noelle, about Vanessa, about my mother and father, about Tyson, and about what I had gained, and what was lost forever, and how all I had to show for it was a life confused by love and honor and obligation.

As the liquor took hold, the moon evolved from a big rock reflecting a distant light to the keeper of truth, waxing and waning as light clouds flew past it, sometimes clear, other times partially obscured from view.

I fired up the Z and drove into town toward Skye's apartment, hoping I could find it in my inebriated state. I located the apartment complex without incident, but after I parked and started walking, I realized I had no idea where I was going.

Through a lighted window, I saw a group of five or six people sitting around a table talking. I knocked on the door. One of them rose and opened the door as the others looked on with interest.

"Can I help you, young man?" he asked with a smile.

"Yeah," I said. I noticed he had a thick book tucked in his hand, his finger holding his place. "I mean yes, sir. My friends are having a party..." I realized I was slurring my words.

"Would you like to come in?"

"No. Thanks." My breath reeked of alcohol. "I'm looking for the pool."

The man walked through the threshold, leaving the door open as he came into the moonlight. He shifted the book in his hand. The Bible. I was glad to see it. I could have knocked on a different door and been invited in, never to be heard from again.

"I think I can point you toward the building," he said. He either had not noticed or, more likely, was ignoring my state. "Follow the parking lot that way to the biggest building. It's got glass doors." He smiled at me. "Are you sure you don't want to come in for a bit?"

I tried to maintain a sober bearing and shook his hand. "No. Thank you very much. I hope I did not disturb you."

"It's okay, son," he said. "We were just talking about the Lord."

I turned in the direction the man indicated and walked away from the Bible study as gravely as I could.

I could hear the party as I neared the building, a noisy composite of conversation and rock music. A figure of modest height was coming out of the door as I approached. It looked like Francis Cruce, but he did not turn when I called his name. I opened the party room door and went in.

At the near end of the room, a large stone fireplace blazed with gas logs. Through the stereo speakers, Gregg Allman was singing that he was not going to let them catch the midnight rider. I recognized several of the hockey team members engaged in conversation or eating from paper plates or both. There were more girls than guys, which would have been unusual for any other cadet party not organized by jocks.

I walked across the large room, following the aroma of pizza. Water-soaked partiers wearing swimsuits came and went through glass doors that, from the strong smell of chlorine, obviously led to the indoor pool.

I tried to hide my surprise when I locked eyes with Vanessa. She smiled briefly, which caught the attention of the cadet standing with her. He glanced over his shoulder. Philip Quince. Dusty Durskan was chewing on a carrot stick at his side.

Vanessa tilted her head. Following her attentive gaze, I spied Skye near the far wall at a long table arrayed with catered cold-cuts, pizza, fruit, and a large tray of largely untouched raw vegetables.

Skye's wet blond hair was slicked back. Water dripped from his well-proportioned body, forming a growing puddle at his feet as he piled pizza slices on a paper plate that seemed ready to collapse from the weight. He was naked except for his academy-issue whitey-tighties. "BOOK" was printed in black permanent marker on the crotch in mock compliance with the cadet regulation requiring all military clothing to be tagged with the owner's name.

He moved to the end of the table, opened one of several coolers stacked on the floor and extracted a can of Coors. He turned and, ignoring the prominent sign that warned "No Food or Drink in Pool Area," took his pizza and beer through the glass doors. I crossed beyond the threshold to find him descending the pool steps with his meal.

Throwing back his head for a long swig of beer, he caught sight of me and raised his eyebrows. He placed his plate on the pool's edge.

"What's up?" He looked to the glass doors. "Melody with you?"

I shook my head. "Does a chicken have lips?" I sat on the slatted wooden bench a few feet away. "She knows you're here, though. Probably suspects I am, too."

He took a bite of pizza. "Want a beer?"

"In a minute."

"It's free."

I nodded.

"Well then, strip and jump in," he said.

My head was swimming from the Southern Comfort. "I would if I had your balls."

Skye's free hand disappeared into the pool water. "Nope. Still got 'em."

I glanced around the pool room. "Was Cruce here? I thought I saw him leaving."

Skye took a bite of pizza. "He was a chickenshit like you. Wouldn't get in the pool either."

I suddenly felt very tired. I was not looking forward to the long lone drive back to the Academy. I lowered my head. "Can I ask you something?"

Loud yelling noises from the front room made me jump. I glanced at Skye who did not move. I stood and followed some of the partiers through the glass doors outside.

"That sonofabitch!" a voice I recognized as Quince was yelling from the parking lot. "Did anybody see him?"

I walked up beside Vanessa who was hanging back with Dusty. "What's this about?"

Vanessa looked at me and smiled. "I'm not sure."

"Some guy on a motorcycle," Dusty said. "We saw him through the window, hanging around Phil's Vette."

Quince was running toward his car, a bright yellow Corvette Stingray. I followed him a few steps, drunken curiosity winning out over the more sober voice in the back of my head that was telling me to stay put. I stopped short when Quince bent to the ground and picked up a familiar-looking bag.

"What is it?" Dusty asked coming up from behind me.

Quince held up the bag. "Sugar!"

Dusty nodded in understanding.

Quince eyed the bag in disgust. "That asshole was going to put sugar in my gas tank!"

"Do you think he got any in?" Dusty asked.

Quince examined the bag. "It's still sealed."

"Bastards!" Dusty's use of the plural encrusted the whole thing in a conspiratorial clump.

The partiers that had responded to Quince's initial surge from the building were beginning to disperse, making their way back inside.

"Did anybody recognize him?" Quince yelled after them.

Those that bothered to respond did so in the negative.

"I can't believe a cadet was trying to kill my car!" Quince said, turning to me.

"You think it was a cadet?" I asked. "On a motorcycle?"

"Who else could it be?" Dusty growled.

"How would anybody know you were here?" I asked.

Quince looked back at Vanessa. "She has an apartment here."

"Oh." Now I understood. "You were invited to the party."

Dusty shook his head and glanced at Quince. "We were just hanging in the apartment and heard music. We decided to check it out."

His story seemed contrived. I thought of Skye in his whitey-tighties and wondered if Vanessa was already at the party when Quince and Dusty showed up.

I realized Quince was saying something to me. "Gene! Have you?"

I shook my head. "What?"

"Have you seen Skye?" His eyes were on fire.

"He's in the pool." I glared at Quince. "You're not trying to pin this on him?!"

Quince shook his head and surprised me with an apology. "Sorry." His eyes registered doubt.

Vanessa took his arm. "The guy on the bike looked kinda short to me." She glanced in my direction. "Did you see?"

"No," I said. I would not be a witness. I would offer no theories.

I knew there were cadets who kept motorcycles illegally, stowing them in the garages that came with their equally illegal apartments. I had overheard Tomi Evans brag of such an arrangement.

I glanced around the onlookers and realized I had not seen The Tomi. Being the hockey-hound he professed to be, I could not imagine him missing this final senior year bash. Perhaps he had gotten a better offer. I envisioned Evans and Melody together in his 2+2 and tried to brush the idea from my mind, or at least into its recesses.

Quince walked toward his car, seemingly unwilling to leave it unguarded. Vanessa glanced at me, smiling weakly as I turned away.

Back inside, I found Skye toweling off and getting dressed. "What was all that about?"

"Quince thinks a cadet on a motorcycle tried to kill his car," I said.

"Really?" Skye seemed unphased by the idea.

"Yeah."

"Well, for the one guy with the balls to try, I wouldn't doubt there are dozens who wish they could."

I tried to make eye contact. "That's kinda hateful, isn't it?"

"It is." Skye set on the bench and pulled on his loafers.

"Somebody knew he was here," I said finally. "Any hockey jocks you know keep bikes at... Matilda's?" I thought I knew the answer.

Skye stood and zipped his pants. "I couldn't say." He leveled his eyes on mine. "Is that what you wanted to ask?"

I shook my head. "Never mind." I pivoted to see Vanessa returning to the party alone. "Later, man," I said. "Have fun."

I left Skye and the others, walked outside and fired up the Z for what I was sure would be a risky drive back to the Old Dorm. I lowered the windows in hopes the cool air would sober me faster, or at least keep me alert.

I shoved Melody's tape into the player. Alone with my new "driving music," I had plenty of time to formulate numerous scenarios of what exactly Vanessa Cardewey could have shared with Skye's little sister.

CHAPTER FORTY-NINE

I think we sometimes formulate plans in casual disarray because we wish to deny the importance of the consequences.

I stumbled into my room, rousing an angry Nathan as I hurriedly threw a few necessities into my olive drab laundry bag faux "backpack"— a crumpled flannel shirt, a canteen of water, some canned peaches, and two old blankets. I tossed the bag unceremoniously into a corner of my closet and hit the rack amid Nathan's continued grumblings.

The parade the next morning, while conducted with the usual somber professionalism, had its humorous glitches, if you knew where to look. One of the senior hockey team captains was also a squadron commander. He had imbibed heftily at the party and was showing signs of a significant hangover. From the corner of my eye, I watched him lean in a way that made me think he was about to puke, but he held it in like the tough jock he was supposed to be.

Skye seemed in marginally better shape. He was less vocal than was his norm during parades, although he did whistle along with some of the music. When Dusty sought to quietly admonish him, Skye whispered hoarsely, "Hey, Dusty. Knock knock..."

Performing a surprise inspection before the parade, Dusty Durskan had found my crumpled duffle bag and subsequently written a Form 10 for "closet in disarray" which resulted in four demerits, putting me on the cusp of Conduct Probation.

I was mulling this over in my mind as I grabbed the bag. I threw in my toothbrush and toothpaste as an afterthought, wrenched the bag closed, signed-out for a weekend pass at the CQ desk, and walked down the deserted hallway to the stairwell. I raced down the stairs, taking them two at a time before exiting onto the Terrazzo.

The day was clear and quite warm for the first April weekend following one of the mildest Colorado winters in recent history. It was a good weekend to celebrate the birth of the Air Force Academy by getting the hell out of there. The sky over the mountains was as blue as I had ever seen it, and there was not a whiff of wind. I hurried up the ramp on the west side of the Chapel.

When I got to the top, Melody was sitting on the low wall, her feet dangling, her head turned away from me, her eyes on the mountains. I thought to sneak up on her. I always liked getting a rise out of people by doing that. But she turned and looked squarely at me as if instinctively aware of my presence.

A green backpack with a matching tightly rolled sleeping bag was leaning nearby against the granite wall. A pale lightweight coat was folded next to her. I focused for a brief moment on the sleeping bag. We had not discussed the possibility of overnighting in the mountains.

She smiled her glowing smile and lowered herself from her perch. She was wearing an oversized buffalo plaid shirt—possibly Skye's—that was tucked into loose-fitting jeans. She wore a brand of hiking boots that I wished I could afford. Her long soft dark hair was braided into two ponytails and constrained at the crown by a scarlet headband that matched her shirt. The starfish necklace dangled at her chest.

"That's three demerits for being tardy, cadet," she said. She eyed my laundry bag knowingly.

I groaned. "Don't even joke about that. I'm on thin ice as it is."

Melody put on the red insulated vest she had been sitting on, zipped it, and smiled again as she turned to grab her backpack and coat. She pushed the coat through some straps and lifted the backpack with her neatly stowed gear to her shoulders.

"Where do we begin?" She pulled a thin pair of gloves from a pocket of the vest.

I pointed to the path that led through the small rise to the west of the Chapel. "That way," I said. I looked back at her. She had donned the gloves and was interlacing her fingers to fit them on tightly.

"I hope you don't need those," I said. "I didn't bring any."

"You've got pockets."

I nodded. "And matches." I retrieved my sunglasses from my coat and put them on.

She turned away and walked around the small parking lot to the path. I started after her, and my eyes fell almost immediately to her legs and then to her rear. If I had not known her as well as I thought I did then, I would have sworn she was putting a little extra hip action in her walk.

I followed her in silence to the place where the pathway emptied into the boulevard that led from the Cadet Chapel and Harmon Hall.

"Left, I'm guessing," she said, stopping to look back at me.

I overtook her, heading toward the Lawrence Paul Picnic Area and the mountains beyond.

She caught up with me. "I'll just stick with you."

We crossed Academy Drive into the trees next to the small lake romantically named "Reservoir Number Four." As we passed the rustic looking Lawrence Paul Lodge, I conjured a brief glimpse of the past. We were on the same path Vanessa and I had taken a year and a half before.

Beyond the Lodge, Melody and I picked up a trail worn into the mountain by other explorers. It followed the valleys, mostly, making our adventure easier to navigate. The edge of the trail was highlighted with golden currant bushes.

"Those are pretty," Melody said, noting the yellow trumpet-shaped flowers. She stopped and lowered her backpack to the ground, leaning it against a bristlecone pine, then picked several small clusters of the little currants. "What are they?"

"Yellow flowers," I said.

She laughed. "They didn't teach you anything about flowers during survival training?"

"They taught us not to pick the purple ones."

"Why those?"

"Columbines. The state flower. A hundred-dollar fine."

"Oh."

"You can eat them raw. They're even sort of tasty. Takes about four thousand dollars' worth to make a meal, though."

"Have you ever eaten one?" She began to weave the flowers into a sort of diadem.

I frowned guiltily and turned my gaze to the trail ahead of us. "I had a five hundred dollar breakfast once."

"Didn't you feel guilty?"

"No," I said, looking back at her. "I was hungry."

She laughed as she examined her growing crown of currants. "What about these?"

"I don't know... maybe a nickel each."

"Why so little?"

"They're early bloomers. There's lots of them. Late bloomers are better. They arouse more anticipation."

She winked and smiled.

I watched her anchor her braided flowers into her headband.

"Do bumblebees like columbines?" she asked.

"Would it have been better if I ate the bees?"

Melody carefully stretched the band back on her head, adorned now with a halo of the yellow flowers. Satisfied with her fresh look, she donned her backpack and took to the trail again, turning her head briefly to confirm I was following.

"Do you have any particular destination in mind?" she asked.

"I want you to see something," I said simply. "It's no big deal, but not many people go there, especially cadets."

"Sounds mysterious."

"Not really. It's just pretty. You'll know it when you see it."

"Is it that steep bunch of rocks up there?"

I looked where she was pointing.

"That's Eagle Peak," I said.

"That's where we are going?"

No," I answered. "That's a tough climb. And it's slippery."

"Slippery?"

"Loose rocks."

"Have you been there?" she asked.

I nodded. "With Skye."

"When?"

"Last fall, before it got too cold."

"Like now?"

"It was colder than today. There was snow."

"Well, then, can we go there?"

I shook my head. "I can take you up there next weekend if you want." She smiled. "I think I could get there on my own, if the trails are like this."

"How do you mean, 'Like this?'"

"Well worn. No new ground to break."

"It gets steeper," I said.

"Too steep for a girl?"

"That's not what I meant." I looked toward the peak. "It can be risky," I said, "even where the trails are. Just because it's been done before doesn't make it any easier."

We ascended quickly on the trail that curved where it needed to. At one turn, I thought I recognized the place where Vanessa and I had camped, but I was not sure. There was no need to mention it anyway. Many people had been this way before, so, as Melody had implied, we weren't blazing any new ground.

We turned southward below the peak. Our trail was almost level now. Small boulders and fallen limbs impeded our progress at times, but it was all navigable. As we came over a small rise adorned with Colorado blue spruce trees, Stanley Reservoir appeared below us.

"Oh!" Melody said. "There's a lake down there!" She looked at me, her eyes bright. "Is this it? Is this the place?"

I nodded and glanced at her. "Treasure."

She looked at the little lake. "I wasn't expecting this up here!"

"You don't have anything like this in Nebraska?" I kidded her.

"I never get tired of the exceptional."

I considered that for a moment. The past four years had hardened my emotional skin, turning it thick and calloused. Few things struck me as exceptional anymore.

We walked down the ridge, losing sight of the lake for a short time. When it came back into view, we were nearly on top of it.

"This is so beautiful!" Melody said bouncing her gaze between me and the lake.

I resisted the urge to spurt out something stupid, like, 'Not as beautiful as you.' "I thought you'd like it," I said.

She continued down the incline into the valley, and I followed her, watching my step as we went. The last time I had been here, I was nearly on top of a rattlesnake before it let me know the danger I was in.

I had considered asking Skye if I could borrow his Magnum for the day, but that would have led to him asking why. I would have had to explain that it was so I could take his sister into the mountains, and that would have been no good. I didn't care much for guns anyway, despite my Texas breeding.

I was trying to watch in front of where Melody was going, but she was walking swiftly away from me.

She pointed to the dike. "Is it a lake or a reservoir?"

"It's a reservoir lake," I said.

"What's a reservoir doing out here? In the middle of nowhere?" She turned to look at me. "What's the water for?"

"For cadets to discover. I found it last year."

"With Skye?"

"No."

"Oh," she said.

I sensed she was picturing me here with another girl. Maybe several other girls. I could honestly have said she was the first. But I said nothing.

Melody turned away and lost her footing on some loose gravel. I grabbed her gloved hand and steadied her. She started toward the water still holding on. Maybe she thought I had done that on purpose. After a few seconds, I released her hand to adjust my bag.

We walked up onto the modest dike and stopped again.

Melody took off a glove and put her hand in the water, swirling it with her open palm. "Look how clear it is! Are there fish?"

"Probably. I've never fished it."

"Why not?"

"I wouldn't hike all the way up here just to kill something," I said. I felt a little disingenuous, trying to appear above the common man with his less than romantic reasons for doing things. I really would have liked to fish that lake. I was raised on the notion that any body of water, however small, deserved a few hopeful casts.

I thought of Skye's sailfish. I would have kept more than a picture.

"It's not as cold as I expected," Melody said. "Maybe we can swim."

I laughed. "That water can't be more than 50 degrees."

"Well, I just might try it anyway."

"Let's go over there," I said, indicating an open area to the south.

She glanced where I pointed. "Wouldn't we be warmer on the north side?"

I pulled my sleeve away from my watch. It was mid-afternoon. "Depends on how long we stay. There are more trees there. Probably more firewood."

"Can we make a fire?"

"I thought we would."

"I mean, is that legal?"

"It is as long as we don't get caught."

I looked around. "It looks like we've got the place to ourselves. I'm tired of worrying about what you can and cannot do anyway."

Her eyes, her lips, her face... all of her seemed to be laughing. She took my bare hand in hers. "I'm with you."

I picked up my laundry bag with my free hand and held hers until we got across the dike. I released her hand to look at my watch. Less than five minutes had passed. We both knew that.

We walked around the lake until we came to the small open spot on the southwest side. There was ample evidence of previous campfires. Melody adjusted her headband with the currants as she gazed across the calm water of the little lake. One braid of her hair flowed down her back, and she stroked the other one now as she gazed out over the water. The bulk of her down coat, heavy pants and hiking boots camouflaged the girlish figure I knew was keeping warm beneath them.

She bent over and opened the front zipper of her backpack. "Are you hungry? I've got hotdogs with buns, and marshmallows."

I lowered my bag to the ground and looked at her. "You were planning on a fire all along."

She raised her hand like a boy scout. "I came prepared. Any preferences?"

"Hotdogs sound good." I gazed around us. The only dead wood was small and scattered. I started gathering what there was.

Melody placed her backpack against a fallen dead pine and started her own pile of firewood. "We should swim before we eat."

I laughed. "You really want to go swimming... in freezing water."

She looked out over the lake. "It's not that cold."

I shook my head. "You swim. I'll watch."

"You're going to miss out on a lot in life if you're just a spectator."

NOR TOLERATE AMONG US

"That's like practicing bleeding," I said. "I don't need to experience hypothermia to know I don't like it." I pulled the two blankets from my pack, making it considerably lighter. "Here, spread these."

She took the blankets and gave me a closed-mouth smile.

I got the fire going, then said, "I'll see if I can find something bigger to burn." I turned and followed the ridgeline south. As I scoured the dry earth for dead wood, I struggled to clear my mind of more stimulating thoughts of Melody. I conjured the image of Skye and the promise I had made to protect his sister from the lascivious horde of horny cadets amassed on the other side of the mountain.

When I returned to the small clearing, I did not see her. The blankets were spread in the open not far from the trees near the fire. I scanned the lake with some concern, not wanting to believe she would jump into that frigid water alone. Still cradling the firewood, I walked toward the edge of the lake.

"Hi," Melody said softly from behind me. I turned to see her glowing face peering from behind the towering trunk of a large conifer. She stepped toward me, looking directly into my eyes. I watched her over my left shoulder and, inhaling sharply, tried hard not to stare. My heart leapt as it does now when I've had too much red wine.

Her long braids were tucked neatly into the headband that held the yellow currants. She had shed her coat, pants, and boots, clad now only in the plaid shirt that covered her down to mid-thigh. I lost my grip on the logs which fell from my arms and abraded my hands.

Melody approached me slowly, locking her soft brown eyes on mine. She stopped, standing very still, watching me as my eyes involuntarily traced her body from her graceful neck to the curves of her chest and her hips to the socks that were still on her feet. Embarrassed by my own brazenness, I raised my eyes to meet hers.

"Can I trust you?" Melody asked.

"Always," I heard myself say in a voice made raspy by fickle salivary glands.

"I'm going in. If I start to drown, you must come in and save me."

I picked up the wood. "We're gonna need a bigger fire," I said without looking up. "Before we go in."

"You're going, too?"

"I'd rather freeze to death than try to explain how I lived to tell the tale."

The dry wood caught quickly and was soon crackling noisily.

Melody walked to the water's edge and threw off her shirt, revealing a camisole that did not quite cover her panties.

Her scream when she hit the water was playful and loud, making me look around involuntarily to ensure no one else was there.

"It's perfect!" she said.

I stripped to my boxers and the USAFA T-shirt with my last name on it and took a step into the water. Fighting with all I had not to recoil from the cold, I took another daring step. "Oh, yeah," I said. "Perfect."

Keeping just her head above the water, Melody swirled her way toward the middle of the lake. I crept further into the frigid wetness, thinking that her northern upbringing held a distinct advantage over my southern propensity to avoid such glacial environs. Fighting to keep my breathing regular, I lowered myself to my neck and breast-stroked toward her.

"How long do we have to stay in to prove we can do this?" I yelled.

Treading water, she rotated toward me and said, "You're free to quit whenever you want."

I caught up with her and circled around, trying to get more blood flowing to my extremities. "Is this a test?"

"A test?"

"To see if the Texas boy can hang with the Nebraska girl."

She threw her head back and laughed then smiled at me. "How could you hike all the way out here and then not jump in?"

"Quite easily," I said. But I knew what she meant. Too often we creep timidly to the edge of life only to fall short of embracing the real thrill of living. I thought of the phrase Skye had etched inside his senior ring. "Celebrate Life." That was certainly a motto worthy of them both.

We circled around each other, treading water like two gunfighters waiting for the other to flinch. Finally, Melody said, "Had enough?"

My body was numb below my neck. I looked back at the fire. "I could go another hour at least," I said.

"So could I. I'm just thinking about you."

"Well, if you insist." I started toward the shore.

"I'm afraid I must," she said, following me. "For your sake."

At land's edge, I got out and threw a gray blanket over Melody as she emerged from the icy water.

"Thanks," she said shivering. "You take it." She pulled the blanket from her shoulders and handed it to me.

"Your lips are blue," I said.

She pursed her lips before allowing them to broaden into a smile. She reached into her backpack and retrieved a colorful hooked wool blanket and draped it over her shoulders.

"That's nice," I said.

"Gram made it." She wrapped herself in the blanket and shuffled to the edge of the fire.

I cloaked myself in my gray blanket and stoked the burning wood. We stood side by side as close to the flames as we dared. When the blood began to flow again through our veins, we retreated a bit. I blew into my clutched hands as Melody took a seat on the dead pine.

I lowered myself next to her, feeling sadly platonic yet somehow relieved. The combination of frigid water and Gram's extended presence had served to quell any wayward imaginings.

We sat in silence watching the sun drifting lower in the west as the glow from the fire warmed our shivering bodies.

Melody scooted closer and leaned slightly against me. I shivered from something that was not cold. Neither was it remorse. Whatever it was, it was not pure.

I was suddenly aware of Melody's gaze. I turned my head. Her bright eyes questioned me above a close-lipped smile as she edged closer. She cocked her head, and I touched my lips to hers.

Never in my life had I felt a sensation so soft and so open. Yet, there was something noncommittal about this brief kiss. Rather than removing barriers, she seemed merely to be repositioning them.

"I'm getting hungry," she said, her eyes laughing, her face retreating from mine.

"So am I."

She grinned. "I could eat a dozen hotdogs!"

"Or a king's ransom in columbines."

She rose from the tree. "I'll get the franks and buns."

I dropped my blanket on the dead pine and put my jeans on over my damp boxers. "Could be more wood over there," I said pointing.

She smiled and opened one of the packages. "We'll need sticks to cook the meat on."

"I've got a knife," I said. "I'll cut some when I get back."

"I can do that," she said. "Give me the knife."

I pulled it from my jean's pocket and reluctantly surrendered it to her. "Don't hurt yourself," I said. "It's a long way down the mountain."

I finished dressing, grabbed my laundry bag, and walked away from the camp, taking a new path through the trees. I don't know how long I searched in a contemplative fog before I spotted the first useable dry branch. It wasn't very big, and I knew we'd need more. This was going to take some effort. Regretting yet again my failure to bring gloves, I put the smaller limbs in my bag. I gathered an armload of the bigger logs, making sure I had enough to make me look strong but not so much that I would drop them. I hurried back toward our camp, uncertain what this day would bring.

Melody was sitting on the fallen pine near the fire, tightly tucked in Gram's blanket, her bare shoulders partially exposed. I noticed her camisole and panties hanging from a pine limb. In her free hand, she held two sticks with wieners that were beginning to blister.

She smiled as I approached. "They're almost burned," she said. "The buns are there." She indicated a flat rock near the fire.

I placed a couple of the bigger logs onto the fire and retrieved two buns.

"No fixings" she said. "Unless you brought some." She let me take one of the sticks.

"I left the ketchup and mustard in my other laundry bag," I said.

"I'm too hungry for it to matter," she said, taking a big bite.

We ate in silence as the golden embers made their escape above us.

"Want more?" she asked, putting another wiener on her stick.

"Sure."

She took my stick, skewered a frank on it, and handed it to me.

Staring into the fire, she said, "Are we staying the night?"

I looked across the lake to the low-setting sun. "It's too late to head back now," I said. I threw some more small sticks on the fire. "We don't want to be going down in the dark."

The fire grew again as the new wood took. We sat close together, watching the flames rise gently into the evening air.

She blew on her hotdog to cool it. "I'm glad I can trust you, Gene," she said.

CHAPTER FIFTY

As the sun dipped below the ridgeline, I gathered more wood plus a big dead log that I dragged into the middle of the blaze in hopes it would burn all night. Or at least glow warmly. I pulled live pine branches from the nearby trees and laid them on the side of the fire opposite the fallen tree. I spread a gray blanket on top and tucked it in a little at the sides.

"Looks like you've done this before," Melody said.

"Survival training," I offered as a guilty memory of Vanessa stung my mind. I unzipped and opened Melody's sleeping bag, making it big enough for both of us. I billowed my other blanket over it.

She stood and walked around the fire. "What else did you learn?"

I rose from my work. "That sleeping nude is the best way to preserve body heat."

Melody stood a foot or so away, her head turned up. She opened Gram's blanket and dropped it behind her on the makeshift bed. I caught my breath and bit my lower lip, trying hard not to stare. The starfish necklace alone adorned her naked body. She stepped to within a few inches of me, her searching eyes peering deeply into mine.

It was clear she had been thinking about this for some time. It was not a spur of the moment impulse fed by a sexual urgency. She would later tell me she had deemed me to be worthy from the first time our eyes met. And she had been trying to make herself worthy of me. This I found embarrassing—I knew who was worthy and who was not. Now she was facing me with everything that was her and nothing that was not, the unspoken question filling the narrow physical void between us and seeming to echo against the mountains.

She placed her naked body against my fully clothed one. I knew she could feel my arousal, but she took my desire to mean more than mere lust. If I wanted her, I wanted all of her. She was offering it all to me—her intelligence, her strength, the dance of life in her eyes. It made me feel at once good and guilty. I craved it, and so it was, above all else, the one thing I most needed to reject.

Wordlessly, she unzipped my ski jacket and opened it very slowly. She was giving me every chance to do that which she most feared. She lowered my coat from my arms and pulled herself close to me. I could feel the violent, rhythmic pounding of her heart. All else was soft. Putting my arms around her, I placed my cold hands against the small curve of her back. Lowering my lips to hers, I felt months of forced resistance falling from me.

Melody pulled me toward the blankets, then released me and lay on her back with her arms stretched toward me. I undressed quickly in front of her, but she never seemed to look lower than my shoulders. As I lowered myself beside her, she broke our silence.

"Gene. I'm still a virgin."

I pulled slightly away. "Then maybe we should..."

She placed her hand gently against my lips then reached to Gram's blanket and pulled it over us. "Hold me."

Millions upon millions of people have felt the feelings that consumed us that evening. Which is good because I could never adequately describe them. Yet so much was different. Missing were the unspoken questions of lust and desire. Rather, her body asked, 'Do you like my heart so close to yours, my innocence so completely entrusted to you?'

We kissed and whispered and touched each other. She wanted to hold me close, to gaze into my eyes, feel my weight on her. But she was less ready for anything beyond that. She was where she wanted to be, and she was happy.

Something caught her attention. "Gene! Look." She pointed to the southeastern sky.

"What?" I said, disappointed by the interruption.

"You see it? The moon is turning red. It's a blood moon. That means a lunar eclipse tonight!"

I rolled away some and looked where she was pointing. "It's almost as beautiful as you," I whispered.

We did not sleep much, but only dozed. The full moon rose above us, adorning our little world with a soft glow as if to say it belonged to us alone. Sometime after midnight, Melody pushed the blankets away and stood with her back to me. I watched her move, the curves of her body undulating as she worked her way into her jeans before disappearing beyond the soft glow of the fire. When she returned, she did not undress.

"It's cold out there!" she said as we snuggled in our makeshift bed.

Shivering slightly, she pulled in close to me, kissing me briefly before uncovering one of her arms to point to the eastern sky.

"You can just make out Cygnus," she said.

"What?"

"The eagle that flies along the Milky Way."

I tried to seem as interested in her description as I was in her. "I think I see the Milky Way," I said. "Because it's milky. But where's sig us?"

"Cygnus. Do you see that cross of bright stars?"

"I think so." I was unsure what I was seeing. I kissed her deeply and put my hand on her chest, rolling her gently onto her back. "Are you warm now?"

The night grew suddenly darker.

"The eclipse!" Melody said. "It's starting!"

I rolled to one side and looked where she was pointing.

"See how part of it is darker?" She moved from me slightly. "It's not a total eclipse. We can see the stars better now!"

I looked up. "I see the eagle."

"Uh huh," Melody said. "When I was a little girl, Gram told me that the Oglala call the Milky Way *wanagi tacanku*—the ghost road. It's the path of those who have gone before. They're met by an old woman who looks at each one's life, assesses his or her deeds, and determines if they were good or bad. The good souls follow the ghost path south beyond the pines. The bad souls fall—actually are pushed off a cliff."

"Oglala heaven and hell," I said.

"There are evil spirits, but there is no concept of hell for the Oglala. What evil exists resides in us."

She touched my shoulder softly.

The night felt profoundly singular, like something that could happen only once. Life, I thought, could be good, starting now. "There are so many stars," I said. "Millions... or billions."

"Plus galaxies," Melody added.

"I can't believe there isn't someone else out there."

"You mean God?"

"I mean other people of some kind on another planet. It could be the universe is filled with trillions of lonely sentient beings."

"Maybe two stargazing lovers are looking up at us just now." She kissed me.

"Are we lovers?" I asked. "Without making love?"

"You can't make love," Melody said closing her eyes. "It has to be there already."

I nodded and kissed her cheek.

"Have you seen the stars tonight," she sang softly in my ear. "Would you like to go up on a deck and look at them with me?" She kissed me. "I love you, Eugene Oliver Townsend. I will always love you."

I knew better than to ask her why. We held each other and watched the moon without talking.

I began to get angry at Skye for putting me in a position where I felt false honor hindered my freedom to live as I chose. In that way, he and the Academy were one and the same. I was angry with Noelle and Vanessa for manipulating my emotions. Noelle who did not want to be protected. And Vanessa who only wanted me to know she wasn't. I really hated God for taking my mother, especially so painfully. And I was angry with myself for not being stronger.

I remember Melody's soft sweet voice reminding me that she was a virgin and imploring me to be gentle.

Two kinds of shadows are cast during a lunar eclipse. The penumbra merely obscures the moon, while the umbra cloaks it in darkness. Throughout my life, I would struggle against the shadows of my own character, as all men must. Against the shadow of doubt that obscures truth in the mind, and the umbra of fear that eclipses it totally.

We create the shadows because we doubt ourselves, and we mistrust others because we fear the light. As the shadow of the earth can only cover a moon when it is at its brightest, so it is with us, when a harsh truth intrudes upon our being, all too often we pull the blinders of superstition and intolerance over our mind's eye, embracing a desperate lie.

We feed our wolves and cling to the dark madness of the umbra.

I awoke feeling cold. The sky was turning red from a sun that was yet to appear, the fading embers of the fire glowed from the breath of chilling air that came off the lake. I pushed myself up. It was Palm Sunday, but I would not be going to church.

Melody was dressed and sitting at the water's edge with her back to me, her hair braided, her coat wrapped around her. The moon descended in the red sky to the west in one of those moments most people rarely experience, that time when the sun and moon give the morning sky a veiled luminescence from opposing edges. Gram's blanket was folded and balanced on Melody's backpack. I dressed quickly, retrieving my boots from near our bed. I stood, put on my coat, and walked down to Melody.

"You're up early," I said. I was not surprised.

She lowered her head for a moment before looking out over the smooth water.

"This is beautiful," I offered.

She continued her gaze toward the horizon. "I wanted to see all of this morning before we head back." She turned her head to look at me. "I want to remember this place, this first sunrise, this feeling... always."

"Are you hungry?" I asked. "I can get the fire going again."

She shook her head. "That will just make it harder to quench before we leave."

I sat beside her, holding my knees in my arms. "Back to the real world," I said.

Melody smiled sadly. "Imagine if we didn't have to."

I nodded and gazed out over the lake to the setting moon. "Are you okay?" I asked.

She looked away for a moment. Then she turned and embraced me, her head resting on my chest. "It hurts," she whispered.

I fought not to recoil. "I'm sorry," I said. "I didn't mean for it to."

She lifted her head and gazed at me. "Oh." She lowered her head to my chest again. "No, not that." She paused. "I mean, it did a little, but it got much nicer."

I squeezed her gently. "For me, too."
She returned my hug. "It just hurts to have to be so secretive."
"Well..." I began.
She placed her soft finger against my lips. "We must."

Descending from the mountains, I suffered the fretful highs and lows that youthful emotion alone can invoke. We spoke infrequently, and then only about simple things—the sound of the wind through the boughs, the smell of springtime pine, the distant song of a secretive bird.

I searched for the right words, the right mood, the right approach to reconstruct the closeness we shared only hours earlier. But squinting against the clear morning sun I could find no pleasant afterglow.

Watching her walk beside me, I composed an indelible picture in my mind, her face reflecting the sunlight, her body a perfect organic fit amid the rocks and trees.

I hoped we might discover a cozy place to stop and spread the blankets, but that place never appeared. When we did pause to rest, or pretend to, Melody would turn and embrace me, holding me as if to never let me go. But her embrace did not give way to arousal. Something was missing.

I was ill equipped to delve into the complexities of a young mind in love. She had told me she loved me. I wondered if she still did. I returned her innocent ardor with a tight hug and a light caress, but it felt awkward.

Trapped somewhere in the cool mountain air lay the seminal question we neither desired to be asked nor answered. It was like an open secret, a shared unspeakable dream. To speak of it threatened to create a wound that, once opened, could only bleed out.

And so we continued down the path unsure of where we were, oblivious to where we were headed.

CHAPTER FIFTY-ONE

I did not talk to Melody the following week. She had the numbers of the pay phones in the squadron, but she had never called there before, except, I think, to talk to Skye. With the weekend approaching, I wandered down to Skye's room and casually asked how his sister was doing.

"I haven't heard from her for a while," Skye answered.

"Neither have I," I said. "Maybe she has a boyfriend."

Skye nodded solemnly. "It was bound to happen sooner or later."

"You mean she does?"

"She's sort of alluded to a guy." He placed his hand on my shoulder. "I'm sorry. I really hoped you two might hit it off."

I shook my head in surprise. "You did?"

"I think she likes you." He seemed genuinely apologetic. "But I'm not sure she knows what she wants. She's still a teenage girl."

I nodded but said nothing.

Dusty Durskan wrote me up again. My next two weekends would be spent at the Academy serving confinements. Thirty minutes before I was to start my first of four two-and-a-half-hour confinements, the CQ came to my room and told me I had a phone call. I ran down to the payphones and picked up the one off the hook.

"Hello?" I said somewhat breathlessly.

I recognized Melody's laugh on the other end. "There you are!"

"Here I am," I said.

"For a while I guess. Skye said you are confined or something. What does that mean?"

I groaned. "It means I'll be spending the next two weekends here."

"The next two?!"

"Thanks to Skye's buddy Dupert."

"I've heard that name. I don't think they're buddies."

"They aren't."

She paused longer than I wanted her to before saying, "Well, maybe my grades will improve."

I wanted to tell her I was sorry, and that I wished we could be together now. But something in my head made me think she might actually have another beau out in the real world. Maybe it was better that way.

I glanced at the Casio watch Momo had given me as an early graduation present. "I've got to get to my room soon," I said, "or I'll be confined until I graduate."

She was silent for another long moment. "Well, if you've got to go." She sounded tired, like she hadn't been sleeping much.

"I've missed talking to you," I said. "Can I call you next week?"

She laughed in a way that seemed forced. "You can try."

I did try to call her dorm a few times during the week, but no one seemed able to find her. On the verge of flunking both Astrophysics and my last Military Training class, my social life, such as it was, seemed a distant memory. Still, I had a lot of free time to consider all I had done wrong to make Melody so suddenly distant. I imagined plenty.

A second weekend passed with no call from Melody. I didn't want my insecurity known to anyone, especially myself, but I was beginning to lose interest in everything except graduating and driving back to the salt marsh for what would surely be my last visit of any consequence.

Near the end of the third week in April Skye came into my room, interrupting my studies, urgently beckoning me to follow him. I marked my place in the Astro textbook and trailed him out of the room to the stairwell, his favorite haven for secret discussions.

His face was distorted, as if an inner demon had taken control of his countenance.

"What," I said flatly.

"Have you talked to Melody lately?"

"It's been a while. I can't reach her. I know she's got finals..."

"She thinks she may be pregnant," he interrupted.

I tried to appear calm even as intense panic spread to the edge of my being.

"How..." I began. "That can't be." I felt myself slipping into a sickening abyss of guilt and betrayal.

"I know my sister," Skye said.

"I'm sure you do." I waited for the accusation I knew was coming.

His face betrayed a rage rising slowly from the depths of disbelief. "This guy she's been seeing... some asshole..."

I thought it better to confess, to insist on Skye knowing what I was certain was the truth. "Look Sky..." I began.

"He may have raped her!" I had never seen Skye so animated. "I'm going to pound his ass!" He looked at me, and his eyes burned silently.

All that remained was the confession he seemed intent on hammering out of me. I began to feel defensive. Almost self-righteous. I had only done what any red-blooded American boy would do when the girl he thought he could love offered herself to him.

"Skye..."

"It's not your fault," Skye interrupted quickly as if reading my thoughts. "But she refuses to talk about it. About anything." He looked away, shaking his head in confusion and disgust. "My gut tells me whoever it is goes to CC."

I was taken aback. "Why CC?"

"An uneducated guess."

"It couldn't be a cadet?" I asked simply. Maybe I wanted to get caught. Maybe I craved the confession they say is good for the soul.

Skye closed his eyes tightly. "You've got to tell me if you know."

"How could I know?" I asked.

He opened his eyes and looked at me. "Does she talk about anybody? When you're together?"

"We haven't talked about anything in a while," I said truthfully.

"It could be Fattafred."

I was caught short by the accusation. "The Tomi?"

"She's gone out with him, I think."

"When? Are you sure they've... been together?"

He glanced sheepishly at me. He seemed smaller.

An angry flush suddenly consumed me. In my misguided hubris, I had believed Melody could only be interested in me. Could I have misjudged her so completely?

Skye rubbed his furrowed forehead. "If it *is* a cadet, you can bet he'll be protected by that murder of crows that pose as academy lawyers! They'll slander her just to get him off."

I nodded. No matter what happened, Melody would be ruined.

"I'm sorry I brought up Fattafred," Skye said distantly. He touched my shoulder and his eyes softened. "I really don't think Melody would have anything to do with... someone like that."

"What is she going to do?" I asked, my heart in my throat.

"I don't know." He looked away to the stairwell door. "But I can't imagine her having some slimeball's kid. If she refuses to tell me the guy's name, I'll take care of it."

"What about your parents?"

Skye gritted his teeth in determination mired by fear. "This is something they will never know." He looked at me to make sure I understood. "You've met my father. Melody would never be able to face him again. And Mom..." He shook his head. "It would be more than she could bear."

I was desperate to reach Melody. I called the phone in her dorm and told the girl who answered that I was her uncle.

After a few minutes, Melody picked up the receiver. "Bill? How'd you get this number?"

"No," I said. "It's me."

"Gene," she said simply. "You lied?"

"I prevaricated. Are you okay? Why have you been avoiding me?" I hoped she would tell me what I already knew, and that I would not have to confess I had heard it from Skye.

"I'm... I just haven't been feeling well." Her voice was distant and restrained.

"Was it the cold? Or the water?"

"Have you talked to Skye?"

"What?"

"Have you talked to my brother?"

"About what?"

"About me being pregnant."
I swallowed hard. "You know you are?"
"It could be something else."
My body flushed in the hope that everything would be all right.
"No," she said. "That's not true. I can feel this."
I fought for breath, caught in the undertow I had refused to believe existed.
"How long?" I asked hoarsely.
"How long have I been pregnant? Three weeks."
I said nothing.
"It can't be anyone else," she said, as if reading my thoughts.
I was at once frightened and enlivened to learn the truth.
"I know you did not plan for this to happen, Gene."
I swallowed hard. "What are we going to do?"
"I don't know." She paused, and I could hear the breathing that accompanies the onset of heartache. "Skye can't know you had anything to do with this."
I felt a quick flare of indignation. "Melody, I am quite capable of taking responsibility for my own actions."
"So am I," she said simply.
"What will you tell him?"
"Something else."
"I want to do the right thing," I said weakly. "This should be our decision together."
"No," she said with finality. "It's my choice."
As I hung up the phone, I felt the wolves circling, their bared fangs of truth threatening to rip my future to pieces.

"Have you taken the GRE?"
I looked up from my notebook. "What?"
"Have you taken the GRE?" Skye repeated.
I nodded. "Two months ago. But I don't remember much."
Skye shook his head. "I need your help." His eyes were pleading.
"Of course," I said a little too quickly.
"I found a guy for Melody. In Denver." He paused and looked away, his eyes reflecting a thoughtful silence. "She's not completely onboard with the idea, but I think she realizes... well, anyway... after... she'll need

a place to go. To get... until she feels good enough to go back to school."
He looked at me.

"Matilda's," I said.

I can still see the pain in Skye's eyes. I knew some of his hockey buddies had used the apartment more or less as a brothel. The idea of taking his sister to that den of iniquity must have weighed heavily on his mind.

"I thought you were against abortion," I said scornfully.

Skye's jaw tightened. "No more than God."

"God?"

"The bitter waters. God ripping the babies from the wombs of the Samarian women." Skye glared at me as if I was supposed to understand what he was saying.

I looked away. "What do you need?"

"We're going to Denver on Friday. Then back to the apartment. That first night will be hell. I can't stay with her. I signed up to take the GRE Saturday morning, so I have to sign in by 2300."

Again I nodded in understanding. Like most things at the Academy, once you signed up for something, it became a mandatory formation, one that could not be missed without consequences.

"You want me to stay with her."

His eyes were pleading. "I need you, Geno. I know it won't be any fun, but I think she'd feel better with you there. I know I would."

"Okay," I said as noncommittally as I could. "I've got to serve my last confinement Friday. Two and a half hours starting at Evening Call-to-Quarters."

"Then you'll be free."

I nodded slowly.

"Good. Meet me there around ten. That will give me an hour to get back here and sign in."

"That'll be tight," I said.

He watched me without speaking.

"Friday. 2200. Matilda's," I said finally.

He turned to leave but pivoted again to face me. "You know what's funny about all this?"

I caught my breath before saying, "Nothing comes to mind."

Skye's lips formed a sad smile. "I'm still a virgin." He embraced my shoulders and looked into my eyes. "Thanks, Gene." He nodded, released me, turned, and walked away.

CHAPTER FIFTY-TWO

That Friday was not good for me. I did not sleep the night before, and my final English test was a disaster. In desperate resignation, I rationalized that a decent grade in English would not make me a better fighter pilot. Skye did not mention the plan again. It was understood that I would do my part.

Evening came, and with it a terrible sense of foreboding. At each passing minute, I became more uneasy, uncertain I could cope with being in the same room with both Skye and Melody. I glanced at the digital LED display on Momo's watch. Time was my enemy. I wished it to pass quickly and yet not at all.

When my confinement was over, the CQ came to my room and told me I was released. I signed out, grabbed an extra set of civilian clothes and my Dopp kit of toiletries, and stashed the lot in the Z. I did not want to wait in my room for Skye to call one of the squadron payphones, which he would inevitably do if I did not show up at the apartment.

I went to the Richter Lounge and ordered a pitcher of beer. When it was gone, I decided to drive to the Springs. I thought I might still be able to face the inevitable, and the beer helped. Yet, the closer I got to the South Gate, the weaker my resolve became.

A half mile or so from the Gate, I did a U-turn and drove back to the Cadet Area. I parked on the street below the dorm and lumbered up the stairs in a daze.

I entered the squadron through the wide metal door. Detecting neither sound nor movement, I held the handle to quiet the door closing behind me. The hallway was completely empty, the squadron like a ghost town occupied by the lone CQ who rose from his desk in the far corner and disappeared into the latrine.

Eying the daily sign-out log, a residual thought crept its way forward from the umbra of my mind into the realm of conscious action. If I could not protect Melody, I could at least save her brother. I flipped the pages until I found the line where Skye had signed out that afternoon.

My eyes focused on my watch, concentrating on the numbers as I fought to ignore what this would mean. Gripping the pen, the tip hovering just above the sign-in sheet, the space between point and paper slowly closed as my impaired brain zeroed in on the act.

One of the payphones rang behind me, sending my pulse racing as my hand jerked upward. I glanced left and right before etching 2222 in the empty box. Releasing the pen, I pushed the door to the stairwell open, ignoring all stealth as I escaped downward and outward to my getaway car.

I arrived at Matilda's before midnight, but I did not see Skye's car. I stopped near the apartment and sat idling for what may have been fifteen minutes before realizing that the more time passed the less likely I was to do what Skye had asked of me.

I circled around the apartment complex until I spotted his Champagne Metallic Alfa Romeo in the shadows on the back side of an adjoining apartment building. There were several cadet-looking sports cars in the lot. Skye's Alfa was parked next to a Porsche 914. I figured another cadet girlfriend had an apartment nearby. For the briefest of moments, I toyed with the idea that the entire Academy hockey team was lying in wait somewhere, ready to beat the crap out of me.

By now, Skye was certainly wondering where I was. I drove on and parked in a blind corner some distance from the apartments. Skye would have to leave sometime for the GRE, and I knew he would not get into trouble for signing in late.

I set the parking brake, killed the engine, and reached behind the passenger seat to retrieve the half-empty bottle of Southern Comfort that had been stashed there since the hockey party. Unscrewing the cap, I took a long swig, feeling the warmth of the whiskey flow soothingly down my throat. I rolled down the window. The air was cool and fresh and smelled of spring. The clear night showcased a brilliant moon.

"Have you seen the stars tonight," I sang softly to myself. I took another drink.

I thought back to my night with Melody, feeling a painful twinge of regret. I played the night over in my mind.

We had stayed warm by holding each other, our bare chests melded so closely that I could not really touch her the way I wanted to.

I remember waking sometime after the eclipse and kissing her cheeks and eyelashes. When she turned slightly, I had moved my hand down her bare stomach to her pants and begun to unzip them when I felt her hand on mine. I could not tell if she was encouraging my touch or arresting it in search of certainty.

I took another long drink and closed my eyes.

Even as the booze made my head swim, it seemed to clear my mind of a delusion I had been living since that night. Melody said she loved me. I wanted her to want me. I thought the first time might be hard, but it would get easier after that.

I remembered her whispering, "We have to be careful." I had assured her I would be gentle, but as I thought of it now, it seemed she was fighting her own confused emotions of arousal and concern.

Desire hijacked my reason, filling my mind with a blind need to have Melody want me completely or not at all. I had pulled away to look at her face in the moonlight. Her lips were open, her eyes bright, her brow raised in anticipation. I could feel her aroused body welcoming mine, her young mind trusting me to know what was right. To protect her. To protect us.

My head was swollen with the Southern Comfort, my eyes rolling as if trying to keep up with a very still world. I sighed aloud to relieve myself of my thoughts. Redemption would have to wait until morning. I needed a place far away where I could rest, to return to the apartment in the morning when I was sure Skye would no longer be there, and Melody and I would be able to talk alone.

I closed my eyes.

When I awoke, the sun was well above the horizon. I looked at my watch. It was nearly 8AM. I blinked myself into consciousness and drove back to the other side. Skye's car was no longer there. I parked and checked my hair in the mirror and my breath in my hands. Both were bad. I took some toothpaste from my Dopp Kit and squirted it between my lips, slushed it around, then opened the car door and spit the goo on the white stripe of the parking space.

At the apartment, my key unlocked the door, but when I pushed to open it, the chain on the inside arrested further movement.

"Melody?" I said under my breath. When no one came to the door, I tapped on it, softly at first, and then louder. I saw movement inside, and suddenly Melody's face appeared through the space. With but a sliver of her face exposed, I saw the pain. Blackness lined the bottom of the eye that bore the teardrop-shaped scar May Belle had given her.

Before I could ask her to unhook the chain, she said, "Gene, this is not where you should be right now."

I had anticipated this. I assumed she would be hurt because I was not with her for the procedure. "I want to take care of you," I said.

She closed the door. I heard the chain move and the door reopened, but she stood between me and the dimly lit room beyond.

My eyes went involuntarily to her stomach, as if that was the place where I would notice the change. She was barefoot, wearing Skye's plaid shirt. I looked into her eyes, and when she did not move to allow me in, I said, "I'm sorry, Melody. I want to talk. To apologize."

"Now is not the time," she said, looking briefly over her shoulder into the dark room. She leaned toward me and whispered, "I can't talk about... anything."

"So," I said. "It's done?"

She closed her eyes and lowered her head. "Skye said you would be here last night."

I was flushed with guilt. "I was supposed to be. But I couldn't bring myself to face..." I paused. "...your brother." I held my breath before exhaling sharply. "When did he leave?"

"Early."

"Can I come in?"

"Please don't ask again."

"I can't let you stay here alone."

Melody shook her head and glanced back inside the room. For a moment, I thought she was going to move away from the door. I thought I detected movement in the shadows. The faintest whiff of Hai Karate escaped through the opening.

"Someone else is here?" I asked.

Her nod was barely perceptible as she whispered, "Why did you... break your word?"

I did not know where to begin. Why had I done things I swore I would not do? Why had I crossed a line I once promised not to violate?

"I've never seen my brother this way," Melody said.

"I'm sorry I let you down." My weakness made my words guttural. "I should have come..."

Her forgiving gaze was a salve for my anguished eyes. "There will be a time when I'm ready to talk," she said. "But my brother needs you the most now." She glanced away. "He can be... fragile sometimes." She eyed me tenderly. "Please go take care of him."

"What about you?"

She reached through the opening and touched my arm. "We will see." She retrieved her hand and began to close the door.

I lowered my head and turned to walk toward my car. I stopped with my back to her, hesitating for one desperately hopeful moment.

"I love you, Gene," Melody called to me.

My shoulders ached like they had after the cross exercise at the beginning of basic training. When I turned to look back, the door was closed, and I heard the latch being put in place. I slid into the Z's driver's seat and locked the doors. When Skye returned, I would be gone.

CHAPTER FIFTY-THREE

My backslide became a landslide. Melody's words played over in my mind. I tried to talk to Skye, but he never seemed to have time for me. He avoided me, altering his routine to ensure our paths did not cross.

I wanted to go back to Melody. I wanted to believe she was protecting me and that Skye would understand once I was able to explain why I had failed him.

But Skye never asked me why I did not show up. He was dealing with other concerns that overshadowed my flawed friendship.

On Tuesday, almost a month to the day before we were to graduate, the CQ knocked on my door, summoning me to the AOC's office. When I entered, I was surprised to see not only Major Wainwright, but also Quince, Dusty Durskan, and, standing in the corner, Skye. My first thought, after I suppressed a sudden flow of panic, was of my bad idea the previous Friday, and how devastated my father was going to be when I told him I got kicked out for an honor violation a month before graduation.

"Cadet Townsend," Major Wainwright said sourly as I entered. I turned to see Skye's back as he left the room. Durskan rose from his chair and noisily closed the door behind Skye.

"Take a seat," Wainwright said, indicating the empty chair across from his desk.

It was then I realized that Eric Salter, now the Wing Senior Honor representative, was also in the room.

I sat down, trying to remain calm but ready to confess my complicity and exonerate Skye of any implications. I would plead drunkenness and perhaps the resulting blurred vision that would cause me to think I was signing myself in when I accidently signed in Skye instead.

"Cadet Townsend, Cadet Salter has some questions for you," Wainwright said. "I am here merely as an observer."

Sure, I thought. That's why we're in your office with the door closed.

"Gene," Eric began, "did you do anything Friday night? After you were released from your last confinement?"

I knew I had two choices. I could come clean right then, or I could delve into an irrevocable tale of deceit and outright lies. At least we were on a first name basis for my crucifixion.

"I went to Arnold Hall," I said. "To the Richter Lounge."

"Is that all?"

"I also went to the Springs."

"Did you come back to the squadron?"

"Yes. Briefly."

"What time?"

"Uh, around 2230."

"But you did not sign in then."

"What?" No other words came to mind.

Quince handed some papers to Salter. I recognized them as sign-in sheets. Salter flipped through them a little too dramatically. "You were on a weekend pass, and you signed in Sunday afternoon."

I nodded my head thinking there was enough rope in the room as it was. The less I said, the less chance I had to serve as my own hangman.

"Why did you come back? Did you plan to sleep here?"

I felt a surge of indignation. "That's an improper question," I said, citing the phrase that was essentially the cadet version of pleading the 5th. Where a cadet bedded down when he was signed-out was no one's business. Or at least it should not have been.

"Please answer the question, Cadet Townsend." This from merely the observer Wainwright.

I glanced at Salter. We had not spoken to each other since our altercation a year earlier, but there were rumors floating around that his fiancé had broken off their engagement. Perhaps she had experienced certain... primordial desires that did not involve him. I shook my head. "I left again."

"Were you away from the Cadet Area overnight?"

I decided my best defense was to answer their questions honestly if I could. "Yes."

"Where?"

"In my car, actually."

Quince leaned forward in his chair. "Were you ever at the Regal Apartments?"

I eyed him for a moment. "You know I've been there. I was there when you were at the hockey party." I looked back at Eric.

Quince shook his head. "I mean on the evening in question."

I nodded at him again, trying to read his eyes. "For a short while."

"Why were you there?"

"I know a girl who has an apartment there. But I didn't see her car that night." It was the first of many half-truths.

"You left," Quince said. It was a statement.

"Yes." I turned to Major Wainwright. "Sir, should I be asking about legal representation about now? Don't I have the right to know what this is all about?"

Wainwright shook his head. "You're not in trouble, Gene." He leaned back in his swivel chair. "Did you see Cadet Book while you were at the apartments?"

I flinched. "No, sir," I answered honestly, looking directly into the major's eyes. It was the first direct eye contact I had made since the inquisition began.

"Was his Alfa Romeo parked near you?" Quince asked.

"No."

"At what time did you leave?"

"I don't remember." I was beginning to understand that timeline was important. "Sometime around midnight, I think."

Quince turned to Wainwright and nodded almost imperceptibly.

"Thank you, Cadet Townsend," the major said. "You're dismissed."

"They wanna boot me," Skye said simply when I went to his room. "What!" I said. "Why?"

Skye held his head in his hands. "Quince saw my car," he said through his palms.

"What does that matter?"

He glanced at me. "They say I signed in and left again. I swear Geno! I did not sign myself in!" He looked at me like he was soliciting a confession.

"It must have been an accident," I offered weakly. "Someone probably did it by mistake."

Skye inhaled and held his breath for a moment. "I may have implied that I did." He looked away. "Though not in so many words." He paused. "I did not lie. It was more like... a slick nontruth. When I saw someone else had signed-in beside my name Friday night, I just sort of let it go." He looked out the window. "My car was parked in the back. I didn't think anybody had seen me."

The ensuing silence rose in crescendo, filling the room with words neither of us had the power to utter.

Finally, Skye shook his head wearily. "I don't understand why they're doing this!"

"You're not going to get kicked out," I said. "This will all get straightened out. And we'll go to Al–capulco after graduation. You can teach me how to fish."

He did not look at me. "My parents, my dad, will disown me."

"That can't be true."

I could see he really believed what he was saying.

"Does Melody know what's going on? I'd really like to talk to her."

He shook his head. "I put her on a bus. She's going to stay with Gram for a while." He paused. "She really didn't want to go."

I tried not to think this was meant to hurt me. I had transgressed, that was true. And perhaps he knew. Maybe he sought to punish me. I felt something welling in my soul.

Skye leveled his gaze at me. "You were serving confinements that Friday, weren't you?"

I cringed. "Yeah. I'm sorry I didn't make it."

He nodded thoughtfully. "On our way to Denver, I thought I saw a blue 280 following us." He scowled. "But that couldn't have been you."

I was floored to think he could even consider such a thing. "I wish I could have been there," I said.

406

Skye closed his eyes. "Those hypocrites! Those... chickenshits are questioning *my* honor!" He opened his eyes slowly and turned his gaze out the window, immersed in self-pity.

In the days leading up to his honor board, we did not speak again. Neither of us could find the words.

"WE WILL NOT LIE, STEAL, OR CHEAT, NOR TOLERATE AMONG US ANYONE WHO DOES."

CHAPTER FIFTY-FOUR

The room where Skye's honor board was held may have been flooded in light, but in my mind's eye I see a dimly lit dungeon. From the shadows, a perimeter of uniformly dressed cadets silently contemplated what the one lone figure seated at the long wooden table could have done to find himself the focus of such intensity.

Skye was hunched over, his hands folded to support his chin as he stared straight ahead. He had lost weight, and his eyes were sunken and sallow. His tie was askew. His uniform shirt seemed too large for his neck, like the man inside had become a little boy. I imagined him watching his life like a home movie projected on a wall, rewinding and replaying the scene that had brought him here. It was Skye as I had never known him, captive and beaten, submissive, resigned. As I watched him, admiration was replaced with something that bordered on contempt. It roiled in my stomach like a long-chained beast at last smelling the stench of freedom.

Lewis Carpenter joined him at the table, patted him on the back and opened a folder labeled "Defense." As the representative of the accused, Lewis was restricted in his ability to present arguments, cross-examine witnesses, receive all the information the board members had—essentially the absence of disclosure. The right to remain silent would not come into play unless Skye was actually charged with a violation of military law.

Eric Salter and another honor rep—the prosecutors—sat at an adjacent desk. Facing them along a long table, Francis Cruce sat with his fellow honor representatives and one Air Force major. Six of them would have to vote "guilty" for a conviction.

The board would not be interested in the circumstances, just the facts. If it was determined an honor code violation had occurred, nothing else would matter, regardless of the situation. The whole truth did not need to be revealed. Just enough to prove Skye had been caught in a lie.

I thought of all my petty lies—the 'I love you's,' the 'I'll be there's,' the 'I'll call tomorrow's.' I was sure there were plenty of cadets in this room who were just as guilty.

The board began with Skye. Although I do not know if this was the main intention, questioning the accused first kept a potential liar from countering what other witnesses testified and kept the accused from asserting the other cadets were liars in front of the honor board members.

Salter studied his notes for a bit longer than I thought necessary before he finally asked, "Cadet Book, did you take the GRE?"

Skye sat straight in the witness chair. "Yes."

"When?"

"Saturday before last, about ten days ago."

Salter nodded solemnly. "Because you were taking the GRE, weren't you required to sign in by 2300 hours the Friday night before the test?"

"Yes."

"Did you?"

"No."

"You did not sign in..." Salter glanced at his notes, but I knew he did not need the reference, "shortly before 2300?"

"No. I stayed downtown in C... in Colorado Springs until early Saturday morning when I returned to the dorm and changed into my uniform to take the test."

Salter held up the paper from the log. "I have here the sign-in sheet for that evening." He showed the register to Skye. "Is that your signature?"

Skye looked at the paper longer than necessary. "Yes. I signed out at 1423."

"That is your handwriting?"

Skye looked again. "Yes."

"And here," Salter pointed. "It shows you signed in at 2256."

"I did not."

My mind snapped out of sync with a foggy memory.

Salter studied the sheet. "The handwriting looks the same for both numbers." He handed the sheet to Skye.

Skye looked the sheet over. I could not help but think he was looking for handwriting from other cadets that might match those next to his name. Was he looking at mine?

"Several of these numbers look alike," he said finally.

"You are saying you did not sign-in? That another cadet signed in for you? Maybe to cover for you?"

"I did not sign in," Skye said simply. "How could I ask another cadet to sign in for me? And risk two honor violations?"

"So another cadet lied on the sign-in sheet?"

Skye shook his head. "More likely a drunken one wrote on the wrong line." I expected him to look at me, but he did not.

"But all the sign-in blocks are filled," Salter said as he took the sheet from Skye and perused it. "And there are no other sign-ins at 2256. If you signed in on the wrong block, realized your mistake and signed in at the correct block, wouldn't you erase the mistake?"

"I would."

"I think any cadet would," Salter said.

Skye lowered his head.

I had been drunk, but my memory of the time was clear. I knew, or thought I knew, that I had written 2222 in Skye's sign-in block. The numbers had glowed from my digital watch like an omen.

"Were you in your room at any time that night?"

"No."

"You say you were in Colorado Springs. Where in Colorado Springs?"

Skye paused briefly. "An apartment."

"Whose apartment?"

I followed Skye's eyes as he scanned the faces of the cadets who were there to observe. He stopped his search momentarily on the group of hockey players near me. He looked back at Salter. "My apartment."

"You maintain an apartment downtown?"

Skye nodded. "Yes."

"Against academy regulations?"

"Yes."

Salter put the sign-in sheet on the prosecution's desk and turned again to face Skye. "Where is this...?"

"The Regal Apartments."

"Was there any particular reason why you stayed there the night before the GRE rather than come back to the Cadet Area?"

"I fell asleep."

"Did you go anywhere else that afternoon or evening? Did you leave the city?"

Skye's head shot up, and his eyes fell on mine. "Yes."

"Where did you go?"

I saw Skye glance briefly at Cruce who faintly nodded his head. "I went to Denver for a while."

"Why did you go to Denver?"

Skye looked around as if expecting someone to step in and protest that his every waking minute should not be subjected to scrutiny. No hero came forth. "I wanted to," he said simply.

"To do what?"

Finally, Lewis Carpenter stepped in. "I don't think Cadet Book has to account for every minute of his life."

Salter looked at Cruce who indicated his agreement with Lewis.

Salter smirked but nodded in tacit assent. "So, you returned to your illegal apartment at what time?"

Lewis stood. "Is this necessary?"

"It is," Salter put in quickly. "There is evidence that Cadet Book went to Vandenberg Hall after returning from Denver, signed himself in, and then went to the apartment downtown."

"I did not," Skye said.

Salter turned to Skye. "You'll have your chance to make your case, Cadet Book. For now, answer my questions only."

"I request Cadet Salter show more courtesy!" Carpenter snapped. "I believe Cadet Book deserves that."

The major nodded at Salter.

"Was there anyone there with you? Your girlfriend?" Salter asked.

"I don't have a girlfriend."

"Were any other cadets there then?"

Skye looked at me, the hurt reflected on his face. "I expected someone to meet me there earlier, but he never showed."

"So, you were alone."

Skye buried his head in his hands before looking up into Salter's narrow eyes. "Yes."

I knew Skye had told Quince and the AOC he had been alone. He could not change his answer now. I guess he thought it wouldn't matter.

Salter turned to the board members. "We can dismiss Cadet Book."

From his seat at the center of the honor board members, Cruce said, "Cadet Book, if you or your counsel would like to say anything in your defense, you may do so now."

Skye glanced briefly at Carpenter before saying, "I did not return to the Academy Friday night. I did not sign myself in. I slept at the apartment and returned early Saturday morning to take the GRE."

Cruce nodded and said, "You can return to your seat."

As Skye slumped noisily into his chair, I lost myself in my own musings. I waited to hear my name called as I stared at the ceiling. When I looked down, Quince was on the witness stand.

"Cadet Quince, did you see Cadet Book at the Regal Apartments on the night in question?" Salter sounded like a Perry Mason wannabe.

"Yes, I did. Well, actually my girlfriend saw him first."

"Does your girlfriend know Cadet Book?"

"She's actually my fiancé now."

"Congratulations," Salter said with a subtle tinge of bitterness. "What is her name?"

"Vanessa Cardewey."

Quince must have noticed my reaction, or perhaps anticipated it, because he looked directly at me for just a moment. I detected a mocking satisfaction in his eyes as he answered Salter's next question.

"How does she know Cadet Book?"

"She used to hang out with members of the hockey team. Before we met."

"How did your girlfriend happen to see Cadet Book?"

"She has an apartment. At the Regal."

"Did you also see Cadet Book? At the Regal Apartments?"

"Yes."

Salter clasped his hands in front of himself and took a step toward Quince "Are you sure it was him?"

"Yes."

"How can you be sure?"

"Because I saw him get out of his car, a gold Alfa Romeo with a cadet parking sticker."

"You saw him along with..." Salter eyed his notes. "...Vanessa?"

"Yes."

"At what time?"

NOR TOLERATE AMONG US

"Around 2100 hours."

"Was he alone?"

Skye flinched.

"There was a girl with him."

"Did you see the girl's face?"

"No. Vanessa did."

"So you cannot give direct testimony that he had a girl with him."

"I believe my girlfriend."

Carpenter stood. "This court can consider neither the fiancé nor her words. I need remind no one she is not bound by our honor code."

There was a perceptible shuffling by some of the cadets present.

Salter nodded. "You, yourself, never saw that the person with Cadet Book was a girl?"

"No, sir."

Skye jerked ever so slightly which caught my eye. He glanced at Cruce, and something seemed to pass between them.

"If they were together, how did you see Cadet Book?" Salter asked.

"When my girl... my fiancé told me she had seen them, I went outside and saw two people going into the apartment. Cadet Book came back out to get something from his car, and I recognized him then."

"Why were you so curious?"

Quince opened his palms. "I had seen him at a party at the pool house a few weeks earlier." He paused. "He knows Vanessa. I thought about maybe seeing if he wanted to come have a beer or something."

It was all pretense, but it made Quince look good, even noble. There was no legitimate court on earth that could convict Philip Quince of a lie of the heart.

"You changed your mind?"

"He went back into the apartment so quickly, I figured he didn't want to be disturbed, especially if there was a girl with him."

"But you did not recognize the girl."

"No, sir."

Lewis rose abruptly. "It has been established that Cadet Quince did not know the sex of the other person."

Cruce nodded. "Could you rephrase your question, Cadet Salter?"

"That won't be necessary," Salter said, turning his attention back to Quince. "Did you see anyone else?"

414

"Sometime around 2330 hours, as I was getting ready to leave Vanessa's apartment to come back to the old... to Vandenberg Hall, I saw a blue Datsun 280Z pull up near where the Alfa had been."

I felt Skye's eyes coming to rest on me.

"So, you did not spend the night there?" Salter asked Quince.

Quince straightened himself. "Of course not!"

Salter peered at him.

"No, sir," Quince corrected himself. "I finished putting my laundry in my car and went in to tell Vanessa goodnight."

"The Alfa Romeo was not there when you left?"

"It was not."

Salter nodded again. "Did you recognize the 280Z?"

"I wasn't sure, but I thought it might be Cadet Townsend's car."

I flushed with the idea that I was about to be snared, that this whole ordeal was meant to nail me.

"Did anyone get out of the car?"

"It wasn't there long. I never saw anyone get into or out of the Z." He steepled his hands. "Cadet Townsend did tell me later he was looking for an ex-girlfriend."

"And when you left, the 280Z was no longer there," Salter said again.

"No, sir. That car was gone."

"Thank you, Cadet Quince."

Suddenly, his testimony was ended with no questions from Carpenter. Salter did not ask about the meeting in Major Wainwright's office or what I had said there. Quince made it sound like the conversation had only been between the two of us.

I was called next.

"Cadet Townsend, did you go to the Regal Apartments on the Friday night in question?"

"Yes."

Again, the Salter stare.

"Yes, sir," I said.

"Did you see Cadet Book there that night?"

"No. Sir."

I avoided looking in Skye's direction.

"Did you see a girl there?" Salter asked.

I frowned at him. "I did not see anyone there."

"Did you see Cadet Book's car in front of the apartment?"

"No, sir," I said, repeating what I had told the others earlier.

"Cadet Book's Alfa Romeo was not parked in front of the apartment when you were there?"

"No," I said. "Sir."

Salter did not understand then what I was answering. He expected a confirmation that Skye's car was not there, and he assumed as much to be my intent.

"Cadet Book has said he was alone at the apartment," Salter said. "A witness has said he saw another person go into the apartment with Cadet Book. Do *you* know who that person was?"

It hit me then. They knew what I knew. Perhaps Vanessa had seen me at the apartment the next morning. Maybe Quince had lied and never left. Or maybe he came back later. Regardless, this was not simply about signing-in or not signing-in. Sky had told them he was alone. They knew someone else was with him that night. They knew who it was. They were just looking for me to confirm it.

I had descended deep into Whit's proverbial box canyon with no valleys in sight.

I glanced at Carpenter. Why did he not jump in? Why did he not say anything? I turned to Skye. He was watching me with the intensity of a cornered dog. He did not shake his head. He gave me no signal. He simply looked on as I dismantled his life.

"If anyone else was there," I said. "It would most probably be his sister."

Salter seemed surprised, as if this was an unexpected revelation. He turned away and looked curiously at Skye. "And why would Cadet Book's sister be there? Did he leave her there that night?"

It occurred to me that explaining everything might just make sense of it all. They would see what Skye was doing and why and would agree that this was an extenuating circumstance and so let the whole thing go.

"He would not leave her."

Salter whipped around to stare at me. "What do you mean?"

Carpenter's chair slid loudly as he rose. "This is conjecture. Cadet Townsend has not stated for certain that he knew who the person was."

Cruce nodded and looked at me. His eyes were intense, his countenance sour. "Cadet Townsend, do you know who other than Cadet Book was also at the apartment?"

I nodded.

Salter's gaze was insistent. "Was Cadet Book's sister with him?"

I could not bring myself to look at Skye. "That's why he would not have gone back to the Cadet Area to sign-in."

Salter approached me. "Why do you think that?"

"Because I don't think Skye would have left her under the circumstances."

"But you said his car was gone."

"I did not see it parked in front of his apartment. It may have been parked around back."

Salter raised his eyebrows in realization. "What circumstances?"

I felt a flush of rage, but it was not just because of Salter and his impertinent questions. It had angered me to imagine that Tomi Evans—or someone like him—could be involved. And if it was just me, that would mean she considered me unworthy after all. Every beat of my heart told me neither could be true. Melody had said it was her choice to make. I was not so sure.

"Skye has been under a lot of stress," I said.

"Why?"

"His sister has not been feeling well."

"Is she sick?"

"Not exactly."

"What then?"

I paused, avoiding Skye's eyes. "I think she had an abortion."

The room went silent.

"Skye was trying to take care of her," I said. I could hear the pleading in my voice, so certainly everyone must have as well. "He would not act this way unless there was such stress on him." I wanted to help Skye. I was ready to face the truth.

The major spoke up suddenly. "Gentlemen, we will stop the questioning there. Cadet Townsend, you are dismissed."

"No sir," I said insistently. "I need to speak."

"No, Cadet Townsend. You've said enough."

Again, they were one question short of the truth. For me to say I was the one who signed-in Skye would constitute a lie. But I had intended to, nonetheless. And it would be my lie and my honor on trial, and Skye would be exonerated because they would understand why everything happened as it did. I might even get off with a warning from the commandant if I passed it off as a drunken mistake.

But Salter and Quince had everything they needed. They were uninterested in me.

I turned to Cruce who was nodding my dismissal. His face was dark, his eyes encircled with black rings as if he had forgotten how to sleep. He lowered his head.

Eric Salter addressed the members of the board. "Gentlemen. We have lies covering more lies." He turned briefly to stare at Skye before turning again to face the board. "Whatever leniency you may have considered I believe is no longer appropriate."

I had told Tyson in what seemed another lifetime that I would not let anyone lie about him and get away with it, that I would protect him because that was what the honor code was about. I don't really believe Skye wanted to get away with a lie. He just wanted it all to make sense, to be understood as necessary, and, therefore, tolerable.

But this wasn't about protection, it was about retribution, about cleansing, about eliminating undesirables from the cadet wing. Philip Quince and Eric Salter and little Dusty Durskan had targeted Skye, and their poisonous arrows had at last found their mark.

I recalled an abbreviated version of St. Paul's writing that Cruce had once quoted in his attempt to sooth me. *'Whether in pretense or in truth ... I rejoice.'*

After the honor board, I went to find Skye. His room was dark, except for a small candle lit on his desk. He was slumped in his chair, a beaten man. A beaten kid, his life's path ruined. He did not look at me as I entered, but he gave no indication he wanted me to leave.

I sat on his bed, leaning forward, my hands clasped between my knees.

Finally, he raised his head. Black circles hung like two half-moons beneath tormented eyes that glowed bloodshot in the dim light. "They voted against me," Skye said.

I nodded. "All of them?"

He slowly placed his hand to his head and rubbed his patrician brow. "Except for Francis... Cruce." He turned his gaze on me, and I felt as if he could see my soul.

"I'm so sorry," I said. "I'm sorry about... telling them about..."

Skye waved his hand, cutting me off. "No matter."

I was stunned to hear him brush off what I thought had been my most damning of words. As I studied his sullen face in the flickering light, it hit me. "They already knew about Denver."

Skye nodded and leveled his gaze on me. "Someone must have seen us go in the clinic."

"Do you know...?"

He breathed in deeply. "It doesn't matter. Quince's testimony was the clincher. He's the only one who could say that he saw me go into the apartment with... someone else that night."

For the longest time, Skye looked at me saying nothing, as if waiting for something from me. Finally he opened a desk drawer and pulled out a thinly rolled cigarette.

He offered me the joint. "Want a hit?"

I leaned away. "Where'd you get that?"

Skye smiled sadly. "Bad Company."

"I'll pass," I said, glancing beyond the shadows to the door.

"It'll keep," he said, putting it back in the drawer.

I began to calculate how much longer I could stay in the room.

Through my silence, Skye said, "For the record, I did not sign myself in." He rested his eyes on the emptiness behind me and sighed. "But I think I know who did."

I had expected him to ask why I told the board about Melody. I was ready to field that question. "Who?" I asked weakly.

He turned to look out the window into the night. "Quince said he didn't spend the night at Vanessa's apartment." He looked at me. "I think that chickenshit would sell his soul to keep me from graduating."

"You don't think he came back just to see if you signed in?" I said. "And then sign you in if you had not! That makes no sense. He would be taking quite a chance."

Skye shook his head. He dropped his head into his hands.

"You know who signed you in," I said thoughtfully. "And it wasn't Quince or any of his confederates." I paused as if in a trance. "That leaves an accomplice... a friend..." And then I knew.

Skye raised his head slightly. "A secret can only be kept by one person. Add one more, and the secret becomes a lie. No one has a good enough memory to be a successful liar." He turned away. "I never thought it would matter. Never imagined it could come to this."

Skye's face showed no emotion, no hint of anything. After a long moment, he closed his eyes as if he could no longer look at me. "If there is a god... if this is His plan... he knew all this was going to happen." He held out his arms. "Why not just tell me and not waste my time?!" He placed his face in his hands again.

I rose and walked out in silence, his words echoing in my soul.

CHAPTER FIFTY-FIVE

I awoke fitfully the next morning, feeling worse than I ever had in my life. I went to the window and opened the curtains as I had seen Skye do many times before, but I could declare nothing good about the day. I dressed slowly. I wanted to go to Skye, to say goodbye, to say I was sorry. I wanted to say things I knew I would not have the courage to utter. I wanted to know if he still believed there was no such thing as truth.

Once I said my goodbyes to Skye, there would be no one else I wanted to talk to. I laid out my combat boots and canteen, thinking I might take a hike to spend the day alone in the mountains.

I padded down the hallway in my socks to Skye's room. He was not there. His clothes were still in his closet, his suitcase lay open and empty on the freshly waxed floor. His bed was stripped of sheets, and his blankets were folded neatly at the foot of the bed. I spotted a piece of paper with my name on it.

Reaching for the paper, I heard a distant "pop." The hair on the back of my neck bristled, as if my body understood before I did.

More pops now discernible as gunshots reverberated through the air.

Within seconds, Dusty Durskan ran into the room, dressed in Service Bravo.

"Where's Book?" he asked.

"I don't know," I said.

Dusty's eyes widened, and he hurried away down the hall.

The shots seemed to have come from outside. I trotted back to my room and put on my combat boots.

I ran down the stairs and onto the Terrazzo where I followed some cadets running up the Chapel ramp.

Early-bird tourists were gathering with several cadets in the rounded parking area near the Chapel, pointing toward one of the spires. Others were gesturing to the shallow hill behind it. I ran past them, across the road, beyond Lawrence Paul, and into the mountains. When I got to the steeper path that led to Eagle Peak, I stopped. I was already out of breath.

To this day, I cannot understand why I hesitated there for even a moment. Laziness, I guess. Or lack of spleen. It would be a steep, tiresome climb, and I rationalized to myself that I needed to conserve my energy.

But my rational side was overshadowed by my knowing side.

As I caught my breath, I realized I was at the sheer wall that Skye and Salter had tried to climb together. Skye had saved Salter there, but Salter had not returned the favor. In fact, he had done all he could to destroy his savior. I gathered my resolve. I could not let Salter win. Or Quince.

The day grew darker as billowing clouds blocked out the sun. A misty haze seemed to envelope my skin and my thoughts as I started up the steep grade. It was incredibly difficult and bloody. I kept cutting and abrading myself on the harsh rock, at times losing my footing on the damp earth and gravel. I stopped to rest once or twice more.

When I finally came to the clearing, I saw Skye standing at the outcropping where we had both stood in what seemed a lifetime ago. His arms were stretched out wide like a cross, his head raised upward, as if asking one last time for some sign of purpose or import that would demand his life continue. The magnum was in his right hand.

I called to him.

He turned without lowering his arms and looked directly at me. No smile, no frown. He acknowledged me as neither friend nor nemesis.

"Skye!" I yelled. "Skye! Give me the gun!"

As if coming out of a trance, he dropped his arms and locked his eyes on mine.

I reached out my hand, encouraging him to put his hand or the gun in it. Either would be fine with me.

Skye placed the barrel of the revolver against his temple and squeezed the trigger.

The cylinder rotated and the hammer fell, but nothing happened. He squeezed again without effect.

He shook his head and lowered his arms.

He smiled sadly and tossed the gun at my feet. I stepped forward, shuffling toward the edge.

"Skye," I began, "come back with me."

He spread his hands again, leaning ever so slightly backward, and the thought crossed my mind that he had been waiting for me to stop him from this insane self-sacrifice. It seemed Fate and I had worked together to save Skye Book from himself.

"I'm so sorry," I said as I took another step and bent to retrieve the weapon.

His body folded toward the edge. He tilted his head, keeping his eyes on mine as he angled away from me.

Then he was gone.

No sound, no scream, no movement to stop himself.

I felt my knees might buckle at any moment as I staggered to the precipice.

For what seemed much more than the few seconds it probably was, I stood there, meditatively pondering what it was that had transported me to this moment. I looked out over the Academy to the plains, raising my eyes ever higher to whatever lay beyond. I was on the edge, and there was no fear. I could feel Skye's spirit urging me to join him. One more step, and this truth would never be recorded.

I closed my eyes. I felt those of the world on me. I was the center of everything. What was that supposed to be? What was I supposed to be?

I opened my eyes and stepped back.

A hundred feet below me, I could just make out Skye's broken body splayed upon a flat, craggy rock, his face upturned, his arms outstretched, his brow bloody. A small cedar had caught him on his left side, causing his body to lean slightly to the right.

I gazed down at Skye's gun, still in my hand. I raised it high above my head and squeezed the trigger, thinking that a signal might get the attention of those down below us. The shells were spent. I hurled the gun as far from the peak as I could into the trees below.

Attempting to scale the edge was suicidal. To go down and climb the face of the hill seemed impossible. I yelled, certain I was calling to a corpse, but irrationally hopeful he was still alive and would survive until I could find a way to save him. I retraced my steps down the mountain.

Movement caught my eye as I rounded the corner at the sheer wall. My heart leapt in a brief moment of hope before I realized the person coming toward me was two small to be Skye. His head was low as he worked his way up the path. He looked to be in great pain.

I held up.

"Frank... er... Francis?"

Cruce had neither seen nor heard me. He stopped and focused his eyes on mine. "Geno." He shifted his body to look around me.

"What are you..? I began.

"I thought Vincent might have come up here." He looked at me. "I guess not."

"Vincent? Oh... Skye." I studied him for a moment. "He did," I said. "He did... go up there." I indicated the path behind me.

Cruce nodded. "So, he's... at the peak?"

"He's not," I said. "He... fell."

Cruce stared at me, searching my eyes. "What... how could he fall? Where is he now?"

"We can't get to him," I said. "I'm going for help."

A clap of thunder echoed from the west. We turned to see the black clouds rolling in across the mountains.

"Is he okay?" Cruce asked.

I started again down the path. "I don't think so."

"We should go get him!" Cruce said, grabbing my arm, halting my progress. "The storm's coming."

I shook off his arm. "We can't get to him," I repeated. I turned away down the path, walking as quickly as I could.

"I'm going up!" Cruce yelled.

I did not look back.

Emerging from the shadow of the valley, I trotted down the pathway and crossed the perimeter road to follow the long boulevard to Harmon Hall. The first gust of the storm was bending the small trees in the grassy median strip. I went through the glass stairwell doors of the administration building and raced upward, taking the polished steps two at a time. Rushing into the hallway of the second floor, I yelled rather incoherently at the first person I saw, a female airman carrying a handful of manila folders with bright red tags on them. I told her a cadet had fallen from Eagle Peak and was probably in very bad shape.

The airman stared at me for a moment, stunned at my presence, then said she would let her superior know. I yelled that we needed a rescue unit right away—I don't know why I called it a unit. She shuffled her folders and disappeared through a solid wooden door. A lieutenant colonel appeared shortly and began asking me questions. I told him I would lead him or whoever came with me to the last spot I had seen the cadet. He instructed me to wait and disappeared again behind the door. I doubt now if much time had actually passed, but I began to imagine he had forgotten about me.

I retraced my steps down the stairs and walked outside, crossing the pavement to the Chapel. The doors were not locked. I went in.

At the far end of the sanctuary, the huge silver-winged cross hung in silent accusation as I glanced around the empty space between it and me. I don't know why I thought I would just see some chaplain waiting for me to come to him. I retreated outside and walked slowly back to Harmon Hall.

A small group of men had gathered outside the glass doors, one of them my lieutenant colonel.

"I was afraid you ran away," he said.

"No, sir," I answered.

"Where'd you go?"

"To find help..."

He nodded solemnly. "We've called Search and Rescue. They'll be here ASAP." He looked at me. "Did someone shoot at the Chapel?"

I shook my head. "I don't know."

I turned away to look at the mountains. Dark clouds obscured the peak, and the rain was now constant and coming harder. "My friend is still up there," I said.

"We'll find him," he said.

I nodded. "His name is Francis Cruce. He's not the one that fell."

His gaze was stern as he wiped the rain from his forehead. "What's he doing up there?"

"Looking for his... for our friend."

He glanced to his right as a blue Air Force van braked to a stop in the open area beyond the perimeter road. "We're on our way up." I could see he was evaluating me. "It might be best if you go back to..." He looked at me again. "What squadron?"

"Evil Eight," I said. "I mean Eagle. Eagle Eight." I did not move. "I should go with you. I know where he is."

He put his hand on my shoulder, and his countenance softened. "You said he fell... a long way?"

"Yes, sir."

"And he was... is your friend.'

I nodded.

He squeezed my shoulder. "Go back to your squadron. Wait for my call. Tell your AOC."

I bowed my head. "Okay."

I watched as the group of men, joined by those in the van, walked rapidly into the mountains and away from me.

When I returned to Skye's room, I was surprised to find Quince there, standing near Skye's bed. He turned to me as I entered.

I realized there were two other pieces of yellow paper on the bare mattress next to the one with my name.

I glanced at Quince and lifted the paper with his name on it. Beneath it was a small Bible with a bookmark. A passage on the page was highlighted—the one in Exodus about baring false witness. I handed it to Quince who silently eyed the book.

I felt a flood of emotion I could not quell, a flash of red in my eyes, a pulse of hate in my heart.

I reached for the small stack marked for Cruce but decided not to disturb it. Under the paper with my name I found the picture I had taken of Skye on Eagle Peak, along with a pair of gold Second Lieutenant bars, his compass, and the hat Gram had woven out of plastic bread bags.

"I'm here to escort the former Cadet Book," Quince said, tossing the Bible back on the bed and turning to me. "Do you know...?"

My fist across his face interrupted his casual words. Quince reeled toward Skye's bed, blood from his lip splattering the wall beyond. He sat awkwardly against the headboard, bright red blood dripping from his distorted mouth onto the Bible and the bare mattress.

I stood over him, my body shaking with rage. I longed for a pugil stick to shove into his throat. "I don't ever want to hear his name come from your lips," I hissed. "Not ever. For all I know, you set him up!"

Quince wiped his lips and gazed at the blood on his fingers. He tried to stand, but I held my hand at his face, inches from his nose.

"You hid behind the honor code! You used it to destroy a beautiful human being."

As I stepped away, Quince rose from the bed and walked to the sink, turning on the spigot. He put his hands into the flowing cold water, and the diluted blood slowly washed down the drain. He took Skye's washcloth from the side towel rack and put it to his lips, dabbing to stem the flow of blood and wipe away the dark clotting residue as he angrily eyed my reflection.

"You'll burn for this," he said. "I'll make sure it never leaves you."

"I'm burned already," I said.

The lieutenant colonel called my squadron that evening to tell me the storm had forced them to call off the search. He said they found Cruce shivering beneath a rocky overhang near where I had last seen him. It had taken some convincing to get Cruce to go back down the hill with them.

The next morning, an ad hoc team made up of cadets, officers, and enlisted men started up the trail, but another strong storm rolled over the mountains from the west, and they were forced to wait.

In late afternoon, the skies cleared and the team renewed their search. They found nothing at the place where I said Skye was. There was telltale evidence of a shoe and some torn clothing, but no body. If there had been blood on the rock, the storm had washed it away. Perhaps he had tried to get down the mountain himself.

The holes in the Chapel were soon discovered, and the investigators put dowels in them to triangulate where the shots had been fired. The wooden sticks converged toward a point at the top of the small hill between the Cadet Area and the perimeter road. Two concentric circles of stones are near there, now. I have no idea why. From the God's eye view, they look like a pagan monument. Or the center of a target. A bullseye.

As evening of the third day fell, I was taken into the AOC's office behind a closed door, and he, along with the team commander, interrogated me about the events as I had reported them. The team commander asked me more pointed questions. I became aware that I was under suspicion for Skye's disappearance.

I stuck to my story because it was true, but I could tell they were skeptical. They asked about the Honor Board and my testimony. They were concerned that my confessional about Skye and his sister might have caused Skye to lose control of himself.

They told me Harold Book was coming to the Academy to get Skye's things. When asked, Harold had assured them I was a good friend, if not Vincent's best friend. I pitied him, although I had no right to. Everything he had worked to attain, everything he was desperate to hold onto, was being negated by life.

Saturday afternoon, slumped in a recliner in the squadron TV room, I watched Seattle Slew win the Kentucky Derby. I remember entertaining bizarre thoughts, imagining what that horse's spleen must look like, and thinking the only way to know for sure would be to cut him open. When the race was over, the other cadets in the room filed out quietly, leaving me alone to my thoughts.

I expected at any moment for someone to come for me. I was the last to see Skye alive. I had assaulted a fellow cadet. And I had secret sins incapable of being hidden with the passage of time. But time passed and nothing happened. It was the harshest sentence possible.

CHAPTER FIFTY-SIX

Word of his disappearance spread quickly among the Wing, and the vacuum created by Skye's fall sucked the soul out of so many who knew him. Denial, whether sincerely expressed or not, ran rampant. There would be those who refused to believe that Skye had died, saying rather that he had resigned or gone permanently Over The Fence, or that the authorities decided not to continue the search because doing so would make Skye a martyr and create havoc. Some even joked that he had transmuted to become Nino Balducci.

Tomi Evans declared to anyone who would listen that he had known Skye well, that they had been good friends, that he would miss Skye more than was possible for the rest of us mere mortals. Following six years in the Navy, Fattafred became a businessman like his father. He married four times, each wife younger than the last.

Philip Quince tried to rewrite Skye's story, distorting the things Skye said and did, decrying Skye's shortcomings as a cadet which inevitably led to his downfall. He even tried to convince people that Skye would never have mustered the gall to jump, that he must have fallen... or been pushed. The picture he painted was self-serving and ridiculous. Still, some came to think what Quince said could be true because he was, after all, a good cadet.

But destroying the heretic does not destroy the argument.

I knew the truth. And that truth was far more complex than anyone understood. Skye *was* pushed. He was pushed out of an intolerant world by menial children not yet ready to be men. He chose to take what remained of his life after being robbed of the most critical part of it.

Francis Cruce avoided talking about Skye, or the honor board, or of anything else of consequence, although I could tell there was something he was trying to bring himself to tell me. Shortly after graduation, the Air Force exposed his malady and quietly dismissed him into a world that found it difficult to tolerate his lust for life.

He wrote to me some years later, while I was stationed in Spain, to say he was sick. Despite his weakened condition, he hoped to take a trip through Europe and promised to look me up. Perhaps the dry air of Spain would do him good. In the meantime, he wanted me to know he loved me as a brother, and that the world was a darker place without Skye Book. I do not know how he found me. The postmark was as obscure as his life had become.

That was the last I heard of him until Walt Whittaker wrote me to "brag" that, after cramming four years of college into seven, he had finally graduated and was enrolled in Officer Candidate School. He also wrote that he had finally married "program chick." Whit signed the letter "Waldo F. Dumbsquat." He added a postscript, asking if I knew that our friend Henry Francis Cruce had died of complications from pneumonia. I cried for the first time since leaving the Academy.

If there is a silver lining to the shadow of this cloud, it is that Skye never had to live through Iraq, or 911, or Afghanistan and then Iraq again, or the divisiveness created by an unconscionable greed for power that continues to feed the contest for American souls.

When Tyson went away to the Mideast wars, what came back was not him. Like Skye, he was forever altered, betrayed by a world driven not by courage and honor, but by fear and greed. I've heard it said a squirrel is just a rat with better PR. I think Iraq was that squirrel.

My father suffered with Tyson from the time he returned home until the morning he decided life wasn't any good anymore.

"It's my cross to bear," Dad said to me just days before Tyson put an end to his pain. "It's not right for the people who send others to war to have a good time while young soldiers are dying in battle. Those that owe their country the most are those that have been here the longest, not those that were never given the chance to live. The next time our leaders feel the itch to sacrifice men and women to be butchered, they should do as David Brinkley suggested and declare war from Arlington Cemetery."

In the twilight of his years, my father became the strongest man I have ever known. He reconciled his life, despite the suffering that comes with living and the pain accrued because of it. He faded away in quiet dignity, at peace with the secret you cannot share, the truth you can only learn for yourself, and the accrued wisdom you can neither give away nor take with you.

I was proud to have been able to call him my father.

There are so many wonderful things about the Academy and its legacies that have survived being compromised by the flaws of human nature.

Mattie LaForce, a charter member of "Bad Company," would fly fighters until he died in one, choosing to stay with the disabled jet to steer it clear of an elementary school. He exemplified what was good about the place. As did Lewis Carpenter, and Joshua Steinway. Even Henry Francis Cruce. And Walt Whittaker, who made it through Officer Candidate School to receive his Air Force commission as a "ninety day wonder." He graduated first in his Undergraduate Pilot Training class, later attended the Air Force Fighter Weapons School, and flew the F-15 in combat in Iraq, receiving the Distinguished Flying Cross.

Other graduates would do heroic things, like saving the lives of 155 people in the "Miracle on the Hudson;" or breaking barriers to become the first female four star general, or first female Academy superintendent; or become the first woman to be on an expedition crew, spending over 160 days on the International Space Station.

Thank God we are resilient. As an institution, as a country, as a people.

The Cadet Honor Code has been amended since the time I lived under it. To "We will not lie, steal, or cheat, nor tolerate among us anyone who does" has been added the Honor Oath, "Furthermore, I resolve to do my duty and to live honorably, so help me God." It is good to resolve to do your duty and to live honorably. But you cannot kick someone out for failing in their resolution to do their duty, nor for those lapses where one might not live as honorably as another might think he or she should. It can even be tolerated. Maybe it was just a way of throwing God in the mix.

Still, if that had always been part of the code, Quince may have chosen to live more honorably.

And I would have done my duty.

And perhaps Skye would be teaching history somewhere.

I heard from Melody only once after it was all over, when she sent me a package. Inside was a note written in her hand informing me that Gram had died. It seems she just stopped caring about living and encouraged death to take care of that inconvenience. They "planted her," as Melody wrote, on a nice little green hill with a pink garden of gaura. She wrote that in the late spring, the bees danced with the gaura in the warmth of the sun. Gram would have liked that.

There was also a dreamcatcher in the package. "Hang this above your bed," Melody wrote. "Dream on and be at peace."

Peace.

The last time I saw Vanessa was in Arizona. I was shopping at the Williams Air Force Base commissary, looking for something to make myself for dinner. Turning down an aisle in search of the cheaper meat, I was surprised to see her ten feet from me, a package of ground beef in one hand and chicken breasts in the other.

"I'd tell you to go with the chicken," I said from behind her, "but it looks like you already did."

She whirled around and, seeing me, smiled that fun smile I remembered when our eyes first met at Lawrence Paul.

"You would?"

I nodded. "Who knows what they churned up to make that," I said, pointing to the beef. "On the other hand, you can be fairly certain that, at least at some point, what they call chicken probably had feathers."

"Maybe." She put them both in her cart. She seemed undecided as to whether she should hug me.

"How is it you're here?" I asked.

She tilted her head. "You don't know?"

"Hence the question."

"I thought you... I'm married. To Philip Quince."

I truly had not anticipated that. I had come to assume that once anyone came to know Quince, their only real desire would be to get as far away from him as possible. A brief thought of opportunity flashed in my head, one of ridding the world of a cancer.

"I had no idea," I said.

"Shortly after graduation." She flashed a small diamond for me to admire.

"Under the sabers?"

"What do you mean?"

"The Chapel. The full cadet saber-bearers deal and all that."

"Oh. No. It was a little more private."

I glanced at her belly, and she caught my glimpse.

"Not that private!" she said, laughing.

I'm sure I reddened. "I like your dress," I said.

"Right."

I looked around for her husband.

She touched my arm, drawing my gaze back to her. "I was so very sorry to hear about..." Her voiced trailed into silence. There was sincerity in her eyes. Perhaps the beginnings of a tear.

"Me too," I said. "There were times when I imagined you and Skye might end up together."

Vanessa laughed sweetly. "Skye and me? That was never in the cards. I was not Skye's... type."

I nodded, my mind drifting away for a moment. "Francis Cruce..."

Vanessa smiled warmly, as if anticipating my thoughts. "Just good friends, I think." She paused. "Like you and I were meant to be."

I fought to deflect a flash of restrained anger. "How does your husband feel about the way things turned out?"

"It bothers him, I think. But we never talk about it."

"Then how do you know?"

"Because we never talk about it."

I nodded. "When yours is the key evidence that leads to... all it led to, I can understand."

"I'm surprised it mattered that much."

"You're kidding."

"No. I don't know what he could say. He only knew what I saw."

I looked at her, my mouth falling open for a moment before I asked, "What do you mean?"

She gazed at me with interest. "Well, all he would be able to say was what I told him. I'm surprised they would even allow it."

"He never saw Skye that night?" I asked. I fought against the rage rising to the surface.

She shook her head. "When he went outside, Skye's car was gone."

I am certain Vanessa saw the anger in my eyes. "He testified he was there," I said through gritted teeth. "He said he saw them and his car."

"No. He would have told me." Vanessa's eyes widened as the implication settled in. Within the space of a few seconds, her face went from confusion to disbelief to understanding.

'By their fruits you will know them,' I thought. I glanced around again for Quince. Perhaps he was hiding in the produce.

"He's not here," she said simply.

I turned to leave and felt her hand once again on my arm.

There was fresh pain in her eyes. "I'm so sorry," Vanessa said. "I didn't... I couldn't know." She kissed me on the cheek, and I detected a trace of Vaseline.

"I did care about you, Vanessa," I said. I wanted to add 'You did not marry a good man.' I refrained.

I guess she decided that, anyway. A few months later, Quince passed out while on a solo flight in the T-37. The scare led him to SIE, a self-initiated elimination from pilot training. Not long after that, Vanessa Quince became Vanessa Cardewey again in her own form of SIE.

I know it should not have, but that news pleased me. Vanessa Cardewey had introduced me to The Garden of the Gods, and to Fargo's. And almost to love. It seemed now I had returned the favor by burdening her with my misery.

Quince's last assignment was a desk job at Incirlik Air Base in Turkey. I ran into him there once while flying fighters out of Torrejon, Spain. We tried not to remember each other, but when that proved impossible, we agreed to have lunch together.

We talked uncomfortably for perhaps an hour. He talked as if there was nothing between us, that the past was just that. Not for a single moment did the thought seem to occur to him that what he had done was morally despicable, and that the invisible vault in human beings we call the soul was, in him, utterly bankrupt.

It was then I began to formulate a plan of action I felt might prove redemptive for me.

He got out of the Air Force shortly after that, having served a little over 5 years. It was rumored he went to the "Holy Land." Perhaps seeking redemption. Or a scapegoat.

He dropped out of sight for a while before I tracked him down in Alaska.

What I had in mind seemed easy enough. I felt the world could tolerate him no longer, and it needed me to do something to restore the balance. I sensed it was my duty. When I confronted Quince, I reveled as I watched his eyes turn from recognition to knowing to fear. Perhaps he knew his time had come.

But I realized then that, with him gone, the only one left would be me. I left him in disgust, never doing what I thought I would do. Our souls were burned, and nothing of this world could raise them from the ashes.

Men often live out their lives that way, it seems, when they do something that mars their existence for the rest of time. They cannot start over, they cannot erase the past, nor can they hide it from themselves no matter where they run or who they become. So they continue to live the lie.

But the truth does not always set you free. Perhaps that is what makes this story so hard to tell, because I must go to that edge and then transcend it, seek what I don't wish to find, knowing all along the wolf lurks inside me in all its ugly, soul-wrenching glory.

It took me half my life to understand what went wrong. It wasn't the place, certainly not the idea. It was failings in the integrity of men. Flawed men who put a self-serving face on what they thought the place should be.

Our fatal flaw, as it turns out, is that we are mortal creatures. And as mortal creatures we have only one mind in which to comprehend life. We cannot tolerate alternative possibilities because if another way of thinking is true then our own becomes the lie. So we fight for what we need to believe, desperately hoping we have not wasted it all.

That is why I think belief in God is not a matter of reason at all. I think it is a matter of accepting the possibility that something so powerful as a Creator of a universe could care about the most flawed adjuncts of his creation. Perhaps we do need God in some form.

NOR TOLERATE AMONG US

But we have no need for Satan. We are quite adept at creating our own hell.

I have often wondered why Skye didn't handle the whole thing in a different way, one that would have been better for everybody. I was never sure if he believed I was his Judas. Who was he trying to save? Was it Melody? Or me? Maybe Francis Cruce? The world needed Skye so much more than it needed his sacrifice. Maybe he had to die a violent death because that is the only thing that resonates with mankind.

Among the things Skye placed neatly on his bed, I found a poem he left behind for me. Let it serve as his eulogy.

He titled it *"Anti-Hymn."*

Perhaps if I close the door
A little more
Everything will be fine.
Perhaps if I close my eyes
To all the lies
I'll open up my mind.
Perhaps if I close to doubt
All that's without
Believing only what's within
Perhaps I'll find
Inside my mind
No meaning left for men.

Maybe he was right. Maybe truth exists only because of lies. A lie is something that is not, and in the universe, there exists nothing that is not. To say we are searching for truth in the world would be to imply that the universe seeks to lie to us. That is impossible. What exists simply is. The universe needs no distinction between what is true and what is not.

Until you put Man in the equation.

EPILOGUE

"The more you love, the more you love more."

Walter Oscar "Whit" Whittaker

I felt pressure on my shoulder and a dampness on my forehead. The back of my head hurt as did my side. Despite this discomfort, I opened my eyes as if awakening from a deep regenerative sleep. Cadet Wesley was looking at me intently, his countenance showing both concern and relief.

"Are you okay, Father?" he asked.

"What?"

"Are you alright?"

I felt a soft hand on my arm. "You fainted," a voice as soft as the hand said. "Are you hurting anywhere?"

I lifted my head and saw I was lying atop the red blankets on the cadet bed. I reached my hand to my waist and tried to rub away a sharp pang. I moved my other hand to my head and felt the wet handcloth. I brushed it off and tried to push myself upright.

"Don't sit up before you're ready," my classmate's wife said. She eyed my neck. "Perhaps we should... can we... is it okay to loosen your collar?"

I looked at her, closed my eyes tightly and opened them again, taking in a deep breath. I could smell the wool of the red blankets and the hint of the lady's perfume. "I think I'm ready."

I was helped to a sitting position, and I turned to put my feet on the carpeted floor, locking my arms to support myself. "What happened?"

"You passed out," Cadet Wesley said.

"My hip hurts."

"You hit the desk corner," said another voice.

I stood up.

"We've called someone," the lady said. "A doctor, I think. You should wait."

There was nothing more to wait for. I had waited long enough. I stood and walked toward the open door as the lady tugged gently at my arm. "Just to be careful," she said.

I shook my head. "No, I'm okay."

I removed her hand and looked into her eyes. She blinked and smiled warmly as if thinking this would convince me to stay.

"Thank you for taking care of me," I said.

"Father, you really should wait," Wesley said.

I unbuttoned my cotton collar and removed it. "I'm not your father," I said. I placed the stiff white strip in his hand and walked out of the silent room.

The sun was high, and the bike's seat was hot.

I unlocked the saddlebag to retrieve my helmet and jacket. I searched along the bottom for a small cardboard box I had long ago labeled "old but important pictures" and pulled out two faded photographs. One was the picture I had taken of Skye at the edge of the peak, and the other was a forever youthful Melody smiling at me as she hugged the statue of the jackalope. It was the only real picture I had of her. I returned Skye's picture to the box and tucked the one of Melody securely in a brace on the windshield.

Every day of my life since that last spring in Colorado, I had endured a myriad of moments where I fought to keep Melody beneath the surface of my mind's eye. By stubborn self-righteousness, until this moment, I had been fairly successful. I wanted to believe Melody's last words to me.

Even if she did mean them once, she would never speak them to me again.

It had been just a fleeting moment in time, one brief spring, long ago, forever past. I envisioned her on Fireball, galloping ahead of me toward the bluff. I was overcome for just a moment as I indulged myself to mourn my past. How much happier my existence could have been had that vision been an everyday reality.

I saw her now as I had that spring afternoon when I kissed her, secretively hoping her brother would never know. The angle of the sun— neither too high nor too low—the way it reflected so beautifully in her eyes that appeared brown until you looked deeply enough to see the green around the edges. But it had been a false spring, too hot too soon. The yellow currants were proof of that.

I ceremoniously adjusted the rearview mirrors, laughing to myself as I thought there was no need for looking back now. It was then I saw the bump on my head and the small scratch that accompanied it. Looking into aging eyes that seldom smiled, I caught a glimpse of something new. Understanding, perhaps, or acceptance. I gingerly strapped on my helmet and fired up the Indian.

I drove out the North Gate and turned left, glancing over my shoulder for one last view of Eagle Peak. It seemed far away and unaffected by all that had occurred in its shadow.

Gram once told me the Oglala believe the wanagi of a dead person lingers in the place where it dies and attempts to lure its family and friends to go with it. It beckons them to follow, like the corpse of Gregory Peck's Ahab strapped by harpoon lines to the great white whale.

The speed limits were higher now, so I rolled the power on, scarcely aware of the eighteen-wheelers sharing the road with me. Everything flew by so much faster. I was unsure where I was going exactly, but wherever it was lay to the north. I concentrated on my path, believing it to be true.

I rode without stopping until I was in Wyoming, and then only briefly for gas and personal needs. In Cheyenne, I programmed Chadron in the GPS and pressed on. I needed to see if Gram's gaura was still there, dancing with the bees.

After that, with any luck, in a day or so, I'd be in Custer.

As the sun disappeared to the west, the moon rose from my right, illuminating my path like a beacon. The road was not quite as abandoned as before, but I was alone just the same. Driving past the grass and dry dust of the Nebraska plains, I imagined a star shining in the distance, beckoning me onward.

What makes a person yearn for the past? Is it because thinking it was meaningless dangles him perilously close to the madness that lurks at the edge of the soul? Or does he merely wish to rearrange the pieces, to see, finally, the good buried beneath?

I found the house as if I had just been there yesterday. By the light of the rising full moon, I saw the gray fence and the yellow flowers. I stopped the car and closed my eyes, trying to feel something of Gram.

The moment passed. I dismounted, draped my helmet over the sissy bar, and walked briskly up the sidewalk to the freshly painted entryway, no longer afraid of anything Fate had to offer.

The little house seemed at once aged and timeless, old but well maintained. That was good. It was worthy of such care. I thought how perfectly fitting it had been for Gram's life, with just enough room to live, unlike the ostentatious houses owned by so many people today who, like Harold Book, build mansions to make a statement that says "see, my life is large and wonderful because I have large and wonderful things."

Light escaped through drawn curtains in the front room, and there was the faint timbre of classical music. I thought it would be okay to knock on the door, despite the evening hour. Perhaps I could explain to whoever waited inside my reasons for wanting to see just a little of it, to see inside once more, if only for a moment. To remember what I had seen there, and what I could have been because of it. I hoped I did not appear too rough, and I briefly lamented having given up my collar. It might have eased my path in gaining admittance, although that was no longer honest.

I laughed softly to myself. Perhaps at long last I would get my shit together.

I swung the screen door open, knocked, and let the screen close again.

The Baroque music faded.

The face that opened the door was a distant memory.

Three decades had come and gone, but I still recognized the soft brown eyes, one with a tear-shaped scar that had grown more prominent than I remembered. She shifted the sleeping toddler cradled in her arms.

It took her a moment to see through the years, but the warm smile on her face was quick and genuine. She pushed the screen door open and stepped aside to let me in as if we had performed this ritual every evening for the past thirty years.

Corralling a tear, I said, "Is it okay?"

She nodded. "It has been for some time."

I entered and looked around briefly, taking in the pleasant mood of the small front room I remembered so well. The mantel of the fireplace was adorned with years of photographs, keepsakes, and dust, some the same, some different. The walls remained tastefully garnished with framed pictures and Lakota regalia. I recognized Skye's Spanish guitar on a stand in the corner next to the upright piano.

And there was something new. A portion of the wall opposite the fireplace now displayed numerous clocks, each unique in shape and size and all set within a minute of each other. I thought back to the living room wall of the Stanquist home. What had mattered to them was crosses. Of most importance to Melody, it seemed, was time.

"Those are still good seats," Melody said, pointing to the two aged wingback chairs near the window.

I looked at them and could almost see Gram sitting comfortably in one as she explained her world to me. "Does it matter which...?"

"Matter?"

"Is one your favorite?"

"Depends on the sun."

She placed the sleeping toddler on a loveseat near the fireplace before drawing back the curtains of the cased window. The soft glow of moonlight spread throughout the room. "Harley?" she asked, gazing into the night.

I shook my head. "Indian."

She flashed that indelible smile as she took the seat near the window. I sat in the chair opposite her.

"I'm sorry..." I began awkwardly. The brash impetuosity of all this was suddenly quite evident to me.

Melody seemed unphased. "I knew you'd find me."

I cringed. "I didn't think you wanted me to..."

She nodded.

I clasped my hands and lowered my head. "I had no idea where you were, really," I said.

She nodded. "Skye said you had a girl in Texas."

I shook my head.

"Oh."

I scanned the pictures on the walls. "Your folks?"

"Both gone."

"I'm sorry."

"I miss them."

I looked for telling memories of matrimony and shared experiences. There were several pictures of horses—one I recognized to be Fireball with a smiling young boy in the saddle. My eyes stopped on a free-standing framed picture of a handsome man perhaps in his late twenties hugging a pretty girl who was not Melody. At the top left corner of the simple frame, hanging by a chain, was the now tarnished starfish necklace.

She seemed to understand my search.

"Gene, I never married."

That hurt more than anything else she could have said. I wanted to ask why, but I knew the reason. I looked again at the picture and caught my breath.

"Yes," Melody said. "Your son."

I felt my chest tighten. "All this time... you didn't... it never..."

"I'm sorry I lied to you," she said with unquestionable sincerity. "I would have told you later." She glanced away. "Had things been different."

I looked at the sleeping young girl on the loveseat.

"That's little Olive," she said. "Olivia. Your granddaughter."

I felt the blood rush from my head. I hoped I would not faint twice in one day. "She's beautiful," I said.

"She's a good kid. Like her father."

"How old?"

"Almost two."

"What did you tell him? Our son."

"Everything. Over time. As I thought he was ready. I filled in the story when I thought it was right."

"Does he hate me?"

She gazed at me with a sudden sadness. "He never said so."

I saw the tear forming in the corner of her eye.

"What happened?" My own voice sounded faint.

"There was a rally. A protest, really." She looked away, her eyes flickering momentarily as her mind replayed a vision she must have invoked many times before. "Olivia was staying with me." Her eyes met mine. "They knew it was dangerous, but it was important to them. They never came back."

"Oh, God! Why didn't you write me?"

"To tell you what? That you had a son but now he was dead?"

My tears came in a flood. "I'm so sorry!"

Melody rose from her chair and came to me, kneeling at my feet, taking my head in her hands. She touched the bump on my head. "You hurt yourself."

It was the story of my life. "I fell."

She lowered my head and gave a healing kiss to the future scar. "I'm not sorry for what I did," she said softly. "I am sorry I did not tell you. But I was afraid it would hurt too much."

I dropped to the floor and put my head in her bosom.

"Why would you want to protect me?" I asked through tears I could not control.

She turned my head so that my eyes met hers. "Because I could never stop loving you."

"You could have found someone else."

She shook her head slowly. "I didn't want anyone else."

I looked at our granddaughter. "How long has... how..."

"A year last August."

"So, she doesn't really understand."

"No. But we'll tell her over time. When we think she's ready."

"Maybe she shouldn't know who I am."

"I think she should. Olivia should know her grandfather, Eugene Oliver Townsend."

I gazed into Melody's soft brown eyes. "And then what?"

"And then we'll see."

THE END

AFTERWORD

This is fiction. A fiction framed in reality. A fictional depiction of factual circumstances. There is reality and there is fantasy. Some events are real. Some people mentioned are real. But the characters of the story are creations of my mind, as are the events that involve them. Still, the circumstances under which these fictional events are depicted will be familiar in one way or another to every cadet that has attended or is attending the United States Air Force Academy.

In certain cases, I claim artistic license in altering the chronology of real events for the benefit of the story, but that makes them no less real.

In the year of the publishing of this novel, the 65th Firsties are into their senior year at USAFA and the 68th class is beginning its Doolie year. As the number of graduated commissioned officers approaches 50,000, so much has changed and yet so much remains the same. This is as it should be with any noble institution. Ideally, the strengths remain, while the weaknesses are addressed within the changes brought by time.

In any given year, there are approximately 4400 cadets in attendance, and each views the Academy from within his or her own, unique paradigm. Some, upon leaving, don't want to talk about the Academy, and may even wish to erase it from their memory. Others recall their time there with great affection, as the greatest college experience imaginable. And some famed people who left before incurring a commitment will maintain they never quit the Academy, but merely transferred to a different university. You may read into that appeal what you will.

For me, this novel has proven cathartic as I find myself feeling a little of both extremes. In no way do I mean to disparage cadets or the institution itself. Quite the opposite. A brief turn in my writer's garret exposes an obvious pride in my alma mater, and a kinship with my classmates and my fellow graduates.

Still, I, like most cadets, both graduates and those who left early, look back on the Academy years feeling a complexity of emotions. I have therefore struggled with the utmost care and consideration to depict the love/hate relationship so many cadets share with the institution.

I am reminded of the adage to "forgive and forget." I have to take exception to some aspects of that pearl of wisdom. To learn, we must remember. We may move on, but we must never forget. If we forget, then what was the point?

That is not to say we should dwell on what is past. It does no good to fret about what could have or should have been. The past is just that.

Acceptance to change at the Academy has been slow at times. Some things have changed only when the institution was forced to do so. The "Bring Me Men" ramp remained so named for nearly 27 years after the first women began attending the Academy. It was a tradition with a meaning broader than the words, but it was conceived when women attending a military academy could not be. Even the most conservative among us can see the problem with this.

When the era of "Bring Me Men" came to a definitive close, those aluminum words were removed from the ramp leading to the parade grounds and ceremoniously replaced with the unpoetically verbose *"Integrity First - Service Before Self - Excellence in All We Do."* Not as romantic, but certainly more appropriate, being as these have been the approved core values of the United States Air Force since 1995.

The honor code has been amended with an added phrase that is more of a pledge, blurring the line between ethics and morality.

The demographics of the wing have been altered, which is for the better as our culture progresses. The military academies especially needed women, and our country needed for them to be there.

And tolerance of individuals? I could not tell you as I am not living it now. Perhaps no one can.

As for the Institution itself, I believe it strives to be the ideal, all the while knowing the impossibility of such a thing. It works to graduate the best leaders the military can know. It strives to be fair—knowing the limitations of the human factor—to be noble, honorable, and nurturing (despite what some may say). It encourages strength of mind and body, although it may at times be subjected to a misguided approach formed from individual influences. It espouses integrity and strength of character. I believe that character grows from standing strong against untruth and respecting others who do as well. Poor character is exposed in people who chose to demean and degrade those who refuse to share their narrow, prejudiced, and at times capricious perspective of the world. That is, in my opinion, the ultimate form of cowardice.

There is a tinge of hamartia in each of us, a fatal flaw waiting to surface if we allow it. Recently, the first openly gay commandant was relieved of duty. I have no problem with a commandant who also happens to be a lesbian if she can do the job as well as a straight male. As of this writing, I do not know why she was replaced. I suppose the circumstances will out over time. We are forever learning.

Great strides, I believe, have been made at the Academy—my visits there emphasize that. The institution has matured, has learned, has grown. But human shortcomings remain the constant that cannot be completely removed from the equation. Sadly the scandals speak for themselves: cheating, sexual harassment, assault, rape.

There was and is at the Academy, as anywhere, a desire by some to influence the attendees beyond the call and purposes of the institution—and with rank comes a perceived privilege to influence by coercion and force—religiously, sexually ...

There remains the fear of scandal, of weakness, of things getting out of hand. This is understandable, but fear should not be the driving force for doing what is best for the cadet wing.

And so it is that I wrote this novel because I wish people to think and act wisely within any aspect of life, whether time-tested or not—to realize the effect on not only those they touch, but of their legacy as well. No one knows the whole truth. No one should embrace the lie that claims otherwise.

That being said, my narrator does speak from a particular paradigm.

But that's just his opinion.

ABOUT THE AUTHOR

Charles Williams is a United States Air Force Academy graduate, a former F-4 and F-16 fighter pilot, and a retired Delta Air Lines captain. He was the coach of the Niceville High School Forensics Speech and Debate Team for eight years and was the Northwest Florida State College Collegiate High School Forensics Team coach for another three. He was also the director of the Niceville Drama Department for four years, during which time he wrote two comedic plays entitled *I, Xombi* and *13-13-13* which were performed on stage by members of the Niceville High School Drama Troupe.

He has been honored to receive several awards in the speech and debate community, including being named the Florida Forensics League Coach of the Year, a Diamond Coach recognized by the National Forensics League, and was inducted into the Gator Guard by the University of Florida Blue Key Speakers Bureau. He also coached the National Forensics League Poetry Interpretation National Champion of 2013.

This is the third novel Charles has published.

He continues to work on new projects, including a coming of age novel involving high school forensics speech and debate students who must deal with a school shooting.

Made in the USA
Columbia, SC
17 October 2022

69617228R00276